Old Steve Boy⸺ arranged my escape quay, the *Sea Warrior* me. "Captain Sterret is redemptioner, but he w⸺board. Would to God I had the ten pound⸺ to pay for your passage."

"Somebody in America'll redeem me," I assured him. "I'll work hard until I've paid the fare."

His seamed face darkened with worry. "Ah, you are so young you wring my heart. And far too lovely for your own good—like a magnolia when 'tis but half opened. Those wide French blue eyes are like water too deep and too clear. And your chestnut hair. I'd swear you were of noble blood . . ." he broke off suddenly, and I turned to see Tet Kester looming in the doorway, his lustful eyes small and mean.

"Ye got ter make up yer mind and soon, girl," he threatened drunkenly, "or, by God, I'll come up to yer room. That's it—I'll take ye tonight!"

I thought of the jeweled poinard tucked at my waist. If I had to draw Kester's blood with its bright, sharp blade, I would. I was going to America. Nothing would stop me from becoming the lady I was meant to be . . .

Novels by Annabel Erwin

AURIELLE
LILIANE

Published by
WARNER BOOKS

Aurielle

by
Annabel Erwin

WARNER BOOKS

A Warner Communications Company

WARNER BOOKS EDITION

Copyright © 1979 by Annabel Erwin
All rights reserved.

ISBN 0-446-91126-7

Cover art by Melissa Duillo

Warner Books, Inc., 75 Rockefeller Plaza, New York, N.Y. 10019

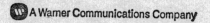A Warner Communications Company

Printed in the United States of America

Not associated with Warner Press, Inc., of Anderson, Indiana

First Printing: May, 1979

10 9 8 7 6 5 4 3 2 1

For Sharon, with love

Avrielle

Chapter
1

"Blesset child, where are ye?" Moll's strident voice
came dimly to my ears where I lay on my flat little stomach
in the garret, poring over the well-worn book of Shakespeare's plays. A ripple of fear coursed along my spine and
I closed the book with a frightened thump. Moll sounded
angrier than usual and she often boxed my ears when I
was not fast enough to please her.

I rose hastily and stuffed the book quickly into the
rough knapsack, bulging now with everything I owned,
which was not a great deal.

Excitement at the prospect of escape tonight rose to
blend in a heady mixture with terror as I looked down at
the bag. I had first learned to read when old Steve Boyette,
the crippled sailor who was now the kitchen cook, had
introduced me to *The Tempest*. The book he had given me
was one of my most prized possessions.

Dust motes sparkled lazily in the air where a shaft
of late evening sunlight penetrated the dirty dormer window that looked out over the roof of the Boar's Head Inn.
The odors of roasting meat and baking bread came to my

nostrils and Moll's voice rose once more, impatient and even angrier. "Blesset, I know yer up in the attic! I need yer to he'p serve!"

Blesset. How I hated that name Moll had fastened on me! Moll called everything blessed, even when she cursed. But she had said, "Ye don't know Aurielle's yer name an' Blesset's good enough fer ye!"

"I'm comin'," I yelled, hastily pushing the knapsack back into the shadows under the dormer. My English was singularly awful despite my ability to read, for I had grown up in the gutters of Portsmouth, played in the dirty cobbled streets with other urchins in that English port city. The French that Moll had said I spoke in my baby voice was long since forgotten as the years rolled by.

I took the steps lightly. Excitement and fear still gripped me, leaving no room for hunger. If all went as planned, I would be well away from all this tomorrow! I took the dark hall that led from the back stairs to the kitchen and met with Moll's scowl. I ducked as she swung a hand at my head.

"Blesset, 'twas a sorry day when Steve give yer that book fer y'own. 'Im an' 'is books an' 'is eddication—pah!"

Now she grumbled, "Ain't been a April so 'ot since you come, back in the spring o' eighteen 'undred." Her little jet eyes on me were shrewd. "That was when old Boney was jis' gettin' 'is start. Cor! Them was 'appier days. 'Ere, Blesset, carry them plates inter th' tables."

I knew England was locked in a life-or-death struggle with Napoleon Bonaparte. Men at the bar talked of it all the time, sailors and soldiers alike. Silently I took the stack of heavy dishes from Moll and went into the large dining room of the inn. I saw the bar beyond was crowded with men from the ships that lay in the harbor beyond the inn. I put the dishes down carefully. From the mantle I took flint and struck fire to oil lamps on the tables, one by one, my mind far away from these regular chores.

It had been April when I had come to the inn, Moll told me, relating the experience when I reached ten years of age, which she thought old enough to grasp the import of her words. It had resulted in a flood of persistent questions on my part.

10

No, she didn't know who the Englishman was. "I don't know why yer so set on 'im bein' yer pa, Blesset. Ye wasn't no more'n four. There wasn't nothin' on 'im but that blesset note. An' 'e was out of 'is 'ead—burnin' up with fever. Ye can't believe nothin' 'e said. Lucky none o' us caught that fever—it killed 'im quick enough." Then with a cruel smile, "Yer nothin' but a little bastard, Blesset, an' that's a fact."

But I had persisted until she finally went to a cupboard in our room and produced the torn and yellowed note. It was in English. *I am discovered and I must flee for my life. Take Aurielle to England with you. Tell her how beloved she is to us and that she is never to forget her mother is of nobility. She is the*—The rest was torn away. Was it my mother who wrote those words, so desperate and fearful, so full of love? I fantasized a different story about those facts every day. In the end, I convinced myself that my mother was alive somewhere grieving, for she did not know where to find me.

I continued to nag Moll with questions as the days slipped by. Exasperated, she would reiterate, "The note was all 'e had on 'im, 'cept'n that little dagger. 'E never called yer name—if it *is* Aurielle." She came down hard on the name and it sounded like Au'rl. " 'Ow could Tet Kester do nothin' else but bury 'im behind th' inn, 'im unknown an' dyin' like that? Tet was afeared 'e'd be blamed fer 'is death. Now get busy at yer chores."

But that note, written by someone probably long dead to someone else now long dead, reposed among my treasures in the knapsack, along with the yellowed but finely embroidered cambric dress I had worn when the man I was sure was my father had brought me here.

But his poniard—ah, that beautiful and deadly dagger with its jeweled and silver monogrammed haft—was tucked at my waist even now. Moll had given it to me grudgingly and only when she realized I was more woman than child at twelve. For four years now, the poniard had been my recourse in moments of danger. It had fended off advances from street urchins, from passing sailors and soldiers, and from amorous clients in the Boar's Head Inn.

"God an' th' devil, Blesset, yer must be daft with the

11

spring—" Moll hissed, passing me with the beef haunch cut in twain and on two big platters, one in each hand. "Get on back inter the kitchen this minute an' bring them loaves o' bread. Tell Steve ter roll in a new barrel o' ale for Wiggins at th' bar, too."

I did as I was bid, for I saw Tet Kester looking at me from the main stairway to the rooms upstairs. It would be Tet Kester I would be happiest to leave. I made a wide circle beyond the stairs. Tet was not afraid of my poniard. Indeed he had threatened to confiscate it and I had lied to him, telling him Moll kept it for me. Moll knew of this lie but made no effort to help me stay beyond Kester's reach.

In the kitchen, Steve limped up to me, a tray of loaves in his gnarled hands. He whispered, " 'Tis the *Sea Warrior*, Blessed. 'Twill be at the end of the quay." Steve Boyette was well spoken, a man of obvious education, and had I been able to spend more time with him, no doubt my speech would have been less offensive.

"I know," I replied low, aware of the sharp and beady observance of the two maidservants. Marianne's little club-footed boy clumped crookedly to me, holding up his chubby hands. "Later, Billy," I murmured, dropping a quick kiss on his golden curls. His mother turned to the brick oven where Moll's pies were being removed with a long, flat board. She stood stolidly while Jane, the other maid, plucked them out, pads on her hands against the heat.

Steve rearranged the loaves fussily, whispering, "Captain Sterrett is well aware that you are a redemptioner, Blessed, and I have told him you are Moll Stuart's daughter. Would to God I had the ten pounds to give you to pay for your passage."

"It don't matter," I replied sturdily. "Somebody in America'll redeem me. I'll work 'ard until I've paid me fare an' then some." I observed the maids going into the hall carrying the pies. For a moment Steve Boyette and I were alone.

His seamed face darkened with worry. "Ah, Blessed, you are so young you wring my heart." His thin throat worked with emotion. "And you are far too lovely for

12

your own good, with those wide French blue eyes—like water too deep and too clear. And your chestnut hair! 'Tis a shining foil for your white skin." His faded eyes brightened. "I'd swear you were of noble blood—" He broke off and I turned to see Tet Kester standing in the doorway.

Steve bent his head obsequiously and I scurried quickly toward Kester with my tray of loaves. The baby, his clubfoot tucked under him, crouched against the wall, his eyes upon Kester. Even as I moved, Kester was able to reach out and touch my high, firm breasts by seeming accident as he reached for a loaf.

He smiled, revealing a mouthful of crooked yellow teeth and said low, "Blesset, by God, ye got ter make up yer mind and soon. I bin sleepin' cold. I'll come up to yer bloody room and take ye—tonight, by God!"

With sudden boldness I said, "I'll come to ye termorrow night, Tet." By tomorrow night I would be long gone. I moved away with a seductive smile. He caught his breath, his face flushed with passion, and he murmured, "High time, ye little tart—"

Tonight I will be forever beyond his touch, I thought grimly. Ambition was a towering, all-consuming fire in me. I was *better* than Tet Kester, better too than the common backwash of humanity that peopled the Boar's Head Inn. Steve might *think* me of noble blood, but I *knew* it. In England's tightly knit caste system, a girl without a name, who was likely a bastard, no matter how beautiful, would find only backdoor liaisons.

That was not for me! I meant to climb in the world— the new world that lay far across the Atlantic.

Late that night, I lay in my cot beside Moll's. She slept heavily scarce two feet from me. I waited an hour, then another. A light rain fell, then stopped, and through the single window in our small, ugly third-floor room, I could see intermittent moonlight.

At last, with a stealth I had acquired over the years, I slipped from the cot and silently donned the chemise, the petticoats, the dress I had worn that day, one of the only two I possessed.

I did not put on the worn half-slippers. I carried them as I made my secret way to the garret. There, I retrieved my knapsack and struggled to sling it over my slender shoulder.

I thought of Moll and drew a deep breath of relief. She had become increasingly rough and cruel over the last months. She had slept with Tet Kester until her coarse attractiveness failed. Now she was jealous of my youth and Kester's open desire and admiration.

But Billy! My heart caught as I thought of that little crippled boy who loved me as well as his own clubfooted mother and tears stung my eyes. Stooping, I wound the laces of the little slippers about my ankles as I perched on the last step of the stairs.

I thought of all Moll's railing, her accusations and her cautioning, as I made my way through the silent inn to the doorway. She had reiterated so often the dire consequences of sleeping with a man and now she was ready to turn me over to Kester and bastards be damned. But it was Marianne's confinement that had made me intensely wary. My virtue was more from fear than from morality on my part, for like any sixteen-year-old, I was curious about the vague stirrings and longings that invaded my dreams.

I slung my old cloak about my shoulders and I did not look back as I stepped into the night. The transient moon made livid the pools of water standing in the street where cobbles had sunk to form potholes. I kept close to the buildings, a darker shadow among others that pervaded the silent street.

It was a long walk, near a mile to the quay, and I would have to search for the *Sea Warrior* among the many vessels whose masts forested the harbor.

Since England was at war with France, she had clamped an embargo on the ports of many nations. But Steve Boyette had said, "Captain Sterrett is an astute trader. He carries flags of many nations in his hold and changes his flag to suit his waters. Actually, you might call him a smuggler, Blessed, but he is an old friend to me and he will see you reach America, you may be sure."

When I came at last to the wharf near the end, the night air was bitter chill and a fog was rolling in from the channel. It was cold and moist against my face, but it did not cool the urgent heat of my desire to be aboard. *Slowly,* I told myself. *There is plenty of time before dawn.*

It must be near three thirty of the morning, I thought, peering through the fog to read the names on the prow of each ship I passed. It was thickening so fast I knew a moment of panic, fearing I might search until dawn and never find the *Sea Warrior.*

Leaning forward dangerously near the wharf edge, I passed the *Anemone,* the *Richard,* and the *Gull.* I was nearing the end of the pier when there loomed up a dark vessel with a gangplank extended to the wooden wharf beneath my feet. *Sea Warrior.* It was dimly but plainly visible, and I dragged in a great breath of relief. Shifting the knapsack to my other hand, I mounted the plank. It gave off a shrill creaking under my hastening footsteps. I fairly flew up the remainder, for I felt the sound would bring out sleeping sailors and God alone knew who else.

On the deck, a feeble lantern glimmered on a hatch, its rays a poor defense against the swirling fog. But as I approached, I saw a flight of stairs beyond and a light emanating from them.

My hands were cold with nervousness and my heart beat in strange, rapid bursts as I took those steps. I passed closed doors on either side of the passageway. At the end was an open door from which the light came.

Reaching it, I saw a man with a full dark beard seated at a table. His head was bent as he pored over maps and papers before him. I rapped. He did not look up as he made a brusque response.

I cleared my throat and said, "Sir, are ye Cap'n Sterrett?"

He looked up swiftly then and his black eyes took me in. "I am."

I was shaking slightly. "I'm—th' redemptioner—I—"

"Ah, yes. Moll Stuart's daughter, old Boyette tells me. What's your name? Blessed, did he say?"

"It ain't," I replied defiantly. "Me name's Aurielle Stuart." I came down harshly on each syllable and vowel and the name sounded hard on my lips.

"Hmmm." His bright little eyes went over me leisurely, surprise mingling with annoyance. "Boyette didn't tell me you were a beauty. I'll thank you to keep away from my crew during the voyage."

"Ye mean I must make th' whole voyage—inside?" I was dismayed.

"Nay, but you'll come out only when I tell you. Can't have a piece like you stirring up my men."

I set my mouth. "Ye can be damn sure I'll discourage 'em," I said in my gutter language. "They'll leave *me* alone." My father's poniard was hard against my side and I spoke with complete confidence.

He laughed shortly. "By God, I believe you. I've looked on bergs in the North Sea not half so cold and hard as those eyes o' yours. Come on, I'll take you to your quarters. I'm doing this more as a favor for Boyette than for the money you'll bring. You're the only passenger. I don't like passengers."

He came around from behind the desk carrying his lantern and shouldered my knapsack, saying brusquely, "Come along, miss. I'll show you to your quarters."

Stilling my trembling, I followed him back down a flight of steps and, after that, still another flight down into the bowels of the ship. A sour, ugly odor smote me, and in the light of his lantern, the captain saw my short, straight nose wrinkle. "You'll get used to it," he said dryly, and opened a door on a narrow, stuffy room with two bunks built into the wall. There was a table with a cracked pitcher and bowl upon it, and the linen looked soiled.

Cleanliness had always been a passion with me. Moll had often railed out at my frequent bathings and laundering of my clothing, which she insisted wore them out before their time.

"This place looks dirty an' *used,*" I said accusingly.

"Hell, yes, it's been used. What do you think you are, miss? A queen's lady-in-waiting?" Then lighting the single candle beside the pitcher and bowl, he eyed me narrowly. "Are you sure you know what a redemptioner is? You're even less than indentured. There isn't *anyone* wanting you in America."

My chin rose. "Certainly," I replied coolly. Steve Boyette had told me. Redemptioners were whites who left Europe without a contract specifying the number of years they would be required to serve in return for the cost of their passages. I would have to redeem myself by agreeing to a term of servitude to whomever would pay this bearded smuggler his fee. I would not be permitted to leave ship at all until someone on the shore paid that fee and papers were issued confirming my servitude.

"Can I wash this beddin' 'fore I use it?" I asked.

"No, you can't. Not until this vessel is well underway. Then on a sunny day with a spanking breeze to dry it, I might let you scrub it up in here a bit. Now, if you're smart, you'll crawl into that bunk and catch some sleep. You're aboard only because my friendship for old Boyette makes it so." He turned to leave, then wheeled back, lantern swinging. "There's a tinderbox on that shelf up there. The first mate, Mr. Timothy Tucker, will see you get water and food." He was gone, closing the door on the fetid little room.

I longed to open the door but refrained. Some seaman might come prowling down the passageway and bumble his way into this stinking little hole. I examined the door for a lock. There was none. Fully clothed, I lay back on the bunk.

I was still wide awake when the dim shouts of the men who clambered on deck to let out the sails came to my ears. I had snuffed the candle to save it, so the room was black as pitch, without a touch of relieving light. My long journey to America was not to be a pleasant one.

Three weeks out from England, I realized at last that I would never be permitted to scrub the bedding or the room. There was not enough water for such niceties. I was miserably aware that my person smelled almost as abominably as my bunk. It was all I could do to cadge enough water to scrub my face and limbs in the meager confines of the bowl.

We had passed through two spring storms in which the ship wallowed heavily, but I was not seasick. On fair days, in the evening the first mate, Tucker, a thick-shouldered, thick-necked man, fetched me above and let me walk the decks. I looked forward to these periods as a starving prisoner would to food. Tucker, who had a broad, flat nose, was letting me know that he found me appetizing despite my dirt. He had a great drooping mustache that always looked distastefully wet.

One day when he brought my supper and a mug of ale, he leaned near and ran his hand along the curve of my back, cupping my right buttock as he whispered suggestively, "I can make your life a lot easier, Aurielle, if you'd be nicer! I could bring you tidbits from the cap'n's table—even get clean bedding for you." The hand slid back up to my waist as I moved back, the plate and mug in my hands. I twisted away fiercely, spilling some of the ale.

"Keep yer filthy 'ands off me, ye bloody scum! I ain't fer the likes o' ye!"

He scowled, his lip going down at the corner. "You think you're so damned fine! You aren't anything but a redemptioner—a stinking pauper, you are, and *you* putting on such grand airs." He went out, slamming the door hard, causing the candle to flutter.

But as the days went by, he grew bolder still, and more persistent, and I kept my poniard at my waist morning and night.

We put into the Azores, the Indies, and later at Martinique, whose seaport city I was permitted to look at from shipboard only. The captain had become more lenient, letting me out of my malodorous room more often during the day, for I ignored the impudent sailors with an icy remoteness that put them off effectively. I was greatly relieved not to be beholden to Tucker now for my outings.

We took on fresh supplies at the stops we made, and I noted that the flag at the top of the mast changed frequently, as Captain Sterrett paused with his cargoes and took on new ones.

Then, at last, we entered American waters and the captain had Tucker bring me a large bucket of water and a bar of handmilled soap. I knew we were nearing our final destination and he wanted me to present as good an appearance as possible in order that he might up his fee for my passage.

I rejoiced in the bath, and in that miserably small

bowl I managed to wash my hair and bathe myself entirely. I then donned my only other dress, which I had saved for the occasion.

Sterrett's cargo now was spices and silks, as well as delicate French china, which he traded for in Martinique. Now he proposed to make a small fortune as well as rid himself of me in New Orleans, a city on a great river, he said, that cut through the whole of the American continent.

But evening came and, as I strolled the deck, I realized that we would not arrive in New Orleans that day. Indeed, we were becalmed, the wind having died, and we moved at a snail's pace on the still waters of the sea.

"It isn't the sea," Tucker responded to my remark. " 'Tis the Mexican Gulf." His eyes roved nervously over the horizon toward the setting sun.

"What're ye lookin' fer," I asked, unable to keep contempt out of my voice. "Are ye scairt o' somethin'?"

Stung by my tone, he took my arm roughly and pointed to the north. " 'Twould serve you right, you proud piece, if Lafitte himself took you. He's a pirate and he'd bend you to his will, you may be sure."

I jerked from his grasp and stepped back. "No man'll bend *me* to his will."

He laughed under his breath. "So you say, you uppity wench—so *you* say," and to my great relief, he left.

I looked up at the flag hanging limply from the mast and saw it was French now. I grinned to myself. Steve Boyette had taught me enough history to know that the Americans had clung to their friendship with France because of her help during their revolution against England more than thirty years ago. They would welcome Captain Sterrett to their shores, unaware of his true allegiance—if true allegiance such a man could possess.

The sun sank below the rounding line of water in the fiery west and we sat aimlessly on the still surface. It was late June and the air about me in this latitude was warm and tropic.

A grizzled sailor I had seen often in my walks came up beside me and spat over the side. "A braw evenin', miss," he said.

"Yes," I replied, indifferent and cool. Even though

19

this man was old enough to be my grandfather, I had never returned his friendly smiles.

"Ye'll soon see the river, ma'am," he said respectfully. "She's a queen, the Mississip—a lady queen an' a whore bitch."

He said it quite naturally and I was unoffended, for it was the language with which I had grown up. " 'Ow c'n a river be both?" I asked idly. There was a dreaminess in the air, a kind of glamour in the stillness.

"I lived in N'Orleans fer two year oncet. That damn river's so beautiful by moonlight it makes yer heart ache— an' by day she brings a king's ransom down from the north, ever kind o' animal skin in the world an' God knows how much produce. Cotton enough ter set ever wheel an' mill in England spinnin'." He paused, his eyes narrowed on the northern horizon.

"That sounds like a lady queen—not a whore bitch." I was interested in spite of my wariness.

"Ah, but she brings the Kaintucks—great brawly men with knives to carve out a man's gizzard. An' when it rains, she brings floods an' fevers to kill a man in 'is own vomit. Bronze John, they calls that fever. Turns a body yeller as gold. An' the fights she gives harbor to! Them bloody Frenchmen—Creoles they call theirselves—fancyin' their aristocracy, darin' a man to fight 'em over a word, a move, er maybe th' way yer wear yer hat. Oh, she's a bloody bitch of a river all right."

I laughed. "Ye make 'er sound like a person." Then slowly, "I think I'm goin' ter like livin' by that river."

"I'd 'a stayed in N'Orleans—but I made one voyage too many on an American ship an' a British man-o'-war stopped us. Took off all th' Englishmen an' a few native Americans, too. Th' American government don't like that —impressin' their seamen. One day I suspicion they'll go to war over it."

"God and devil! I'm sick o' war!" I swore. "That bloody Napoleon's give us enough o' wars. Everything in Britain's been goin' fer th' army an' navy. I'm glad ter get away from it."

He shrugged. He was too old for the British Navy now and was evidently long ago reconciled to his lot in

20

life. He did not look at me with the raw desire I had seen in the others' eyes and I knew a fleeting regret for my earlier coldness to him.

"I wish ye well, ma'am. Yer fair—fairer than any girl I ever see." He began tightening a rope, for the breeze had suddenly freshened with the sinking of the sun. I stayed until darkness was fully upon us, then I made my way reluctantly to my narrow room below.

A bud of joy pushed its way into my heart. Tomorrow I would see that river of passions, that broad, swift-flowing river on the banks of which I would make a new life for myself. I slept and dreamed of it.

Some deep, primeval instinct wakened me, even before I heard his heavy breath. I wakened not slowly but all at once, with every sense quivering and alert. Then I heard his smothered movements as he stealthily approached my bunk. The rank odor of him reached my nose and I drew myself up into a tight ball at the back of the narrow bunk, feeling for the poniard that never left my side.

The bed gave as his hands fumbled in the linens, seeking my body. By his smell I knew unerringly that it was Tucker.

As his hands roved the bed, he smothered a curse and whispered hoarsely, "You're here, you little bitch. Now where the hell—" And suddenly he was touching me. As his hands closed on my shoulders, I drew the poniard.

"Let go o' me, ye low bastard," I whispered in my gutter English, " 'er I'll slit yer bloody throat."

He laughed triumphantly, his hands slipping over my breasts to seize my waist and draw me to him. "So no man'll take you, eh? Well, I'm going to, if I kill you in the doing of it. No one'll know or care."

We wrestled silently in the blackness. Then, in our panting struggle, his face came down on mine and he pulled at the neck of my gown, tearing it with a rip that was loud. I screamed. His great hairy hand found my mouth and clamped over it, while with the other he fumbled with my nightdress, pulling it upward.

With the fluid dexterity of an eel, my hand slipped between us and I drove the poniard into his broad chest.

21

It was such a slender and sharp weapon that it went into him with the ease of a hot knife through butter.

He gave a low grunt, the one hand closing spasmodically on my face and the other on my thigh with agonizing tightness before they both relaxed. With a deep sigh, he fell across me in the bunk. My hand had not left the haft of the dagger and I tore it from him as I struggled against the inert weight above me.

God and the devil, he was heavy! I panted silently as I worked to push myself from under the man. At last, I twisted out and away, staggering to my feet in stygian darkness. Silence was all about me. Had no one heard my piercing scream? With the poniard still in my hand, I sought the flint on the shelf above the bowl and, with trembling hands, lit the candle there. As it guttered to a flame, I looked down and was shocked and repelled.

My torn nightdress was red with blood across the front. Shuddering, I pulled the garment over my head, only to see that the blood was horribly smeared across my breasts.

Frantically, I poured the last drops of water from the pitcher into the bowl and began to bathe the blood from my bosom, hands, and the long, thin blade of the poniard. I donned my clothing hastily, then turned to my bunk where Tucker lay, face down.

I tugged at him, rolling him over on his back at last, with one great leg trailing on the floor. The front of his shirt was blood-soaked and his eyes were shining slits in the candlelight. His breath was a hoarse rasping now, which seemed to fill the small room. A great horror flooded me. I had meant to drive him away, that was all. I started to put my hand to his breast, blindly seeking a pulse. I stopped short as I realized that it was his left breast from which the blood welled.

Sickness crept through me. *I had killed a man.* I could not believe it. I, who wept over the stray mongrels that begged at the Boar's Head, who took up for every skinny waif on the streets.

Terror followed swiftly. Punishment would be sure and quick, for there was no one to come to my defense. It would do no good to tell of his attempted rape, his threat to kill me. I could imagine Captain Sterrett's reaction to the death of his first mate at my hands. It would make no difference to Sterrett that Tucker would have killed me readily enough. If I had killed him instead, I would pay for it. Murder. That's what they would call it in England. I might well hang.

Oh, if only I could hide him until we made port, I thought impractically. Perhaps under the bunk. No. Sterrett would miss him and the crew would be set to search for him in every nook and cranny. If I could somehow drag him up and heave him overboard—I discarded the frantic notion. I could never manage so big a burden.

The New World and escape were almost within sight, I thought with fresh anguish, yet with one blow, I had lost it all. By stabbing blindly at Tucker, I had thrown away my chance. I sat down weakly on the opposite bunk and pondered my fate. How long did I have before they would come searching for Tucker? I flung myself across the bunk and gave myself up to the healing flow of tears.

Suddenly I froze. My tears dried. From above had come the sound of shouts, hoarse and forceful, cries and orders, and the ship shuddered as a gun roared out from her side. I jumped to my feet. They were firing a cannon from the *Sea Warrior!* That could mean but one thing. We were under attack!

The volume of noise grew and the small cannons roared repeatedly. All at once a great crashing sound came to my ears. A mast falling? It had to be! The sound of cannon balls smashing into the *Sea Warrior* grew explosively. Lighter gunfire cracked in the background.

Then slowly and with an unsteady hand, I took my poniard, dried it carefully, and tucked it at my waist and out of sight. The ship shook under the broadsides she was taking. If I had killed Tucker, it now appeared that in swift retribution I would be blown to bits. All the guns on the *Sea Warrior* were thundering now and the sound of falling timbers mingled with the agonized screams of the wounded.

I stood there, with the candle glimmering across the blood-soaked Tucker, and it was borne in upon me that in the holocaust going on above, anyone, *anyone at all* could come below and find me with the body. Renewed terror crawled through me and I set the candle on the table by the bed. My breath was coming in quick gasps and I was flooded with the superhuman strength that only wild fear can release.

I seized Tucker's thick shoulders, then slipped my hands beneath his arms and tugged hard. I must hide him! I must! With a heavy thud, the inert body sprawled to the floor and I began to shove him into the narrow space between the bunk and the floor. Dear God! He was too big! No, no—the body was sliding at last under my frantic efforts. Panting, gasping, I pushed him farther, until the great, heavy body was out of sight. I rose, seized the blood-soaked covers, and pushed them in upon the body. Then I tore the blankets from the bunk and spread them over the half-hidden corpse.

I backed away. To the casual eye, nothing could be seen but the stripped bunk. Turning, I caught up a single blanket from the other bunk and flung it across the bare mattress. There! The room looked much as it had before Tucker had entered. Sobbing for breath, I sank onto the bunk across from the one under which I had hidden the body.

I do not know how long I sat thus, with the candle guttering low in the dish, before it came to me that I could not stay there another moment—not even if it meant going above and getting my head blown off.

The candle gave forth a last flicker and I was in total darkness. Rising, I felt my way to the door and stepped into the black passageway. Closing the door, I took a slow, shuddering breath. The vessel trembled as it took another ball, and the odor of smoking timbers came to my nostrils. There was a dim light at the end of the second flight of stairs. I lurched suddenly as the cannons roared and I put a hand to the wall to steady myself.

I climbed slowly, dreading what would meet my eyes. The light increased as I neared the opening to the deck. It was early morning! It was the light of dawn filtering down between the brilliant flashes of gunfire.

I stood at the opening to the deck and recoiled at the horror I saw there. The dead lay scattered about. Three

24

masts had fallen and two sailors lay crushed beneath them. One was the old seaman who had told me of the river. I glimpsed the attacking ship. I had never in my life seen one like her. She was a slim vessel and her sides were lined with cannon, big ones, while smaller ones were mounted on the deck. I noted her beautifully formed prow as she slipped by to rake the *Sea Warrior* with those cannon.

I squeezed my eyes shut against the sight of the fire and belching smoke.

I glanced again at the attacking ship to see it had made a graceful turn and was bearing down upon us once more with deadly accuracy. I could see the men aboard her now, firing at the sailors on the *Sea Warrior* with long, slender guns. Two of our sailors fell and a bullet thudded into the wall beside me.

I turned in sudden panic to retrace my steps, but the smell of smoke rose to meet me strongly. Somewhere below, the *Sea Warrior* was afire.

Fresh fear welled up as I clutched my skirts and returned to crouch on the first step. I longed to run out on deck to escape the acrid smoke that was seeping up just below me, but I knew it would be suicide to do so.

Complete disorder reigned on the deck of the *Sea Warrior* now, with the remaining sailors hiding behind hatches, piles of rope, barrels of molasses, any protection against the fatal fire from the beautiful vessel that was now alongside. Sailors aboard her slung out grappling hooks and pulled the *Sea Warrior* closer, and I saw the first men leap across to board us.

I looked up then at the flag that fluttered above her prow. I did not recognize the brilliant colors in the rising sunlight. The *Sea Warrior*'s men were creeping from behind their hiding places now, holding their hands above their heads. The groans of those lying wounded on deck were terrible to hear. I looked again at my friend lying beneath the mast and noted that his leg appeared shattered and his abdomen impaled by a large splinter from the mast. His seamed face was contorted with pain. I could stand his suffering no longer.

Oblivious to the loud voices about the ship, I leaped

from my hiding place in the companionway and ran to his side. Stooping, I said, "Be still—ye're losin' blood! I'll bandage yer leg where I c'n reach it," and I seized a petticoat beneath my dress and tried to tear a strip from it, but it would not yield.

His smile was ghostly. "I'm killed, ma'am—th' mast's stabbed me guts through."

I put the petticoat in my teeth and tore off a wide band of white cotton. I was struggling to bind his leg tightly when a quiet and cultured voice above me said, "Mademoiselle, you will please rise and come with me—join the crew for interrogation. We have men who will care for the wounded."

I looked up into a dark French face, with eyes the color of my own under his dark tumble of hair. He spoke again, the eyes complimenting me, "You are the only lady aboard? Or are there more below?"

"There ain't nobody at all below," I replied quickly, thinking of Tucker lying in his hasty and temporary grave beneath my bunk. Had I been saved from the consequence of my own folly by these extraordinary events?

"That's as well, *certainement*. We shall have enough difficulty retrieving the cargo, for this ship is afire." His English was flawless and only faintly accented.

As he spoke, I saw his sailors herding the handful of men left alive across to their ship. As the *Sea Warrior* wallowed heavily in the rising wind, the Frenchman put out a brown hand to steady me, and two heavily muscled men with bare chests began to lift the mast from the old sailor. I looked down into his still, white face and knew it was too late now. Sadly, I obeyed the Frenchman's orders to follow him.

Boarding planks had been placed from ship to ship and he steered me to one of them. It shivered as I put my foot upon it and I drew back. "That's a bloody poor walk. I'll fall off fer sure," I said, pulling my arm from my captor's hand.

He caught it again, his fingers like iron. "I will catch you, mademoiselle, if you come to fall," and I was forced to traverse the shaky plank. Once we were aboard, he added, "You will sit here"—motioning to a coil of rope—"until I return."

I noticed then that the victorious sailors who had made their way into the *Sea Warrior*'s hatches and companionways were returning with cargo on their backs, in their arms, and in some cases, by twos carrying the great boxes that contained anything from silks to silver and china. There was a steady stream of them passing back and forth between the ships, and I wondered nervously if they had come upon Tucker. But the acrid odor of burning timbers grew stronger in the air and I drew a long, hopeful breath.

Looking up, I saw a man directing the sailors from the bridge. *Pirates,* I thought suddenly, struck by the obvious revelation. Despite the gaily colored flag atop the ship's mast, I had been captured by pirates, a cutthroat breed of men, rapacious, ruthless, and cruel. My breath shortened as I looked more closely at the man on the bridge. He was very tall, taller than the Frenchman. Black hair gleamed in the early sunlight and narrowed dark eyes were set in a hard, lean face. His breeches and the soft leather boots that came to his knees were as well made as those of the dandies who sometimes frequented the Boar's Head. He did not look to be French. The strong, bold nose made him appear the bird of prey that he was.

The Frenchman approached again, his smile revealing fine white teeth. I drew myself up stiffly and, before he could speak, I said, "Yer pirates, a'course. What d'ye mean ter do with me—us?"

The handsome Gallic features took on a wounded air. "*Vraiment,* ma'amselle, we are not pirates. We are privateers under Captain Quentin Kincannon. He carries letters of marque from Cartagena. We knew your vessel for English immediately, despite your French flag—and we—America is at war with England."

"Oh, lor'," I groaned. I had left one country at war only to reach another. I had refused to think of myself as English entirely, for my father—he *had* to be my father—carried a note that implied I was half French.

"That distresses you, ma'amselle?" the Frenchman asked politely.

I looked at him more closely. He had a thin, straight nose and his handsome features were patrician. His black slanting brows made him look somehow familiar. His tall, slender figure was quite elegant in black boots and fitted breeches. His silk shirt was open at the throat and flowed gracefully to his thin, powerful wrists. I became aware that he was very attractive.

"Cor'!" I responded in some confusion. "War makes life harder. All o' th' money goes fer th' fightin', leavin' but little fer th' rest o' us."

"Not in our Louisiana, *chérie*. We have plenty of everything. Now—you will please remain here, for *mon capitaine* will want to question you when he finishes with your crew." He paused and glanced up at the man on the bridge above us.

I sat back down, this time on a barrel, and looked about me at the milling mass of men. My eyes strayed again to the man above me and I was suddenly struck by the appearance of a slim figure beside that of the captain's. *It was a woman!*

She was clad in breeches and boots, like the men about her, but her full breasts strained against a white cambric shirt and a cascade of red-gold hair spilled from under the seaman's scarf about her head. There were golden hoops in her ears and she was quite beautiful. She held a flashing sword in her hand. Her slim waist was bound by a wide red sash.

The Frenchman, examining the tablet he was marking, turned to go again and I caught at his full sleeve. "Yer have wimmin in yer crew aboard this ship?" I asked incredulously.

He followed my eyes and laughed. "Only Roxanne. She's the captain's—ah—protégé and a good girl in a scrap."

"Her name is Roxanne?"

"Roxanne Deveret."

I was caught by her last name. Deveret. So she was French, like me.

"I am French—my mother was French, highly born," I said defiantly.

He lifted his black, winged brows. *"Vraiment? Comment vous appellez-vous?"*

I shook my head. "I was raised English. I can't—remember much French."

"What is your name?"

"Aurielle. Aurielle Stuart," I said, speaking the consonants and vowels with my customary harshness.

"How do you spell it, ma'amselle?" he asked sharply.

I spelled it out for him slowly and his blue eyes widened. "Ah, that is a lovely name, ma'amselle, but you do not say it correctly. It is a soft name, almost an endearment. Like a word of love," and on his tongue the word was beautiful. He softened it to a gentle, enchanting sound. *Aurielle.* I was exultant. At last, an educated man had spoken my name. No more Blesset. I was Aurielle, almost a word of love.

As he turned away, I spoke the name aloud once, then again, savoring the sound of it. I looked after the tall, handsome Frenchman gratefully.

Then glancing up at Roxanne Deveret, I saw she was looking intently at me. At that moment, she leaped gracefully down from the bridge and strode lithely toward me. Something deep within rose to the challenge in her eyes. My back stiffened and my own dark, slanting brows rose in disdain.

Stopping before me, legs apart in a swagger, she sheathed her sword expertly. Deep hostility sprang up between us on the instant. "What were you doing aboard that ship?" she asked peremptorily; her big green eyes with their fans of tangled lashes were imperious. "You are the only woman, they tell me." Her English was faultless and not even accented.

I returned her stare coldly. "It ain't fer the likes o' *ye* to question *me!*"

Her hand went threateningly to the hilt of her sword and I put my hand to my waist where the poniard snuggled. "Who are you?" she asked roughly.

"Aurielle Stuart," I replied tartly, "an' who are ye that asks?"

She laughed suddenly. "You're an ignorant piece,

29

even if you are beautiful. You'll give me no trouble. Where were you bound?"

I burned with the insult. Ignorant, was I? Because of my speech. I could probably read as well as this impudent female pirate. "I ain't goin' ter answer yer questions, wench. Ye don't have no say-so over me."

Roxanne Deveret looked at me contemptuously. "You'll be surprised at the say-so I shall have over you." She glanced back at the tall captain who was conferring with my French captor. "Captain Quent and I are—we're sort of partners and he often gives me charge of some of our prisoners. I plan to make life hard for you on Grande Terre, Aurielle Stuart. Maybe you'll run away into the swamps!" Her laughter was merry now. "I've done it with others and they've never been heard from to this day."

"Ye won't do that with me, ye scum. I'll do ye in!" I said fiercely.

"Oh ho," she responded, still laughing. "The English tart has some fire in her!"

"I'm half French and ye'll get burned properlike if ye try to do *me* in." My voice was so cold and hard it was alien in my ears. My hand was on the poniard, and already in my mind I was closing with her before she could draw her slender sword.

"We'll see"—her cheeks dimpled with her smile— "when Captain Quent interrogates you. He may give you to me for my personal maid."

"I'll not be maid to ye, ye dirty pirate."

"We'll see," she replied arrogantly and strode away.

I sat on the barrel once more, boiling with anger. Order was being established on deck as the few prisoners were herded below. Still, it was a long time before the tall captain approached me, his black eyes intent on mine.

When he stood before me, I rose so as not to look so far up at him. It was useless. He was still over a head taller no matter how heartily I wished to meet him eye to eye. I had formed a deep antipathy to him already—him and his whore, Roxanne. I felt certain I knew what her hold was over him.

"What were you doing aboard that English vessel

in American waters?" he asked abruptly in a deep and astonishingly cultured British voice.

"I'm a redemptioner," I replied belligerently. "I'm ter be—I was ter be redeemed in New Orleans an' serve out a term fer payment on me passage."

"It appears that I have redeemed you, miss. What can you do that's useful—outside of your obvious physical charms," he added with a cynical smile. "Perhaps we can use you at Grande Terre."

"By God, ye'll send me on ter New Orleans! I don't plan ter be useful ter th' likes o' ye. Pirates an' cutthroats!"

He threw back his head and laughed heartily and he did not deny my accusation. Instead he said, "But you owe me for your passage and you must pay. And it appears you're very prideful for one with such humble beginnings —the daughter of a barmaid."

I lashed out in fury. "I *ain't* Moll's daughter. Me mother was of th' French nobility—an' me father a—a— lord's son!" I improvised this latter rapidly. The girl named Roxanne had drawn up beside him and just behind her stood a giant black man, whose dark brown body was stripped to the waist. Like the girl before him, he wore gold hoops in his ears. His strong nose was broad and flat and his lips wide. His close-cropped jet hair was peppered with gray at the temples only.

The captain was amused. "Sterrett tells me you—"

"I don't give a damn what *'e* says," I blazed. " '*E* don't know me and *you* don't know me! I'll not stand fer ye laughin' at me—" I pulled the poniard from my waist and backed away from them.

The captain was on me before I could move, the poniard in his strong hand as he imprisoned my two in his free one. "The little butterfly has a stinger, Ulysses. Here, take it," and he tossed my prized weapon to the tall black man.

I pulled from his grasp and delivered a stinging slap across his sardonic face, then rushed at the man he called Ulysses, seizing his thick, sinewy wrist and tugging at the haft of my father's dagger. "Give me that," I panted. "It was me father's."

The captain peeled me off the black man easily, and

Ulysses did not smile. It was futile to struggle, so I stood there, breasts heaving, cheeks hot with fury.

"Here, Ulysses—let me see that," the captain said, holding me with but one hand about my wrists. He caught the poniard from the man midair and held it by the point, examining the haft closely. In the early sunlight, diamonds and rubies glowed, returning fire to the sun in shafts of glittering beauty. "J.B.S.," the captain murmured, scrutinizing the carved silver at the base of the precious stones. "There's a goodly sum in jewels on this thing."

"Thief that ye are, I suppose ye'll take me father's poniard from me," I said, with biting contempt; my heart was sick at the thought.

The cynical smile curved his lips. "Nay, since it is your father's legacy to you." The words were heavy with irony. "But I think I should keep it for you until I can be sure you'll not be sticking it into any of us. How old are you, Aurielle Stuart?"

"I don't kn—Sixteen!"

Roxanne Deveret cried triumphantly, "You don't really know! You're a bastard, I'll wager!"

"Ye shouldn't judge every woman by yerself," I flared and tried to twist once more from the grasp of the man who held me, for the girl rushed at me, hands like claws.

Ulysses caught her easily. "Here now, Mademoiselle Roxanne, we have taken her weapon. You would not hurt one who is defenseless." He was very gentle with the girl and his voice was deep and faintly accented.

"I'll kill that one!" she cried huskily, her tawny hair blowing in the rising breeze. Her face was scarlet and her green eyes flashed fire.

I smiled cynically. So my barb had struck home—and no doubt we were two of a kind, I thought bitterly, with neither of us knowing our parentage. I did not know what the initials J.B.S. on my father's poniard stood for—nor indeed, if the dagger had truly belonged to the young man who died so long ago in the upper regions of the Boar's Head. But in my mind the S stood for Stuart. That Moll's name was Stuart had been purely coincidental as far as I was concerned. Now I taunted, "If I 'ad me father's dagger, you'd not be so free with yer threats!"

Roxanne ceased struggling in Ulysses's strong, gentle grasp and I became aware of the captain's hands on me. They were not gentle and the blood was cut off from my hands where he gripped them; his fingers in my shoulder were like steel prongs.

"Let go o' me, ye low scum," I gritted, pulling hard against his hold.

"What's your word worth, Aurielle?" he asked soberly and, despite my anger, the soft new sound of my name was sweet to my ears.

"Once given, 'tis worth me life."

"Then give it to me that you'll not try to wound or escape us, that you will serve us to pay for your passage, and I'll let you have your father's dagger and your freedom aboard my ship."

I looked up into the bronzed face and the hard, uncompromising dark eyes. A sudden prank of wind blew his black hair across his forehead. The corded column of his strong throat rose from an open white shirt; dark curling hair covered the hollow at the base of his throat. "Well?" he prodded.

"You 'ave it," I said, my voice still constricted by anger.

He handed me the poniard, his smile cryptic. "Tell me, Aurielle, have you ever really used this on man or woman?"

I felt the blood leave my face and my eyes flew to the towering flames that engulfed the *Sea Warrior,* half a mile away now, consuming my victim. "No," I lied too quickly. Then with defiance, "But I would if I 'ad to."

"So?" His face was solemn but his eyes suddenly twinkled. "And I was going to let Roxanne look after you, but I don't think that's wise now."

"I *will* look after her, Quent," Roxanne said swiftly. "You know I've needed a maid――"

"I'll not be a maid ter *her*," I interrupted warningly. "If I'm to keep my word, ye'll 'ave ter give me yers—that I'll have naught ter do with that—woman."

The captain's eyes were hard once more. "Nay,

33

Roxanne. You need a maid no more than I." Though he had released me, where his hands had touched still stung. "You keep to yourself, Aurielle Stuart—and Roxanne, you leave her strictly alone." Then he spoke roughly, to me again. "You owe me now, miss, for your passage. We'll talk about your working it out when we reach Grande Terre tomorrow evening."

Roxanne's green eyes were full of passion as they rested on Quentin Kincannon; then, as they moved slowly away and toward me, they blazed with hatred.

With cutting insight, I said, "Ye needn't worry, Roxanne—I don't want 'im," and I looked at the captain, whose mouth went down in a dry smile, and added contemptuously, "I wouldn't 'ave 'im on me life!" But my flesh, where he had touched me, remembered the feel of him.

Suddenly she was rocking with laughter. "And let that be a lesson to you, Quent! There's one woman who's not ready to swoon in your arms!"

He shrugged and said over his shoulder, "There are many of those, Roxanne," and Roxanne Deveret bit her full lower lip.

I turned away, tucking my weapon tenderly against my narrow waist. Then I glanced back at the captain's tall, slim-hipped form speculatively. A privateer. What was that, I wondered. Probably another name for pirate. And did he sleep with Roxanne Deveret? Very probably.

I sat down on a square box with French words written across it and let the freshening breeze have free rein in my tumbling chestnut hair. In the bruising events that had followed one upon another during the last twelve hours, I had not thought to try to put it up and it fell almost to my waist in a faintly curling mass. I stared over the prow of the ship—I didn't even know its name—to the north, willing a horizon to appear. But the endless stretch of water remained unbroken.

Chapter
2

I was conscious of being tired as well as hungry, for I had little sleep the night before, thanks to the rapacious Tucker. I shivered in the hot sun, remembering how smoothly the dagger had slid into his chest—too easily!

Suddenly the Frenchman came up and seated himself on the broad box beside me, a tablet in his hand. "Ma'amselle Aurielle, are you growing hungry?" he asked in his soft, easy French voice.

"Yes," I admitted. "I ain't had nothin' ter eat since yesterday." I looked at him more closely. The soft white shirt with full sleeves graced a chest of magnificent proportions. His blue eyes were merry under arched black brows and his clean-cut mouth suggested tenderness. Altogether he was a very handsome man.

"We will soon dine. The cook in the galley is preparing food now for the captain and officers. The crew eats in relays when we are sailing.

"Are we far from this Grande Terre?"

His white smile flashed in the sun-browned countenance. *"Mais non.* You will see it and Grand Isle by tomorrow evening with this brisk breeze."

"An' who is that Roxanne woman? 'Ow come she's got so much say-so on this ship?"

His laugh was rollicking. "Ulysses brought her to Barataria, they say, from Saint Domingue during a slave insurrection in the islands. She could have been no more than two. He snatched her from a burning sugar plantation and they barely escaped with their lives. He didn't know who she was and he has been her guardian ever since. It was he who named her Roxanne Deveret."

" 'Ow old is she?"

He shrugged eloquently. "Who knows? Sixteen— seventeen, perhaps eighteen."

"Does she sleep with Captain Kincannon?" I asked bluntly.

His laugh was low and tolerant. "Again, who knows? She loves him, *certainement,* but *mon capitaine,* he is a restless man. He does not like the ties. When we have a market up the bayou, all the New Orleans ladies and gentlemen come to buy from us, and the ladies make sheep's eyes at him, but he does not notice."

"He talks so good," I said grudgingly. "He must of been schooled somewheres." I envied him and Roxanne their cultured speech.

"It is said he is the youngest son of a Scottish lord— the Earl of Kincannon. He never speaks of it; only once he told me there was not room at home for him and an older brother, so he came to America to seek his fortune. And when he has made enough at privateering, he plans to go to New Orleans and make a great deal more in business ventures." He paused, the blue eyes intense. "Are you not curious about *me,* Aurielle. My speech is better even than his—"

"Oh, a'course I am—I—what's yer name?" His smile was so beguiling it threw me in a flutter. And my name on his tongue was velvet soft, as if he had spoken it often and with love.

"I am Monsieur Cheviot—Rodeur Cheviot, *chérie,*" and he took up my grubby little hand and kissed it lightly. "And I am very old by your standards—thirty-six."

"Rodeur—that's a strange name."

"It means rover in English—one who wanders, who has no home—a vagrant."

36

" 'Ow come you talk so good an' have such lovely manners?"

His eyes were veiled suddenly. "I learned much in Paris—before I left." There was a heaviness, a sadness in the words.

"It must of been a good school?"

"The best, Aurielle." His infectious laughter rang out again, dispelling the sudden gloom. "Now ask all those other questions that are still in your eyes."

"Then tell me what are these Grande Terre and Grand Isle places?"

"They are islands at the mouth of Barataria Bay, our home port. We belong to Jean Lafitte's—ah—navy."

I followed his eyes and turned to see Captain Sterrett and what remained of his crew in a bunch before Captain Kincannon. I noted they were not bound, but some of them carried packets and casks in their arms. They were murmuring among themselves and there was an air of relief among them.

"What's bein' done ter them? The captain ain't goin' ter kill 'em?"

"The captain's going to put them afloat to make their way."

"What?" I cried. "Jus' set 'em adrift in the middle o' th' ocean?" I ran to the ship's rail and peered down at the boat that had been lowered.

"Non, Aurielle," Rodeur Cheviot, following, replied with a touch of exasperation. "They shall have sets of oars. And you will observe they are provisioned. Further, this is not the middle of the ocean. It is more than Gambio, the Italian who sails out of Barataria, does for his captives. He shoots them and throws their bodies to feed the fish. These men can row themselves to the Mississippi and from there to New Orleans."

"Or a storm could come up an' drown 'em all," I replied.

He shrugged as the men made their way down a rope ladder to the boat that bobbed below. It looked appallingly small. "Aurielle, I'll wager you hold no love for those men," he said shrewdly. "Now were they so good to you?" I felt blood leave my face as I recalled Tucker. Rodeur went on, "And Beluche never takes a prisoner—"

37

"You don't—Captain Kincannon don't take 'em neither," I retorted.

"Now what would we do with prisoners at Barataria, Aurielle?" he asked reasonably.

"At least they could make their way from there to New Orleans by land, couldn't they?"

"Chérie, there are the *prairies tremblantes,* the floating prairies of grass that will not bear the weight of man, between Barataria Bay and the city. There are alligators and quicksand, a thousand bayous and inlets where a man could lose his way and his life." His mouth curved upward again and his smile was reckless and winning. "Believe me, they are much better off where they are."

By now the men had manned the oars and appeared to be in good spirits and happy that they were spared death. I leaned against the rail and looked up at the Frenchman and said a touch arrogantly, "I got ter make my own way t'New Orleans after I work out my redemption. I don't plan on bein' ignorant an'—an' coarse all me life."

"You may like Grand Isle and Grande Terre and not want to leave. We are all free agents there and live as we please—for all Governor Claiborne issues proclamations and threatens to run us out for smuggling. All New Orleans patronizes our market—the Temple—in the swamps. And Jean and his brother Pierre do a brisk business in the city. They have friends in high places there, but Grande Terre is their kingdom."

"I think yer smugglers an' pirates," I said with a little smile, "an' I plan to school meself so me talk'll be as nicey nice as an eddicated person. Pirates ain't gentry."

"Gentry, eh? And education? Worthy goals. I'm sure you will achieve both. You are indeed part French—I feel it—and the French are very quick, very astute. You will learn rapidly."

"You're damn right I'm quick. It won't take no year fer *me* to become a lady!"

He smiled his charming French smile and said gently, "Aurielle, the first thing you must learn is that no lady swears. Cursing in a woman is a signpost pointing to the gutter."

My face stung as blood mounted it. I would have to watch my language very carefully. All those filthy epithets I had picked up in the streets of Portsmouth would have to be wiped out.

His eyes on me were speculative and there was something else there that I could not name. "I will teach you, little Aurielle, at Grande Terre, while you work out your passage. I am fluent in both French and English."

"Oh," I gasped, "would ye?" I knew a hot surge of hope and joy. "I know I c'n make meself useful to work out me passage, Mister Cheviot. I'm a fine cook and I c'n bake delicious breads an' pies—ol' Moll saw to that!" I rushed on, "Yer talk's fair beautiful, Mister Cheviot—the way ye pernounce me name." Sudden fear caught me. "Oh, what if Cap'n Kincannon decides ter redeem me in 'is market below New Orleans? He c'n get as much as fifteen pounds."

"I am Captain Kincannon's lieutenant, his first mate, his keeper of records, and I am a very good swordsman, so I double as sailor, soldier, and record keeper, and I can tell you now that fifteen pounds is worth less than a farthing to us. A good baker would be worth a thousand pounds."

A new fear assailed me. "Then what if he—wants me ter work fer mor'n a year?"

"To pay a fifteen-pound charge? *Non,* Captain Kincannon is an honorable man. You shall be released after a year—while you learn to read, write, and speak beautifully."

"I c'n read already," I said proudly. "I've read all th' plays o' William Shakespeare." Then forlornly, "But I can't talk it—I don't know how ter pernounce half o' them words an' ever'body around me talked like I do, 'cept'n Steve Boyette."

"Ah, since you read, half your battle is won. You'll not know your own voice, ma'amselle, in six months. You shall see!" And giving me another warm, admiring smile, he left.

My eyes followed the tall, graceful figure and I dwelled happily on the prospect of receiving schooling at his hands. He seemed a gentleman, too, not like Timothy

Tucker, who would have brutally raped me. I repressed a shiver and glanced back to the south, but the sky was clear now. There was no trace of smoke, not even a floating timber in the distance. Tucker was safely at the bottom of this gulf. If he had succeeded, I might even now be carrying his child!

It took nine long months to make a baby and then you were never free again. Remembering Marianne, I knew it *hurt* terribly to birth a baby. *That* had thrown a proper scare into me! There would be no babies until I had married and married someone rich and highborn, a man who was gentry, by God, and who could keep me in silks and satins.

Oh, I should be grand—and no one, *no one* would ever know my low background, or that I didn't really know my mother and father. I would overcome it all! All! Ambition burned higher and hotter within me after Rodeur Cheviot's promise of education. *Education*. There lay the road to respectability, the road to New Orleans and marriage with the richest and finest man in the city.

I did not eat with the men. Rodeur Cheviot brought a plate to me where I sat in the lee of a stack of boxes lashed to the deck of the vessel. He sat with me while I ate, telling me about life in Barataria.

"Many of the men have families there—and children, too. I think you will like it, for it is a clean place, none of the filth of a big city."

I ate greedily and mostly with my fingers and I saw his fine nostrils distend slightly with distaste. I slowed, embarrassed by my lack of manners. Taking up the fork, I attempted awkwardly to use it, glancing at him from time to time. His face softened and he murmured that he would teach me many things and I knew table manners was on a growing list of subjects in which I would need instruction.

"You will sleep in my cabin tonight, ma'amselle," he said softly and I stiffened, a forkful halted in midair.

"I won't!" I said fiercely.

"You misunderstand, Aurielle. I will sleep in your place on deck. You will be far safer in my cabin than up here where the men sleep in clear summer weather."

"Oh," I let my breath out in relief. "Ye're very kind, Mister Cheviot." I felt I owed him an apology but I did not know how to phrase it. I smiled at him uncertainly. "Thankee."

I stayed on deck, however, until the stars were out before Rodeur approached and showed me to his cabin. He had left a full pitcher of water beside the bowl on a commode table. His bunk was spacious and the linens were fresh and clean. There was even a mirror above the commode table, a luxury that informed me my hair badly needed attention. I set about remedying all the hardships I had endured. I took up his comb and brush and brought order to the tangled mane on my head. Then I took up the bar of soap beside the bowl and sniffed it ecstatically. Oh, but I should have a bath—a good bath even though the water was cold!

I began to strip by the light of a lantern which swung from a low beam above my head. I wished briefly that I might wash my hair but regretfully decided against it as the water was insufficient and I did not dare go out for more.

Standing nude, I began with my face and ears and slowly worked my way down my body. Though the hour was late, I took my time, enjoying the small luxury of soap and clean water as I finished with my feet.

It was at this moment that the cabin door was flung open and Quentin Kincannon, holding several sheets of paper, said, "Rodeur, what is this you have down here? A case of khol—"

He broke off and we stared at each other in amazement. Then his eyes slipped downward from my frozen face and slowly he reached behind him, closing the door. His upper torso was bare as if he, too, had been readying himself for the night. For some reason the fact that he was barefoot frightened me as much as his eyes, which were black and brilliant now that they had traveled back to mine. The papers in his hand fell to the floor as he came lithely toward me. Neither of us spoke. He smiled, a white, irresistibly heart-warming smile, and for an instant I was helpless under its impact on me.

As he drew near, my paralysis broke and I seized the

41

rough towel from the bunk, but before I could cover myself, he ripped it from my hand. We began to struggle silently, our breaths mingling hot and fast, like animals in a death struggle. I was no match for the big man and he flung me down upon the broad bunk as he divested himself of his breeches. Driven by fear, I fought desperately beneath him, my fingers raking the mat of black curling hair above me, my breath coming in gasps.

He forced a knee between my legs and his face came down, his mouth fastening on mine with fierce urgency. His lips were cool and his breath was warm and sweet and I felt my own lips tremble under his demand. I was unprepared for the sudden desire that swept me, but in some dim recess of my brain I knew I must not succumb and I lunged away from him, dislodging his knee. By now I was sobbing for breath.

His superior weight was inescapable, and slowly he drew me back under him and forced my legs apart even as I drew them upward to drive them down forcibly against him. He caught my flailing hands, first one and then the other by the wrist, pinning them down behind my head, holding it immovable between them. Once again his lips came down upon mine and this time they were hot and not to be denied. My struggles grew feebler, my breath ever faster.

"Mother of God, I ain't never had no man," I sobbed. "Ah, God help me!" As surely as I drew breath, I would be pregnant by tomorrow morning and carry this man's little bastard for nine long months. All my high-flown plans for the future were drowned in this torrent of desire, for I was succumbing slowly but surely. I gave one last despairing cry, "Oh, I don't want no bastard child—"

His grip loosened and I looked up into the dark, impassioned face above me. In the lantern glow my eyes were swimming with tears so that I could not discern his expression; still I felt him moving away.

He said thickly, "You mean to tell me a trollop like you still has her maidenhead?"

"I ain't no trollop an' I ain't never been took, willin' or unwillin'!" I was weeping harder now.

"I'll be damned," he muttered, rolling over and pulling on his breeches. "And I thought you were naked to tempt me." He laughed suddenly, cynically. "And maybe you were—but all these tears have certainly dampened my ardor."

I sat up, timorously clutching the bedsheet to me. "You mean you ain't goin'—yer goin' ter let me—off?" Tears dried and my wildly beating heart began to slow.

"That's right," he said, giving me a dour look. "I'm going to, as you so romantically put it, let you off. I have no taste for maidenly tears. Fod God's sake, blow your nose and wipe your eyes!"

I did so on the bedsheet and he began to laugh suddenly as he drew his breeches snug at the waist. "What a contretemps," he said as I slowly wiped my face. "Well, keep your virginity, Aurielle. I prefer more willing partners." He stooped and began picking up the papers he had dropped to the floor.

I was still sitting in the bed, the sheet drawn up to my chin as he strode away. At the door he paused. "I suggest you bolt this, miss. Someone else may come looking for Rodeur after I'm gone."

As soon as he closed the door behind him, I leaped from the bed and shot the bolt home. I stood there looking down at my firm and pointed breasts, my flat stomach and curved hips, and I realized suddenly that I was faintly disappointed. There had been a moment there, when he kissed me—Hurriedly I put the thought from me.

I went to bed, but sleep was a long time coming. My body tingled with newly found sensations and I could not keep myself from imagining what it would have been for me, held tenderly in his arms. When at last I slept, in my dreams I saw Kincannon again at the moment he stepped inside the room, big, tanned, with the fragrance of the south wind in his hair—I had smelled it and it had registered indelibly in my mind.

In the mornng when I woke, I faced the undeniable. I was deeply attracted to Quentin Kincannon and I must shore up my vows to hate him for his cynicism and his seizing of me last night. I would forget his mouth, his touch, the warm smell of him.

I dressed hastily and went on deck. Everything looked

bright and good to me, the polished morning sunlight, the sails bellied out in the freshening wind, the breakfast of dried fruit and bread, washed down with coffee. I spent the whole day roaming the decks and watching the horizon slide by.

I avoided Kincannon scrupulously, wishing devoutly I never had to lay eyes on the man again in my life. With equal assiduousness I went out of my way to keep from meeting with Roxanne Deveret. I certainly did not want her captain, I told myself. But I did not want to look into those green eyes and tell her that again.

The sun was setting when I caught my first glimpse of the islands. I noted one island was low in the water, a long, flat stretch of beach, then grasses and finally a stand of twisted green trees, all of them leaning away from the sea. Another stretch of land lay on the other side of this island, making a narrow opening into the body of water beyond.

Rodeur Cheviot, having tallied up the booty and conferred lengthily with the captain, had again come up beside me as the land appeared. Pointing, he said, "That's a *chenière*—a stand of oaks on a higher ridge. We'll sail around to the back side of this island. Our little city is there. Lafitte has his *maison rouge* there, though some of the privateers have their houses on Grand Isle as well." He went on to explain their little commune and how each shared in the profits of privateering.

"What's the name o' this ship, Mister Cheviot?"

"It is the *Wind,* ma'amselle."

I looked ahead, where the ship was cutting smoothly through the water in the evening breeze. Rodeur moved closer to me so that his warm hand brushed mine before he took it loosely in his own. His eyes followed mine and he said, "This is a clipper ship, Aurielle—a new kind of vessel made by the Americans in the Boston shipyards, far to the northeast. All the privateers would own her and *mon capitaine* plans to sell her to the highest bidder when he leaves for New Orleans. The *Wind* can outrun anything on the high seas."

"So I seen."

"Saw, ma'amselle," he said in a soft, tactful voice.

"Saw. My first lesson," I laughed. Then, "Where'd th' cap'n get this ship?"

"She was coming in from Africa with a load of slaves last year and ran right into Captain Kincannon's old galleon off the coast of Charleston. Since she was American, he meant only to satisfy his curiosity—but when he found she carried slaves—" He shrugged. "It is against the new American laws to run slaves into the country and so Quent merely saved the government the expense of prosecution—and took the *Wind* as his pay for the favor. He had her cannons mounted in New Orleans."

"And the slaves?"

"He brought them to Grande Terre, where the *bos* took care of them."

"You mean he *sold* them at the—what is it?"

"The Temple. *Oui, le bos* sold them to some very good plantation owners who will see they have a good home."

"And work hard th' rest o' their lives," I retorted. "At least I'm supposed t'be free after a year." I paused, then, said "An' th' captain plans to sell th' *Wind* an' go ter New Orleans?" I felt a sudden powerful curiosity about the tall, dark-eyed man who had forced himself on me, then had the goodness to refrain from rape. He was as great an enigma as this blue-eyed Frenchman with his obviously false name.

"*Oui.* Even as yourself, ma'amselle, our *capitaine* has a desire to become part of the—ah—more legitimate part of this country we have adopted. He has almost the money for it now."

"A few more piratin' o' vessels an' 'e'll 'ave enough, eh? 'E knows 'tis piracy, or 'e'd not be wantin' respectability."

"*Non.* He says there is more money to be made in so-called respectability," Cheviot replied lightly. "And he is right, of course. Among what you call gentry, men kill each other over fancied slights and rob each other in what is called legitimate business every day."

"Just th' same, what you done ter th' *Sea Warrior* was piracy," I insisted.

"You are obstinate—as well as very beautiful, Mademoiselle Aurielle," he murmured.

His French voice was music to my ears and I muttered, "Well, I ain't sayin' you *all* are bad." I didn't want to discourage this handsome gentleman pirate who had it in his power to mend my poor speech and lack of manners.

We were silent as the ship approached the wind-and-wave-swept beaches and swung with beautiful precision between the low-lying islands into the bay protected by them. Unfamiliar vegetation lay beyond the reeds. I was to learn later that the stiff, spiky plants were palmettos and the tall, raggedy, broad-leaved ones were banana trees. Beyond them, in deep shadow now, lay orange and lemon groves.

The sun was sinking and the long, warm twilight had set in as I glimpsed the settlement of oddly constructed little houses with palmetto-thatched roofs that were flung back from long beaches and longer log piers. Myriad red-sailed fishing boats mingled indiscriminately with the oddly assorted larger vessels tied up at the piers.

The *Wind* eased up alongside a sturdy, weathered pier and the sailors made her bow fast. The ship had been seen approaching long before and now a motley collection of humanity was boiling about on the beach and along the pier. There were women and children among them, and the men looked rough and hard.

Rodeur Cheviot left me with a murmured, "Pardon, ma'amselle."

I observed Captain Kincannon and Roxanne Deveret, followed by the man of color, Ulysses, spring from the ship's gangplank to the pier where they were met by a tall, slender man dressed in black. He was well built with broad shoulders that tapered to small, booted feet. In the dusky light I saw a narrow black mustache below a long, straight nose. Instinct told me that here was one of the Lafittes of whom Cheviot had spoken.

I watched him narrowly in the twilight as he moved gracefully among the mothers and their children who were screaming with delight as their sailor fathers swung them in their arms. Then the four stood still among the moving crowd, conversing intently with each other.

I watched it all with interest, realizing that there was order among these lawless men, even if there was only a semblance of order among their moored ships and their primitive dwellings. I leaned forward, relishing the prospect of lessons here under the erudite Rodeur Cheviot, and as I did so, the Frenchman approached the four.

He gestured broadly with his hands and I was sure he was informing Lafitte of the spoils they had taken from the *Sea Warrior*. Cheviot glanced up at me as he spoke. The other four looked up and then I saw that Lafitte's eyes were dark and shining. Roxanne's green ones flashed as her brows drew together, but Lafitte leaned toward her intimately and I immediately sensed a bond between them. Kincannon broke into a laugh, but Rodeur appeared earnest as he spoke. What were they saying? My back stiffened and my palms grew moist.

At last Roxanne, flanked by Ulysses and the man I took to be Lafitte, strode up the pier, passing my perch without a glance. Rodeur and Kincannon took the gangplank and reboarded the ship, coming directly toward me. The sailors had long ago furled the sails and made the vessel tight for the coming night. They would unload her captured goods with the morning light. They had lit four oil lanterns that I could see hanging from masts and along the forecastle; the light from the sky was fading fast. I saw Cheviot take a lantern from its hook as they approached.

Reaching me, Kincannon spoke without preamble. "Aurielle, I have made Monsieur Cheviot your—a—protector," he wore a faint smile, "while you work out your passage. He tells me you are an excellent baker and our communal cook, Antoinette Desmottes, can use you. She has long quarreled for a helper."

"My protector?" I said cautiously, looking up into the charming face of the Frenchman. His smile was engaging and warm.

"Indeed," said Kincannon. "He has a very tight little house and he would share it with you while he goes about teaching you the rudiments of good grammar—when he is not on duty with the *Wind*." I wondered suddenly if he had *told* Cheviot about—last night.

My hands grew cold. I had *counted* on Rodeur

Cheviot. "I can't do that," I said bitterly. "I'm willin' ter work fer my keep here—but I ain't sleepin' with no man! Babies come from that."

Kincannon's laughter rang out, his eyes twinkling in the glimmering lantern light as he slapped Cheviot on his shoulder. "By God, she's right, Rodeur! And I don't think *you* are anxious for parenthood, my friend—least of all fatherhood of a little bastard. You see, your favor is rejected, a new role for you."

"Favor?" I burst out heatedly. "A favor that'd ruin me!"

"Ruin you?" Kincannon's voice was suddenly cold. "Surely you would not expect him to *marry* such as you?"

Rage swept through me like a sheet of flame and I brought my hand up with lightning swiftness. It cracked across Kincannon's lips with stinging force. How dared he speak as if I were some low creature, some scum from the gutter?

He caught my arm in an iron vise, twisting me about, bringing me to my knees before him. "That's twice you've done that, you little tart. This time you shall pay for it!" His face in the dimming light was white and I realized with shock that his rage was as great as my own and suddenly I exulted in it.

"I'll do it ag'n, when I get th' chance," I spat, although the pain in my arm was so great my eyes filled.

"Quent," Cheviot took his arm, "you will do her damage. I think your little joke has gone far enough, *mon ami.*" His voice was gentle and the laughter had faded from his face.

Slowly the grip on my arm lessened and I looked up to see Kincannon fighting for control of his temper. He had not told! Nor would he, I thought triumphantly. He said, "I do not understand your gentleness, Rodeur, with this wench." Then between his teeth, "And you, miss, keep out of my sight—or I'll give you the walloping of your life."

I scrambled to my feet as he turned and strode away. "I have never seen him in such a rage before," Cheviot said thoughtfully. "You must not provoke him further, Aurielle."

"I don't know why not," I replied, still furious. "He spoke of me as if I was a who—as if I was scum, an' I ain't, damn it. I'm as good or better—better'n him!"

Rodeur was silent as he guided me along the deck toward the gangplank, and the lantern in his other hand cast out spears of light before us. Stars were thick in the rigging above us and the night air smelled sweet. His big, hard hand on my arm was strangely comforting. I wondered apprehensively if I might find myself drawn to this man who would be my teacher, so much that I would succumb to the very thing I feared. I had my course mapped out in detail, and an alliance with the winning Rodeur Cheviot was not part of my future.

"Were you really jokin', Mister Cheviot?" I asked cautiously. " 'Cause I ain't goin' to sleep with no man."

"*Chérie,* Antoinette Desmottes is my cook and housekeeper. You will have a separate room in my house, the same as she. Quent was amused by your reaction to my being your—protector and he carried it a bit far."

Then our feet were in soft sand and we walked swiftly up the beach toward the winking lights in the windows of the houses beyond.

"What will ye teach me, Mister Cheviot?" I was full of emotion and I wanted to throw my arms about the man and kiss him, so grateful was I.

"History, writing—penmanship, mathematics. But most of all, I shall try to mend your speech, my dear. It is atrocious."

"I know," I said humbly, and as we made our way to the house that nestled among dark treelike shrubs, he talked of my errors in speech and I absorbed his words like a sponge. As we reached the door of the weathered little house, I vowed I would put "ing" on all words requiring such. I would watch my tongue closely.

"We will have a real lesson tomorrow afternoon, Aurielle, when I am finished tallying up our cargo as it is put in the warehouse," he said as we mounted the narrow wooden steps. He gave the open door a sharp rap and called, "Toinette!"

There was a rustle from the back and the sound of flying feet and a thin, sharp-faced woman rushed into the room. Cheviot put his lantern down on the table beside a candle fluttering there and said, "We have had a most successful run, Toinette. And I have brought you back a helper."

She drew back, suspicion on her narrow little face. Her hair was pulled back in a most unbecoming fashion, I thought, and her small bright eyes were hostile.

"Who is this?" Her voice, like Cheviot's, was lightly accented.

"Mademoiselle Aurielle Stuart. She is a redemptioner and, as part of our spoils, she will work out her passage."

"Pah! She is too young and far too pretty to be of any use. She will be chasing the men and they will be chasing her!" She eyed me with active dislike.

"I'll do no sich thing," I retorted, meeting her half-way. "I'll serve out me year an' then I'm goin'—ter New Orleans."

"She will live in my house, Toinette," Cheviot said, with his endearing smile, "for a little while anyway. There is that extra room at the back—"

"She'll live *here?*" There was outrage in the question.

"It is Captain Kincannon's wish, Antoinette, and mine as well." There was iron in his words.

"Madame, I'll be very quiet an' I'm a good baker—one o' th' best. Ye'll see." I spoke with sudden subservience in an effort to mollify the woman.

"Pah! You are too young to be good at anything," she retorted. Then sharply, "You have no baggage?"

"All me things went down with th' *Sea Warrior* when she was captured by Cap'n Kincannon." All but the poniard, which nestled unseen at my waist.

"I'll have no dirty wench in my house, ma'amselle! But one dress—and you look none too clean now!"

I looked around and saw that the little cottage was spotlessly clean, as was the slender woman before me. I drank in the clean fragrance greedily.

"I will secure a wardrobe for Mam'selle Aurielle in the morning, Toinette. She wishes to receive an education and she will be my student." Cheviot smiled again warmly. "And I know she will profit much from your association.

50

You are so perceptive and so well read—a true lady, Toinette."

I laughed silently. What a rogue was Rodeur Cheviot! I must watch myself because he stirred me unwillingly. Already I bore him an affection. I reflected on this as Antoinette Desmottes bridled and murmured, "That is probably quite true, Rodeur." She gave me another less haughty glance and added, "*I* have some old but clean dresses you may have. You will mind your place, young lady. I will tolerate no impudence."

"Mademoiselle Aurielle is under my protection." Cheviot's voice was suddenly cold and commanding. "She is to be well treated."

"I thought she was to *assist* me," the woman said, taken aback.

"She is. But there will be days when she will be studying with or without me during her schooling. She is to be no slavey."

Antoinette Desmottes's thin black brows drew together as she said, "Of course, Rodeur, I understand." Then to me, "Come. You must bathe before you sleep in this house. There is the smell of the ship about you." She looked back at Cheviot. "I would recommend the same for you, m'sieu, when we are through."

I had noted that along the walls of this room there were many shelves lined with books, more books than I had ever seen in my lifetime, and they stirred a vast hunger in me. There was a beautiful polished desk, intricately carved, and yet, for all its beauty, at home in this primitive house. In the center of the room there was also a large, lovely, round mahogany table, gleaming with a high polish. There were other furnishings, equally pleasant, but the books entranced me most of all. I wanted to read them, each one, and vowed I would as I followed the woman to the back of the small house.

"You will wash all that hair, too—what was your name—Aurielle?" She began to drag a large hipbath into the center of the room and got down towels and soap from shelves built along the walls. Then she pulled me with her into the windy darkness back of the house. "Come, Aurielle, we will draw water for your bath. You will have to use cold water tonight, but you can be thankful the wind is strong from the gulf or you would be initiated to mosquitoes since it is summer."

The bathwater *was* cold but refreshing, and the soap the little Frenchwoman had given me was coarsely made but fragrant. I had scrubbed my hair lavishly and it was still damp on the pillow. The strong, sweet gulf wind blew through a broad open window beside my long narrow cot, carrying the living smells of the sea to my nostrils. I stretched luxuriously in Madame Antoinette Desmottes's borrowed nightdress. It was, like everything about the woman, immaculately clean. She was a tyrant, supervising my bath meticulously, even giving me a brush with which to scrub my nails. She had brought out three cotton dresses and two petticoats, while Cheviot took his turn in the tub. These dresses were plain and severe.

"We will let them out to fit your bosom," Antoinette had remarked, adding disparagingly, "You have scarcely any backside." Then with a grim laugh, "But I'm sure you will take up with one of the men before long and your *derrière* should be a deal larger next year."

"By this time next year, madame, I'll be gone."

Her laughter was suddenly mocking, "And that might well be true also. There can be but one Roxanne Deveret."

I had made no reply, but now I lay on my virginal cot and sleep took me even as I swore that I would be no Roxanne Deveret, but the most envied woman in all New Orleans.

The following morning before dawn, my reluctant benefactress roused me. It was time to start the fires and begin preparing breakfast for the unmarried men of the *Wind*. She was more talkative as I dressed. She had lost her husband at sea three years before. It was Captain Kincannon who had arranged for her to stay on as cook for his men in the bay village. Then she and Cheviot had formed their alliance. "I am a good housekeeper and it is good to work for the man in his house," she said, laying out my meager wardrobe. "It keeps the other brutes away from me. You shall have your hands full warding off their advances, Aurielle."

She supervised my donning of her ill-fitting dark blue muslin dress and petticoats. All of them, dress and petticoats, had to be bound around my narrow waist with a broad band of guinea blue callico. This added a touch of rakishness to my costume and made a place for my poniard, both of which Antoinette disapproved.

I asked about Cheviot and she said brusquely, "He left even earlier to supervise the unloading of the *Wind*—and the storing of the cargo in the warehouses."

Dawn was just breaking when I followed her out the back of the little house, down unpainted wooden steps, and up across the sand to her brick oven. The outside kitchen, under a heavily thatched roof, boasted a large brick fireplace with a spit across it for roasting. There were two weathered wooden tables for us to use preparing food under this roofed area which had but one wall, the one containing the fireplace with its back toward the sea. There were many cupboards lining this one wall on either side of the brick fireplace and Antoinette threw two of them open.

"We must have breakfast ready by eight. Twenty-one men of Captain Kincannon's crew are unmarried. Here are our supplies for bread and biscuits—flour—sugar—I keep my yeast in this jar, here."

I looked back down the beach toward the other houses. One, built up higher in what Cheviot called the *chenière*, was distinctly reddish in color and much better constructed than the primitive dwellings scattered out below it. Antoinette followed my gaze.

"That is *le bos*'s house."

"*Bos*—Mister Cheviot mentioned that word."

"That is what we call Jean Lafitte. He—and sometimes his brother Pierre—live in that house."

"If Jean is *bos,* what is Pierre?"

"Ah, Pierre, he likes the good life. He helps his brother and he has a fine house in New Orleans with a big enclosed garden. He lives there with Marie Villars and his children."

" 'E's married?" I asked.

She shrugged. "*Non,* I did not say that."

I looked at the house far up in the *chenière* thoughtfully. "What's that big buildin' with a fence around it, 'way over yonder?" I motioned toward it.

"*C'est le barracoon*—the slave warehouse."

I was repelled. "I heard ye traffic in slavery!"

"Slaves are very profitable for the Lafittes and for their captains. They will be taking them by skiff to the market soon."

"But Ulysses is a black and he is free."

"New Orleans is full of free men and women of color, Aurielle. They win their freedom in many ways. Ulysses is guardian to Roxanne. He would lay down his life for her and she would lay down hers for him."

"Hmmn. She don't seem th' kind ter do anything unselfish."

Her little smile was enigmatic. "Roxanne is a strange girl—when you come to know her. Very unpredictable."

"I don't plan ter know her no better—"

"Come, Aurielle, we must start the breakfast," and we fell to work.

While I worked, I glanced about me and, looking to the north, I saw what Antoinette said were orange groves, the fruit like golden globes shining beneath the darkly polished green leaves. There were banana trees behind Rodeur Cheviot's little house, too. There were big green-and-gold bunches of the crescent-shaped fruit hanging temptingly under the tough, fringed leaves.

In less than two hours, we had a great steaming pot of what Antoinette called grits. She had sliced an enormous ham and fried it in two great iron skillets over the fire. In the oven, which was still hot from the fire she had built in it the previous night, my biscuits were a beautiful golden brown, light and high.

From the south, there approached a stream of sailors, some bearded, some clean-shaven, and I recognized several of them from yesterday aboard the *Wind*. Antoinette wiped her beaded brow on the sleeve of her coarse muslin dress. There was one, I had heard his name, Durket, a giant of a man with a sandy beard and unkempt hair, who had fixed his eyes on me at the time of my capture and had scarcely taken them off, even as he went about his duties on board the *Wind*.

I saw him now, burly and muscular, approaching with some of his American companions as they came brazenly up to the kitchen itself, ostensibly to sniff the freshly baked biscuits and to joke with Antoinette, but their eyes slid over me with interest. Like the men at the inn, they moved nearer, and the one called Durket pinched my bottom.

I whirled on him and he received my bread paddle with great force on the side of his head. "Hell and be damned!" he shouted. "Toinette, you've a spawn o' the devil in yer employ!" and he clapped his great hairy hand to his reddening cheek.

Antoinette Desmottes gave him a wintry smile. "Do you not know she is under the protection of Rodeur Cheviot?"

"That damned Frenchman with his handy sword?" and with another curse he went off to join the others, still rubbing his face. Apparently he spread the word among the rest of the men, for they eyed me with some trepidation after that.

Mid-afternoon we again fed the men of the *Wind,* with the exception of Captain Kincannon. They sat about on the sandy ground in groups of two and three. Roxanne Deveret was there and her flashing green eyes were malicious. As I handed her a wooden plate of food, she grinned impudently.

"You look a fright in old Toinette's dress with your hair skinned back like hers—a proper scullery maid." Her laughter was mocking.

I flushed with anger. Antoinette had pulled my hair back and pinned it firmly with great wooden pins and we had not had time to let the bosom of the dress out or to take up its voluminous folds. "Ye ain't no ringin' belle in them tight britches, either. Ye look like a boy."

"I could never look like a boy, you English gutter-snipe," she retorted in a rollicking voice, "and you've no idea what freedom these breeches afford me."

"Freedom from Cap'n Kincannon's attentions anyway," I jeered and was rewarded by a glittering stare of fury. But I had shut her up. Shortly after that, she took her plate and went off down toward the beach.

Rodeur came with the others for the noon meal, although a little late, his sunny smile directed to Antoinette and me. "My apologies for being late and missing breakfast, too, but I have been tallying up our profits in the main warehouse." He gestured toward Grand Isle. "We will soon have to go to the Temple and dispose of it. Mmm, your breads have a delicious scent, Aurielle."

"I told ye I was a good baker." I was glad to see him, more glad than I had thought to be. His was the only truly friendly face, unless I chose to call the rapacious desire in the eyes of the others friendly. "When'll ye start me lessons?" I asked, filling his plate generously. The men seated under the banana and orange trees watched us curiously. Antoinette went steadily about her pots.

"This very afternoon, after you and Toinette finish here." He took his plate, adding, "Did you not notice my fine library?"

"I saw all them books. Have ye read 'em?"

"All. And many more when I was a student in Paris."

I noticed Antoinette's inscrutable black eyes on Cheviot. She was still faintly pretty though I thought she must be past thirty. She looked at him from beneath her bristly black lashes as he went on, gesturing with his fork. "I have many books of history, poetry—Greek mythology."

"How fine," I murmured, taking up my bread paddle as I prepared to pull the last of the hot loaves from the brick oven. "I been wantin' ter read history. Ol' Steve Boyette tol' me lots o' it." I bent to the iron door, opened it, and thrust the paddle under the four fat loaves. "Jis' a minute an' I'll cut ye a hot slice o' this."

"I'll wait." Then he laughed suddenly. "I see Toinette has done her best to hide your beauty. That dull blue frock is scarcely your dress. I think I can do better for you later."

"You will make it harder for her," Antoinette said warningly. "Already the men cannot keep their hands off her."

"Who has dared to touch her?" There was a quick rage in the quiet voice.

"Durket, for one," Antoinette said dryly, "but she let him have the bread paddle to the side of his head and I told him she belonged to you. It turned him back some-what—temporarily."

"I don't care how I look," I said firmly, "until I get ter New Orleans. Then I want ter be beautiful and talk properlike."

He laughed. "Your eyes are like stars when you speak of it. And you will need money for that sort of entry."

My face fell. "I know it," I replied disconsolately.

Afterward, as Antoinette and I gathered up the wooden plates and implements, which we scrubbed clean with sand and water, I asked, "How did you and Mister Cheviot"—I hesitated and added delicately—"come ter this arrangement?"

"When my husband was lost at sea, he left me with only a little money in the bank at New Orleans, but not enough. That same fall, my little house blew down in a hurricane. M'sieu Cheviot had this house, but no house-keeper—and Captain Kincannon wanted me to stay on as cook for his men." She shrugged eloquently. "So m'sieu and I came to an agreement."

"Ye sound mighty cool an' businesslike. Do ye—are ye—"

"I am fond of him, that is all." Then abruptly, "I lost my little son with a fever three years ago. You might say all the real love that was left in my heart died then, too."

"I'm sorry," I said inadequately.

She favored me with a cynical smile as we stacked the plates in readiness for the evening meal. Then we walked together back to the small house. There were batten blinds on either side of all the windows, well made and pushed back to permit the sweet gulf air to enter, but ready to be pulled tightly closed in stormy weather.

I followed Antoinette into her bedroom, asking, "How old was your little son?"

"But three."

"I—left a babe almost that age in Portsmouth—I loved him dearly."

"Yours?" she asked incredulously.

"No, but I had the care o' him and he come to mean much ter me." I glanced at a strange white netting in one corner of the room on a pile of tall sticks. "What is that stuff?" I asked.

"A *baire*. You have one in the cupboard in your room. Most of us have them. You drape them over the bed when you sleep on still nights, to keep the mosquitoes from eating you up."

"What are these mosquitoes?"

"Small and terrible insects that buzz about your face and body and stick a long, pronged nose into your flesh to draw blood, which they feed on. They make life miserable during much of the spring and summer."

"They sound dretful," I murmured.

"They are dreadful—ah, I hear m'sieu—best you go in for your lessons now." There was a pregnant pause, then, "I would caution you, Aurielle. Take care with Rodeur. He is a subtle man and you may well find your deepest affections stirred."

My feelings exactly, I thought in silence as I said, "I will—and I will be ready to help you with the supper when the time comes."

Antoinette said, "No hurry—I have already put a great roast on the spit."

I left her and found Cheviot in the main room pulling books from the shelves and placing them on his broad, polished desk. He looked around, smiling. "Come, *ma petite,* I plan to teach you French along with correct English. You shall be a most accomplished young lady." His long, thin brown fingers were flipping the pages of a heavy volume. "If you are truly half French, as you say, the language should come easily."

I sat down near him, the fresh, clean scent of his skin and clothing coming to me on the gulf wind that coursed through the house. It set off an explosion of new emotion and I put down an absurd desire to creep into his strong arms and be comforted. Antoinette Desmottes was very right. I would have to watch myself carefully or I would come to love this man before ever a caress was exchanged.

I took up the book, and our lessons began.

Chapter

3

Two days went by; first, Rodeur Cheviot had me read aloud from an English history while he meticulously corrected my pronunciation as I read. I was very halting and I despaired of my recalcitrant lips that invariably took the wrong accent, but I was so eager the time passed swiftly.

"You have a good grasp of what is transpiring," Cheviot said encouragingly. "You understand what you read even though you cannot pronounce it correctly."

The third day we were seated side by side, very close, when there came an unexpected interruption. *"Vraiment!"* The word came from behind us at the open door to the little house. "You really *are* giving the English wench her lessons, Rodeur—I should have come later when it will be more interesting, I'm sure."

We broke apart, turning to look at Roxanne Deveret who stood there, her copper hair blowing in the wind, derisive laughter on her red lips. She did not wear her sword and her white shirt was open too low, revealing the deep curve of her full breasts as she leaned an elbow negligently against the door. "Do not let me stop you, Rodeur.

I will leave so you can—study more *intimately*—a more delicious subject," and she turned away.

"Stay," I said loudly as Rodeur flushed a dull red. "Ye must'a come fer some reason. Maybe ye needed lessons worse'n me. Ye could use some manners, ye little bastard!" I was in a fury at her insinuations.

She turned in a flash and darted through the door like a slim flame, but I was ready. The poniard was in my hand and her eyes widened as they caught on the shining dagger. Then she seized my wrist in a grip of steel and we fell to the floor, rolling over and over. I could feel the rough planking against my back as we came to a stop at the door's edge.

Then Rodeur Cheviot was above us, his strong hands under Roxanne's arms as he lifted her easily from me. She would not let go of my wrist and she pulled me upright with her as she screamed imprecations at me as foul as any I had learned in the Portsmouth gutters.

I threw back my head, my hair tumbling to my waist as the pins fell from it, laughing exultantly. "Ye ain't no lady," I taunted, "fer all yer pretendin' to talk so fine. Mister Cheviot, ye can teach *her* in yer spare time, too."

"Drop that knife, you little bitch," she cried as I twisted my wrist from her grip. Cheviot had firm hold on her flailing arms. I noticed his face was pale now and his blue eyes brilliant on my poniard. Something we had done had shocked him. I felt it intuitively.

I slipped the poniard into the band at my waist. "Ye needn't worry," I said coolly. "I ain't goin' ter stick ye unless ye come after me agi'n."

"I shall skewer you on the point of my sword, you filthy wench!"

"No, ye won't," I said with careless bravado, my heart pounding with exertion. "Me poniard'll—"

"Good God, Rodeur!—What's going on here?"

All three of us turned to see Captain Quentin Kincannon towering in the open door. Rodeur was the first to speak, still gripping the struggling girl. *"Hein!* But I am glad to see you, *mon ami.* Here, take your protégé."

But Roxanne was suddenly still in Rodeur's arms, flinging back her hair. "I am glad to see you, too, Quent.

60

This *bête sauvage* attacked me—and Rodeur has helped her."

"Oh, what a liar ye are!" I expostulated, outraged, but Cheviot broke into sudden wry laughter and Kincannon joined him. I began, "That ain't a word o' it true—" What was a *bête sauvage*? Even in my rage I marked the words. I would ask Rodeur.

"We all know Roxanne takes large liberties with the truth, Aurielle," Rodeur cut in, still laughing, thrusting the girl toward Kincannon. For all his laughter, I felt he was troubled. I had a strange rapport with this mysterious Frenchman and I knew he was deeply disturbed. The captain caught Roxanne's small hands in his. "Come now, why have you created such a hue and cry, my pet?"

"Quent, she did attack me—" She broke off, tears filling the beautiful, thick-fringed eyes. Suddenly she pulled from his light grasp and ran out the door. I looked after her as she took the sandy ground in long strides with her little booted feet.

"Why don't ye run after yer whore—yer *pet?*" I laughed scornfully.

He stared down at me, anger rising like dark fire in his black eyes. "If you called her a whore," he said deliberately, "I don't blame her for attacking you."

I laughed. "I called 'er what she is—a little bastard. An' you should'a heard what she called *me.*"

"Aurielle," Rodeur cut in smoothly, "I can never teach you to be a lady if you keep using such language."

Kincannon's mouth went down at one corner in a sardonic smile. "Rodeur has told me of your fantasies. The finest gentleman in New Orleans, the finest lady, the finest house. Rodeur, you'll never succeed."

Before I could lift my hand, Rodeur caught it easily, *"Non,* Aurielle. I cannot have you slapping *mon capitaine* again—nor do I want him walloping you as he's promised—"

"A good walloping would do her a world of good, Rodeur." The captain's eyes were glacial and a little muscle along his jaw quivered. "But I came for the additional list of our goods in the second warehouse on Grand Isle. Jean and Pierre want to go over it with me." His eyes swung back to me, "And I caution you, miss. One more blow from your coarse hands and I'll take you back in the *chenière* and lay a stick across your bottom."

My coarse hands! Involuntarily I looked down at them. They were rough and red from the sand and water, from the mixing of breads and pies, from the hard work I had done most of my life. I bit my lip and turned away as Rodeur returned from the carved and gleaming desk with two sheets of paper which he handed to the captain.

I glimpsed the fine, lacy handwriting, spaced in even columns across each sheet. Ah, what lovely marks, symbolic pictures of all that was charming, cultured, and elegant! How could my rough hands ever turn themselves to such writing? My chin went up automatically. I would accomplish it. My resolve hardened under Kincannon's contemptuous eyes. And someday, some wonderful day, I would meet him again and in a ladylike way I would tell him to go straight to hell. My spirits rose at the thought.

Kincannon's face showed pleasure as he scanned the list. "We did well, Rodeur. I shall soon sell the *Wind* and go into business in New Orleans."

Rodeur's face was sober. "You shall be much missed, my friend. I have not made up my mind which of the captains shall receive my services."

"Why will you not accompany me when I leave, Rodeur?" Kincannon asked bluntly.

"You know my desire to rove, Quent. Like you, I do not desire the ties—and business would tie me down completely."

"Ties like that we can handle. I think it's more than that with you," Kincannon said sharply. "I think you are running away from something—something you might find in New Orleans."

Cheviot smiled brilliantly. "I have been running away for many years, Quent. I like the life of a *rodeur,* the dangers, the pitfalls, and the triumphs make me forget—and bring a measure of peace to painful memories."

Kincannon shrugged. "I hope you will change your mind before I go. You are invaluable to me. I shall need you in my business ventures—that practical French mind of yours."

"I will think on it." Then he added cheerfully, "You and the others are set for our games tonight, *n'est-ce pas?*"

I looked up alertly. What games? I found the life, the ways here at Barataria vastly interesting.

Kincannon said, "You are too shrewd a player for me, Rodeur, but I shall be here with the others. I know Jean and his men think to take us both."

"Antoinette will arrange refreshments and I have two unbroken packs of cards from the city. And the brandy we took from the *Sea Warrior* is superlative."

He laughed. "I will see you after dark." Then, without a glance in my direction, he strode from the house. Cheviot and I stood in the door watching the tall, lean form take the sandy path rapidly.

"Before we resume our lessons, Aurielle," Cheviot said abruptly, "let me see that—dirk you drew on Roxanne."

"That's my pertection," I said defensively as I drew the knife from my waist. I feared he meant to relieve me of it. "It's saved me many a time." I handed it to him and he turned it slowly, examining it carefully. I said with a touch of belligerence, "It was me—my father's. 'Tis all I have left o' 'im—of him. I lost the note from me—my mother when the *Sea Warrior* went down."

His face had paled once more as he held the knife and I was suddenly filled with apprehension. "What is it, Mister Cheviot?"

His voice was rough with emotion. "I know this poniard. It belonged to a friend of mine in Paris, long ago."

"Oh," I cried joyfully. "Then you knew my father!"

"If he owned this poniard, I did. Where is he now?"

I launched into the story of my arrival at the Boar's Head Inn in 1800, recounting all that I knew of the unfortunate Englishman who had been my young father, ending with, "Now you can tell me his name since ye—you knew him. What does the J. B. S. stand for?"

He was silent a long moment, looking at the poniard; then he said slowly, "John Bayard Smith, and you are right—he was of the English gentry. What did the note from your mother say?"

From years of poring over it, I recited readily, " 'I am discovered and I must flee for my life. Take Aurielle to England with you. Tell her how beloved she is to us and that she is never to forget her mother is of the nobility. She is the—' " I stopped, my throat thick. "That was all. The rest was torn away. Oh, Mister Cheviot, I just know me mother wrote that to me father. I'd give anything ter— to know what else she said."

He was silent so long I grew worried and pled, "Please tell me about me mother an' father—they was married, wasn't they?"

"Oui. John said they were married." His blue eyes were veiled and his face closed against me. I started to speak again and he lifted his hand. *"Non,* ask me no more questions, *ma petite.* You know I have left my past behind. I will speak no more of it."

"But me mother—"

"I have told you all I know."

"But you haven't! Tell me how they looked—did you know when I was born to them? What was her name and why did my mother have to flee for her life?"

He reached out and drew me to him and my head was scarcely above his heart. I could hear it beating heavily. He laid his cheek against the top of my head and whispered. "No more, *ma bien aimée.* No more."

My arms closed convulsively about his waist and I realized I was weeping. "You *can't* stop now," I choked. "You *knew* them. You must tell me."

"I will tell you this and no more—and you must swear never to pry into my past again, nor reveal what you know of it. Have I your promise?" He pushed me away and looked into my eyes sternly.

"Yes," I whispered over my tears. "If you will only tell me a little more."

"Your father—and this poniard is proof enough— was with me during a very bad time. We were trying to put the King of France back upon the throne. Though I never met her, John told me he was married to the most beautiful woman in all of France. Our little band of nobles was discovered by Napoleon's men and we fought for our lives—were scattered, and we fled, I to the New World and he to his native England." He broke off abruptly.

"But my mother! What became of her?"

"I can only assume she too was found out and must have fled France. Or she died, *peut-être.* Who knows? It was very dangerous in those days when the populace rose against the Convention and Napoleon put them down."

"You never saw her—even once?" I asked, tears streaming down my face.

"Non," he said roughly. "I have told you all I can, *ma petite."*

I went back to my chair beside the desk, controlling my sobs determinedly, the open book a blur before me.

Behind me, Rodeur Cheviot gave vent to a stream of French oaths, then said, "It is enough for today, Aurielle. We will take up your lessons tomorrow." He moved with restrained violence to put the poniard beside the open book. "There is your father's poniard, *chérie*—I am sorry it opened old wounds in both of us," and suddenly he was gone.

I put my head down on the desk and gave way to hard sobbing. In a moment or two I felt a hand upon my shoulder, feather-light. I jerked upright and whirled around to face Antoinette Desmottes.

"Do not cry so hard, little one," she said with unexpected compassion. "At least you know now that your parents were married and your mother beautiful."

"You listened?" I said accusingly.

"I always listen," she replied calmly. "It saves time and sometimes it saves trouble."

"Me name's Aurielle Smith—I know *that* now. Me father was John Bayard Smith."

"You would be a fool to tell the others."

"Why?"

"If you change your name now they will all think you flighty and be more convinced than ever that you were born out of wedlock. Besides, you cannot expect Rodeur to reveal so much of his past in order to corroborate your claim—he is a fugitive—and you gave him your promise."

"That's true," I said dejectedly. "I can jis' hear what that Roxanne would say about me."

"Oui—now come and have a cup of tea with me before we prepare supper."

I followed her obediently out to the open kitchen and found she had already put a pot of water to heat over the fireplace beside the roasting meats. Another large pot held more of the grits. There was a great bowl of oranges upon one of the tables and she said, "When we finish our tea we must peel and separate the oranges, to make a bowl full for the men to eat with their supper."

Antoinette seemed suddenly to have lost all her hostility to me with the discovery of my sorrowful background. Over the pewter mug of tea, I told her of my life at the Boar's Head and she nodded sympathetically.

"Even with all you must do to help me, *chérie,* you will find it better than that. And remember, we must all lose our fathers and mothers someday. You lost yours sooner than most, but now you can look to a better future for yourself." She hesitated, then added, "Remember what I have told you about Rodeur. You do not wish to find yourself carrying a bastard child to New Orleans with you when you go."

"I ain't goin' ter do that!" I replied heatedly.

"You looked very comfortable in his arms, and he is a man who can charm the birds from a bough—worse, he is a man who can *wait.*"

"I think ye do him a bad turn with yer talk. He ain't like that at all!"

Her shoulders lifted eloquently as she sipped the last of her tea from the mug. "It is only that I would advise you," her voice grew reflective, "and there is something very endearing about you—vile language and hot temper notwithstanding."

"Yer kind," I said sincerely.

"My advice is to learn from Rodeur and his books and not from Rodeur the man." She laughed suddenly. "Tonight you will learn what such men do for amusement without women."

"What?" I asked curiously.

"They will come to our house tonight, their pockets jingling with gold, and they will play a game *le bos* learned from *les Américains.* It is a game of cards called poker.

You will see some well-known men of Barataria when we serve them their brandy and refreshments." She rose to her feet saying, "Come, I must turn the roasts," and the two of us put aside our cups and fell to preparations for the evening meal. We stayed busy until near dark, when at last the crew, well fed, disappeared into their various haunts.

When we finished dining, we cleaned the dishes with sand and water and left the outdoor kitchen.

Entering the house, Antoinette said, "Go and brush your hair, *ma petite,* and put on that pink cotton dress— the one I let out in the breast. You will want to look presentable as we serve the men later when their card games start. I think you will enjoy helping me in this."

I felt very dressed up, for Antoinette was astonishingly adept with a needle. The pink dress was drawn snug across the breast to fall in full folds to the floor. Luckily, her little feet and mine were the same size and she kindly gave me a pair of half-slippers with little wooden heels. And to my further surprise, she came into my room and dressed my hair in a very becoming fashion. Then she took me to her room where she had the luxury of a great oval mirror with a gilt frame.

"Yer a very marvel with th' needle an' me hair," I said with gratitude, staring at my reflection. "I didn't know ye knew so much."

"Do not say 'ye', Aurielle. The word is 'you,' " she replied. Then, "Before I left France for the New World with my husband, I worked in one of the great couturier's houses in Paris. But I come by my knowledge of coiffures by nature." She paused. "If these were the common run of sailors at the house tonight, I would dress you very dowdily. But it will not hurt your standing to look lovely for Jean and Pierre Lafitte and their lieutenants. They are mostly gentlemen."

When the men came, one by one, to the house, Rodeur greeted them at the door, and from our place in the storeroom at the back, Antoinette and I could hear their deep voices and hearty male laughter. I peeked around the door to see them sitting in chairs about Cheviot's beautifully polished round table. I recognized the two brothers, side by side. Pierre was as tall but much heavier than Jean.

Antoinette answered my whispered questions. "That one so short and powerfully built is Beluche, a close confident of the Lafittes. The man beside him is Dominique You—as merry as a Christmas pudding. He's a very strong man and no one is so good as he with cannons or any kind of gun."

I peered around the storeroom door. "That last one—with the black beard—"

"That's Belli. Him I do not like. Jean tolerates him because he is a good privateer—as far as prizes go. He is a very cruel man." Her voice was brusque with dislike.

I peered again at the six men around the table. There was a lantern just off center of the table and I saw Cheviot take up the two packs of cards and break the seals on them. As he began to deal, he called over his shoulder, "We need brandy, Toinette—and refreshments."

Antoinette handed me a wooden platter she had prepared, with cheeses upon it, and, taking up a bottle of brandy and six glasses on a wooden tray, she bade me enter first. There was a moment of silence as the men registered my presence.

I put the cheeses down beside Cheviot with my lashes lowered; Jean, handsome in his dark piratical way, said, *"Mon cher* Cheviot—you have turned the little English bramble into a rose." Then gallantly to me, "You are very beautiful, mademoiselle." His teeth gleamed whitely under his little black mustache.

"Thank you," I said huskily, for I was aware of Belli's ferocious black eyes on my bosom and I suddenly smelled danger. All of them were looking at me, Kincannon with mocking cynicism, Dominique You with pleased surprise, Beluche with a warm smile on his swarthy face, and Pierre with a kind of lackadaisical admiration. I noted one of his eyes canted to the side and it gave him the odd appearance of looking two ways at once.

As I turned to leave, Jean reached out to catch my arm casually. "Stay, little one. I would talk to Kincannon with a view to your serving out your indenture at the red house. I've no maid and your presence might pique that elusive jade, Roxanne." He was laughing and his face took on a twinkling and engaging expression.

"I couldn't do that," I replied, alarmed. "I'm bound to the cap'n an' Mister Cheviot fer a year." There was no real lust in Lafitte's face, only mischief.

"I'll give the cap'n fifty pounds fer her," Belli said suddenly, his voice gutteral. My heart lurched downward. So much money!

Cheviot had stiffened but his face was impassive. Kincannon laughed carelessly as he replied, "Nay, Belli, her services are not for sale," but there was a thread of steel in the words.

Surprisingly, Antoinette spoke up pleasantly. "I could not do without her—so much help is she."

I cast her a grateful glance. I could not look at Belli with his little button eyes and the wet red lips shining in his heavy black beard. I started to leave, but the light-hearted Jean spoke up again. "Why not let her be the stakes for the winner this evening, *mon vieux?*"

Beluche gave a great guffaw. "Jean, you are too cocky! I will take you down a peg." He had a heavy French accent. I stood poised, a trembling in my limbs. All my plans to be schooled, to be free of male molestation hung in the balance! Even Antoinette was frozen, still holding the brandy bottle.

Dominique You, black eyes brilliant with laughter, said, "I will beat you all! I will win the mademoiselle—Jean, you only want her to make Roxanne jealous."

"The mademoiselle is not the stakes in this game," Kincannon said, and this time his voice was chill and hard as ice.

"No," said Cheviot, speaking for the first time. "Her term of service is pledged to Quent—and I am her protector."

Belli gave a great roar of laughter. "Protector! *You?* Why your prowess with women is too well known, Cheviot. That is to laugh!"

"All the same, Belli—Jean, my good friend—the girl is not to be bought or gambled for." Kincannon's voice was easy now, even pleasant, but the others looked at him and murmured agreement. I had the feeling that Kincannon was his most dangerous when he was most pleasant. *He's not going to let the others do what he almost did to me,* I thought with a cynicism of my own.

I slipped back into the storeroom and Antoinette followed me. Her hand shook as she set down the brandy bottle. "Animals! All men are animals! I feared for a moment that—"

"I know," I said, remembering Kincannon's cold, level eyes. "I'm still a little afraid."

"Do not be. Quentin Kincannon is a dangerous man to cross. I have never seen his equal in swordplay."

The laughter at the table was sporadic as the cards were dealt, and there was talk of the warehouses on Grand Isle filled with merchandise. Their voices were quite audible to Antoinette and me as they played. I heard Jean Lafitte say, "The goods from the *Sea Warrior* should bring you at least sixty thousand American dollars, *mon ami!*" And I peered around to see Jean slap Kincannon on his shoulder.

Antoinette said exasperatedly, "When I said they were all gentlemen, I didn't think of Belli—that beast."

"You—you think they'll—he'll not get drunk and give me up to any of them?" I asked somewhat tremulously.

"*Mais non.* Kincannon and Cheviot are of a mind on that and you are a very lucky girl. And Cheviot—he is an easy man to live with, patient and kind, though a little headstrong."

"I ain't goin' ter live with him!" Why did Antoinette bring that up so constantly? Was she jealous under that tolerant exterior? "If yer afraid I'll take 'em from ye, ye can rest yer mind. I ain't!"

She laughed softly. *"Non, chérie.* Ours is an arrangement of convenience. He is not mine, nor am I his, and I am not jealous of him. It is only that you are so young and untouched and he is an older man, but young enough to know hot passions." It came to me then that Antoinette had become fond of me and I was suddenly filled with humble gratitude. No woman had ever offered me any kind of friendship and I determined to please Antoinette in every way I could.

The hour grew late and the laughter from the main

room more ribald, interspersed with good-natured arguments. They talked of going to the Temple soon and disposing of their great treasures. I found myself wishing I could go too and watch.

"I'd love ter go ter th' Temple," I said to Antoinette as we sat in the roughly made chairs.

Her face lit up and she cried, "That's it! You shall make money to enter New Orleans properly—and that's the way you shall make it. I've been doing it for years!"

"What?" I asked excitedly.

"We'll take breads, pastries, tarts, and pies to the Temple and set up our own little stall together. You shall sell them to the aristocrats as I do. That will put extra money in your pocket, for I will share half and half with you!"

A flood of joy swept me. I jumped up and hugged the thin shoulders of the little Frenchwoman in wild exuberance and gratitude. She said, "I will make a leather bag for you like mine and we will slowly fill them—I, to add to my money in the Dessaultes Bank of New Orleans —and you to start yours."

"You are *good,* Antoinette," I said humbly.

"There is something about you, Aurielle," she mused, "something that sets you far above the common drab."

The men called for more brandy. I took it in and saw them with their long, sharp knives cutting pieces off the cheeses and eating with relish. I was careful to stay as far from Belli as I could, straining to pour his brandy from a distance, but he turned his bearded face to me, the wet red lips pulled back in a smile. I did not return it as I took my leave.

Much later, Antoinette smiled faintly. "Ahhh. I think you have impressed *le bos* that you are a very nice young lady and he will be glad to allow you to sell with me at the Temple." She leaned back in the slim, straight chair, her slender spine flat against it. Then she added, "Now, *chérie,* you may go to bed. Your eyes look very heavy."

I left her for my nunlike little room, passing through the room with the men, but so absorbed were they in their game that they were unaware of my passage. I disrobed in the dark with only the faint light of stars from the open

71

window to guide me. It was still and very hot, for late July was upon us and I heard the menacing buzz of mosquitoes about me. I went to the corner cupboard and drew out the *baire*. I crept under it and listened to the frustrated insects as they buzzed about it.

The laughter from the big room in front was still frequent and interspersed with heartfelt oaths, but it was good-natured cursing. In a matter of minutes, those sounds blended with the buzz of the mosquitoes and I was in deep slumber.

Captain Kincannon stayed in port for two weeks and Antoinette and I did not get to the Temple this time. They were selling only the slaves and no one but a few of the rough sailors and the Lafittes went. Antoinette told me it would be better to wait and go when all the merchandise was sold as well, for there would be many women who came to buy the silks and liquors, china and silver at that time.

Rodeur Cheviot was meticulous in spending a few hours each day with me. He was very patient and we pored over the books as he gave me instructions.

"I just got to learn!" I said passionately.

"I must learn," he replied gently.

I repeated his words with my new accent and new-found knowledge and it was surprising how easily the French came to me. It struck a long-unused chord in my brain and I was able to speak short sentences haltingly even that first day. And I learned that a *bête sauvage* was a wild beast, so I marked up one more grudge against Roxanne Deveret.

Then when Rodeur went out on a voyage, he left instructions and Antoinette saw that I had many hours to spend with the books that covered the walls of that big front room. Without the crew to cook for, our chores were minimal during those warm summer days of 1812.

I became familiar with the routine on Barataria Bay, meeting the jaunty fishermen and their wives as well as many of the women and children who lived there, always awaiting the return of their men. The other privateers came and went and only a few days passed between one or the other of the ships coming in, either to refit for another voyage or to bring in prizes.

One day as I was returning from the smaller warehouse on Grande Terre where provisions were kept for the community, I passed the great bull-necked Durket. I looked straight ahead and strode purposefully with my sacks of meal and flour, but he reached out with a great hairy arm and caught my elbow.

"Here, now, miss, can't yer pass the time o' day with me? I'm what ye might call an admirer o' yours." His hand was hot on my arm and his grip strong as I tugged to get away.

"Let go of me, sir," I said between my teeth. "I ain't —I'll tell Mister Cheviot you accosted me if you don't release me."

"Accosted, eh?" and he let out a guffaw of laughter. "Wal, now, if I'm to have the name, I might as well have the game," and he jerked me forward as the bags of supplies flew from my hands.

I twisted in his grasp and my poniard flashed into my hand. But at that moment a cold, even voice spoke. *"Qu'est-ce qui ce passe?* Durket, get your hands off mademoiselle."* It was Jean Lafitte accompanied by his plump brother. I looked at them with undisguised relief.

Durket's hands fell immediately and he said angrily, "She was makin' eyes at me, *bos.* What's a red-blooded man ter do? I thought 'twas what she wanted."

I picked up my sacks and said breathlessly, *"Merci,* Monsieur Lafitte," as Durket stalked off toward the warehouse. "He lies, you know."

"Oui. I'm sure of it, ma'amselle." He doffed his black broad-brimmed hat and his brother smiled with one eye looking away from me.

"Alors," Pierre said in his soft voice, "how are the lessons these days, mademoiselle?"

"Très bonnes," I replied proudly. "I am becoming more proficient each day." There, I had used my new word for the day. Proficient. And I was putting "gs" on my words with remarkable regularity.

"Your voice is very musical," Pierre said gallantly,

his wandering eye still looking in the other direction. "Very musical."

"Thank you," I replied demurely. "Madame Desmottes says that you are goin'——going to have a market at the Temple soon."

"Oui, as soon as Captain Kincannon returns from the voyage he starts today. We have only a few slaves, but we will have much merchandise to sell to the New Orleanaise," Jean said.

"I would love to see——all those fine people," I said wistfully.

"You will, ma'amselle, you will. Madame Desmottes tells me you will have excellent breads, tarts, and pastries to sell." Jean smiled whitely as he replaced his fine black hat. The brothers had swung into step, shortening their strides to match mine as we made our way along the path.

"I'm sure they will be superlative," Jean said and both brothers doffed their hats once more, as if I were a highborn lady, leaving me exhilarated as they turned off on the path toward the red house.

As I swung along the path to Cheviot's house, I noted two swarthy men seated on the narrow porch at the front. Drawing nearer, my eyes narrowed. It was Belli and another captain named Chighizola, both Italians. They were a pair who came often to Antoinette for pies. They paid her well and now they sat there in the blazing sun munching on the pastries with sullen expressions.

I slipped around and entered the house from the rear, dropping my sacks on the table in the storeroom. Chighizola, who had lost part of his nose in a saber duel, so it was said, was dubbed *Nez Coupé* by the French. Now I stepped lightly into the front room where I could hear their surly conversation.

Belli was growling, "I'm goin' before the council next meeting an' demand we be allowed to take the American vessels. The last one I took was beeg——reech. And the wines! Ah! Silks and spices, chests of silver! An' *le bos,* he give me hell. Him an' his patriotism, bah!"

"We'll have it out next council meeting at the red house, Belli. The other captains will see the sense of it," Chighizola said, wiping his mouth with the back of his hairy hand. There was underlying violence in their voices as they rose and made their way from the house.

I went into the storeroom where I found Antoinette had returned from the well with two buckets of water. Before she could put them on the table I was telling her of the conversation I had overheard.

"Those two," she spat. "They are not privateers! They are pirates, bloody and cruel. *Le bos* would do well to rid Barataria of the pair of them."

"I met with the Lafittes as I left the warehouse. They say when this voyage of the *Wind* is over, they will have a big market at the Temple." My voice lifted joyously, "Tell me again about the Temple, Antoinette."

She smiled as she emptied the sack of meal into a box for storage in the open kitchen cupboards. "It is on an ancient Indian burial mound of snow-white shells in the massive *chenière*—the oaks and magnolias are huge. Legend has it that the Indians performed human sacrifices there long ago."

"How do people know in the city when there will be an auction?"

"Why *chérie,* the Lafittes post handbills about the city and anyone can come and buy anything from slaves to silks and china."

"*Post handbills?* For smuggled goods!" I was astounded.

"*Mais oui,*" she grinned. "*Le bos* is popular in New Orleans. No one but the governor frowns on smuggling."

Impulsively I seized Antoinette and whirled her about in my exuberance. "Oh, Toinette, we shall make pouchfuls of money! I feel it in my bones. I can hardly wait—and to see all those elegant Creoles and highborn people."

"Humph. They dress elegantly and put on fine manners, but they have their troubles even as we do."

Quentin Kincannon's ship, the *Wind,* came in less than three weeks later with a rare prize. He had captured a Spanish galleon bound for Florida and filled with treasures, mostly gold. He was followed in shortly by Belli, who had intercepted a slaver and the barracoon was full once more. The camp was pulsating with the good fortunes

75

of the privateers and everyone was looking forward to the sale at the Temple. Jean Lafitte sent two men with his brother Pierre to New Orleans to post the handbills and the auction at the Temple was set up.

During the week before going to the Temple, several things happened. First, Rodeur brought me three dresses from the captured galleon. They were Spanish in style but very becoming and far too rich to wear about Barataria, but I dreamed over them as they lay in the chest he gave me. I told him of the conversation I had overheard between Belli and Chighizola.

He said, "We are having a council meeting at the red house today. There is a little unrest among the crew and their captains. And those two are troublemakers," he finished disparagingly. Then his blue eyes began to twinkle. "Jean will cut them down to size."

"What do they want?"

"Belli and Chighizola wish to declare all vessels fair game. *Le bos* will take only the ships of Spain and England. He considers himself American—for now, anyway."

After the conversation, I spoke to Antoinette as we were preparing the evening meal. She laughed dryly. "*Le bos says* he wants to take only vessels from warring nations."

"Don't you think he speaks the truth?" I was surprised by Antoinette's faint contempt, especially since I had come to think of myself as American.

She laughed as she stirred up the fire beneath the long spit on which were strung a number of fat game birds. "Carthagena is supposed to be at war with Spain and Lafitte's captains sail under Carthagena's letters of marque. But I will tell you this, my innocent—there are things that go on at Grand Isle and farther down Grande Terre I would not like to see. I have heard of fair women captives —and there are unmarked graves on Grand Isle. Dead women, like dead men, tell no tales. Who is to know what country a vessel sailed from when she is safely at the bottom of the sea and all her crew with her?"

"But Captain Kincannon set the *Sea Warrior* survivors free with provisions and not too far from the Mississippi River," I said.

"Captain Kincannon is an exception, at least where open murder is concerned. But he, too, is a ruthless man, *ma petite,* even if he doesn't take part in the debauchery on Grand Isle. He plans to leave Barataria a rich man one day, and soon. He is a different cut of cloth."

"Debauchery," I repeated. That was one of the new words I had learned but recently. It meant extreme indulgence of one's sensual appetites. "What do they do when they debauch?" I asked curiously, setting my breads on the paddle to slip them in the oven.

She shrugged. "Some of these men are beasts—they drink themselves senseless or wild on their captured wines and it is said that some bring their women captives along with their booty from captured vessels and drag them nude through the camps before they have their way with them."

"God and the devil!" I burst out. "And Lafitte lets such go on?"

"He and Pierre—they do not go to Grand Terre when such things are happening. They go only during the day to inspect the warehouses and their merchandise." Her voice was dry and impartial.

"Do you think this council meeting will do *any* good?"

"*Peut-être.* We shall see."

When the meal was nearly ready and my loaves and pies were baking slowly, we walked around to the front of the house. By now the crew would usually be arriving, so we went to see what was going on the bay side that kept them. A large group of men were gathered about Lafitte's red house far up the beach and on the *chenière.*

"Let's go up there," I said, my curiosity aroused. There were even women and a few children on the outskirts of the thick knot of men.

"They are waiting for the council to finish. Our diners are late because of it. Lafitte will come forth and tell them —I'll wager—that they may not raid the American vessels." She laughed sarcastically. "Pierre and Jean fancy themselves great gentlemen—very civilized. And they are smart enough to keep from getting too far in trouble with the American government. Come along, we will see."

We walked swiftly along the sandy ground, our feet in their light slippers sinking into it and taking on an uncomfortable amount of sand. When we reached the crowd, I noted that there was muttered conversation among the men, truculent and argumentative.

"They are Belli's and Chighizola's men," Antoinette murmured. "A murderous-looking crew, *n'est-ce pas?*"

One bronzed giant with a yellow bandanna bound about his black head was gesticulating, a pistol in his hand. The women were very quiet and kept the children near their skirts.

We had no more than glanced about, when the door to the house opened. I saw the two Lafittes first, followed by Dominique You, Beluche, and Quentin Kincannon. I glimpsed Roxanne Deveret behind him. More captains filed through the door after them and they all stood a moment on the little porch, looking down on the crowd of sailors before them. The late sun was blistering along the back of my neck and shoulders and the bay behind us glittered like polished brass.

"You will take no American vessels hereafter," Jean Lafitte said clearly. He had a pistol thrust in his waist and his hands were on his hips. "We make war only on the Spanish and the English."

The bronzed giant let out a stream of oaths and shouted, "You can't tell us what to do! We serve Belli and we'll take all the vessels—any of them, by God, and you can go to the——"

In the wink of an eye a pistol shot sounded and the man pitched forward, his own gun flying from his hand. Not a word was spoken as the impassive Jean Lafitte put his pistol to his lips and blew the curling smoke away. Belli, beside him, was scowling blackly but he said nothing.

"It has been decided," Lafitte went on in a measured voice, "the first man who brings goods from an American vessel will be hung without trial."

The sailors picked up the body of their dead comrade silently, one at each of his arms and two at his feet, and carried the limp body to a skiff at one of the piers. The crowd melted and Antoinette and I turned away.

"Belli is the one he should have shot," she said

quietly. "Instead, he will roam the seas and he will not turn away from an American ship. You shall see."

"And run the risk of hanging?"

"*Oui*. M'sieu Lafitte may have put the fear into many of them, but Belli and his comrade Chighizola are brutes."

I looked out on the glittering bay and saw that the men in the skiff were rowing the body of their comrade to Grand Isle, which stretched out to the west. In the sudden silence that had fallen, we could faintly hear a high, keening wail from the barracoon. The captured slaves were hungry and homesick.

"They'll bury him on Grand Isle," Antoinette said cheerfully, "and good riddance. We are very lucky to have Rodeur and Captain Kincannon as our protectors, you know."

I felt gooseflesh prick along the backs of my arms as I thought of the women unfortunate enough to fall into the hands of Belli's and Chighizola's men. I was suddenly grateful that Kincannon had shown nothing more than extreme irritation toward me since that hot and abandoned night aboard the *Wind*—but Rodeur! Ah, I was becoming more and more fond of him. He was always kind and gentle, treating me as if I were a lady. I did not keep my guard up with Rodeur. Ours was a deepening friendship. I *trusted* Cheviot instinctively.

Chapter 4

September was fading into cool nights before it was decided there would be a general sale of merchandise at the Temple. Jean Lafitte announced it the day before we were to go, and that evening found us preparing to leave before dawn the following day.

I was wildly excited and Antoinette and I spent the evening wrapping our crusty loaves and crisper tarts for transportation. Cheviot wandered in and observed our diligence with a little half smile. He looked exceptionally handsome in a new pair of boots and breeches that fit him exceedingly well.

I felt a warm sense of security knowing he would propel our pirogue through the twisting maze of bayous to the Temple. Rodeur's pirogue had been made by the French fishermen and it was a huge cypress log, smoothed and honed to a fine finish. It was larger, too, than most, which meant we could carry everything we needed, for we would spend the night at the Temple before the people arrived the following morning.

Before dawn I was up, donning one of the silk dresses

Rodeur had given me. It was the deep French blue of my eyes and I couldn't resist asking if I might peer in the mirror in Antoinette's bedroom. At the time, I felt my appearance couldn't be improved on, though the gown was uncomfortably elaborate.

Later, Rodeur was hefting the sacks of breads and tarts, taking them by twos to the pirogue at the mouth of the bayou. It was a long walk and while he was gone, under Antoinette's instructions I brushed my hair until it crackled and gleamed and put on a pair of the new blue faille half-slippers that Rodeur had brought with the dresses. They were a shade too large, but I laced them tightly about my ankles.

Fall was coming. It was in the air, damp and cool, as Rodeur returned for the last two sacks of breads. This time, we went with him.

By daylight's first pale rays, we were well on our way up the bayou, with Rodeur wielding the paddle strongly. There were dozens of pirogues and skiffs carrying every description of booty. Three broad skiffs bore blacks, those newly come from Africa and captured by Belli but a few days ago. They looked belligerent and dejected at the same time. There were women among them who wept occasionally.

Now I looked into their untamed faces as the sun slowly rose over the bayous and the *prairies tremblantes* and felt great pity and sorrow for them. They spoke not a word of any language I knew.

I asked Rodeur about this as the sun dispersed little pockets of mist in the swamp on either side of us. He shrugged without pausing in his rhythmic strokes with the paddle. "They will learn eventually."

"It's wrong," I said angrily, "to sell human beings."

"And weren't you yourself sold—for a mere passage fee? *C'est la même chose.*"

"No, it isn't the same. I will be free when my year is up."

"And so may the slaves win their freedom," he replied.

I was silent, for as the sun rose higher, the sights and sounds about us were fascinating. The watery forests on either side were filled with life and I kept crying out in astonishment as each new creature met my gaze. Antoinette was very patient in answering my rapid-fire questions. Egrets with filmy plumes flew about among the trees, looking like graceful ladies dressed for a ball. Indeed the birds that inhabited these giant cypresses and oaks were myriad and colorful beyond measure.

Rodeur, in response to my happy ejaculations, said cynically, "There are other creatures in the deeper woods, *ma petite,* that you would not find so entrancing."

It was late afternoon when we reached the Temple and I caught my breath at the beauty of the isolated spot. Even the roughly constructed warehouse for the temporary storage of some goods in case of rain blended into the untrammeled beauty of the place.

Rodeur pulled the pirogue up to one of the piers and tied the prow to a post. We began to unload. Activity took on a feverish eagerness as the corsairs brought up their goods and began to spread them out beneath the trees for their customers to browse over the following morning and afternoon. Many of the privateers, including Kincannon and the red-sailed fishermen with their great tubs of shrimp and crab, had come up the night before and readied much of the merchandise. The fishermen would sell hot spicy seafood to the customers from their huge iron pots over fires already laid.

Antoinette and I went up into the *chenière* seeking a proper spot to display our fresh, crusty breads and pastries —Antoinette had even baked mince tarts.

We were all tired by dark and after eating heartily of good food brought and prepared, we were ready to lie upon our rough pallets and sleep until daybreak. In the cool, open air, I slept deeply and refreshingly, rising early with Antoinette to don the remodeled blue silk dress and prepare my coiffure with her help.

The whole camp was abustle and I was amazed at how temptingly the privateers had laid out their wares. The blacks had spent the night herded in the warehouse under guard and looked most pitiable to me as they came out to eat. The spiced scent of the freshly boiling crabs and shrimp made my mouth water. Oysters they would serve raw, from containers beside the boiling pots. These fishermen were very jolly and cut from different cloth than the predatory corsairs, though they lived unconcernedly side by side with them at Barataria.

"Ah, look," Antoinette pressed my arm, "here come the first of the New Orleanaise."

I looked up to see a man on horseback, followed by a wagon with a black driver on the box. "He has come to buy slaves," Antoinette said. "There will be many of them. And the women—ah, you shall see their dresses and riding habits—they will be along soon."

We went back to our place under a towering magnolia and arranged the loaves and pastries on the cloth spread beneath them. In a short while, the wealthy planters and even more wealthy merchants and their wives came to the Temple. Soon there was a great hubbub of voices and much excited bargaining.

I was so fascinated I simply sat and stared. The women were beautifully dressed and coiffed, exquisite in the latest fashions. The whole affair took on a gay carnival air, one of laughter and joy. I thought of Governor Claiborne, who was trying vainly to stop the flow of this contraband merchandise. It all seemed so free and pleasant, I found myself almost in agreement with Rodeur, that the governor was a fool and these people, who were buying merchandise much cheaper, were the smart ones.

The two Lafittes, along with Beluche and Dominique You, had arranged a sort of portable bar which they had brought out in sections from the warehouse nearby. They were allowing the gentlemen in their sleek pantaloons and fine weskits to sample the wines that were for sale. One man caught my eye, for he was exceedingly handsome, with black, curling hair and a long, straight French nose. From his bearing I knew he must be someone of great importance.

Kincannon stood nearby, his narrowed dark eyes flicking over the crowd. He had arranged for his men to set up their wares on a long, broad table, but much of the boxed china and silverware was on the ground beside the tables of silks, jewelry, perfumes, dainty decanters, and what appeared to my dazzled eyes to be a thousand treasures. Women were clustering about them now, their silken skirts brushing against each other.

I noted Roxanne Deveret's hostile glance taking in my refitted frock with scorn. She wore her tight pantaloons and knee boots arrogantly, her full and pointed breasts provocative beneath the white silk shirt that was always open too deeply at her throat. With sudden passion, I hated the French blue silk that hung about my ankles above my too large shoes.

"Antoinette," I whispered breathlessly and with anger, "I am the shabbiest woman here."

She gave me an astonished glance. "You look *très gentille,* Aurielle," she replied reprovingly. "Would you look like Roxanne, strutting about in men's clothing?"

I would with all my heart, I thought as I moved the golden brown loaves nearer the tarts and pastries. Then, sitting back upon the log just back of our display, I secretly observed all the young men, their muscled legs strong and symmetrical in boots and breeches. From beneath the thick fringe of my lashes they all looked beautiful and unattainable. I stared at the young women who hung on the arms of the young men. There were older people among them, arrogant as the young with the arrogance that only money and security can bring.

Ah, if I only had a dress like that girl in the pale pink silk trimmed in darker pink satin—a web of lace over her bosom and a matching pink parasol; she simpered up at the handsome young man I had noted earlier at the bar. There was an older woman with the two now, a woman of imposing hauteur, with snapping black eyes and a tight mouth. The glance she bent on the tall, handsome Frenchman was as full of love as that of his bridling companion. His mother, I realized, with quick intuition.

Antoinette, who had followed my glance, said scornfully, "Creoles! What a stiff-necked, prideful lot they are!"

"Just what is a Creole—aside from being gentry?" I asked curiously.

"The true Creoles are the direct descendants of the marriages between the Spanish nobility and the French nobility who came to Louisiana—some of them near a hundred years ago. Their vanity is enormous—thinking they are better than the rest of us!"

The young man glanced my way idly. I was staring so fixedly our eyes held. His face was as beautiful as a Greek coin, his black hair gleaming in the dappled sunlight. There was a vitality, a dashing charm in that handsome face that drew me irresistibly. For the space of a heartbeat a smile trembled between us before I let my lashes fall. He must be someone highborn and wealthy, I thought excitedly, and I yearned to know him. I felt the heat in my face and knew my color was high and I tossed my head spiritedly as I bent to further arrange the loaves.

With my face lowered, I saw only his polished boots with the pantaloon straps beneath the high arches of his small feet as he came to stand before our wares.

"*Maman,*" his voice was deep and musically authoritative, "do we not need some of this smuggler's bread and pastries?"

I looked up then, my eyes meeting his once more, and a sharp thrill of premonition shot through me. Antoinette took charge at once and I stepped into the background. "M'sieu, smuggler's breads, like smuggler's wares, are of the best. See? I will cut a loaf and a tart that you may sample. Madame?" She sliced a loaf and a bit of tart swiftly and proffered them to the imperious mother, who took them and daintily bit into them.

"Hmmm, *très bon,* Valier. Here, give Lisette a bite," she said to Antoinette, who hastened to do as she was bid.

They stood talking among themselves, the girl, who had a pretty but vapid face, hanging on every word the man spoke. I glanced at him quickly to see that his black eyes were still on my face and they were twinkling wickedly. I looked down, knowing my double lashes were thick black crescents against apricot cheeks. The Baratarian sun had been kind to me. I did not freckle but turned instead a pale, translucent gold.

The woman bought several loaves and half a dozen tarts and Antoinette put them in a thin cotton sack with a drawstring top. She had made over two dozen such sacks with her swift French fingers days ago for this moment.

"I shall pay the young one," the man called Valier said to Antoinette with a laugh. "Has she worked hard on these good pastries?"

"Oui," replied Antoinette. I said nothing but held my rough little hand out and he dropped two gold pieces into it, and the three of them moved away. He did not look at me again.

I heard his mother say reprovingly, "You are too generous, Valier. They are not worth twenty dollars—"

His reply was lost as they drifted away, and Antoinette said with cynical satisfaction, "He can well afford it. They own the Dessaultes Bank of New Orleans, as well as much property."

"Dessaultes—is that their name? Tell me about them, Antoinette."

"The girl with him is Lisette Poliet. The Poliets are an old family, very aristocratic, also connected with the bank, and Valier Dessaultes is the head of the Dessaultes properties—and a hot-headed, break-neck man he is in his personal life." She looked after them a moment as they disappeared in the crowd. "It is said he pursued Dolores Ysidro until her father—who did not approve of the match, being Spanish and much more aristocratic than the Dessaultes—sent Dolores away to Savannah, where she married another. His mastery of swordplay is unparalleled."

"Has he much money?"

"Very much money and he is not led around by that high-nosed mother of his either, though she is a strong-willed woman."

"I thought him—wonderful."

"You dream high, *ma petite.* Creoles do not marry out of their class."

"I plan to be of their class when I reach New Orleans—"

Roxanne swaggered near, saying, "Give us two tarts, Antoinette." She was accompanied by a woman who put the Dessaultes out of my mind the moment I looked at her.

"You will pay for it," Antoinette said firmly.

"Oui. Here," and she pitched a gold coin worth many times two tarts down upon the sheet.

Antoinette picked it up unhurriedly, then handed two mincemeat tarts to the girl. "One for you and one for Madame Chaille," she said, her voice cold.

I could not tear my eyes from the lady, whose poise was that of a woman about thirty-two or -three, though she looked ten years less. Her hair was dark mahogany with red lights, the same color as mine, and her features were classic. Her smile was enchanting as she bent it upon Roxanne when the girl handed her one of the tarts. I felt a strange emptiness that was waiting to be filled—and it was with a rush as the woman bent her smile upon me. "Delicious," she murmured, her cornflower eyes never leaving my face. Indeed, it crept upon me that we looked somewhat alike.

"Comment vous appelez-vous?" she asked.

"Aurielle—Stuart," I replied huskily.

"I am Madame Ondine Chaille and it seems we resemble one another, *chérie.*" The lovely face wore a brilliant smile and I thought I had never seen such serene and gentle kindness on anyone's features. Her lips were not so full as mine and her face a touch narrower, but we could easily pass for sisters.

"You are much more beautiful, Ondine," Roxanne said as the two walked away eating their tarts. I looked after the swaying figure of Madame Chaille with the bud of an incredible hope in my mind. Her dress was exquisite, her wide-brimmed hat of white silk was like a flower on her pretty head.

It was then I noticed a powerful black man who had been at her side, for he looked back at me a long time before he turned to follow Madame Chaille. His shoulders were enormous and I saw his eyes were slightly elliptical, giving him a strange, foreign look, somewhat like an ancient Egyptian prince I had seen in Cheviot's history books.

"That's Sebastien," Antoinette volunteered, as we looked after him. "He is a majordomo, her confidant, her protector. She brought him with her from Paris years ago. Roxanne says she is a widow and there is a certain mystery about her past."

"She is from Paris?"

"So Roxanne says. It is whispered that she escaped some dread punishment when she came to New Orleans."

"Who whispers that?" I was brimming with curiosity about the beautiful woman I resembled. A hundred questions trembled on my lips.

"All my information comes from Roxanne—and sometimes I overhear the men talk when they come for cards at Rodeur's," Antoinette replied, shaking her leather pouch. It jingled comfortingly. "She—Roxanne—brags that Madame Chaille would like to set her up in New Orleans society—that she is her great friend. Roxanne gave her some diamonds once, a matched set taken from a Spanish ship. But Roxanne says it is because she is what she is that Madame Chaille likes her—a woman of independence."

"She looked as if she liked me, too," I remarked, and Antoinette laughed cynically, her sharp little fox's nose wrinkling. "But she *did,*" I insisted, "and we do look something alike. What became of her husband?"

"Who is to say? I have told you all I know."

"But you haven't," I protested. "Tell me about where she lives and her house—who works for her?"

"Cease!" Antoinette threw up her hands. "She lives in a very grand house on Chartres Street, so Roxanne says. She has visited there. This is all fool's talk, you know. No one in New Orleans will remember any of us, once they are back in the city." She rearranged the tarts to cover the two that were missing. Then, "Look, here come three ladies to buy from us."

We were kept busy through the noon hour and sold all we had brought. Indeed, we could have sold twice as much, I thought regretfully as we seated ourelves to watch the rest of those about us sell their prizes. Antoinette counted up our money.

But I was thinking now of Valier Dessaultes. He had admired me, I knew, but he had dismissed me for the nonentity I was. Antoinette was right. No one would remember us. *God and the devil!* I thought furiously as I looked up through the trees beyond to glimpse Madame Chaille examining the china at Kincannon's table. *I will escape all this, as I escaped the Boar's Head!* I would go to New Orleans. Nothing should stop me. Patience, the most difficult of all virtues, I would learn. I bit my lip.

Having sold out, I was now afforded the dubious pleasure of watching all the monied people from New Orleans buy and buy and buy. Madame Chaille lifted a silver teapot and held it up to examine the silversmith's mark, and her white silken sleeves fell back to reveal beautiful, slender arms, a gold jeweled bracelet twinkling on the left one.

Back from the scene of all this merry activity, I saw the carriages, surreys, and curricles that had brought these fine people to the Temple. Their blooded horses, sleek and well cared for, leaned their arched necks to the ground to nibble at the vegetation growing there.

There were some Negroes among the shoppers, some carrying baskets for their white mistresses, but some who were free were buying as eagerly as their white counterparts.

"Look, they are getting ready now to auction off the slaves." Antoinette pointed and farther down in the *chenière* I saw them coming from the warehouse. They were not bound and they came forth almost eagerly, glad to be out of the confines of the rough building.

I felt a kinship with them. We were all of us strangers in a strange land, each of us bound to serve others for the most part, and all of us yearning for freedom and a good life. In a moment, several had mounted the little square platform of planks over logs. Two giant seamen stepped up beside them and the auction began.

There was a great crowd about the platform now, mostly men, with women on the outer perimeter. Some of the Creole women stayed where they were, pulling at bolts of satin, brocade, muslin, and various silks. Even so, the attention was focused on the auction and the two auctioneers and their goods. I turned my head as the bidding began. Then as the bidding rose to a crescendo, Antoinette said, "Come, little one, let us eat while this unpleasant business is conducted."

"I'm not hungry," I replied.

"Then here—divide our earnings."

So while the black men and women in their loincloths and shapeless dresses were stepping down one by one from the platforms as they were purchased, I counted out the money.

Much later, when the auction was over and the blacks had joined others of their color in the wagons, I realized that I was indeed very hungry. The steaming pots of seafood and gumbo made by the fishermen and their wives gave off the most delicious fragrances.

"Are you ready to dine now, my hot-headed little friend?" Antoinette asked good-naturedly, motioning toward the pots. "It will cost us but little of what we have made."

The sun was lower in the sky now, the air growing cooler, and the buyers, glutted with their purchases of cloth, silver, jewelry, food, and flesh, were forming an exodus. I had surreptitiously watched Valier Dessaultes and when I could not see him, I had looked for the incredibly lovely woman known as Madame Ondine Chaille, who already in my imagination had become dear to me.

I thought wryly what a romantic fool I was, as the French fisherman thrust his dipper into the steaming cauldron and came up with the wooden ladle filled with shrimp.

So Antoinette and I stuffed ourselves on the pink and firm shrimp, followed by still warm, cracked whole crabs with sweet, clean white meat. I took a seat under a huge magnolia whose leathery leaves rustled in the rising fall breeze.

Suddenly I saw Valier Dessaultes steering the two women, his mother and the girl, Lisette, toward a polished black carriage drawn by two gleaming black horses. He spoke to a black man seated on a wagon behind the carriage. The wagon was filled with purchased goods. Two young black women he and his mother had bought were perched on two heavy boxes of fine Spanish Madeira. The black driver flicked a whip over the two strong horses that drew the wagon and turned it slowly around as Valier assisted his mother and Lisette into the carriage. I watched moodily as the entourage followed the others departing.

The little stalls and shops on the tables and ground were nearly empty and the men of Barataria were jubilant. I saw them hefting sacks full of gold and others, still larger, stuffed with greenbacks.

I glanced back at the last departing Creoles as they followed each other slowly down the trace that meandered off beneath giant trees that towered almost a hundred feet in the air.

"How far from here to New Orleans?" I asked

Antoinette as I licked my fingers. The gumbo was delicious and full of mouthwatering bits of seafood and a vegetable called okra.

"Five miles to the batture at the river. Come, Aurielle, we must make a place to sleep later. We will leave for Barataria at dawn. Are you not tired?"

"No," I replied rebelliously, still staring down the trace. There was no sign, no sound of those richly clad Creoles now. I saw Jean Lafitte and his plump brother Pierre before the table where the bags of money had been emptied. Kincannon joined them as they divided it up. A shaft of the sinking sun struck his dark, tumbled hair as he stood laughing down into their faces. He held a large leather bag in his hand and I knew that much of the gold and the new United States currency would fill it.

Rodeur came up and flung himself down beside us, holding up his own leather pouch, bulging with his share of the proceeds. Only the fishermen did not participate in the division, keeping the money they had made from their steaming cauldrons.

"I saw you," Rodeur said, smiling, "looking at Valier Dessaultes, little one—and very ardently, I might add."

"Tell me about him," I said, my heart beating fast. Antoinette, who had already told me about him, gave me an amused and dour look.

"He is as near to royalty as New Orleans can boast, among the French—though not the Spanish. He and his mother live in one of the finest houses in the city—on Toulouse Street, not far from our estimable Governor Claiborne's house," Rodeur said slowly. "He is well educated, he owns a bank and much property. He is skilled in all the social graces." Rodeur's eyes narrowed on me and his lips tightened. "In fact, he meets all your requirements, chérie." He paused, then added, "And he has killed nine men on the field of honor."

"Field of honor?" I asked blankly.

"These Creoles are very gallant, Aurielle. Their honor is easily offended and a duel follows. That is the field of honor. They are nearly always fought on the outskirts of the city. One place often chosen for duels is sous les chênes—under the oaks, where many men have died."

91

Suddenly Kincannon loomed over us. I looked up into the hard dark eyes and sardonic smile. "How would you like it, Aurielle, if I had sold your redemption to one of the great families of New Orleans? Just think—you could go to the city if I had. And I could have sold it for as much as a thousand dollars, probably to Valier Dessaultes if I had offered you. I saw you two looking at each other." His voice had an edge to it.

"I can't imagine why you didn't," I retorted, my eyes locked with his in anger. Always, when I was near him, the intimacy we had almost shared hung in my mind, tempting as ripe fruit, but forbidden by my will.

"I should have," he retorted mockingly, "but Rodeur tells me your bread is very good indeed and he has grown —fond of you."

Rodeur was looking from one to the other of us and his little smile was unreadable as I said, "And Rodeur assures me that after one year of making that bread, I shall be free!"

"Ah—how your speech has improved. I am astonished. Since Rodeur's excellent tutelage, you do not sound at all like the low creature you are." Before I could answer, he was gone.

Rodeur, at my side, murmured, "Now, Aurielle, no lady would scowl as you do at this moment." I looked into his smiling face and my own smoothed slowly. I owed him a great deal and that knowledge was in his narrow, twinkling blue eyes.

"I would see some of your dreams come true, *ma petite*—but I do not think they will with Dessaultes. The man is reckless and—they say—he loved another too well and lost her."

My little smile was secret. If he had loved once and lost, he could love again—and win. I rose, took my empty bowl back to the fisherman and his wife, then returned and sat back down slowly beside Antoinette as the dark blue shadows crept across the shells, fading their whiteness to a dim glow in the dusky light. Fires about the perimeter took on new cheery brightness as the late September chill set in. Laughter echoed, deep and husky from the men, high and shrill from the women. Satisfaction and pleasure emanated from the little camps. It had been a very successful sale and all the Baratarians were pleased with themselves.

A great orange moon lifted itself slowly above the impenetrable trees and stretches of marsh and reeds, spilling light on the black water of the bayou beyond us, sending fingers of gold in little splinters over us. Rodeur got to his feet, unbuckled his sword from his waist, and went into the deeper forest to gather wood. Antoinette and I, full of good food and yawning, sat upon the log.

When Cheviot had a fire going, we put our hands out to it and found the heat relaxing. Antoinette, muffling another yawn, said, "Rodeur, I am going to make down our pallets now. It is high time we rested."

"But I am not sleepy," I protested, looking down toward the bayou where a group of men and women were laughing and talking.

"Then why have you been yawning?" she asked severely.

"It's all that food," I replied mutinously. "I would like to go down there where all those people have gathered. Listen, someone is singing!"

"Come, Aurielle, we will join them," Cheviot laughed. "Let Toinette make down the pallets—she is the sleepy one."

I followed him joyously across the shells to where the main body of men had gathered around a big fire. I saw Kincannon sitting on his heels, talking with Jean Lafitte. Beluche and Dominique You were listening to one of the sailors who had lifted a fine baritone in song.

> When we are enchanted by love
> Farewell to all happiness!
> Poor little Mamzelle Zizi,
> Poor little Mamzelle Zizi,
> She has sorrow, sorrow, sorrow—
> She has sorrow in her heart . . .

Everyone quieted down, listening to the story told in song by the French sailor. It became apparent there were many verses, all dealing with the unhappiness of the little French girl whose lover was stolen by a beautiful quadroon named Callalou. As he sang, I noticed several brandy bottles being passed among the men and women alike. Sated on food, with money in their pockets and leisure time in which to enjoy both, all were becoming a little heated with the liquor passed and the blazing fire before them. I noted Roxanne, seated near Kincannon, listening intently to the song, her full mouth drooping with sympathy as the singer finished.

> Callalou's a shameless jade
> She wears dresses of brocade,
> Lures the lover of Mamzelle,
> Sorrow, sorrow in Zizi's heart.

There was much clapping, and in the firelight I saw Belli and Chighizola taking great swallows from the bottle and passing it to Durket who crouched beside them, his face redder by firelight, his black brows, which met in the middle of his forehead, lifted in appreciation of the singer.

The singer sang on, this time a lively French tune with saucy words, but the others talked and laughed among themselves, bragging over who sold the most. I saw Roxanne Deveret tilt a bottle to her lips and take a dainty sip. Cheviot left me and went to talk with Kincannon, so I sat down on the cool damp earth to watch the others make sport with each other.

I was thoroughly enjoying it when I became uncomfortably aware of eyes fastened on me. I glanced around the group seated back from the fire and encountered the shining black eyes of Durket. I looked hastily away, but felt his stare still. Where was Cheviot? Still talking with Kincannon. It was then I saw that Roxanne Deveret was looking at me, too. She would glance at Durket and then back to me. I sat still, wondering at the fear the man stirred in me. Around the fires, the people were growing more heated in their exchanges and I saw several violent embraces taking place among the men and their women.

Durket sat still as a rock, never taking his eyes from me. The crowd was breaking up now into arguments, some good-humored, some not. The lovemakers were growing more passionate and moving off into the shadows. I shifted uneasily.

Suddenly, lithely, Durket was beside me, his great arms closing about my waist and his large, moist mouth was pressed to mine. I heard Roxanne's delighted laughter dimly. I struggled with great violence, drawing back, but he pressed his mouth, now wet, against my throat and a great scream welled out of it, freezing those about us into immobility. By now the two of us had risen to our feet and were swaying before the fire in a wild flow of attack and resistance. I did not see him come, but Cheviot was suddenly there.

"*Sacré bleu!* Durket, you are mad—let go of her!"

The two men were suddenly locked in combat and I stepped breathlessly away. Durket was the larger of the two and his great hamlike hands clenched into fists and lashed at the tall, slender man, who had no weapon. He landed a blow with jarring force on Cheviot's jaw and he went down under the onslaught like a felled tree. Then Durket lunged at me, his arms closing about me, lifting me off the ground, and he took great strides toward the woods, my screams ringing in the air. By now, all of those left about the fire were watching with interest the struggle between us.

Abruptly I was dropped to the ground bruisingly. And Durket lay sprawled beside me, Kincannon standing over him with the point of his sword at the man's throat.

Durket glared up at him and growled, "What's she to you and Cheviot? By God, nothin' but a nameless little bitch. Why not give her to me?" Then slowly, "I'll give you all my share of today's profits for her."

"Get up," Kincannon said pleasantly, but his eyes in the firelight were twin flames.

The man got to his feet as catlike as he had fallen on me. "You don't care nothin' about her," Durket protested. "I've seen you treat 'er like dirt—I'd keep 'er. Build a house fer 'er."

"You struck Cheviot," Kincannon said. "For that I would kill you. Get a sword."

The man's face blanched. "Now, Cap'n, you know I ain't no swordsman. Pistols is my game."

"Get a sword."

"Aw, no. Now, Cap'n, I'll make it right." He walked

95

rapidly to where Cheviot had risen to his feet, shaking his head to clear it. The bruise on his jaw was swelling now. "Cheviot, I'm sorry I hit yer," Durket growled. "But th' girl's all I want. I'm willin' ter pay ye fer 'er."

"She is not for sale, *chien!* Not to you or anyone else. Stay away from her or I'll kill you." Cheviot's voice shook with fury.

Kincannon had followed and now he said, "Shall I save you the trouble, friend Rodeur?" The sword swept about Durket's huge frame and the coarse face paled.

"Ah, *mes amis*—a leetle quarrel over a girl. *C'est un rien, un vetille.*" Dominique You spoke softly. "Let us put away weapons—no harm has been done. Durket is a good sailor—a good privateer."

Lafitte and his brother drew up before us. *"Alors, mes amis*—Ma'amselle Aurielle is safe. Let us forget the contretemps."

Kincannon prodded Durket's stomach gently and the man shrank. "You will leave the girl alone after this, Durket. Otherwise, Cheviot or I will have your head."

"I will. I swear it!" The others who had come to watch were drifting away. Beluche slapped Kincannon on the shoulder jovially.

"You are a quick man with that sword, *mon vieux*— you may be sure we will all give ma'amselle a wide berth now."

I was still trembling slightly when Cheviot took my arm. "I think it best you go to bed now, *chérie*. The drink has affected the judgment of the men." Then ruefully, "That *bête noir* took me on without my sword. I was not much use as your protector. If it hadn't been for Quent——"

"I don't see how Roxanne stays free of them," I interrupted shakily as we made our way toward the dying fire beneath the tall magnolia.

"Roxanne is rarely without her sword. The men learned long ago that she has Kincannon's protection. They are used to her. They are not used to you and you are beautiful."

Antoinette was sitting upright on her blankets and

she said acidly, "It is no more than I expected, Rodeur. Come, Aurielle—your blankets are ready."

I said not a word but slipped between them fully clothed. I didn't care if the blue silk wrinkled beyond repair. No clothing of mine would be removed in the chill night with those terrible sailors all about the camp. I was shaking with nerves, but within minutes, I was deliciously warm and slept soundly despite the wild cries of the nocturnal creatures of the swamp. I slept until dawn when an exceptionally noisy alligator's bellow awakened me.

I was depressed the whole of the trip back to Barataria, sitting disconsolately behind a swarthy sailor from Kincannon's *Wind,* while he methodically plied the paddle. Rodeur was not with us, for he and Kincannon, along with the Lafittes—and worse, along with the taunting Roxanne and her guardian, Ulysses—had gone in three big pirogues to New Orleans. Roxanne had come out of the warehouse clad in a green watered-silk dress with ruffles peeping from her pelisse, which made the ensemble enchantingly beautiful.

Antoinette had been brisk. "Did you not know they are going on to the city today? *Le bos* has sent several bales of cinnamon and other spices and a box of fine linen shirts to his blacksmith shop on St. Philip Street." She laughed shortly as she added, "They go to sample the city's pleasures and make a little more money."

"I should think they'd be arrested the minute they are seen!" I burst out, angry that I should be jealous of Roxanne.

"Non, chérie. You forget their powerful friends— lawyers among them. And no order has yet been issued for the arrest of the Lafittes."

Now I stared moodily out at the strange yellow lilies of fall that occasionally dotted the shore like golden stars, contrasting sharply with the ugly alligators, some of them fifteen feet long, that could be seen where a tip of land met the bayou. I was silent most of the long trip back, Antoinette finally giving up the effort to cheer me.

When we were safely back in Cheviot's small house, Antoinette followed me to my room where I flung myself disconsolately across my narrow cot. She stood looking down at me reflectively.

Then she asked, "Have you the leather pouch with your money, Aurielle?" She patted the little bag at her waist, heavy under the weight of coins. "They are very fat, *n'est-ce pas?*"

"Yes," I replied dejectedly, holding mine in my lap as I sat up, "but I shall need a thousand times that to accomplish what I desire."

She looked at me for a long time, then the hard little sparkling eyes softened. "When my Faubert was lost at sea and our little son died in the plague of fever, I thought of returning to New Orleans." Her face was so sad I felt a lump form in my throat.

"Ah, Toinette, I am so sorry!" I reached out and caught her hand impulsively.

"Oui. But I am a good cook," she shrugged eloquently, "and Captain Kincannon has been kind to me. He pays me well for my services—and I like keeping house for Rodeur Cheviot. He pays me well *aussi."*

"What do you do with your money?"

"Every two or three months, either the captain or M'sieu Cheviot takes it and puts it in the Dessaultes Bank of New Orleans for me. I have over three thousand now."

I looked at her with new respect. "Why, Toinette, you could go to the city and live very well! You could cook there too, you know."

"And I can do coiffures beautifully—and sew marvelously well," she replied calmly. "But I know no one in the city any longer. Here I have friends—I have my job. I am established. It is not a bad life."

I said nothing but the seed was planted. Possibly I would not go to New Orleans alone. This crusty, thirtyish woman would be a fine chaperone. A mantle of respectability. We had become fond of each other over the months. When the time came I would be very persuasive and Antoinette Desmottes might well accompany me. And the money! Ah, if only I could persuade her to lend it to me, I would pay it back double when I married well. Confidence poured through me in a golden flood. I was almost cheerful by the time we ate our supper.

Chapter
5

Life on Grande Terre went smoothly for the next few weeks. Kincannon and Rodeur, with Jean Lafitte, Roxanne Deveret, and the tall black Ulysses, returned from their sojourn in New Orleans, leaving Pierre, I presumed, with his Marie Villars in their fine house on St. Philip Street.

As the days slipped by, ships came and went, and captured riches filled the warehouses on the island. The few ragged palms whipped in the fall winds off the gulf. The sailors and their *bos* made regular trips to the Temple and again to the city, where further business was transacted.

Another slave ship was brought in, and the barracoon was again filled with the bewildered unhappy black men and women. Barataria was prospering as it never had before. Talk of the governor taking action had faded.

Antoinette and I went only once more to the Temple during October and because mostly slaves were being sold, we saw none of the people we had seen the first time I went. We had returned with our leather pouches jingling cheerfully. I had counted my small hoard numberless times, but each time all the gold and silver in it came to no more than a hundred and fifty American dollars, which was disheartening, for I was chafing under the slowly passing days of fall. I studied my books with renewed fervor and intensity.

November came with chill rains followed by brilliant sunlight and almost summer warmth. I thought longingly of Antoinette's three thousand dollars, but I had not yet nerved myself to approach her regarding my hope that she would go to the city with me.

Shortly after the first of November, the news spread throughout the village that Captain Quentin Kincannon was making good his determination to leave Barataria for more legitimate enterprises having their center in New Orleans. He sold his beautiful ship, the *Wind,* to the highest bidder among the privateers. That happened to be Belli, the corsair with the fewest scruples.

When Kincannon set out in his pirogue for the city, he was followed by two skiffs containing all his personal belongings and poled along by two sailors. He carried on his person his sword, his pistols, and two leather bags heavy with gold. He left at dawn on the morning of November ninth and I walked down with Rodeur and Antoinette to see him off. Roxanne and Ulysses were there as well, and she looked sullen and angry.

On our way back to the house, after Kincannon had pushed off in the bayou, I noticed Rodeur was frowning. Under the paling sky, he muttered, "I do not know which of these men left—to serve with. I have no wish to go to the city, even though Quent has said he would put me into one of his businesses. He has bought a large sugar plantation out at Pointe St. Antoine—but I am not sure I wish to be so anchored."

"And he did not take Roxanne with him either," I said with curious satisfaction. "No doubt she will become the—ah—partner of Beluche or Dominique You," I added cynically as we reached the house and entered. "As long as her beauty lasts, anyway. Why she hasn't a dozen babies I cannot fathom."

Antoinette murmured cryptically, "Some women cannot have babies, Aurielle, no matter how hard they try. It can happen thus to any woman, even you."

A knifelike fear streaked through me. I was silent at the enormity of such a suggestion. It could not be so! I loved babies; I had mothered the little ones in the streets of Portsmouth, had comforted Marianne's little clubfooted bastard baby, twisted his golden curls about my fingers. I lifted my chin. "Not to me. I shall have a dozen babies," I spoke confidently, "when I marry a fine Creole gentleman."

Rodeur's infectious laugh was deep. "You are much like Roxanne *ma petite*. I know that displeases you, but each of you has an iron will and a temper like a flash fire.".

"I am nothing like that—that," I choked over an epithet and settled for "woman!"

He laughed again, then changed the subject abruptly. "You must sit and eat your supper with me these nights while I am here and let me instruct you on the art of dining daintily. I have watched you use your fingers and become greasy from ear to ear. Very unlovely."

So in the dusk that evening, he attempted to correct my awful table manners and I struggled valiantly to remember all his instructions. It was such an unsatisfactory meal I had the feeling all of it lay half chewed in my throat as I helped Antoinette clean up afterward.

In the house once more, where Rodeur sat smoking his pipe, Antoinette burst out angrily, "This morning Belli asked me to continue to cook for his crew of the *Wind*. I told him flatly no! I have decided to offer my services to Dominique You. He is a jolly Frenchman and has complimented my cooking many times."

"I would much rather we worked for him than that terrible Belli," I agreed. Then to the silent Rodeur I said, "Since the captain has given me over to you entirely, Rodeur, why do we not all work for Captain You?"

Rodeur looked at me broodingly. "We may do that, Aurielle."

But he had not yet fully decided by the following night. After dinner for the three of us, I went once more to pore over my history books in the privacy of my little room. I was thus engaged for more than an hour when there came a rap on my closed door. I rose and opened it to see Rodeur standing tall and graceful in a flowing black cape and a soft hat, the brim turned rakishly up at the side. His vivid blue eyes sparkled with pleasure under slanting black brows.

"I am going with *le bos* and others to New Orleans tonight with much merchandise by skiff—merchandise that Lafitte wants to dispose of at his blacksmith shop on St. Philip Street. I will be gone over a week and I have come to tell you good-bye, *chérie.*" He caught me quickly in his strong arms and kissed my forehead lightly, murmuring, "I love you, little Aurielle."

"And I love you, Rodeur," I replied, returning his embrace and, glimpsing Antoinette's little cryptic smile, I added, "We shall miss you greatly."

"Your voice is so soft now and your words so correct, *ma chérie.* Do you realize how far you have come since first we brought you to Barataria?"

"For which I have you to thank, dear Rodeur. I am so grateful."

"It is late," Antoinette said dryly. "They are waiting outside, Rodeur."

"I'm leaving," he replied, grimacing at me like a boy. "Meantime, practice your table manners." Then turning, "See she keeps up all her studies, Toinette."

"I shall," she promised, "and do not forget our new bread pans, *mon ami.*"

"I won't," he answered, giving her a hearty kiss. Then he was gone in the moon-washed night.

Later, as I made ready for bed, I thought of Valier Dessaultes for the hundredth time, though I had not seen him again at the Temple. As always, hot excitement welled up. Valier had the same endearing arrogance as Rodeur Cheviot, and something besides. There was that intriguing look of brooding violence—with all the background of good blood that Rodeur did not possess. Or did he? I wondered. There was mystery enough about my French benefactor.

Still, I slipped into bed somewhat disheartened.

Valier would probably be married by now to that simpering little wench who had hung on his arm the only time I saw him.

It was a warm night for November and the moon was high and brilliant. The men on their way to New Orleans would be able to see quite clearly all the way to the edge of that vast river, the Mississippi. I had visualized it a thousand times, a great, sweeping river, shimmering in the moonlight, glittering under the sun, dividing us from the city. Nay, dividing a continent! I slept and dreamed of the day I would cross it to that glamorous city with all its forbidden delights and elegant people.

The following morning, after breakfast, I studied my lessons while Antoinette sewed. There was nothing in the dreamy fall day to indicate the tragedy that was to change our lives forever. As the day progressed tranquilly, we proceeded to the chores Antoinette had set for us, and late afternoon found us scrubbing the tables in the open-air kitchen in the bright November sunshine.

It was at that moment that devastation struck. We heard a man's cracked and hoarse voice coming dimly from behind us. It was from the beach side. Antoinette and I paused and the cleaning cloths fell from our hands.

There was desperation in that husky voice and we ran to the front of the house to see a man running, half naked, toward the thickest part of the settlement. As his voice was raised, men began swarming down from the ships in the harbor, women streamed from the houses followed by their children. Antoinette and I looked at each other in consternation. As one, we picked up our skirts and ran down to the beach where the crowd was gathering about the man. We could hear him now and we saw that it was a sailor, Pedro, from the *Wind*.

He was bellowing, "*Le bos,* he is captured—all are captured!" There was blood crusted on one side of his head and down his jaw. His face was drawn and he appeared ready to drop with fatigue.

As Antoinette and I drew up, he was crying huskily, "—and the moon was bright as day. All our pirogues and skiffs were in good order behind us when we rounded the

103

bend and, *Dios!* There was a captain and a company of dragoons! They outnumbered us two to one——" He lifted his naked shoulders and let them fall. "In the fight, I managed to run into a nearby *chenière* across the *prairies tremblantes,* where I crouched until all was over. I heard the dragoons cursing, and in the moonlight I see them bind *le bos*'s hands——and his brother's as well, after our men surrender. Some were wounded——one killed."

"What of the goods, the merchandise, Pedro?" asked one dark-faced corsair.

"They took it all——and all our men, too. The captain——they called him Holmes——bound them all, even the wounded, and said they were going to take them to the city for trial where they would be put into the jail behind the Cabildo and never get out. When I crept back after they were gone, I found M'sieu Cheviot lying dead among the reeds."

"Oh!" I gasped. Not Rodeur! His merry face rose up before me, tanned and handsome, full of vitality, electric with life. Rodeur couldn't be dead! I cried, "Are you sure 'twas Rodeur Cheviot?"

He looked at me then. All these men, villainous and pleasant alike, all their women, knew Antoinette and I were under Rodeur's protection now that Kincannon was gone. There was pity in the eyes of the women. In the eyes of the men there was speculation.

"I saw him at the edge of the bayou, senorita," Pedro said slowly. "I didn't stay to bury him. And anyway, there was no place to dig the grave in the *prairies tremblantes.* I took a pirogue they left without a paddle. I broke off a tree limb and poled my way back——no doubt the 'gators will feast on him tonight."

I shrank in horror at the thought, and the women murmured among themselves. I glimpsed the great hulking Durket looking at me as he licked his shining red mouth wetly. Antoinette's fingers dug into my arm.

"Let us return to the house, Aurielle," she whispered and I followed her blindly, realizing with sudden clarity that I had not known until this instant how much I depended upon Rodeur Cheviot. He had been in the background with his slim shining sword and the pistol at his waist, standing tall between me and the horde of ruthless men who called this smugglers' haven their home. He was my teacher and he had *loved* me. I knew a slash of sorrow and my eyes blurred. Antoinette was weeping and I heard her speak more to herself than to me as we hastened back to the empty house above the beach, "I knew it would come! I knew it—but I am not ready—ah, God—"

When we reached his little house and entered the open door, I was panting. I glanced at all his books—his desk—the shining round table. He would never see them again. A sob tore at me and I blurted from a thick throat, "Whatever shall we do without him, Toinette?" I scrubbed at my welling eyes with the backs of my hands.

She turned back to an open window, looking out beyond the orange trees and oleanders, down to where the crowd still milled about Pedro. She wheeled about, tears streaming down her face, and said abruptly, "I fear for us, Aurielle. With Rodeur dead and Captain Kincannon gone —*le bos* captured. You will be—we will both be fair game for the strongest among the single men."

I felt a crawling along the back of my neck and instinctively my hand crept to the poniard at my waist. Antoinette, blotting her tears with her apron, saw the movement.

"Aurielle, that small weapon will not save you. These men are prepared for—and welcome—resistance. Any one of them would pluck it from you like a straw."

"What can I do?" I asked, panic sweeping me suddenly. I could imagine any one of the huge, hairy brutes seizing me, ripping clothing from my slender body and, like a rutting boar, having his way with me. With *le bos* gone, there would be no semblance of restraint in these pirates.

Antoinette went to a cabinet and took from it a flintlock and began carefully to load it. She said grimly, "I will be ready for any unwelcome visitor tonight. But, Aurielle, you must realize two women cannot hold off the crews who are in port here now. You are so fair— too fair. Perhaps in the morning, we can leave—" She did not finish her sentence and I could not bring myself to ask her how we could do so.

And as we had feared, not long after we had cleaned up the wooden and pewter supper dishes and darkness drew on, he came. He pounded so hard upon the front door the walls shivered. We had eaten inside the house against this moment, and Antoinette had lit two lanterns which she had placed on the round mahogany table.

She opened the door. It was Durket, whose black brows covered his forehead. I heard him enter, but I kept to the back room, cold with fear. I could hear their voices all too clearly.

"Mademoiselle Aurielle has no protector now and I have been made second in command to Belli on the *Wind*. I've come to take Cheviot's place. I have told the others she's mine and I'll see no harm comes ter 'er. I'm movin' in ternight." His voice lifted as he bellowed, "Aurielle, get in here!"

"She will not do it," Antoinette said calmly.

"Yes, she will. Call her in here, old lady," he snarled at the still young Antoinette. I could visualize him standing menacingly over the thin, valiant Frenchwoman. Most of the crews treated him with respect because of his size and his violent temper. Now he yelled, "Aurielle! Get in here or it'll go harder with yer!"

I stepped into the room, cornered but unconquered. "I will have nothing to do with you, Durket. Get out of here at once."

He laughed uproariously. "By God, it's high and mighty we are! Ye'll come ter me now and no doubt like it very well in the end." He moved toward me and I drew the poniard, backing away. He slowed, the sharp little eyes measuring the weapon and my slim body, determining his method of attack. "Ye can't do nothing with that little pig-sticker," he blustered.

"I killed the last man who thought that," I spoke between my teeth as I backed against the wall. "Get out of here, Durket."

He laughed again, and for so huge a man he was horrifyingly agile when he sprang upon me, wrenching the poniard from my hand. I smelled the sweaty stench of him, the heavy rum on his breath, and clawed futilely at his bearded face.

106

There was the sudden roar of gunfire behind him and all at once, his grip on me loosened. He staggered and fell to the floor, an oath cut off half-spoken. I looked at Antoinette who stood with the still-smoking flintlock in her hands. Durket lay inert, my poniard fallen from his great fist. His breath was thick in his throat for a brief moment, then there was a gurgle and the sound ceased abruptly.

For an eternity, we two stood staring in terrified silence at the man on the floor. Then I lifted an oil lantern from the table and held it out over his body. The great welter of blood oozing from his back could be clearly seen.

"You have killed him," I whispered.

"I meant to. But now we will have to leave Barataria—at once, for they will kill me in retaliation and it will go even worse for you. Get your clothes and money together and we will slip to the mouth of the bayou— and start praying we find a pirogue there. *Vite, chérie!*"

I flew to do her bidding. My fingers shook as I shoved my meager wardrobe into a cloth bag. What if they heard the shot and came to investigate? No, no! We were so far from the ships tied at the piers. I had caught up my poniard from the floor and slipped it once more into my waist.

In an amazingly brief few moments we were ready. We carried our leather bags of coins and no more than three dresses in the two sacks slung over our shoulders. We left stealthily by the back door, silently damning the treacherously bright moonlight as we crept across the sandy land, keeping in the orange groves and among the palmettos so as not to be seen. Behind us gleamed fires on the beach and we knew the men were sitting about them, with Pedro recounting further details of the capture of the Lafittes. And no doubt they were all cursing the loss of the rich merchandise.

After what seemed miles, we reached the pier to find that only two pirogues remained tied up there. There were no skiffs. One pirogue was small, large enough for only one person. The other was big enough to accommodate four—as big, indeed, as Rodeur's own. That brought him to mind again and I began to weep silently.

I choked back my tears as I heard a raucous male voice in the distance and my heart began to pound enough to burst as we stowed our sacks in the long pirogue.

"We will take turns paddling," Antoinette said. "That way, we won't tire too much—But here—I have taken the paddle from the little pirogue. We will both paddle until we put a couple of miles between us and *les sauvages!*" She looked back over her shoulder, cocking her head to one side.

We were almost ready to push off when we heard faint noise among the reeds from which we had just come. We froze, still as death in the chill moonlight. The reeds and cane stood tall back of the pier, rustling in the faint wind from the gulf, and my heart sank. Durket had been found and they were coming after us!

"Hurry! Help me push off—untie that rope!" I hissed frantically, and the two of us grew awkward in our haste. The rope seemed hideously knotted.

Then two figures emerged in the moonlight and I heard a familiar voice. *"Bon Dieu!* It is the English tart and Toinette!" It was Roxanne Deveret and her constant companion, Ulysses. He carried a murderous machete at his waist and it cast a reflection back at the moon. Over his shoulder was slung a sack, much like ours.

My hands fell from the rope. "What are you doing here?" I asked, suddenly furious that they had discovered us.

"Evidently the same as you," she replied coldly. "I am going to New Orleans and Ulysses is going with me." She took in the situation with a lightning glance. "And we don't propose to go in that one-man pirogue. I suppose with Rodeur—gone—you and Toinette plan to go to the city, too."

"I have killed Durket," Antoinette said flatly. "We must escape."

Roxanne laughed suddenly, softly. "And I have just run Belli through." The words were spoken lightly. "Ever since Quent sold his ship to that pig, he has expected me to go with the purchase. Tonight he made his move"—

she paused, then added—"Barataria is no place for single young girls without more than one protector, eh, English wench?" Ulysses was busily engaged in stowing their small bundles into our large pirogue.

I cried, "God and the devil! You can't do that!"

"Here, wench, keep your tongue in your head!" Roxanne whispered fiercely. "Do you want to bring them all down on us?"

"But this is *our* pirogue!" I remonstrated, low-voiced.

Ulysses stepped back on the pier, machete in hand, and said quietly, "Get in, mesdames. I cannot fight them all. Quickly now, or we all are lost!"

Roxanne stepped so lightly into the pirogue it scarcely rocked. Ulysses took Antoinette's arm and helped her scramble down into the slim craft. He said, "Come, Ma'amselle Aurielle, step fast. I think I hear them coming this way."

I jumped in so hastily that the boat rocked wildly. Ulysses stepped off the pier into the front of it and caught up one of the paddles. With one slash of his machete, he cut the ropes attached to both pirogues. He shoved the smaller craft out and away from the pier, where it ran into tall reeds and was lost to sight. Then with swift, hard strokes of the paddle, thrust deep into the gleaming water of the bayou, the bigger pirogue skimmed fleetly away from the pier. I clutched the sides in a panic as it rocked slightly. I could not swim a stroke.

We barely made it into the marshy reeds along one of the smaller bayous leading into the bay when the sound of shouts came to our ears. I glanced back over my shoulder at the pier and glimpsed torches held high among the reeds back of it. There were howls of rage that floated clearly across the rippling water.

"Faster, Ulysses," I whispered. "They will soon follow!"

"*Non,* ma'amselle. They will have to go to another pier, find another pirogue, and they do not know which of the bayous I have taken."

"They were deep in wine when we slipped away," Roxanne said, "nursing their losses. Listen!" Already, the

109

voices were dying away to a grumble. "They don't love Belli or Durket enough to search for us." Her light voice was confident. "And I expect they've found only Belli— I know they've not had time to bury him yet."

Antoinette said with satisfaction, "With both Belli and Durket dead, they will no doubt quarrel over who takes command of the *Wind*. Without Jean Lafitte to arbitrate, that could become a bloody discussion."

"*Oui*," Ulysses said as he propelled our slender craft forward with powerful strokes. "There will be more dead before the night is over."

The pirogue brushed against a tall stand of reeds and the silent movement disturbed a heron, which flapped and squawked hoarsely. I glimpsed its snowy feathers gleaming in the moonlight as it flew a little way, only to settle back down in the marsh grass. Before us stretched shining water, which ended abruptly in the blackness of a forest of moss-shrouded trees. In moments we were enveloped in the darkness; still I could discern the shores on either side of us and I was suddenly grateful for Ulysses and his strength, even though it meant sharing our pirogue with this odious girl. An alligator somewhere near gave forth a raucous snort and I jumped nervously.

"A big one," muttered Ulysses, his rhythmic strokes never missing a beat.

It occurred to me then that but for Ulysses, we might not have escaped at all. Antoinette and I could never have propelled the pirogue far enough away to be out of sight by the time the men with their torches arrived at the small pier. I shivered, for it was cold and the wool cape Antoinette had given me was not very warming, as I crouched tightly behind her. I moved nearer to Antoinette, who reached out and caught one of my cold hands in her thin, colder one.

After we had put more than two miles between us and Barataria, Roxanne said curiously, "I can guess why you killed Durket, Toinette, but how?" The husky voice was still low.

"He came to—Rodeur's house. He would have forced Aurielle to bed with him, of course. I shot him in the back as he fought with her. And you killed Belli—with your sword?" she asked with a touch of awe.

"When he came at me, I drew it and pricked the pig in his shoulder. Then when he saw I meant to kill him, he drew his own. It was fairly enough done, with a thrust clean through his heart. He was always a clumsy beast."

"Where was Ulysses and how did you both escape Belli's men?" I asked.

"It happened in the captain's cabin aboard the *Wind*. Belli asked me there on the pretext of discussing a post under his command. Ulysses waited above on deck for me. We even had time to bring some of our things from the *Wind*," she boasted.

Ulysses laughed softly. "Belli was very sure of himself. He had only one sentinel above deck with me. When Ma'amselle Roxanne came above, her sword red with blood, I disposed of him by snapping his neck."

I drew the cape tightly about me, chilled further by the story of ruthlessness told by these two. Roxanne went on, "As you can see, the sight of Ulysses and his machete and pistols would discourage any on shore. Then we cut through the orange groves to the landing near the bayou." She paused, adding derisively, "And discovered you here before us—is your precious virtue still intact, Aurielle?" I made no answer. Her little laugh was suddenly happy as she went on, "But I have something better than virtue. I have money in the bank in New Orleans. Like Quent, I shall never return to Barataria."

"We will not be entirely without money, *chérie*," Antoinette spoke up. "I have more than three thousand in the bank, you know. It will do until we can make more."

"Madame Chaille will sponsor *me*," Roxanne taunted. "On her trips to the Temple, she has often said she would. She admires me because I am—I am a free spirit," she quoted.

I remembered clearly that patrician face, beautiful, sophisticated, and the slender, elegant form so exquisitely appareled—though I had seen her but the one time. *Madame Ondine Chaille*. She had appeared to be everything I wanted to be at her age. Fresh envy burned my throat. Ah, Roxanne was truly fortunate!

Antoinette said slowly, "Do you think—for a fee, of course—you might persuade Madame Chaille to sponsor Aurielle, *aussi?* I shall be her—maid."

"Why should I recommend this creature to Madame Chaille?" Roxanne asked coldly. "Money is nothing to her. She has a fortune of her own."

"Not to her—to you, *ma petite,*" Antoinette said imperturbably, "for using your—ah—great influence with the estimable Madame Chaille."

Roxanne laughed suddenly. "I must admit our problems are much the same. A burning ambition, a wealthy marriage—and both of us likely bastards."

I drew in a swift breath, but Antoinette's cold hand crushed mine in a grip that made me gasp. She said calmly, *"C'est vrai.* And both of you are very beautiful. With proper guidance you will no doubt realize all your ambitions." Then coaxingly. "You know Aurielle has no designs on the captain of your heart, Roxanne. You will become a fine lady and he will no doubt marry you."

In the silvered November night, Roxanne tossed her head. I glimpsed the glinting eyes. Her voice was decisive. "You speak the truth, Toinette. I will take you both with us to Madame Chaille," she hesitated, then added slowly, "and I will try to persuade her to take you both in." Then with a quick, wicked laugh, "And you can give me that three thousand for my trouble. You can draw it from the bank after we reach town. Meantime, I'll take all you have in those pouches at your waist."

"Non!" Antoinette was suddenly the shrewd and frugal Frenchwoman. "I will give you a thousand for the use of your influence and *only* if you can get her to sponsor Aurielle."

"If I succeed in coaxing Madame Chaille into sponsoring your adopted chick, money is the least of your worries. She will feed and clothe all of us and no doubt marry your wench to a very respectable rich Creole."

I bit my lip on the vitriol that rose up. By now Antoinette's hard nails were biting into my tense hand.

She said firmly, "It is a bargain then? You will make an appeal to the madame for Aurielle and me?"

"For only a thousand if I succeed? No, no, Antoinette. I need some money on account, for my efforts alone are worth something. I will introduce you both and that by itself is worth your pouches in advance. I have no liking for your Aurielle, you know."

"Nor I for you!" I burst out, my voice echoing among the reaching magnolias and oaks that now rose up on each side of the bayou. "Toinette, I fear you would be wasting your money."

Ulysses drew up his paddle and turned to us. "Be silent!" His accented voice was deep and commanding. "We do not know who is in the *chenières*—or who may lurk alongside this bayou."

Roxanne, with laughter still in her voice, said low, "And you have a long way to go, wench, before you become a lady. All you have conquered is your speech and I do not know if even Madame Chaille can give you the rest. Here, I'll take that money now," and she reached for the small pouch in Antoinette's hand.

I clenched my teeth as Antoinette handed the pouch over, saying smoothly, "Aurielle is an apt pupil."

Roxanne replied, "You'd better start thinking on a reasonable lie to tell the madame." She laughed again, putting Antoinette's pouch into one of her bundles. Then, "Give me your bag of money, Aurielle. Madame Chaille told me long ago that she would pass me off as her niece from Paris, sadly orphaned by unhappy chance of the pox." I handed my leather pouch to her slowly, my fury rising.

"Then she can pass Aurielle off as her other niece, English and orphaned by the Napoleonic wars," Antoinette said sturdily. She patted my hand and whispered, "Hold your temper, *ma petite amie*. We will receive our money's worth—I have a sixth sense. I feel it in my bones. Once madame sees you closely, she will not be able to resist you."

"That may well be true, old friend," Roxanne said, and I thought she must have the ears of a lynx. "Talk

113

it up. I can use the extra money and Aurielle can repay both you and madame when she marries."

"Three thousand is all that I possess in this world, Roxanne," Antoinette said in rapid French. "You are greedy. You are avaricious. You are unfair." I knew it was against every precept in Antoinette's practical French soul to give up her hard-earned money.

"*I* will pay you the three thousand when I marry well, Roxanne," I said roughly.

"That is not good enough," the girl retorted insolently, "and I am not willing to talk madame into taking you without the promise of Toinette's money. I swear I will whisper to her you have the *petit mal* and she won't be able to get rid of you fast enough."

I shrank. It would be just like Roxanne to tell Ondine Chaille that I was an epileptic. I felt Antoinette stiffen beside me and the words were torn from her. "All right then. I will give you the money—"

"And I shall repay you fourfold when I am wed, Toinette," I said between my teeth. Then I said to Roxanne with an unplumbed depth of feeling, "You—you *bête sauvage!*"

But she only laughed softly and said, "A bargain has been struck between us, *mes amies,*" and I heard a deep rumble of admiration and amusement in Ulysses's big chest.

We were silent, and with tireless strokes Ulysses sped us along the twisting bayou. The moon sank lower in the sky. Once a large gar leaped up from the water before us and fell back with a noisy splash. Nightbirds gave forth their eerie cries. We passed the Temple and I could see the brilliant white shells beneath the trees as we moved along the narrowing vein of water toward the city.

"We were going to stop here, Aurielle," Antoinette murmured, "and walk the river where we would await a ferry."

"Much better we go by pirogue, madame," Ulysses rumbled reassuringly. "This way we stand less chance of encountering others—and we do not have to wait for the ferry. Also, we can arrive by night, when we will be much less conspicuous."

"How long will it take us to reach the city?" I asked him. Though it was now the hour before dawn, I was too tense to feel any drowsiness.

"By tomorrow night," Ulysses responded. "We will pull to shore and rest at dawn. It is farther by way of the bayous, but better to reach the city tomorrow night."

"Do you think they may be searching for us— coming after us from Barataria?" I asked.

"I doubt it," Roxanne replied. "Their desire for revenge will be short-lived. The main reason we should enter by night is if we are unseen, there will be fewer questions that Madame Chaille must answer."

Ulysses was like a dark, shining machine, thrusting the paddle deeply, noiselessly into the water, sending the pirogue forward with smooth, even speed. He was right; it was much farther to the river by way of this twisting, winding bayou than it would have been if we had taken the land route from the Temple. Even so, it was faster than we could have walked.

As dawn drew on, the bayou grew narrower. In the dim, increasing light, I looked at Antoinette and murmured, "We could never have found our way through this," for here there were many bayous branching off in all directions. Still, Ulysses seemed to know which to take and shortly he propelled our craft toward a narrow, sandy spit beneath a thick forest of looming magnolias.

He beached the pirogue swiftly, then jumped out and pulled it farther ashore. We all disembarked and Roxanne stooped to help the tall black man as he pulled the craft into the rank vegetation back from the narrow spit.

Antoinette said, "It would have been bad to have to wait for a ferry and enter by day—a very bad thing for ones who wish to go unnoticed until a debut can be made. What we thought a mischance may prove to be a blessing in all ways."

Roxanne, overhearing with her sharp ears, jeered merrily, "That's right, Aurielle. Once you're seen for

115

the little tart you are—in those terrible clothes—the people wouldn't forget, even if later you wore the finest satin ballgown."

I turned on her hotly. "And I'll wager you are not unknown in New Orleans—as a playmate of pirates! How do you plan to overcome *that?*"

Stung, she retorted, "I was never a playmate. I was a *privateer.*"

"And that qualifies *you* as a lady?" I laughed aloud.

"Ondine Chaille will vouch for me as a lady at the proper time." Then with her merry laugh, "After all, I have come from Paris originally, by way of Santo Domingo and the privateers—born to luxury which followed me to an indigo plantation. My people, who were French nobility, were killed in an insurrection. Can you match that story, Aurielle?"

"Of course," I responded cheekily. "My father, a lord, was killed in the wars with Napoleon and my mother, Madame Chaille's own sister, died of a broken heart, and I have come to my aunt for protection, as all of my family in England have perished."

Roxanne's ready laughter burst forth. "By God, that's almost as convincing a story as mine!"

Ulysses came from the woods where he had been exploring and said, "Come, mesdames, I have found a proper spot for you to rest." He caught up our bundles, Antoinette's and mine, containing but one blanket each, and we followed him back into the trees.

It proved to be a very uncomfortable period of rest, for the ground was cold and moist and penetrated the thin blanket I lay upon. It seemed to creep into my bones. I finally wrapped myself in it, making more than one thickness about me. It did not help much and my sleep was fitful, even though I had not rested for twenty-four hours. I found myself dreaming of Rodeur Cheviot. I could see his haunting smile, always somehow familiar, and I roused twice during the day, weeping. My stomach growled emptily, for none of us had brought food in our haste to be away.

I was not much rested when night fell, and with the coming of darkness, I was sitting up, looking at the others where they still lay in their blankets. Ulysses rose suddenly, greeting me as he set about building a small fire. To my great relief, he brought forth a small coffee-pot and a bag of coffee from his pack.

"It is all I could filch in the time we had," he said, returning from the bayou with the pot full of water. "It will help allay our hunger until we reach the city."

When the other two women rose, we all sat about the fire in the late dusk, drinking hot cups of the slightly salty brew. I began to feel better after a second cup and I looked at Roxanne with a kind of resentful appreciation. She irritated me beyond measure and set me boiling with anger all too often. I didn't really know how we two would manage to reside in Madame Chaille's house together—if that charming lady would accept me. Then I reflected that, after all, learning to control my emotions and my tongue were very necessary to my plans. Certainly Roxanne Deveret would give me constant practice.

I turned to Antoinette. "Did you really mean it when you said you would be maid to me?" I asked, smiling.

"*Oui, chérie*. I would enjoy that, I think. You would be a very tolerant mistress, I am sure." Her dark eyes were luminous and her mouth had softened, making her face quite pretty. I realized with a rush of gratitude that this thrice-bereaved woman had come to love me. I had altered her life and her outlook on life—even as she had saved me from disaster.

During the night, with a lopsided, fading moon looking down, Ulysses propelled the pirogue steadily through the black waters as they twisted and wound their way to the mighty river. In one place it was so narrow that the tall reeds and thicker cane brushed against us and I had a momentary sense of suffocation before we pulled into a broader expanse.

About three hours before dawn, we passed through two large battures, which were formed where the river's current was weakest, silt being deposited and land having been built up on each side of the bayou. Wil-

117

lows, thick as the stars above now the moon had set, dropped to the narrow bayou and spread out through the battures.

Then suddenly, by starlight, we came upon the Mississippi River. A pathway of water twinkling in the pale light spread before us and it appeared as broad as the sea to me. This was the fabulous river of which the old sailor had spoken. It was a river that stirred passions and slaked them as well. I felt my heart swell with awe at the waters slipping by steadily, silently, irresistibly before us. I could barely see the dark shore far across it, and in the dim light there were three little craft to be seen on its broad bosom. Suddenly we seemed very defenseless as the pirogue thrust to the end of the narrows and out into the river itself.

The current could be felt beneath the pirogue and Ulysses's strokes became more powerful as he fought it, keeping us on a nearly straight course for the city that was sleeping beyond. I looked up and down the wide sweep of the river and breathed deeply of the moist wind that rose above the mighty body of water.

Slowly, slowly, we came nearer to the levee that was built up before the city. There were hundreds of craft tied up there, barges, skiffs, flat-boats, and a forest of tall ships' masts. There was little activity at this dead hour.

A few roustabouts and sailors could be seen by infrequent lanterns on board their vessels. I could discern merchandise stacked up along the many wharves—barrels, boxes, kegs, and what looked to be thousands of bales of cotton.

The scents that arose from the levee were so varied and of such a mixture they set my senses tingling. Spices mingled with the smell of coffee beans, peltries, vegetables, and, despite the November chill, the rich scent of ripe fruit. I was at the beating heart of New Orleans—where goods from everywhere in the world eventually found their way either in or out. Excitement gripped me and I had the sudden intuition that danger, even death, lay ahead.

Antoinette and I followed Ulysses's and Roxanne's quickening steps and found ourselves in the midst of a great square. Antoinette whispered, *"C'est La Place d'Armes.* See the flags flying?" And in the pale false dawn, banners stood out from tall poles, caught in the river wind.

"Come along," Roxanne said, again stepping up her pace to keep up with Ulysses. There were only a few people about the Place d'Armes and the streets beyond, each intent on his own destination, and they paid us no heed.

"We want to be safely in Madame Chaille's house before daylight." In her breeches and boots, Roxanne could be taken for a slim boy in the half-light.

We hastened down the streets, houses with wall touching wall along the banquettes, as Antoinette called the sidewalks. The banquettes were wooden and creaked horribly under our feet, but the streets were potholed and dusty here and were difficult to walk upon. Farther down, they appeared to be muddy, so we clung to the wooden banquettes until we turned sharply. "This is Chartres," Antoinette murmured, and her thin hand reached out for my wrist. *"Alors,* the banquette is brick now. Observe."

My feet had already told me. Though the brick was crumbling in many places, it seemed much more solid than the creaking wooden planks. We crossed another street and Roxanne said, "This is St. Philip Street. A few blocks to our left, it meets with Bourbon and on that corner is Lafitte's blacksmith shop. Beyond it, his own shop for our goods."

"Much good it does him now," I retorted. "He is probably in jail, sealed up tight as a mouse in a trap."

She laughed low. "Don't be too sure of *that.* The Cabildo's jail holds no terrors for Jean. By now he and Pierre are long out of it."

I was panting slightly, for Ulysses's strides were long and Antoinette, Roxanne and I were almost running to keep up with him. He slowed abruptly as two men approached in the fading darkness. We passed close by each other and I could feel their curious stares on me as I ducked my head and drew close to Antoinette.

We could hear their steps slow even more behind us and Ulysses took his machete from his waist and swung it loosely in his hand. Their steps took up a faster beat and the big black grunted, "So. They know you have protection, mesdames. It is well."

Suddenly we came upon a tall, broad house that stood alone in its grandeur in the center of the block. It was white in the dawning light; I knew from Antoinette's talk that most of these houses on Chartres were of handmade bricks which were so soft that stucco was used to cover them as a protection against the elements. There was a high fence of fine wrought-iron across a dark space dividing the front of the house from the street. Without hesitation, Roxanne stepped up to the gates and pulled a bell cord that hung there, setting off a distant clang.

We waited fully five minutes, but Roxanne did not pull the cord again. I was growing restive, a queer chill settling about my heart as I stared up at the three-storied house. There was faint light flickering in a top dormer above the balconies banistered in black wrought-iron in a design of many leaves. For some inexplicable reason, as that light was snuffed, I grew colder than the November air about us and my heart beat very fast.

Then suddenly the gates were flung open and we were met by a black man, almost as tall as Ulysses, with equally powerful shoulders.

"It is I, Roxanne Deveret, and Ulysses," Roxanne said. "Sebastien will you take us to madame? These are my—friends." She gestured carelessly to Antoinette and me.

I recognized the man as the one I had seen at the Temple with Madame Chaille. He was clad now in old-fashioned breeches and a full white shirt with a small ruffle down the front. His nose was broad and his small, slanted eyes under their folds of flesh fixed themselves on my face for an instant. I felt the prickle of gooseflesh once again.

"*Bonjour,* Mademoiselle Roxanne. Madame will be glad to see you." His rumbling voice with its heavy French

121

accent did nothing to dispel my uneasiness as his sweeping gesture welcomed us inside.

We stepped into a small courtyard. A fountain splashed at the side and though it was November, the faint scent of oleanders in bloom blew across my face. Around us was a small, perfect garden with banana trees, palms, oleanders, and bougainvillea. We followed Sèbastien up a short curving set of marble steps with another artfully wrought ironwork banister. The sky was becoming very light by now and I could clearly see the carved and polished wooden door recessed behind half columns, an arched fanlight above it. Sebastien opened it, then stood back to bid us gracious entry.

We entered a rather small but ornately beautiful foyer. An oil lamp gleaming on a nearby table sent its golden tracery over the exquisite pieces of fine French furniture that graced the little room. I was mute with admiration, an emotion that blotted out my apprehension.

When Sebastien greeted Ulysses, I had sensed a certain constraint between the two powerful blacks. But then he said, "I will go up and tell madame that you are here," and he stepped noiselessly up the gleaming staircase that rose before us and disappeared around its sweeping and unsupported curve.

Roxanne removed her cape and, flinging herself upon one of the dainty little chairs against the wall and dropping her small bundle of belongings to the floor, murmured, *"Dieu!* But I am starved."

"Madame Chaille will serve us a good breakfast, *ma petite,"* Ulysses said, his smile warm upon this beautiful girl he had raised from a baby.

Antoinette still clung to my wrist like a leech. As I dropped my own bundle and cape in the warmth of the room, I took her thin hand from me and held it firmly. We looked at each other and each found her doubts mirrored in the other's eyes. She murmured, "You are afraid, my Aurielle and I responded an affirmative in French.

Roxanne, with her little cat's ears, said pertly, "And well you might be. Ondine may turn you away despite all my coaxing. And remember, Toinette, you owe me three thousand."

Antoinette's back stiffened. "You haven't introduced us yet and I owe you nothing unless Madame Chaille agrees to take us."

Ulysses had taken a place standing beside the seated girl, his strong arms crossed over his chest. "Madame Chaille is a—" he hesitated, choosing his words as if to keep from offending Roxanne—"a most unusual lady. You may be sure she will give consideration to your request."

"If she has unlimited money," I said disconsolately, "there is nothing I can ever give her in return—when I marry well."

"*Peut-être.* You cannot be sure," he responded. His great dark eyes on me held a kindness that warmed me further toward him. I had long ago decided he was a much more likable person than his charge, Roxanne.

Silence fell and Antoinette still held my hand tightly. We were gambling away her life savings in any event, I thought, ashamed—and all on the tenuous hope that I would marry a rich aristocrat. Madame Chaille would have to lie and dissemble for me. I felt a little sick with anticipation.

From the staircase there came a soft exclamation. We turned as one to see Madame Chaille herself descending. She drifted down the polished stairs in a cloud of white silk as thin as a whisper, but the folds of the peignoir were gathered so thickly she appeared to float. She came straight to Roxanne and took her oval face between her hands and kissed her brow. Then she turned and greeted Ulysses warmly.

"What brings you to my home at such an unlikely hour, my dear little pirate?" There was laughter and pleasure in the cultured voice as well as genuine affection.

"I have come at last to let you make a lady of me—a member of the respectable New Orleanaise," was the laughing response.

"*Bien!* I am so glad! You know I have always told you that you could set society on its ear. Now I will be your *tante* and you will be my bereaved niece, recently come from Paris." Then she turned to us, a slight frown between the perfect dark brows. Her unbound hair tumbled down her back in a gleaming chestnut mass. As I looked into her eyes, I was struck anew by our resemblance. "And who are your friends, *ma chérie?*"

Roxanne drawled, "The girl is Aurielle Stuart. Perhaps you remember buying her tarts at the Temple. She has her own ideas of becoming a lady. And Antoinette Desmottes was the cook for Quent's crew and has now volunteered as personal maid to Aurielle. I promised to introduce them to you with a view to your sponsoring her in society."

Stung, I blurted, "She promised to do it for Antoinette's life savings—three thousand dollars." Madame Chaille was silent, the delicate brows lifted, and I rushed on. "I know if you were to be my patroness, I would meet a man of wealth and then I could pay you well for your kindness."

Ondine Chaille tapped her chin with a slender forefinger. "I remember you—for we do resemble one another and you speak very well—in a low and charming voice." An awkward silence fell upon us and Sebastien, in the background, fixed his strange, elliptical eyes on my face. She added slowly, "You are very beautiful, even with your hair pulled back—so. And in that horrible dress."

"She needs much training, Ondine," Roxanne said disparagingly. "She speaks very well, due to Rodeur Cheviot's training, but she must be taught a great deal more to pass for a lady." She shrugged slightly. "Still, I promised her to use my influence with you. Have I that much influence with you?"

Ondine's clear eyes were thoughtful, then suddenly she laughed. "It would be a pity if the little cook's life savings went for nothing, you naughty Roxanne! I might have two nièces from Paris."

Hope surged through me in a hot wave. "I could be your niece from England, madame. My father was a—a fine English gentleman and my mother was of the French nobility."

Roxanne laughed mockingly. "How do you know?

124

Ondine, she grew up in Portsmouth—worked in an inn there—"

I turned on her furiously. "Our backgrounds are remarkably alike, you chit! You can't sit in judgment on me!"

Ondine Chaille's tinkling laughter came again. "*Violà!* I cannot have two nieces who quarrel with each other and who are cousins! How can I teach you all the graces and arts of culture if you are at each other's throats?"

"You mean you *will* be my patroness?" I cried, joy welling up within me.

"I will be your *aunt*, Aurielle. I think it could be very amusing to have *two* nieces who will make a debut in New Orleans society under my auspices." Her laughter grew and she threw back her dark head; the ivory column of her throat was lovely.

Once more the incredible thought shot through my mind. *We are close kin!* It was idiocy I told myself firmly. Ondine Chaille was a transplanted Frenchwoman, no more, no less. But I found myself wondering when she came to New Orleans and, before I could stop, I blurted, "When did you come here from France, madame?"

"I have been here since 1800. My own country was so torn with intrigue and disruption from the wars, when my husband—died—I left." As she fixed her cobalt eyes on me, I thought exultantly, *I knew it.*

Antoinette had not opened her mouth since she and Madame Chaille exchanged nods. I looked at her, bursting to share my joy with her.

"Then you will actually take Aurielle and Toinette in?" Roxanne asked with a dainty yawn.

As Madame Chaille hesitated, I cut in swiftly. "I assure you, madame, I will be most grateful—and I will make you proud—I swear it." Then slowly and steadily, "And I will repay you *somehow.*"

Her eyes held mine intently and she smiled, revealing a row of even white teeth before she turned to Roxanne. She said decisively, "Then I shall, after all, have two nieces to debut this spring."

I felt the blood leave my face. "Thank you," I

whispered, and forgetting all those about me, I took her slender white hand in both of my rough ones and brought it to my cheek. She turned it quickly and caressed my cheek for a brief instant. And in that instant, the chilling anxiety I had known when I first entered the house was forgotten in a rush of love for her.

"You must all be starved if you have come all the way from Barataria," she said gaily. "Sebastien, I will tell Selina to stir up the fire and prepare an early and very large breakfast! You go wake Tressa, Bonnie, and Catherine as well. I will want them to prepare rooms and serve our guests." Then to us, "Come," and she swept past us as Sebastien began to mount the stairs.

We followed her from the foyer into a cozy sitting room, where coals glowed redly in a fireplace with a glistening marble mantel. Ondine went quickly to the mantel and took up a cloissoné box containing flint and steel and in an instant all the tapers were lit.

Ondine motioned us to a seat, saying, "I will go tell Selina to serve us coffee before breakfast," and, beckoning tactfully to Ulysses and Antoinette, she left the room with them.

Roxanne, seated with easy grace in one of the fine chairs, threw a booted leg over the arm, leaned back upon its velvet cushion, and drawled, "Do you feel at home, wench?"

My back stiffened and I said coldly, "I shall refer to you as a whore as long as you call me wench, Roxanne."

"Alors! Aurielle, then. I cannot have you exposing your gutter manners in foul language since we are trying to make a lady of you."

"We?" I laughed dourly. "I've never heard language any fouler than yours, when sufficiently provoked. You certainly cannot help me become a lady."

A gust of real laughter shook her and she said candidly, "You are right, Aurielle. Ondine will have her hands full despite my knowledge of speech and manners—all of which I learned from Ulysses." Then coolly. "We can be friends as long as I am sure that you and I are not after the same man."

My lip curled at the thought of Quentin Kincannon, but I said nothing as I ran my hands appreciatively over the satiny arms of the small French chair. I was almost successful in wiping out the memory of those powerful arms, the feel of his kiss, the clean smell of his flesh and his wind-tossed hair. But not quite. I would not look at Roxanne.

Ondine Chaille came back into the room, smiling. I looked behind her but I did not see Ulysses or Antoinette and my pleasure again gave way to uneasiness. I began, "Where are Ulysses and Antoin——"

"My child, you do not have coffee with your servants," Ondine said kindly and I felt a slow blush mount my face.

"But Antoinette is not my *servant* and Ulysses is *guardian* to Roxanne," I said uncomfortably.

"Then I misunderstood," she replied coldly, "when each of them said they serve you."

"No, Ondine, you did not," Roxanne said suddenly. "Ulysses can make himself useful—perhaps help Sebastien in his duties. And Antoinette said herself that she would be maid to this wen—to Aurielle."

"That is good," Ondine replied, warmth restored as she settled gracefully back on a satin brocade sofa. "Now, tell me, what brought you finally to accept my invitation, *mon ange?*"

Roxanne said diffidently, "I grew tired of Barataria."

Ondine's laughter was soft and tender. "Ah, tell the truth. You still have that insolent Captain Kincannon in your affections. I have been told he has come to settle in New Orleans."

I hid a cynical smile. Then we were not going to tell Ondine Chaille of the deaths of Belli and Durket that lay behind our flight. Well, I was glad enough to put them from my mind.

"Have you heard of what Quent is doing—where he is?" Roxanne asked eagerly.

She sighed. "Who has not, *chérie?* He has bought the bankrupt Baron de Marnet's fine house on Bourbon Street and is building a great house on a large sugar plantation out among the others at Pointe St. Antoine. He has even set up an importing firm—a shop too!" Again she laughed softly. "He gave a fine ball in his house on Bourbon last week and the ladies refused to attend, though we were all invited. Only the men who are doing business with him came, so I am told."

"Then the Creole aristocracy is not accepting him," Roxanne said thoughtfully.

"Why should they?" There was scorn in Ondine's voice. "A great, tall, and arrogant man from Scotland? He is as bad as the Kaintucks!"

"Mais non, Ondine, he is the youngest son of an earl and his education is extensive."

"A *gentleman* smuggler, eh, *ma bien aimée?*" There was a touch of derision in the words.

"He was never a pirate like Belli or Chighizola— or even Beluche and Dominique You. He was a true privateer." Roxanne's smile was slow and enchanting. "He will be accepted in the end, you may be sure—when he marries a true lady—*me.*"

"Ah. Then you would like me to break the ice for him, *aussi,*" Ondine said quietly, "since you plan to be that lady." Then turning to me abruptly she said, "And you, Aurielle, have you also chosen the man you would marry?"

I felt my face heat up. "I have seen such a one," I replied in French, "but no doubt he is already wed by now."

Her smile was curious. "Who is he?"

"Valier Dessaultes," I blurted, twisting my fingers in the lap of the ugly dark blue cotton dress.

"Oho! You aim high, Aurielle! Valier and his widowed mother are leaders in New Orleans. Almost every charming girl in the city, no, in the whole parish and parishes surrounding, has set her cap for that young man."

"Then he is not wed!" Relief washed through me and I realized suddenly how deeply this Valier Dessaultes had invaded my dreams.

"No, he is not wed. But he almost was once—to Dolores Ysidro. A sad story, that one." As she said this, a tall and beautiful black woman entered. She moved with stately grace and carried a silver tray containing china so thin it was translucent and an ornate silver pot with fragrant steam issuing faintly from the spout. She placed it upon a marble-topped table before Ondine. I noticed a slanting scar along her cheek that failed to mar her beauty.

"Will that be all, madame?" the woman asked impassively.

"*Oui*. Thank you, Selina," Ondine replied kindly. "Now if you and the others will prepare a sumptuous breakfast for my two nieces and their servants, I will be so grateful. They are all very hungry."

" 'Tis on the fire now, madame." The woman's eyes were veiled. "Pearl is up, as well as Catherine, Bonnie, and Tressa. It shall soon be served." She bowed gravely and silently made her way from the room.

Ondine poured coffee and offered us thick cream and sugar, the last a rare treat for me since we used syrup as a sweetener and had no cream at Barataria, and I said so.

"They first started granulating sugar in 1795 here and with the increasing cultivation of cane it is quite plentiful. Indeed, Roxanne, your captain will amass a great fortune from that alone, when this stupid war ends—and if he is as astute as is rumored. Perhaps his money will eventually make him accepted despite his background."

"It is Quent I wish to marry, Ondine," Roxanne said bluntly, "so it is imperative you help him if you would help me."

Ondine shrugged. "I have met him before." She paused for a sip of the sweet coffee. "*Eh bien*—this spring I shall have your debut, little nieces. Captain Kincannon and Valier Dessaultes will be among those present."

"But spring!" Roxanne protested. "So long a time to wait. He will find some other girl!"

Ondine made a little moue. "There are refinements I would teach you both. Little things, but they are the hallmarks of aristocracy. Besides, we want to whet their appetites—let the word spread of your beauty and inaccessibility—your grief at the loss of your parents." She went on as we sat drinking together, listing the arts she would personally supervise.

I observed her through my lashes. There was a delicate blue tracery of veins on her lids and faint shadows beneath the heavily lashed eyes. It was fascinating to me to watch the dainty gestures of her long-fingered hands. And she was so beautiful! I was entranced and worshipful by the time Sebastien stepped to the door and announced breakfast was served.

We followed her floating figure to a great dining salon off the small foyer. The long table was linen-covered and the mellow gleam of sterling and fine china twinkled under a great crystal chandelier that glittered like diamonds.

There was a sumptuous pink ham, its savory slices laid flat beside it on a silver platter, and a huge feathery omelet beyond looked light enough to float off the china plate. There were dishes of curly bacon and light pancakes and at least five crystal bowls of different jams and jellies. There was yet another silver pot of coffee and I had three cups while eating as if I had never had a meal before.

Ondine frowned faintly and I slowed, trying desperately to handle the silverware as if I had done so all my life; still it was awkward in my slim fingers. The conversation between Roxanne and our hostess became livelier.

"Oh, yes, my dear, the Lafittes are out on bond. I personally do not think they will ever come to trial. I have heard that none of their comrades remain in the Cabildo jail either." Her little tinkling laugh sounded. "Ah, well, my friend Jean has said over and over they warred only on Spanish vessels—their letters of marque from Carthagena permitted that, *certainement*."

"I knew it would be so," Roxanne said with satisfaction. "Quent never took a vessel that wasn't Spanish —or English when war broke out between them and America last June."

"But our governor—he is growing most impatient." Ondine's voice was troubled. "He has vowed to incarcerate them all—again. You can be glad your captain has quit their trade, Roxanne."

"How do you find these things out, madame?" I asked, munching on a last bite of pancake.

"My dear niece, you must begin to call me 'aunt' and

I must teach you not to speak with food in your mouth. Sebastien gets his information at the French market when he shops for me."

My blush from her reprimand was slowly receding as a plump, fresh-faced English maid with dark brown hair came from the kitchen with a tray of baked apples in cream which she put at each of our three places. When she had disappeared, I said wonderingly, "And you have white servants as well as slaves?"

"They are indentured, but only for four years. They come frequently to New Orleans, *mon ange*. You can buy them at the levee when they are redemptioners. Bonnie Trelawney and Catherine Bonham, who has an eight-year-old daughter, are redemptioners."

Roxanne laughed merrily. "And now you have a third—Aurielle Stuart!"

"I have paid my passage time over again!" I said, furious that this cheeky girl should make reference to the fact that I had been a redemptioner.

"In six months?" she jeered. "Quent wouldn't say so."

"Kincannon has nothing to do with it. My passage was paid when Rodeur Cheviot was killed! It was to him I was indentured."

"No, you weren't," Roxanne said imperturbably. "Quent only gave you to him to *use*."

"God and the devil! 'E never *used* me!" I was in a towering rage by now. "'E only taught me ter talk—" I broke off in mortification.

"And he didn't do that very well." Roxanne was still laughing.

"Lentement, lentement! I cannot have two nieces who quarrel thus," Ondine Chaille remonstrated. "You are both lovely young ladies. I believe Aurielle speaks very well when you do not bait her so, Roxanne—and you both *must* remember to call me Tante Ondine!"

"You ought to hear her swear, when——" Roxanne began.

I cut in, "You ought to hear *her* swear! She's far more learned in gutter language than I!"

Ondine smiled. "I think you are both well versed

131

enough in it. But you will not use it in my presence—nor elsewhere, I would hope." She laughed lightly. "Ah, but you are both a challenge to my ingenuity. I shall launch you and you will be accepted by all *mes amis*—the best families in New Orleans." Her eyes gleamed with sudden, hot blue light. "How I shall enjoy the deception!" Then briskly, "Now finish your breakfast and we shall go up to my room and plan our strategy."

It was on our way up the stairs that we met the child coming down. Her eyes flew to us and a small gasp escaped her lips as her eyes widened. She had a pale oval face under dark bangs and a thick braid of hair hung over each shoulder. She did not look as old as her eight years.

"Ah," Ondine said in her musical voice, "Bessie." Then to us, as the child stood transfixed before her, "Bessie is Catherine Bonham's daughter. Catherine is a widow and came to America to escape poverty in England."

The child's white, frightened face touched me. I had seen many like it in the streets of Portsmouth. I said warmly, "Hello, Bessie. I know how to make a doll from scraps—I shall make you one."

"When you are not busy with your lessons," Ondine added firmly. Then as we made our way down the long hall, "So you love children, eh, Aurielle? That is a good thing in a wife. It will make you even more desirable to our good Catholic Creoles." We reached the end of the hall and an east window flooded the gleaming floor with light where the velvet rug did not cover it. Ondine said, "These are your rooms, across from each other. Yours on the north, Aurielle, and yours, the one you have occasionally occupied on the south, Roxanne."

I peered into mine and gasped with pleasure. A white woman with dark hair and haunted brown eyes was putting the finishing touches on a testered bed that took my breath with its magnificence. High and broad, it looked as light as thistledown beneath a white ruffled spread that matched the white ruffled tester and silken curtains drawn at each corner. Three polished wooden steps were beside it. A small, thin black girl, who was dusting, turned and placed a beautifully painted chamber bowl beneath the bed, looking up at me with those unreadable black eyes that I had noticed in Selina's dark face.

Roxanne said negligently, "I know mine well from the nights I have spent at your hospitable invitation, Ondine, and it is lovely."

"*Tante Ondine,* Roxanne," she reproved gently, then smoothly gestured, "That is Catherine Bonham, my dear nieces, and this"—she lifted a white hand toward the slim black girl who was now coming hesitantly toward us—"is Tressa, another of my servants."

The black ducked her head and made a little bow as Ondine added, "This is my niece from England, Tressa—Catherine—she's come to live with me on the death of her parents. And you both know Roxanne Deveret—my niece from Paris, who has finally accepted my invitation to make her home with me. My sisters, their mothers, passed away just this year."

Both servants looked at us fleetingly, turning their heads aside and murmuring acknowledgments. Both were gone like shadows in an instant. The indefinable fear that had gripped me at the gate, when we first arrived, seized me unexpectedly.

I asked anxiously, "Won't they know we aren't really your nieces—and spread stories about us?"

"My servants believe what I say. They will *know* you are my nieces." Ondine's voice was cold and irrefutable. "And now, my dears, come with me to my room where I will dress and tell you of my plans for you. Then you may sleep all day, if you like. I know you are weary from your long journey."

I was not in the least weary, I thought, as I followed her back down the hall. Roxanne's lithe stride was also undiminished and her green eyes bright with interest. Near the west end of the hall Ondine opened a door on the most beautiful room I had ever seen—and I can say today that it is still the most beautiful room I have ever seen. It was of great size, spacious in its depth and width. All the accouterments were in the palest of blue. The thick velvety rug on the floor was pale blue, the testered bed, much larger than the one I had just seen, was lavishly equipped and there was a polished box of four steps to reach it, so tall was it. The fall of satin bedcurtains at each of the four posts was rich beyond imagining. Gathered silk gauze fell thickly from all four sides of the bed. I had never seen so fine a *baire!* The delicate French chairs, the chaise longue, the exquisitely carved escritoire with a small mahogany chair before it, the two luxurious sofas were all a tribute to the taste of the woman who occupied the room. I was so dazzled I could not take it all in at once.

Ondine motioned us to one of the intricately carved couches with down cushions of pale blue velvet. There was a low fire in a large manteled fireplace. And when we had taken our places, side by side, Ondine began to speak cheerfully.

"Alors, mes anges, I will tell you what we will do until I have the large ball honoring the two of you. For you, Roxanne, will have almost as much to learn as Aurielle—despite the veneer you have acquired. Your culture must run bone deep and you must control that sharp tongue of yours, or I can do nothing for you."

"I know it," Roxanne responded with the nearest thing to humility I had ever heard in that arrogant voice. "I swear I shall succeed, Ondine."

And I said, low-voiced, "I too, madame—*Tante Ondine.*" I added timidly, "And I swear I shall repay you someday for your kindness."

Her eyes on me were curiously deep and fathomless. "I believe you, Aurielle." On her curved lips my name was soft as silk and fear gave way to excitement. The rug beneath my feet was thick as the down cushion on which I sat.

Ondine's beautiful eyes were still fastened to mine for that long, breathless moment. "I may remind you of that someday, *chérie,* and exact payment. Who knows?"

I smiled back at her and my whole heart was in the words, "You can rely on me *always*—Tante Ondine."

Then she launched into her plans for us in her soft, husky voice and I was fascinated. We would have a dancing master, we would have a tutor in languages, we would have a music teacher. We would be schooled in the arts of enhancing our beauty and receive lessons in etiquette—

and charm—from Ondine herself, as she would trust no other.

"Word will circulate, of course, that I have two extravagantly beautiful nieces, who will make their debut in society this spring. Sebastien can plant the story with the other servants at the marketplace—but I shall keep you closely cloistered. We will take Sunday walks and carriage rides together. I shall introduce you, but you will be demure and quiet until the moment of your debut. Then I shall expect you to be brilliantly charming." She paused, then said firmly,"I want to change you a great deal, polish you to such a fine point that no one—no one, you understand—will ever recall having seen you, no matter how briefly, on a trip to the Temple." She looked fixedly at Roxanne, "Or ever saw *you* in the shops of New Orleans on the arm of either the Lafittes or the redoubtable Captain Kincannon."

That night, I slept snuggled warmly in the high feather bed in the glow cast by the dying fire on the hearth before it. In a while, I dreamed, and in the dream Ondine Chaille put her slim, patrician fingers on my shoulders and looked into my eyes and told me she was my mother. I woke trembling and sweating and I told myself vehemently that I was a fool indeed.

Still, I was a long time going to sleep again.

Chapter
7

From November to the middle of December, we spent our days and nights, Roxanne and I, in that beautiful home on Chartres with Ondine Chaille. We did not leave the house, nor did I want to, since I knew the first luxury of my life and I was vastly interested in the curricula Ondine had arranged for us.

We had a music teacher in the mornings, a thin, fever-eyed French girl named Belle Fontaine, who played the harpsichord in the music room with a storm of passion and had infinite sad patience with Roxanne and me as we stumbled through the scales.

Before noon, we had a session with our dancing master. He was tall and very slender and he had a small black mustache that would twitch when he was amused and he was amused very much of the time. His flashing black eyes were flirtatious. Indeed, Roxanne and I had to be careful with Frederico Echessasse or he would take shameless advantage of the nearness our course in dancing naturally brought about between us.

Our language teacher suffered no such inclinations.

Alfredo Munez was Spanish and he taught us French grammar as well. He was also thin and bright-eyed, but he lacked the patience of Belle and Frederico and spoke sharply to Roxanne and me when we stumbled over the Spanish words he rapped out. He always apologized immediately, for like all the people employed by or serving Ondine Chaille, his attitude toward her was a mixture of deference and a kind of trepidation.

The man who taught us history, penmanship, and mathematics was an American from Boston, a tall, crane-like young man with a thin neck and narrow shoulders. He had come to New Orleans on a flatboat to seek his fortune and had wound up tutoring the children of wealthy families and was very bitter about it. His name was Thomas Rutherford.

But it was our sessions with the dressmakers and with Ondine herself that Roxanne and I most enjoyed. At Ondine's request, I had long ago put my precious poniard in the back of a bureau drawer and saw it only when I laid the freshly washed, handmade, embroidered under-clothing into the bureau drawers. I thought cheerfully that I would never need it again.

As our wardrobe rapidly took shape, Antoinette took great pleasure in supervising mine. Ondine accorded her a rather haughty respect, for Antoinette proved to be an infallible *maîtresse d'haute couture.* In Ondine's luxurious and smoothly run household, Antoinette Desmottes's thin, sharp face took on a roundness and I discovered suddenly that she was not so old as I had at first thought. She confided to me, with her mouth full of pins one afternoon, that she had just endured in silence her twenty-ninth birthday, and her flushed face, as she pinned a basque firmly about me, looked younger than that.

Roxanne was not as content as I. She was chafing under the restraint of remaining in the house, or walking in the beautiful, ornate courtyard at the rear, which was surrounded by three sides of the house. She reminded Antoinette so often of the three thousand dollars she now owed that Ondine at last remonstrated with her.

We were clearing away after the dressmakers had left us in the large second-floor sitting room and Ondine scolded good-naturedly, "*Chérie,* you cannot spend the money yet! I am paying for all these gowns." She gestured to the lovely garments flung over the chairs, the sofas, and even the small polished tables. "There will be time for Antoinette to transfer the money to you when I take you for an outing one day."

But as the days went by, we did not go for an outing, and I passed the time dreamily studying and being fitted. Indeed, the ebb and flow of the household moved smoothly around me, but some primal instinct told me it could not last. Though Sebastien and Ulysses took turns doing the marketing, when I was near the two of them I felt a dark undercurrent of animosity between them. I could not but feel they had known each other before, in some other life, and the hostility between them had followed them to this new one. And though Ulysses was the essense of courtesy with her, I sensed that his repugnance for Sebastien extended to Ondine. His black eyes upon her were unreadable, but I was acutely aware of the vibrations about me. Ondine seemed entirely unaware of Ulysses's constraint and took great pleasure in the gossip that each man brought from the marketplace.

Sebastien reported that the homes of the Spanish and French aristocrats were buzzing with the news that Ondine Chaille's two beautiful nieces had arrived from Europe, and, according to the servants from their homes, there was much speculation about the Chaille relations.

I will never forget the morning Ondine took us into her great bedroom for our first lesson in preparing an elaborate toilette. She seated us side by side on a long bench with a fine, needlepointed cushion before her great mirrored dressing table and introduced us to lip salve, khol, and rice powder. I was absolutely entranced by this sumptuous multitude of beauty aids. There were even dainty cloisonné pots of rouge in different shades and a vast array of crystal perfume bottles that glittered like diamonds in the golden glow of two lamps, one at each end of the dressing table.

Ondine gave us an enchanting smile. "*Mes anges,* perfume is very important. It does no good behind the ears. It must be used—so—only where there is a little pulse. *Ici.* On the inside of the wrist, in the bends of the arms, at the temples. Last, a touch in the hollow of the throat and between the breasts. Not too much! *Mais jamais!* Men are to be tantalized, not engulfed."

By now I was Ondine's willing worshipper, and as she carefully used these enhancements and artifices on Roxanne and me, I watched with awe as each of us grew more and more lovely. For the thousandth time, I thanked God —and grudgingly, Roxanne—for guiding me to her.

Roxanne and I maintained a sort of armed truce between us during these days. Under Ondine's tutelage, we were becoming more and more polite and careful of our speech. Indeed, our politeness itself became a sort of weapon between us, each attempting to outdo the other in saccharine sweetness.

On warm, sunny days, and they were many, we would go into the rear courtyard where the big fountain in the center splashed down over a cherub and into three different bowls until it reached the pool below, which was filled with large, orange-gold fish and a few lily pads. It was here that Selina would serve hot coffee to the three of us on sunny afternoons.

I adored the courtyard, for it was like a small, private world of beauty and I could lie back in the wicker lounge and dream of Valier Dessaultes to my heart's content. Under Ondine's instructions, I was learning to manipulate a fan with piquant dexterity and I would practice here.

I was learning to carry a lacy parasol over my shoulder as well and to flutter my long, thick-double lashes and coo in wonder and admiration. All in all, I was learning not only to be a lady, but a coquette and a siren as well. And I loved Ondine with increasingly fervent devotion for her kindness to me. The aura of mystery about her, the fact that she never mentioned her life in Paris or the circumstances that sent her to New Orleans, strengthened my foolish hope that she might at least be related to me. My intuitive fear when I had first arrived at the Chaille house was long since forgotten.

Once she had remarked lightly on our resemblance and said, "If I had a daughter, Aurielle, I think she might have looked like you." We had laughed together, but she had avoided my searching gaze.

Two weeks into December, just as Christmas was in

the air, I took the eight-year-old Bess Bonham with me to my room after lunch. I had carefully collected scraps from the dressmakers, who were still working on the clothes for Roxanne's and my debut.

"Come, Bessie," I said gleefully, "we are going to make a doll for you today."

The child hung back, looking down the hall fearfully. "I ain't—supposed ter come ter yer room, ma'am."

"Who says so?" I asked, realizing suddenly that the child had been like a wraith about the house. I had only had the chance to greet her and say half a dozen words to her in the past four weeks.

"Madame won't like it. I'm a servant's child." But her big dark eyes looked longingly at the bits and pieces of satin, muslin, and bright silks in my hand.

"Everyone must serve someone—even the highest in the land," I said with a touch of bitterness. "You and I shall make the most beautiful doll in the world."

I kept her with me for the two hours before Thomas Rutherford appeared for our history, math, and penmanship lessons. The doll was almost formed—arms, legs, body, and head ready to be joined together by my needle. I had the pleasure of seeing happiness glow in this child's pale face.

Later that afternoon, Roxanne and I went for our first walk with Ondine. We dressed in two of the frocks she had the seamstresses make for us. They were the latest fashions from Paris, the French dressmakers had assured us, and the waist was at long last making a reappearance in some of them. Our skirts were full over lacy muslin petticoats, with yards and yards of lace ruffling on them. Mine was Ondine's favorite pale blue and the skirt was caught up with saucy bows around draped scallops over a large flounce at the bottom. The neck was cut daringly low and the sleeves full at the shoulders, only to cup tightly at my narrow wrists. Roxanne's was, of course, pale green, which made her eyes emerald, but the style was much like mine. Our pelisses matched the dresses and were flared beautifully to permit them to be seen provocatively.

Antoinette, adroit hairdresser that she was, had done

both Roxanne's and my hair in the current fashion, piled high on top with teasing little curls at the napes of our necks. I had never felt so grand in all my life and wild exhilaration filled me. I was hard put to present a demure face to the people we passed on the banquette, so full of smiles was I.

"We will walk to the Place d'Armes, my dears," Ondine said briskly and we paced ourselves sedately. In the bright afternoon light, I looked at the houses on either side of us with wide eyes. They were extraordinarily beautiful, a blend of Spanish and French architecture.

It was Sunday afternoon and the streets were full of people taking the air as we were. Ondine had decided on walking rather than having her coachman, Jasper, get out the carriage. "You can see so many more and so much more intimately than from the carriage. We will take the carriage in the middle of the week and then you, Roxanne, may at last exact your pound of flesh from poor Antoinette —though I think it very unladylike."

"I can be a lady and still conduct my business," Roxanne replied stubbornly. "You do."

"C'est vrai," Ondine laughed, then smiled brilliantly at two men approaching. "Ah, M'sieu Eugene Poliet and M'sieu Gabriel Villere. How do you do?"

They were young men and they greeted her with great warmth, but their black, flashing eyes were on Roxanne and me. "Ah, Madame Chaille, we had heard you were harboring two beautiful nieces from Paris and London. Will you not introduce us?"

"But of course, messieurs. This is Aurielle Stuart, my dear sister's child from England, and this is Roxanne Deveret, my sister's child from Paris, both sadly orphaned at almost the same time."

We nodded gracefully and lowered our lashes, the epitome of good manners. The men would have stayed to chat further, but Ondine swiftly and tactfully extricated us and as we walked on down the banquette, she murmured, "We are just going to give them a taste of you, my little loves. We will spend no more than two or three moments with any of my friends."

As we drew near the heart of the city, Ondine called

141

to fashionably clad young matrons with prancing children about them. There were more young gentlemen clad in skin-tight pantaloons of yellow broadcloth with long coats of blue and bottle green, thrown carelessly back, the better to show off their embroidered satin waistcoats. As we passed and were introduced to some, they furtively adjusted their starched lace frills and pulled down their flowered silk vests.

We stood smiling politely while they exchanged amenities with Ondine, their sharp eyes straying often to us. They talked of the latest *duello* and last night's opera, their friends and their activities. My wide-eyed fascination was not a pose. I was seeing sights and enjoying conversation completely new to me.

As we reached the Place d'Armes, I saw pushcarts of *bier douce,* ginger beer, for the buying. Beautiful quadroon girls with golden skin swept by in their gowns of silk, with their turbaned black mothers looking neither to the right nor the left. Over toward the French market, I was astonished to see near-naked Indians—Ondine had to tell me what they were—reeling drunkenly, having splurged on liquor the money they had made with their produce and pelts. There were oystermen selling their wares and black women in their bright guinea-blue dresses calling, "Pralines! Sweet, tasty pralines!" with baskets of the confection under their arms.

Suddenly I was electrified by the sight of Jean and Pierre Lafitte, walking leisurely down the street across from the Place d'Armes. Roxanne espied them at the same time and a little gasp escaped her.

"*Sacré bleu,* look at them," she murmured. "As if they had not a care in the world!"

They drew nearer and I saw the tall Jean's black eyes flicker over us and there was merriment in their depths. Ondine smiled at them warmly and said, "It is the Messieurs Lafitte. How good to see you gentlemen," and she introduced us as she had done before.

With their black hats held to their chests, the Lafittes bowed over our hands in a courtly fashion, dropping a kiss upon them. Not by look or word did they betray our previous acquaintance. I was very glad Ondine had made me wear mitts soaked in glycerine and rosewater every night, for beside Jean's swarthy cheek my hand appeared white and soft. But as he looked up, I caught Jean's eyes on Roxanne and for an instant, a white-hot flame gleamed in them and I knew I was right. Jean loved Roxanne. Being the kind of man he was, perhaps marriage was not in his mind, but I knew he desired her. I knew too, by the flush in her cheeks, she was not immune to his charm.

Ondine was saying regretfully, "I am having a ball in May for their debut, Jean—Pierre. But I am asking Governor Claiborne to attend and I know you do not wish to see him, *mes amis*—but you *must* call and have coffee with us in the meantime."

"I would be charmed," Jean murmured, replacing his broad-brimmed hat.

"And so would I," Pierre smiled, his bad eye wandering away from us. They bowed again and left us to continue their errand.

Ondine called over one of the black women with her basket of sweets and bought a praline for each of us. "We will sit in the square and eat them, then make our way back to the house. You two have made quite enough stir for one day."

"I don't know about that," Roxanne replied pertly, her green eyes narrowing on a tall figure approaching on horseback.

Suddenly there was tension in every line of her slender body and she leaned forward, her delicate nostrils flaring slightly with excitement. My eyes followed hers and widened swiftly. It was that disturbing and somehow frightening man, Quentin Kincannon. He sat in the saddle of a powerful bay horse. The sunlight was dazzling on his snowy, ruffled cravat and the superbly tailored buff coat and breeches. His boots, to the knee, gleamed brightly.

Roxanne half-rose from her seat, the pale green dress and pelisse falling gracefully about her. Ondine, occupied with her praline, failed to observe this, and Roxanne started forward, but I caught her arm suddenly.

I dreaded meeting him again, for always in those

mocking black eyes lay the remembrance of the moments of desire shared between us aboard the *Wind*.

Roxanne turned on me, eyes blazing, and for an instant I thought she guessed my guilty secret and would strike me. Then her face cooled and she took her seat once more. The horseman drew near, obviously on his way to the levee. He slowed, a smile white in the sun-browned face. I looked away.

He swept off his rakish black hat and bowed, "Good afternoon, Madame Chaille," and at Ondine's cool nod, his boots pressed against the bay's flanks and he moved on toward the levee with an increased gait.

Ondine said quietly, "I compliment you on your poise during this encounter, Roxanne."

"I wanted to talk to him," she said rebelliously.

"Then I congratulate you on your further restraint," was the imperturbable reply. "You will meet him soon enough. Next time he may be on foot and I will be forced to introduce you."

"You said you'd ask him to the ball—"

"This spring. And so I will, Roxanne. You must learn patience. Observe Aurielle—how patient she is."

I bit my lip and looked away. Impatience was devouring me, had been devouring me for years. My desire to rush headlong into life and bend it to my will was like a consuming flame. Yet I had learned through my short years to hide the multitude of facets that made up my character. That I had managed to deceive Ondine Chaille the last few weeks was a tribute to my smooth face and downcast eyes.

But Roxanne was laughing scornfully, "Aurielle—patient? Pfaugh! What a canard, Tante Ondine. She is as breakneck as I. She has only managed to fool you."

"Whatever she is doing, she is doing it well. I'll vow she won't leap to her feet when we lay eyes on Valier Dessaultes." Then she *had* caught Roxanne's involuntary movement!

"But she'll want to, you may be sure!" And still laughing she rose at Ondine's gesture. The three of us walked sedately from the Place d'Armes. It was to be a week later before I glimpsed Valier Dessaultes.

144

I had finished the doll for Bess Bonham and a dress was in the making. The child was delighted, her big dark eyes gleaming with joy. But her odd surreptitiousness had rubbed off on me. I found myself beckoning her to my room discreetly, when no one could see, and aiding her in escaping back to the kitchen or to the mysterious upper regions of the house, unseen.

Christmas was only four days away now and Ondine returned often from town with interesting packages. At my protests that I had nothing to give her, she smiled gently. "You and Roxanne are giving me the greatest gift of all—release from boredom—the opportunity to pull the wool over the eyes of some of the greatest snobs, the most pompous, the most conceited people in the world. I adore secrets—and you two, *mes anges,* are two of my best secrets." She put an arm about each of us and pulled us lightly to her for a brief kiss. *"Je vous adore."*

A faint discomfort pervaded me at her remarks. What contempt Ondine must feel for her friends in New Orleans to take such delight in deceiving them—in speaking of them so. Then I told myself hastily that she was a great lady with a touch of the gamin in her and *that* I could understand.

"Besides," she continued gaily, "I am doing no more for you, Aurielle, than I am for my adorable and tight-fisted little Roxanne. She pays for nothing, eh, my pretty?" She tweaked one of Roxanne's bright curls.

"Mais non. You will not take my money," Roxanne grinned impudently, "despite my offering to pay. Which reminds me, *when* are you going to take us to the bank so that I can collect from Antoinette?"

"La! Forget money, my Roxanne," Ondine laughed, her blue eyes twinkling, "and let us all take a carriage ride this bright afternoon—perhaps shop a bit, too. With Christmas in the air, you will enjoy all the flurry. Now run get your bonnets and pelisses—and don't forget your gloves!"

Later as we bowled down the rutted, dusty street with the tall, skinny Jasper on the box, I was caught up in the festivity among those on the crowded streets. Ulysses and Sebastien sat stiffly in the seat before the three of us.

They were dressed in bright suits of livery Ondine had purchased for both of them. There was great dignity in both men, and though I felt the hostility between them, as always, I knew security in the presence of Ulysses.

"We will go first and see the activity at the levee," Ondine said conversationally, and she and Roxanne fell to the discussion of parties and balls being held during the Christmas season. I was too caught up in the passing scenes to join in.

Two fine-looking gentlemen passed and I craned to look after them. Ondine, seeing me, said, "That is John R. Grymes and the taller man is Edward Livingston, very distinguished men. Grymes is the district attorney and Livingston is a graduate of Princeton. He is the younger brother of Robert Livingston, who played a memorable part in the purchase of Louisiana from France—too recent, I suppose, for your history books, *mes petites*. I will invite them to your debut." She laughed suddenly. "And scandalously enough they are good friends of Jean Lafitte. In fact, they are his lawyers." She talked on of the two men and I gathered their careers were most illustrious. It seemed odd to me that they were close to Lafitte, whose reputation might be glamorous but was certainly spotty.

The nearer we drew to the levee, the more frantic the activity. Jasper halted the carriage at the base of the levee beside several others and, assisted by Ulysses and Sebastien, we three women debarked and walked up the narrow dirt path to the crest of it.

From the thin, dusty road running along the broad top of the levee, I looked down, spellbound, at the frantic hubbub below. It was a warm December day and the scents that always hung in the air near the river were intensified a hundredfold. There was a maelstrom of produce and cargo lining the wharves and docks below. I could see bundles of furs, great crates containing silks, china, silver, and a thousand luxuries, I knew. I was awed by the vastness of the enterprise before me. The river wind was only faintly cool and the sunlight gentle. Below us, the stevedores, like great ants to an anthill, were carrying goods to and from the tall-masted ships tied up before us.

"I've seen all this before," Roxanne said boredly, "only not so frantically busy. They will do well if they can elude the British blockade."

"We have some very adroit blockade runners, besides your Jean Lafitte," Ondine said lightly.

"I have never seen such," I murmured, fascinated as the great stevedores, black and white, hefted boxes and barrels. I left reluctantly.

"I will have Ulysses and Sebastien bring you one morning after Christmas, Aurielle, and let you stay as long as you like," Ondine told me with a touch of asperity when we took our places in the carriage.

I was still entranced by the Christmas crowds that flooded the streets about us as we clattered down·Decatur, turning on Toulouse Street on our way to the shops. Suddenly, from the corner of my eye, I saw Ondine Chaille stiffen and I turned swiftly. Her eyes were fastened on a woman on the banquette and I saw that the woman was black, tall, and very beautiful, and she was returning Ondine's stare with piercing black eyes. Her nose was thin and high, like the Jamaican blacks, and her head was bound in a scarlet turban. Great golden hoops hung from it where her ears were hidden by the bright silk. Ondine was a statue until we had passed, but when I looked after the woman, I saw she was lost in the crowd.

"Who was that beautiful strange woman?" I asked Ondine.

Sebastien spoke with sudden harshness, "That's a voodoo woman, mademoiselle. Her name is Clothilde LaVaux."

"She comes from Santo Domingo," Ulysses added cryptically.

"Voodoo?" I repeated blankly. "Whatever is voodoo?"

Roxanne gave me a withering glance as if I were abysmally ignorant and I felt defensive and a touch angry.

"Better you do not know, *chérie*," Ondine said quietly. "They are dreadful people who indulge in terrible, bloody practices not to be spoken of—" Her voice was a touch thick and her bright, restless eyes fastened on a

147

magnificent new shop. "Ah, Roxanne, here is the importing firm—the shop of your beloved, Kincannon."

At Roxanne's exclamation of delight, I looked with new interest at the shop which stood out from those about it, being trimmed with newly painted wrought-iron lace. The glass in the windows was glittering from recent cleaning and the objects within that window were rich and varied. I glimpsed silks, laces, small cloisonné boxes, dishes, jewelry, and a myriad of beautiful things.

"May we not go in?" Roxanne asked hopefully, and I knew she was thinking we might see the proprietor.

Ondine shrugged. "You will not see *him, mon ange.* He will be at his plantation. Sebastien told me last week construction is well under way and he has installed a new sugar mill there."

"You didn't tell *me!*" Roxanne retorted with some heat.

Ondine looked at her coolly. "You do not need to be reminded of the man. Shall we go in?"

Ulysses took my arm after the others, and helped me from the open carriage step. Once in the store, I was lost in the treasures, large and small, that surrounded me. In one corner there hung from the ceiling a number of crystal chandeliers, twinkling like hundreds of stars in the pale light. There was one glassed counter that displayed sparkling gems of every kind from topaz to diamond, and I knew suddenly why there was so much of the iron lace about the windows. The clerks, three of them, were hovering near, and I watched as Ondine and Roxanne made their purchases on credit.

Ondine turned to me. "Why are you buying nothing, *chérie?*"

"I am already deeply in your debt, Tante Ondine. I cannot spend your money so freely."

"How good we are—how noble!" Roxanne jeered softly.

I turned on her. "Are you using the money you took from me the night of our escape from Barataria, you trollop?" I hissed. "You haven't been to the bank—so you don't have poor Toinette's savings yet!"

"You know well Tante Ondine will not let me spend

my savings," she replied explosively and the clerks drew back in alarm. "You have such an overweening and useless conscience—" She broke off abruptly as Ondine took her arm.

"*Lentement, mes anges, doucement.* Each of you shall repay me one day, you shall see. And you shall collect in due time from Antoinette, Roxanne. Now keep your voices down and buy what you like."

After that, we proceeded about the shop with a ladylike demeanor that concealed the boiling anger in both of us. I bought Antoinette a length of black watered silk with which to make a new dress and a tiny carved rocking chair for Bess's new doll. For the women servants we bought less expensive beads at a shop farther down the street, and cravats for the men.

Ondine said severely, "Do not buy them too much or you will spoil them. I have already purchased gifts for them."

I wondered what she had bought, but I knew, being Ondine, we would not see them on Christmas morning, for Ondine did not believe in sharing Christmas with servants. And she herself was going to a Christmas ball the night of the 25th. "I cannot get out of it, my sweet ones. I have excused myself from too many soirées, pleading your presence as a reason. But you may be sure I shall talk glowingly of you," she had said.

We purchased handkerchiefs for our tutors and had them boxed and tied with red ribbons.

Surfeited on sights and shops, we arrived late in the afternoon at the Chaille mansion with our treasures and retired to our rooms to rest before the dinner hour.

The days slipped by and Chistmas came and went as Roxanne and I struggled with our lessons, and our teachers drilled into us what knowledge they could. As for the music the dear little French Belle Fontaine taught me, I must admit my skill was poor. Still she taught me a keen appreciation for her talent. When she played for us, her little fingers crashing in chords upon the instrument in the music room, I shivered with pleasure at the beauty of sound reverberating around me.

Roxanne was bored and made no pretense of enjoying her lessons. But to do her credit, she was very sharp in assimilating what was taught her. Our mathematics teacher, enamored of her as he was, took special pains with her regarding her sums and multiplication. She played on his weakness for her unmercifully and teased him until he spent his entire hour with her with his face beet red.

During those long weeks when winter storms lashed the big house on Chartres at night, I sometimes could not sleep. When that happened, I rose and lit a lamp. By its steady glow I studied the books Ondine had purchased for us. There were some that fascinated me, books on philosophy by Greeks, translated into English and French. I struggled to understand them. History came easily to me and I went through those books quickly. Slowly, bit by bit, the fine English poetry, the history, the philosophy began to ring clear in my brain and I realized I was becoming an educated woman. I was that rare thing in the society of the day—a woman who could think.

I began to understand Roxanne better, as well as the patient Antoinette, who had come to terms with life. Among the women I knew, only Ondine remained an enigma to me—a beautiful, dreamlike enigma. And I clung to the hope that she *was* related to me, despite the fact that she gave me no encouragement in that hope.

Though I became better friends with the servants, they remained secretive and somewhat aloof. But the statuesque Selina would smile at me, the scar on her cheek sinking into a crease when I stole into the kitchen for an extra bit of her delicious pecan pie or an orange from the great baskets of fruit that stood on a table by the kitchen door.

But it was Bess I loved unreservedly, with her eyes as big as saucers and her thick braids swinging about her shoulders. I would coax her into my room when my lessons were over and tell her about the things I was learning. I had discovered she was frightened of questions, so I was careful not to ask her too much. I told her about Roxanne deliberately tripping the ardent Frederico Echessasse as they danced and described his antics in righting

150

himself, and Bessie and I laughed together at the scene I painted.

She gasped for breath and bubbled, "Oh, it's been so much better since ye came an' there ain't been no parties er balls."

That jolted me but I kept laughing, even as I examined her startled face carefully, knowing that if I let the words mean anything to me, she would flee. Slowly the fear departed and we played together, I willingly as any child, holding the doll I made and telling Bess a long story about it.

But after she left, I wondered if Ondine worked the servants too hard, demanded too much of them when she entertained.

It wasn't too long after this that I had a really distressing experience with the child. It was the last of January in the new year of 1813 when she came to my room with the doll and the little rocking chair. I noted she kept one hand slightly behind her. I said nothing but waited until she inadvertently handed the doll and the chair toward me. Then I gasped. There was a great gash on the back of the little hand, scabbing over now, but red and angry.

I seized her before she could escape, crying, "Oh, Bessie, dear—you must let me bandage that!"

She twisted in my grasp. "But I had a bandage on it—it fell off!" The desperation of the child communicated itself to me and I felt my own heart beating heavily.

"But, my darling, you must tell me how it happened—"

"No, no! I be clumsy—I fell on a—sharp rock. It's nothin'."

"We should go to Madame Chaille. She is very wise and she will know how to treat it. If you were to get a poisoning of the blood—"

Frantic now, Bessie tugged at my hand and, with a mighty pull, she was out of my grasp and fleeing down the hall toward the stairs. I ran after her a few steps, but at the sound of her sobs beyond me, I halted. I had brought her some terrible distress and I would only bring her more. I turned back to my own room and my books.

Chapter
8

Spring came on and the warm breath of April, filled with the scent of roses, drifted across New Orleans. The news of the war between England and America was unsettling as it came to our ears. We had read in the *Niles Register* that a sixth coalition in Europe consisting of Prussia, Russia, England, Sweden, and Spain had been formed. It sent its forces toward the Elbe, but Napoleon still had an army of 350,000 in Germany and was everywhere victorious. I could not but rejoice, for this meant that England was too busy with the Corsican to throw its entire might at the country I was coming to love.

One bright morning, Roxanne at last persuaded Ondine to take her into town with poor Antoinette, in order to divest her of her savings.

"Come along with us, Aurielle," Roxanne said, amused by my angry eyes.

"I will not!" I retorted as Antoinette stood by, resigned to the knowledge that Roxanne refused to give up her claim upon the money. "You have given up none of your piracy, Roxanne! You are stealing still."

Roxanne laughed and Ondine looked distressed. "You girls must not quarrel over so small a matter. Aurielle, you will repay Antoinette one day soon—and Roxanne is so determined about this."

"It was part of the bargain," Roxanne said stubbornly. "I kept my part of it and now Aurielle wants to weasel out on her part."

"Go on!" I cried. "Go on and take it, you wretch. Toinette, dear, I swear by all that's holy I *shall* repay you soon!"

"I know," the little Frenchwoman murmured.

"Then come along, my dear," Ondine said, smiling indulgently at Roxanne, who stuck her tongue out at me saucily.

I wept with frustration when they had left. Despite Antoinette's pleading eyes, I had refused a last time to accompany them for this robbery. I could not understand Ondine permitting it to happen, when she herself was so free with her largesse.

After the carriage clattered down the dusty street, I saw Thomas Rutherford admitted to the house by Selina. I met them in the foyer, my face flushed from weeping.

"I'm not going to take my lessons today, Mr. Rutherford. Mademoiselle Deveret is not here either—so you may be excused until tomorrow," I said coldly.

He was nonplussed. "But Mademoiselle Stuart——"

"Madame Chaille will not object," I interrupted. "I am—not feeling well today."

He bowed, his Adam's apple working in his long, thin neck. He was obviously disappointed that Roxanne was not here and he took his departure readily enough. Selina favored me with an inscrutable glance and disappeared into the rear of the house.

For a moment I stood uncertainly in the foyer, looking out through one of the long windows by the door. It was beautiful in the enclosed front courtyard where hundreds of blossoms flung their fragrance wantonly in the air. For an instant I felt smothered and then suddenly I opened the door and ran from the house, down the steps, and into the garden. I paused there by the small fountain, looking up where sunlight spilled like gold lace through the ironwork on the Chaille balconies above me.

I dashed a hand across my wet cheeks, wondering hotly what Roxanne would do with poor Antoinette's savings. I knew now that Roxanne had thousands in the Dessaultes Bank of New Orleans. She had implied it in a hundred different ways. She had not come out of her years of privateering at the side first of Ulysses, then Quentin Kincannon, without having amassed considerable wealth.

I pushed through the gate and walked toward the levee slowly. Passersby on the streets eyed me with the leisurely speculation that was accorded to everyone by the New Orleanaise. My dress was palest green lawn with a rather low-cut neck in deference to the tropic climate. I had no gloves, no hat or reticule, I realized, but I did not turn back. I took the streets, my heart growing lighter with each step. I would feast my eyes upon the Mississippi, drink in the excitement that pervaded the air there.

Suddenly a vagrant breeze tugged at my hair. Antoinette had done it up rather loosely, for she had been distraught this morning. Now the heavy chestnut strands were blowing loose. I felt the pins slip with every step. What did it matter? No one knew me yet, no one that I was likely to meet anyway.

I walked faster, the crowd growing thicker about me as I neared the worn path leading upward, and I heard a rough catcall from a group of men with great thick shoulders, wearing small knit caps of red and blue.

I did not glance about as one called out, "Mademoiselle, *voulez-vous faire l'amour?*" His accent was terrible and I was sure it was the only French he knew. I lifted my chin and did not look back, though the whistles and catcalls followed me.

It was then it occurred to me uneasily that I should not be walking to the levee unescorted. Stubbornly I continued. All that frenetic hustle and bustle would take my mind from Antoinette's loss. Ah, God, surely I would marry a rich man and give every cent of it back to her—with *lagniappe*—some besides, as the Creoles would say.

Climbing to the top, I stood looking down on the

milling mass of men and merchandise. As always, my heart soared and excited joy filled me. There were two great schooners moored there today, flying the French tricolor. Blockade runners, I thought. There were the usual hundreds of flatboats, skiffs, and rakish red-sailed fishermen's boats interspersed with the narrow, sleek pirogues.

Like one mesmerized, I began to descend the rough path, drawn by the scents and sights. Slowly I drew nearer the wharves, my hair tumbling down my back now, feeling deliciously cool in the river wind that had sprung up. I sat down upon a small keg that was marked *Macarte Rum*.

Suddenly a great, hairy man with a sandy beard and mustache approached, smiling broadly. "Ah, sweetheart —you *did* wait fer me after all. Ain't you the sweet one!" and before I could move, he caught me in an iron embrace and was pressing his wet mouth against mine. The reek of whiskey was overpowering. I knew from Antoinette's scathing descriptions that this was a Kaintuck, one of those bold, lawless men from upriver.

I began to struggle fiercely, trying to scream, but when I opened my mouth, he thrust his tongue into it and revulsion swept me. I beat upon his huge chest with ineffectual little fists. He reached a rough hand up into the thick hair at the back of my neck and held me immobile.

Then as suddenly as he had seized me, he let me go. I staggered and turned to run wildly away, but I was halted by the curt voice of another man. Looking back, I saw it was the narrow-eyed Quentin Kincannon and he held his sword at the chest of my assailant as he had done to Durket that night long ago at the Temple.

"Get out of here," he said to the man in a quiet, deadly voice.

Pale now and with sweat popping out on his forehead, the burly man said, "Before Gawd, sir, I didn't know she was a lady—with her hair all down an' blowin' in th' wind. I didn't mean no harm."

"Get out of here," Kincannon repeated coldly. Then

to me shortly, "You will wait, miss, until I can accompany you home."

I was poised, ready for flight, the skirts of my lovely little lawn frock in my hands. I looked about us to observe other men eyeing me curiously. What a fool I had been to come to the levee without Ulysses or Sebastien!

"All you men get back to your work," Kincannon said, glancing at the onlookers and sheathing his sword. "And you, Aurielle, come with me." His horse stood beside him, Kincannon held the reins loosely in a muscular hand. He took my elbow and we began to climb the path which horses took up the levee and down on the city side.

"Now, Aurielle, you will tell me what you are doing presenting such a tempting target in such a place. It seems to be a habit with you, this being the second time I have had to rescue you from unwanted attentions."

The foul taste of the man was still in my mouth and instinctively I spat. Looking up, I found the cold black eyes suddenly twinkling with amusement, which angered me. For all his attractiveness, I hated this tall, arrogant man. He had invaded my thoughts all too often with memories of that furious and unwillingly sweet night aboard the *Wind,* when, with a kiss or two more, I would have succumbed to him. He and Roxanne richly deserved each other. Unpleasant people! "I suppose I owe you my thanks," I said grudgingly.

"Something like that," he responded, walking beside me as I detoured to avoid horse droppings. "What possessed you to come to the levee with your hair flowing like a wanton?"

"I was running away—for a little while. Your *pet,* Roxanne, has demanded all of Antoinette's life savings—they have gone to transfer it to Roxanne's account now. She says it's payment for persuading Madame Chaille to sponsor me in society." I added sullenly, "If that day ever comes."

"I'd say that was a bargain. Madame Chaille enjoys the reputation of being one of the most charming, most sought-after and admired women in New Orleans. You are fortunate to be under her wing."

"I know that, but Roxanne has a bankful of money.

Three thousand is nothing to her and everything to Toinette."

He laughed shortly. "Three thousand is a great deal to Roxanne. She is a very avaricious little girl."

"I don't see why you don't marry her. I think the two of you are admirably suited."

"*If* I ever marry, it will be very advantageously. A true lady of good blood."

I laughed scornfully. "Who would have you? I've heard how Creole society failed to come to your ball! Have you chosen the victim of your desires?"

He smiled sardonically. "Nay, but it'll not be a vixen such as you or Roxanne."

"*I* wouldn't marry you if I had to work as a drudge the rest of my life!"

"We are of a mind concerning that," he said with a dry laugh as we drew away from the base of the levee and took the streets on our way to Chartres. "Once I see you safely inside the Chaille house, I would advise you to think twice before flying out of it on the fool's errand of venting your anger. I might not be so conveniently near the next time." Then mockingly, "Do you lock your doors now, or leave them invitingly ajar as you did on the *Wind?*"

I felt my face grow hot. "Oh!" I sputtered, "it was *not* ajar—it was closed! You should have knocked—"

"Knocked? I expected my lieutenant to be there. Certainly I didn't expect you so conveniently nude—waiting for me."

"*Waiting?*" I stormed. "You took shameless advantage of me!"

"At first," he agreed, beginning to laugh again. "Ah, but I think with a little tender perseverance the tears would have dried and our mutual satisfaction reached."

"God and the devil, you are conceited!" The fact that he was right drove my fury to new heights.

"I should think rescuing you, as I have so often, would allow me some privileges."

I was speechless with rage. It had been very embarrassing and humiliating to me that this man had been my rescuer twice now. Three times, if I counted the *Sea*

Warrior, my redemption, and possible murder charges.

He chuckled suddenly. "Your skepticism notwithstanding, Aurielle, I have enough money to marry whomever I choose—*if* I choose. Marriage is very confining and I enjoy my freedom."

"I pity the poor girl you finally choose."

"And I, miss, feel sympathy for the man who becomes ensnared by you."

"I shall make him a good wife—a virtuous wife!"

"Ah, yes," he said thoughtfully as we walked along. "Your virtue. And thanks to my restraint that precious maidenhead of yours is still intact."

His audacity was unbelievable and I turned a flushed face and glittering eyes on him. "What an impertinent blackguard you are—speaking so to a *lady.*"

"Lady?" he mocked. "Under that fine veneer you've labored over, you're still that half-tamed, half-wild cat, Aurielle. You'll never be a lady."

I swung my hand back and up to strike his face with all my strength, but swift as lightning he caught it, holding it easily in a firm grip as he said between his teeth, "Not again, miss," and dropping his reins, he caught the other as it flew up. We stood there on Chartres Street in the warm spring sunshine with the scents of flowers all about us, glaring at each other. I flung my head back, hair tumbling in the light breeze, lips parted and moist with anger.

Then a shocking thing occurred. The touch of his flesh on mine increased my turmoil and my legs grew fluid and weak. He bent his head like a striking hawk and kissed me full on the mouth. It was a swift, hard kiss and the feel of his firm, cool mouth sent a shiver of fire through me. His breath and mine mingled sweet and clean. I could not draw away from the vitality that flowed between us. The weakness in my legs moved to my groin and I felt for a moment I would faint. It was he at last who pulled away, and it opened new fury in me.

"Damn you," I whispered huskily. "You're no better than the Kaintucks—you're worse!"

The astonishment in his eyes equaled that in mine and we faced each other as adversaries, oblivious to the curious people who passed us. Then his dark eyes narrowed and he drew a long breath. "You are a very beautiful woman," he said slowly, as if to himself, "and it is spring."

"Ye're damn—you're very right. It meant nothing. I'm only thankful Roxanne did not see you behaving like an animal! She would hold it against *me*." Then as he caught his horse's reins and we started forward, I added coldly, "You may leave me now. It is only a short block to the Chaille house. My great regret is that I must meet with you again, for Ondine has promised Roxanne that you shall be invited to our debut in May."

He smiled suddenly. "I think you enjoyed that kiss. I did."

"Don't flatter yourself—it was loathsome."

"You are a liar. I was the one who pulled away and only then to see your face."

"Go away," I said, wishing with all my heart I could swear at him. "Go away now, you—cocky oaf!"

Despite his obvious amusement at my discomfiture, his eyes were suddenly knowing and wise. "You are not too young, Aurielle, to know there is an attraction between us. But since it doesn't fit with either of our plans, we will ignore it. Good day." And putting a booted foot in the stirrup, he swung himself up on the big bay and trotted back toward the levee.

I took long strides, unladylike strides, down the block to the Chaille house. With bosom heaving, I entered to find Selina dusting in the foyer. She looked up.

"Mademoiselle! You are all flushed—an' your hair! What has happened to you?"

"I took a walk to the levee. I am in a turmoil over Roxanne taking poor Toinette's life savings."

"That is bad," she replied, her black eyes gleaming. "Reckon th' voodoo might git her."

I stopped. "Selina, tell me about voodoo. What is it?"

"It's—like magic. It come over from Santo Domingo with th' refugees. I hear Sebastien say once that Clothilde LaVaux is a voodoo queen. She got a potion—a powder fer every problem. They say she can give you your dearest wish." She paused and her voice lowered, vibrant with longing—"An' she can kill your enemies—all with voodoo."

"How can that be?" I asked in disbelief.

She lifted her shoulders eloquently and let them fall. "How should I know? I comes from th' back country. Madame bought me five years ago from th' Brouillards. They sol' their plantation an' went back to France." She turned away.

I walked slowly to the curving staircase. Clothilde LaVaux. *That* was the name of the tall, beautiful black woman who had looked at Ondine so piercingly and Ondine had been disturbed. All at once, I realized that Ondine Chaille had been *afraid*. Why? Selina's dark, lovely face was turned away as she moved further to dust another table.

"Wait, Selina," I called softly. "I saw Clothilde LaVaux from the carriage—once. She looked at madame. Do they know each other?"

She gave me a startled glance. "Ever'body knows *of* Madame Chaille. I ain't never seen Clothilde LaVaux." She vanished into the hall.

I paused on the fifth step thinking. It was no surprise that Selina had not seen the voodoo queen. As far as I could see, no servant ever left the house without Ondine, with the exception of Sebastien—and now Ulysses. Yet I was certain Ondine had recognized Clothilde LaVaux and I was equally sure the voodoo queen had known Ondine. More, she was inimical to the woman who was so kind to me.

Suddenly I heard the clatter of the carriage beside the house as it passed through the porte cochere to the stables at the rear. Poor Antoinette! I continued up the stairs and down the long hall to my room to look out on the rear courtyard. Beyond the orange and banana tree tops and the wall, I saw Couri the stable boy unhitching the open carriage and preparing to rub down the horses. The three women, with Ulysses and Sebastien in attendance, had already come into the house.

In a moment, I heard voices in the hallway and I went to the door of my room.

"Your dear Antoinette has been relieved of her excess gold, Aurielle," Roxanne laughed, "all your fuming notwithstanding."

"And I shall repay her, you grasping chit!"

"When you are married to the Dessaultes heir? He and his *maman* are rich—but not nearly so rich as I shall be when I marry Quent."

At the mention of the man I felt blood hot in my face and Roxanne's merriment increased. "Look at you! You have not changed since Barataria, wild and wanton with your hair all atumble and furious at the sound of his name. Truly, Aurielle, you are a great fool. Antoinette is only a servant and she gave the money for *you*. You should be grateful instead of in a pet."

"I *am* grateful," I replied in a hard voice, and Ondine came to me, smiling winningly.

"Mon ange, do not scowl so fiercely. I have some very good news for you." She patted my cheek. "We saw Madame Dessaultes and her son at the bank and they are coming to call upon me in an hour. Antoinette will be along in a moment to help you with your toilette. I will introduce you and Roxanne, but you must be very discreet and promise me you will speak but little, for I had not meant you to meet with anyone before your debut."

My lips parted and my heart gave a great bound. *Valier Dessaultes!* I was to meet him ahead of time—and in the setting I had hoped for. "Oh, madame—Tante Ondine, how good you are to me!" I flung my arms about her and kissed her flawless cheek.

"Oho, how fast the weather changes," Roxanne said derisively. "All smiles and lightness now. I only glimpsed him, for I was busy with Antoinette at the time. I've half a notion to compete for his affections."

I gave her a scornful glance as Antoinette came down the hall. Ondine said reprovingly, "Roxanne, you are much too forward with your ready tongue."

"You are right, Tante," Roxanne replied with mock humility. Then pertly to Antoinette, "Please get Catherine to attend me, Toinette, before you and Aurielle begin."

"Get her yourself," I flashed, taking Antoinette's arm. "Come, Toinette—you shall tell me how the Des-

161

saultes looked." I pulled her into my room, closing the door behind her. "Just think, Toinette, I shall meet him a whole month ahead of time!"

Later in the sitting room, which the servants called the parlor, we were as elegant a trio as could be found anywhere, I was sure. Roxanne wore a deeper green than usual, a lovely dress of gauze over fine muslin, with plaited ribbons fastened to the shoulders and little puffed sleeves. It set off her copper hair beautifully.

Ondine was stunning in a simple white silk with a single rose in palest pink at her waist.

I wore a lustrous pale blue dress of lutestring, as simple as Ondine's in design, but luscious, with gathered flounces at the bottom of the skirt, which was not so full. The prevailing fashion of the moment was a return to the simpler skirts that had been popular ten years before. I did not like it, preferring the fuller-cut dresses, but Ondine was adamant about our remaining in the latest of fashions.

Antoinette had done my hair into a pouf at the back with little ringlets falling from it and clustering near my face. Into the entire coiffure, she had skillfully woven small blue satin ribbons.

Dangling at each of our wrists were the ever-present silk fans, so necessary in this climate. It was mid-afternoon and the long French windows were open on the front courtyard, but the slow, warm winds were vagrant, their fragrance coming to us but faintly. We swished the fans with enthusiasm. Wafting on the flower-scented air was the fine French perfume Ordine had given us.

The bell rang distantly and we could hear the steady tread of Sebastien going to answer it. In a moment he stood in the doorway and said quietly, "Madame Dessaultes and her son, Valier Dessaultes, calling, Madame Chaille."

Ondine rose in a single fluid movement and extended an exquisite white hand as the two, mother and son, entered the room. I had a flashing impression of imperious dignity and iron control over a volatile temper in the older woman.

But it was Valier my eyes sought. He stood well over six feet, his shoulders broad, tapering to narrow hips and very small, finely shod feet. Pantaloons without a wrinkle encased his muscular legs and his face was as darkly handsome as I remembered. He wore rich, dark blue broadcloth and his vest was a paler shade of satin, intricately and beautifully embroidered. The cravat under his strong, olive chin was a cascade of snowy ruffles and his black hair was crisp and faintly curling. Then suddenly he was taking my hand in his, looking down into my up-flung face, our eyes meeting and holding. I knew a moment of fear. What if he remembered that long-past instant at the Temple?

"I have waited for this moment, mademoiselle, ever since I heard Madame Chaille's two beautiful nieces had arrived from Europe." There was not the faintest trace of recognition in those dark eyes.

"You are most kind," I said, breathy with relief as he turned and took Roxanne's extended hand and exchanged pleasantries with her.

But when we seated ourselves once more, I found that Valier had taken a place beside me on the sofa, while Roxanne and the two older women sat in the French chairs around us. The marble-topped table before the divan soon bore the silver service and thin china cups and saucers brought in by Selina, whose black eyes slid over the gathering without expression.

"Young Sylvestre Sartain was killed last evening, *sous les chênes,* Ondine," Madame Dessaultes was saying as she stirred cream and sugar into her cup, "and I thank *le bon Dieu* that my Valier has had no challenges nor made any in the past few months." Her eyes on her son were possessive and loving.

"*Maman,* Sartain was a poor swordsman and he should have thought twice before he impugned the bravery of de Bouille." He laughed dryly. "And you know well that I keep in practice, my dear."

"I know," she replied somberly, "but the Americans —they are bringing a new element to our dueling. They are not satisfied to draw blood. And their choice of weapons is their pistols. A pistol kills."

"Now, *maman,* I have met many of these Americans and they are most amiable. Do not borrow trouble." Then, with a quick smile at me, "Do you have the code duello in England, mademoiselle?"

"Our men are quick to defend their honor, regrettably," I replied, smiling at him from beneath my lashes, "but not, I believe, so often as you do here."

"True. There is scarcely a day when we do not have a duel. I have pinked several. I do not kill, unless the insult is intolerable." His face was brooding and there was menace in it.

"I have heard of your prowess on the field of honor, m'sieu," I murmured, fanning my flushed face. "Nine, I am told."

"Those are only the ones I have killed, but I have fought many duels."

The women about us were talking of fashions and bargains to be had in the shops and I was grateful that this handsome man was confining his conversation to me. "Where in England did you live, Mademoiselle Aurielle? I have been there—a very cold country."

"In London——"

Ondine cut in deftly, "My nieces are recovering from the grief over the loss of their parents, Valier. That is why I have kept them in seclusion for their mourning period. It is better you do not remind Aurielle of home and her loss."

"Ah, I apologize, Mademoiselle Aurielle. What a beautiful name!"

"My mother was French. My father was Lord George Stuart of London," I lied boldly. "He was killed in the wars with Napoleon and my mother died shortly after that."

"Ah, so sad. And you are so lovely, I knew there must be French blood in you. Permit me to say I have never seen anyone so beautiful as you." There was something in those glowing eyes that was unsettling as well as stirring.

"Thank you," I replied, lowering my lashes and sipping from the cup in my hand. I told myself uneasily that no one would recognize the waif from Barataria in the ele-

164

gant young lady who now sat beside Valier Dessaultes.

Madame Dessaultes was saying acrimoniously, "The war is going very badly for the Americans. Their government is in great disarray." She sighed, fanning herself vigorously. "I am glad we are so far removed from it here in New Orleans."

Valier looked at her, eyes twinkling, "Perhaps in the end, we can arrange for Louisiana to be French once more. That would please you?"

"Non, my son. Napoleon is more than I can swallow." She turned to Ondine and added, "I think it far more likely that we will become a British city eventually."

"Then I will go to war, *maman,"* Valier said lightly, smiling. "I do not propose to become a British appendage."

"Do not talk like that, Valier," she replied sharply. "We have no use for the Americans and you know that well, also."

"My dear, they are here to stay. You must accept it. We need not change *our* ways to theirs."

"Jamais! Never will I accept them," Madame Dessaultes said with a delicate shudder. Then, with a piercing glance at me from her anthracite eyes, "You are half English, mademoiselle. Where do your sympathies lie?"

"I am half French as well, madame," I replied softly, "but I must admit my sympathies lie with the Americans. It is a new country, bringing a new freedom for many who are—oppressed and burdened—yes, even persecuted."

"Humph. You are very young—"

"Come now, *maman,"* Valier said with his winning smile, "would you not rather be part of America, which is here, than attached to some country, even your beloved France, so many miles across the sea? Besides, you are much safer here than you would be in France today."

"I suppose so," she replied grudgingly and I thought of the wonderful opportunity that America was affording me and in my heart I silently blessed the beleaguered government on the eastern coast of the continent.

We talked on animatedly of the coming ball next month and those to whom Ondine would send invitations.

"I will have it in the main salon, of course," she said. "It will be very exclusive—I will not have it spill over into the sitting room and dining room. I have engaged the small orchestra of the mulatto musician, Tempe Toulet. You know how well they play, Claudette." She smiled at Madame Dessaultes. Her blue eyes were sparkling and I had never seen her look more lovely. It was as if some inner fire burned at the prospect of festivities.

"Ah, yes, Ondine. It will be the affair of the season," Madame Dessaultes nodded pleasedly.

Before the afternoon visit was over, Valier had asked Ondine if he might call again upon me and take me riding in his carriage. Ondine pursed her lips. "Her parents have been—gone but a year, Valier. Still, I know how impatient you young ones are. I suppose you may do so— but once. And Antoinette will accompany you as chaperone."

We parted with Valier's ardent assurances that in less than a week he would be returning and we would tour the city in his carriage.

As they were standing in the foyer, Madame Dessaultes looked at me closely once more. She tapped her chin with her fan. "You look very familiar to me, Mademoiselle Stuart—you and Mademoiselle Deveret both do," she said in French. "It is very odd for it is impossible that we have met before, coming so recently from Europe."

A cold chill settled along my spine and I said earnestly, "It is a family resemblance, I have no doubt. They tell us that we resemble our *tante*."

She spun her fan open and fanned herself briskly. "Of course. That is it," but I could tell from her eyes that she had not found me too much to her liking. Her son's obvious interest was a deterrent to friendliness toward me and I sensed that she had a much more suitable match for him in the back of her mind.

My determination hardened. Everything about Valier Dessaultes was endearing, his laughter, his twinkling black eyes, his white, flashing teeth, and his magnificent body. I could see he was not dominated by his mother's overwhelming personality. He was his own man and he exuded masculinity. If he chose me, and a thrill coursed through me at the thought, he would marry me and mother be damned.

After they had gone, we sat in the parlor talking of them. Ondine said thoughtfully, "Claudette will never remember seeing you at the Temple, my angels, so have no fear at her saying you looked familiar. I thought you handled that very well, Aurielle." Her sudden laughter was like the tinkle of the fountains in the courtyards. "It pleasures me so to fool her! She is such a stick—so stuffy with overweening pride." Then looking at me, "You will have a mother-in-law problem if you do catch the elusive Valier, my darling, and you might as well face it now. She is a domineering, interfering tyrant—but I can say that Valier is more than a match for her."

"I'll not have that problem with Quent," Roxanne said smugly.

I slanted a glance at her. Her chin was lifted and the green eyes were flashing with desire and hope. A sharp twinge of pity shook me and I looked away guiltily as I remembered the feel of Quentin Kincannon's firm, hard lips on mine and his deep voice when he said *Not you—and not Roxanne.* I murmured, "You will be lucky not to have a mother-in-law, Roxanne."

She looked at me with sudden suspicion as we moved languidly from our seats. "You sound overly friendly of a sudden, Aurielle. Why is that?"

"Nom de Dieu!" I said with my usual annoyance as we stepped into the cooling gloom of the foyer. "One cannot speak a civil word to you, Roxanne. It won't happen again, I assure you."

Her lips curled upward. "Now that sounds more like you."

"And you sound almost as if you like her." Ondine laughed as we mounted the staircase, our skirts rustling as they brushed against each oher.

"Sometimes, I *almost* do—but never quite," and she took the remaining steps quickly, leaving us as she went swiftly toward her room.

"I do not understand the animosity between you," Ondine said quietly.

"It began when first we met—aboard Kincannon's

ship. She is insanely jealous of the man. I cannot understand *that,* for she is a very beautiful girl and could likely marry anyone she chose."

Ondine smiled. "She is beautiful, but not so beautiful as you, *ma petite.*"

I turned astonished eyes to her. "I cannot believe that."

Ondine shrugged. "That is probably the paramount reason I agreed to sponsor you. You are the most beautiful young girl I ever saw."

I looked into the patrician face before me. The resemblance between us seemed more marked to me than ever. My lips were fuller, my slanting black brows tilted more at the ends, my nose much shorter, but the color of our hair, of our clear blue eyes, was the same. Suddenly I thought, *Ondine has extreme vanity—it is our faint resemblance that she calls the most beautiful she has ever seen.* Then guiltily, I told myself that she was kind, thoughtful, and so good to those about her that I did her a grave injustice. What, after all, was a little vanity? Did I not possess a little myself? Still, the thought stirred the old uneasiness that had gripped me on entering this house. Now she appeared remote, aloof, and unapproachable, and I was glad when I entered my room.

Antoinette was waiting to hear about my meeting with Valier Dessaultes. She seized my hands, her face alight. "Did he like you, my darling? Was he as handsome as you remembered? And his *maman,* did she like you? That is so important."

"Yes, he liked me—better than Roxanne, for he sat beside me and has asked to take me riding day after tomorrow." My heartbeat quickened, "He is so strong—so tall! Such a *man!* I should be safe in his arms!" I clasped my own about myself and whirled to the back windows where I looked down on the shining leaves of the orange trees.

Antoinette gave a deep sigh. "Ah, I am so happy. He cannot resist you with your lovely manners, your delicate speech, and all these magnificent clothes to set off your beauty."

"I shall be happy when you and I are in my own home. I—" I hesitated, for my apprehensions were with me still. "I have never felt at home in my life," I confessed suddenly.

"Ah, then you have felt it, too," she replied. "There is something strange about the Chaille servants —about that slant-eyed Sebastien. They do not talk much—they go nowhere. Indeed, I think madame will not let them go anywhere. Ulysses and I spoke briefly of it. He does not like Sebastien, but he is very cryptic about it."

"I wonder why?" I asked thoughtfully.

"He does not say, but I think perhaps he has known Sebastien before. Though I have never seen him do a cruel thing, I have the feeling that Sebastien is very cruel, for all that he worships madame." Antoinette's little pointed face was troubled. Then she shrugged. "It is something I cannot put my finger upon, *chérie*. *Le bon Dieu* knows we should be grateful to madame, for she has been gracious and kind—and extremely generous."

"That is true," I replied fervently. "I love her dearly and I owe her a debt I can never fully repay."

The next day went by slowly and I found occasion to look even more closely at the servants after my conversation with Antoinette. When I suddenly realized I had not seen Bess for several days, I went into the kitchen and questioned Catherine about her. "Where is my little Bessie these days, Catherine? I have not seen her for—it's five days now."

The mother averted her face. "She ain't been well, mademoiselle. I been keepin' her to our room upstairs." Her own eyes had deep blue shadows beneath them, giving them a bruised look. She wore a long-sleeved dress despite the late April heat and she twisted her hands nervously.

"I would like to go up to see her," I said.

"Oh no, mademoiselle!" she replied hastily. "I would not like for you to catch the summer fevers from her."

I knew everyone in New Orleans, and in the

state for that matter, dreaded the spring and summer for the plague of mosquitoes that came with them. Often Bronze John—the death of the black vomit—struck at that time as well. "Do you have a *baire* for her?" I asked, thinking of the gauzy tent I slept under these warm nights, preventing the insects from attacking me.

"I have made such a one fer her."

"It's not a little ailment that keeps a child in bed for a week. Madame should be told—"

Catherine's voice grew pleading. "Please say nothin' to madame—don't bother her with such. You shall see Bess soon, mademoiselle. I promise."

I went from the kitchen slowly. I had never been on the third floor where the servants had their rooms just under the attics. I thought of Bess and her fever as I went to my room, and my thoughts were singularly discomforting.

Chapter 9

I settled my skirts gracefully about me as I sat beside Valier in the open carriage. Jacques, the small nut-brown driver who sat the box, looked inquiringly at his employer, who spoke to him softly in French. Antoinette, under her plain parasol, sat just below and with her back to the driver, while Valier and I faced the front as the carriage moved away from the Chaille house.

"I will show you a New Orleans you have perhaps not yet seen, Mademoiselle Aurielle," Valier said in his charmingly accented English.

"That could be almost any of it," I replied, smiling up into his handsome, swarthy face, tilting my parasol so that its frothy circumference encircled us both rather intimately. "The houses of your city are of a curious architecture. We have nothing like it in England." Truth to tell, I did not know what we had in England outside of Portsmouth near the waterfront, except for the books Rodeur Cheviot and Ondine Chaille had provided.

"Like our architecture, we of New Orleans are

a blend of French and Spanish. My *grand-mere* was Spanish, but the Dessaultes have descended directly from the men under Bienville and Iberville and helped settle this city in 1718." He leaned near, his broad shoulder touching mine and sending a quick, tingling thrill along my spine. The subdued fragrance that seemed a part of him filled my nostrils, evoking sudden hot desire. "Observe," he continued, "yonder is the house of Flamente, who is my fencing master at his academy at Exchange Alley and Conti Street. It has the Spanish windows, all arched, but with French wrought-iron and fanlights over each and every door."

"*Your* fencing master," I said thoughtfully. "He must be a very excellent gentleman of the sword."

Valier laughed, showing his even teeth. "He is a free man of color—a *mulâtre,* if you please, admired and revered and a dandy of great note. He has a truly exquisite collection of cameos in his house, which is the meeting place for all the young aristocrats in town. Though he has probably trained more youths for duels than any other master in Louisiana, he cannot himself take part in any duel either as a principal or a second, for he is not, technically speaking, a gentleman at all."

"I believe that has its advantages. At least M'sieur Flamente will probably live to a ripe old age. I should like to meet him." I slanted an inviting glance at him from beneath my lashes. "You, on the other hand, M'sieu Dessaultes, are so daring—I fear for you."

His little half smile was casual. "Flamente tells me I am his equal—his gift to the dueling world of New Orleans." It was negligently said, but with an authenticity that was chilling. Then he spoke again to the thin Frenchman driving, telling him to take us out the road to Pointe St. Antoine. That name rang a bell in my mind. Suddenly it came to me. Pointe St. Antoine was the area where Quentin Kincannon was building his plantation house.

As the horses clopped lazily down the street that day in May, I listened to Valier's deep male voice, enchanted more by the sound of it and the scents of early summer than I was by the buildings he pointed out. "Privacy is a passion with my people," he was saying.

172

"Truly, it is the rear of our houses that face the street, though we decorate them for beauty—our real living is done in the courtyards at the rear. When you visit our house on Toulouse, you will see that it is much like your aunt's. We take our ease in the rear court-yard—conduct our business over a chilled glass of wine and with courteous and interesting conversation. The Americans are a brash, brusque race of men. They do not understand our way of doing business. I have some troublous times at the bank and at the warehouses in dealing with them. They rudely come directly to the business at hand and once transacted, they are gone. No time for the graces that make life worth living. They miss a great deal."

"I have seen the Kaintucks," I said, with a deli-cate shudder, "and I do not like them. Great burly men with hair sprouting from their heads, even out of their noses and ears!" I was thinking of the lout who had seized me at the levee.

"Ah," Valier said, "we are reaching the outskirts of town. I want to show you some of the sugar planta-tions out this way. Sugar will make us all millionaires, and soon, mademoiselle. And in the Pointe St. Antoine area there are many fine homes and rich cane fields."

I looked down the dark sandy road, the horses still leisurely gaited, and saw beautiful, towering pecan trees with vast stretches of cane, the tall, plumed stalks waving in a gentle river wind as far as the eye could see. We passed a white house, set back from the road a great distance. Valier informed me that it was the home of the Montreuilles, the first of the plantations. It did not look like the houses in New Orleans but was instead made of white-painted cypress with spacious galleries running about the upper and lower stories. Great white columns supported these porches and the overall appearance was very grand.

We passed one after another and Valier spoke the names of their owners, François Languille, Edmond Macarte, Philipe Rodriguez, Louis Chalmet. Each house seemed finer than the last.

Suddenly we heard the thunder of hooves ahead, around a slight bend in the road. Jacques drew back on his reins, slowing the matched pair of bays pulling the carriage. In moments the rider appeared around the curve and I recognized him at once. It was Kincannon, and Valier said, "Ah, it is the *Capitaine* Kincannon, our new and very wealthy resident."

I shot Antoinette a glance and saw her features tighten, but she did not turn around to look. As we drew nearer, each slowed and when we met, horseman and carriage halted. Valier said courteously, "Captain, this is a happy meeting."

I saw the dark eyes rake Antoinette and me, but there was not a flicker of recognition in them. "M'sieu Dessaultes, I am on my way to the city to transact some business with your bank—but you are here instead." His black eyes were on Valier now.

But Valier, punctilliously correct, began to introduce us. "Captain Kincannon, permit me to introduce Mademoiselle Aurielle Stuart and her chaperone, Madame Antoinette Desmottes."

Kincannon swept off his finely woven straw hat and made a deep bow. "Charmed indeed."

"I am showing Mademoiselle Stuart the Pointe St. Antoine plantations," Valier said.

Kincannon grinned. "You are perhaps aware I have installed a new sugar mill at my place farther up the river?" At Valier's nod, he continued. "Will you permit me to show you about the place? The house, as you know, is still under construction."

"Would you like that, mademoiselle?"

"Very much, M'sieu Dessaultes, but I fear it may take too long. I would not care to risk my aunt's displeasure by returning later than she has advised."

From the corner of my eye, I saw Kincannon's lip go down in a sardonic smile which he quickly hid. "Ah, I am sorry. I would enjoy showing you both the place." He eyed Valier contemplatively. "It will scarcely do me any good to go to your offices, since you are not there, m'sieu."

A look of annoyance crossed Valier Dessaultes's olive face. "I have planned this outing with the mademoiselle. My assistant will help you," he said curtly and I had the feeling he would be rid of our unexpected company.

"Forgive me, Monsieur Dessaultes," Kincannon said mockingly. "I forget the New Orleanaise never let business interfere with pleasure."

For a moment I was terrified, for Valier's eyes glittered as if he would strike the tall man in the saddle beside him and I knew that would inevitably lead to a confrontation on the so-called field of honor. Then the Creole aristocrat said merrily, "If you have learned that, *mon capitaine,* you are well on your way to becoming one of us."

"I consider that the greatest of compliments, sir," Kincannon replied without a trace of mockery. He bowed again, his dark hair gleaming in the sunlight. Then, replacing his rakish hat, he said, "I bid you all good day—Mademoiselle Stuart, Madame Desmottes, and Monsieur Dessaultes," and wheeling his big gelding, he was off down the road to the city.

"*Les Américains.*" Valier shrugged and continued in French, "One must make allowances for their lack of manners. That one is more offensive than most. He is a former pirate—or privateer as he would prefer to be called. He fancies he will be accepted by all the older families. A grave misconception on his part. Your refusal to accept his invitation was very well done, Mademoiselle Aurielle."

I bit my tongue on the words that boiled within. *But he is not an American! He is a Scot and probably of much finer blood than yours.* Antoinette's eyes were warning, so I smiled and said gaily, "Ah, M'sieu Dessaultes, you are a great gentleman. I do admire you so very much." I peeped at him from beneath my lashes to find him observing me with considerable warmth.

Indeed, his black eyes on mine were now so intense that involuntarily my own widened until I could feel the stiff, thick lashes pinned against my brows. I lowered them swiftly and murmured that it was growing quite warm. I was acutely aware of his hard-muscled thigh against mine. Opening my fan, I plied it enthusiastically while looking out over the broad alluvial plain as the carriage bumped along the narrow road. We reached an area heavily covered with the ever-present willows and great thick oaks.

Valier remarked, "It is here, back among the trees, that Captain Kincannon is having his new home built." Then in French, "We will turn in here, Jacques. I wish mademoiselle and her chaperone to see the construction underway."

Shortly we drew up before an impressive framework of cypress lumber and found the big layout aswarm with workmen, both black and white. As I observed the beehive of activity before us, I thought Quentin Kincannon's home would probably be more beautiful and elaborate, more magnificent than any of the homes we had seen. His pride would demand it.

Antoinette and I exchanged remarks of amazement at the number of workmen boiling over the framework before Jacques turned the horse back down the rutted lane that led from the construction. I looked beyond the trees at the cane that was already planted about this unfinished home. Kincannon would reap a full crop before the house was ever finished.

We did not go any farther down the Pointe St. Antoine road, but Valier told us that beyond Kincannon's Sugarhill lay Bienvenue, Denis LaRonde's plantation, beyond that lay Jacques Villere's and the last was Jumonville, owned by Charles Villiers.

"Gabriel Villere, the son of Jacques, told me he had the pleasure of meeting you and your *tante* and cousin on a Sunday walk in town," Valier smiled at me.

"Yes, I met him and M'sieu Eugene Poliet, who is associated with your bank, I believe," I replied.

"I was hoping you'd forgotten both those men." He laughed ruefully.

I joined in his laughter and the ride home was very pleasant. The sun was dropping lower in the sky, but its rays were still penetrating. We conversed lightly and I teased him about his reputation with the ladies. He gave as good as he took, lavishing compliments on me with an extravagance that took my breath away. There was no denying it. Valier Dessaultes was interested in me and I knew instinctively that with proper encouragement, I could change it from interest to love.

Later, in the city once more, Valier told Jacques

to slow down; then he asked, "Do you think we—and your chaperone"—he smiled at Antoinette—"might stop for a cup of St. Cyr's famous coffee before I return you to your aunt?"

"No, m'sieu. I told the captain a half truth. I am sure my aunt is expecting us by now. Do you not think so, Antoinette?"

"Oui, ma'amselle," she replied, and we exchanged glances quickly. I knew she was repressing a smile of satisfaction.

"And Ondine has said I may not see you again until your debut," Valier said dolefully. "And I have not showed you half I wished." He was silent for a moment as he sought my eyes. When our eyes met, he said slowly, "I would teach you to love—New Orleans as I do and you would become one of us." The words were heavy with meaning and it was not lost on me.

When we arrived at the Chaille house, Valier came in and spoke with Ondine, who looked lovely in a mauve silk frock. Roxanne did not appear. After chatting a moment, Valier smoothly suggested that he greatly desired to see me again before the ball.

Ondine's delicate brows drew together. "You are a dear boy, Valier, but I would beg you to wait until the ball before you see Aurielle again."

Valier sighed, his piercing black eyes again meeting mine. "I must confess, Ondine, I have never met a young lady with whom I have been so—taken. I look forward to the moment she can accept my invitations freely."

My heart beat fast and exultation swept me. With an intuitiveness that could not be denied, I knew I would marry this man and have beautiful babies. My life would be complete at last.

I went to my room after he left, and, in a dream, I let Antoinette undress me. She corroborated my feelings by saying, "That one is a true gentleman. He will make an ideal husband, little one. I see much happiness stretching before you." She spoke with such authority that I found myself sure of it, little dreaming of the violence and horror that lay before me.

The following morning, I sought Catherine to ask about Bess and found the child in the kitchen, hunched on a small stool beside the door to the rear courtyard. I stooped to her and was shocked by the sight of her pale face and great ringed eyes.

"Bessie!" I cried in distress. "You have been so ill! My aunt will want to call a physician to look at you—"

Catherine knelt beside me, stroking her daughter's thick hair, and said in a low voice, "She's quite well now, ma'am. She don't need a doctor. All I got to do is fatten her up again. No need to worry madame about it." At the fireplace, Selina was very still, and Pearl and Bonnie were openly listening.

"But she should *know* about this!" The servants' awe of and subservience to Ondine nettled me.

"I tol' her," Catherine said. "She seen her yesterday an' give me a tonic fer her."

"Well—I do hope you're dosing her with it regularly. Bessie looks as if she should be in bed right now."

"Oh, no, ma'am," the child murmured. "I feel much better down here. An' I got m'doll ter play with—see?" She pulled the little doll I had made from where it was hidden in her lap. It was easy to see she had taken great care of it, for it was good as new. Then unexpectedly, "Ye be so good, Miss Aurielle. I love ye."

"And I love you, Bessie," I said, hugging her impulsively. "When I have a little girl of my own, I hope she is just like you."

A faint smile crossed the pale, drawn features and I went to my room deeply troubled. It did not seem right to me that the servants never left the house, that they were a withdrawn lot. Even their fondness for me was timid, shown only when we were alone.

Only Sebastien and Ulysses came and went, buying groceries and supplies, doing errands for Ondine and us. There was always that masked hostility between the two powerful black men. They said little to each other, their faces impassive when they were together.

While both were free men, and I knew they were well paid, still I knew their devotions to Ondine and

Roxanne were such that could never be bought with gold.

The three weeks prior to our debut went swiftly and there were more sessions with the dressmakers during that time. Our wardrobes were extensive and exquisite. We went frequently now to the shops, where Ondine bought up dainty little slippers, fitted to our small feet, a series of fans and parasols, hats and gloves, all smuggled in from Paris by the blockaders.

"When you are launched," Ondine admonished, you will need many changes of apparel and all must be in the finest taste."

"I can hardly wait to wear them all! I shall cut such a swathe in society, Quent will not be able to resist me," Roxanne cried gleefully.

I wanted to hope she was right, but I kept remembering that unexpected kiss near the levee and more, that dark, warm June night in his arms. Kincannon's were the kisses of a man who was still seeking the pleasures of women. I was annoyed by the fact that I was beginning to feel a certain sympathy for the headstrong Roxanne.

The day at last came when Ondine went with Sebastien and arranged for the caterers to take care of food and service for the ball. "I haven't enough servants and they are so abysmally ignorant in these matters. I really must buy more and a better grade at the next slave auction—and when the redemptioners come in as well," she remarked as she left us.

Ondine was cultured, elegant, and admirable, and her casual treatment of servants sat poorly with me. I knew there were many more rooms in the third story of the Chaille house and Ondine could have as many servants as she liked. Still, I had too recently left the servant class myself not to be deeply sympathetic with these quiet people, black and white, who served Ondine.

By now, the suspicion that Ondine was closely related to me had taken on substance and meaning. I loved her and our faint resemblance was a source of great pride to me, yet it was laced with the old uneasiness. A hard kernel of decision was forming deep within me and I had touched only lightly on it in my mind. It was the thought of confronting Ondine, asking her outright about her years in Paris, leading up to the burning question—Did she give up a daughter to escape that city and its politics with her life? One day the opportunity would present itself and we would talk intimately. I swore it to myself.

The evening of May 29th, the Chaille house filled with the caterer's help. The air was electric with excitement in my and Roxanne's rooms. I thought fleetingly that I had seen none of Ondine's regular servants with the exception of Sebastien and knew a flash of pity for them. No doubt Ondine had told them to keep to their rooms during the affair. Little wonder they had no confidence in themselves and were such a subdued lot!

I dismissed the thought as Antoinette put the finishing touches on my coiffure. Tonight Valier would see me at my best! My gown was white silk gauze over satin, with tiny silk roses of white down the sides and satin ribbons that floated gracefully from the shoulders. Antoinette had washed my hair until it gleamed. She had piled it high on top, and the tendrils about my face, as well as the two little curls at the nape of my neck, were extremely provocative. By the time I had finished deftly applying Ondine's gifts of rouge, powder, and khol, I looked in the mirror with a touch of disbelief. Could that elegant patrician be Aurielle Stuart, a nameless waif of uncertain origins?

When Roxanne and I descended the stairs together, both of us clad in pristine white, the house was already full of carefully chosen guests. Ondine had told us beforehand that she never entertained any but the cream of society in her home—with the one exception, this time, of Quentin Kincannon.

The fragrant air was warm, warmer because of the many candles and lamps placed strategically about the large salon. We entered arm in arm and a sudden brief hush fell over the crowd of beautifully dressed guests. Then all at once we were swallowed up in introductions.

My head was spinning with names, and I smiled until my cheeks ached. The orchestra played softly from behind potted palms and great ferns with lacy green fronds cascading down.

The strange servants were moving smoothly about the room, carrying crystal and silver trays laden with small hors d'oeuvres, both hot and cold. Still others served tall frosted drinks and slender glasses of chilled champagne.

I had been awed to learn that Ondine secured ice, which had been floated down the Mississippi from lands far to the north where there were mountains that were never without ice and snow upon their slopes. There was even now in the dining room a bowl of punch with several large blocks of this precious cold commodity floating about in it.

The first two men who approached to greet me were the tall Creoles that I had met on the walk with Ondine that Sunday. Gabriel Villere was the handsomest, having a strong nose and a stubborn cleft chin. But Eugene Poliet was much more aristocratic, with thin, sharp features that bespoke his impeccable forebears. It developed that he was the brother of the girl, Lisette Poliet, who had clung so tenaciously to the arm of Valier that day long ago at the Temple. There was also another brother, Philip, who attached himself immediately to Roxanne.

Eugene Poliet took my hand, held it lingeringly after dropping a light kiss upon it. "I have thought of no one but you, mademoiselle, since we met last month," he murmured softly.

"Nor have I, mademoiselle," Gabriel Villere spoke up, his voice deeper and rougher than Eugene's. I recalled then, from my ride with Valier, that this man was the son of the Colonel Jacques Villere who owned the large sugar plantation out on Pointe St. Antoine.

They asked simultaneously for the first dance, but Eugene had a firm hold on my hand and I noticed with some distaste that his grip was slightly moist. "I must meet the other guests, messieurs—but if you would be so kind as to bring me a glass of punch, I would appreciate it. It is so warm—"

As the two men jostled each other toward the punch-bowl, I glimpsed three tall, dark men entering from the foyer. Roxanne swept up to me and whispered, "They're coming in at the same time—your Creole and my Scot." She paused, her voice dropping lower. "And as God is my witness, Rodeur Cheviot is with them—looking very fit for a dead man, I might add." Then she was gone, laughing up into the face of the dark, saturnine Colonel Pierre Denis LaRonde, fully fifteen years her senior and another wealthy planter from Pointe St. Antoine.

I was dumbfounded. Wheeling about, I stared across the room and glimpsed the dark head of the man who had been my friend and teacher. Ondine caught my hand as a wave of joy surged through me. She gripped me with a tightness that brought me to my senses.

She said low, "Aurielle, your face is giving you away!" Then clearly, "Come, *chérie*. I want you to meet our governor, William Claiborne." I followed her a few steps toward a gentleman of great presence; it lay not in his appearance, which was rather innocuous—pleasant, regular features, short hair somewhat disarrayed over a high forehead, and a slight double chin—but in his eyes and the way he carried himself, both of which bespoke his Virginia heritage.

I concentrated on the governor fiercely, keeping my eyes from that dark French face with the reckless blue eyes. I seemed to feel those eyes on me. How could I keep my joy at finding him alive from showing?

Ondine was saying, "Monsieur Claiborne has been our governor since 1803, *ma petite*. And he has governed wisely and well over his varied province. His wife is one of our own Creoles—but she was somewhat indisposed this evening and could not come."

I said concernedly, "Ah, Governor Claiborne, I am so sorry. You must extend her my best wishes for an early recovery." I glanced swiftly back at Cheviot, then away.

"Thank you," he replied solemnly, but there was a twinkle in his bright eyes. "You are quite as lovely as it was rumored, Mademoiselle Stuart. I congratulate Madame Chaille on having *two* such charming nieces."

"You are very kind, sir," I replied, inclining my head

in a half curtsey as Ondine had carefully instructed. But my heart was beating with happiness. Rodeur Cheviot was alive!

"Perhaps you will honor me with a dance?" The governor smiled, holding out his arm to me. Ondine, looking very pleased, motioned to the coffee-colored orchestra and they struck up a lively tune. We swung into the steps of the dance and I silently thanked Ondine for the hundredth time for her excellent tutors.

The dance was a mixture of the quadrille and a minuet and the governor was quite adept, swinging me lightly about as he briskly followed the music. I noted Gabriel Villere and Eugene Poliet at the edge of the dancers, holding glasses of punch and appearing annoyed.

We swung by Kincannon who was holding Roxanne's hands in the dance; her face was radiant. They nodded to us, and the governor, without missing a beat, remarked, "I would caution you and your cousin about that young man. He is not a gentleman for all his elegant appearance. He is an American who has invested in one of our fastest-growing businesses—sugar. I have heard he has bought a house in town as well, but he is a former Baratarian, a pirate if you please." There was a scowl on the governor's pleasant face. "Indeed, I cannot understand Madame Chaille inviting him. She must be unaware of his ugly background."

"How interesting," I replied blandly. I could certainly tell the governor how right he was and that Kincannon was no more American than Napoleon. But after all, Kincannon kept a much more damaging secret about me—and as I thought of it, my heart stepped up a beat. No, it would never do to reveal anything that Kincannon desired kept secret. Evidently he was passing himself off as an American even though his privateering was known. So I simply remarked, "He looks so well bred," and my voice was doubtful.

"Our district attorney, Mr. Grymes, handles his legal affairs. I have great respect for Grymes despite his association with the Baratarians," the governor replied. "But to speak of pleasanter things, tell me how you like our city."

I was able to chat enthusiastically until the music

ended. We stood a moment, still talking on about schooling, with the governor complimenting me on my soft voice and polished accent. I thanked him and, to my intense pleasure, Valier Dessaultes drew up beside us.

"Governor Claiborne, would you permit me to have the next dance with your lovely companion?" Valier's bow was deep and elegant. At Claiborne's assent, the music began again and Valier swept me away, murmuring huskily, "How I have waited for this moment!"

His tone was so warm and intimate I felt a flush of pure pleasure, at which he laughed wickedly. "You are such a delightful innocent, my dear," and his hand was firm over mine as we swung in rhythm with the music. I was virtuous only by the narrowest of margins, I thought, but not so innocent. But Valier should never know, I vowed silently.

Looking up, I saw Rodeur Cheviot swing by with Roxanne on his arm. He nodded imperceptibly at my unrestrained and joyous smile. I had to ride a tight rein on my happiness to keep from calling out to him. As the dance with Valier ended, Kincannon drew up on the pretext of introducing Cheviot.

"Miss Stuart," the captain said with a courtly bow, "may I present my friend and partner in business, Monsieur Cheviot?"

I extended my hand and Cheviot brought it to his lips with an inborn grace, his blue eyes twinkling into mine. "What a pleasure, ma'amselle," he said with his charming, reckless smile. Then to Valier, "It is good to see you again also, Monsieur Dessaultes."

Valier nodded courteously and Cheviot asked, "Would you grant me the honor of the next dance, Ma'-amselle Stuart?" The black, tilted brows lifted.

"Indeed," I said gladly, extending my hand once more as the music began. Valier appeared none too happy and I bent a melting smile on him. "We shall have another later, M'sieu Dessaultes. I shall look forward to it."

He bowed. "And I will be there to claim it, you may be sure." He turned away as I moved toward Cheviot.

It was then, over his shoulder, that I saw Sebastien approach Ondine and she made a little gesture of regret to the man before her and followed the powerful black from the room. Trouble with some of those imported servants, I thought swiftly, still missing the quiet people who ordinarily served us.

Turning to Cheviot, I whispered excitedly, "You cannot know how happy your presence has made me, Rodeur. Tell me quickly how you have been and where. We heard—you were killed last November!"

"I very nearly was, *chérie*. If it had not been for Louis Thibidault and his son, very clever and fine fishermen, I would indeed be dead."

I said low, "One of the men hid in the swamps when the rest of you were overpowered by the dragoons the night you left. He made his way back to Barataria and told us all that he left you dead at the bayou's edge."

"And I lay there in the welter of my own blood until dawn, when Thibidault and his son discovered me while on their way to fish. The two of them took me up, carried me in their pirogue to their little home back in the *chenières* where his good wife, Marie, nursed me until I was able to make my way to the captain's house here."

I looked up at him, tears hot in my eyes. "Thank God for your rescuers, Rodeur. Antoinette and I cried and cried for you."

"Ah, *ma petite*—and I worried greatly for you. The captain tells me that you and Toinette escaped with Roxanne and Ulysses. Roxanne told him as much."

"Yes, Antoinette shot Durket"—I shivered remembering—"when he tried to take me. We had to flee in the night. And you probably know Roxanne killed Belli for much the same reason. We met at the pirogue on the bayou."

"And now you are about to achieve your desires. Ah, Aurielle, you are every inch a lady. I am so proud of you!"

"I could never have done it without your aid, *mon cher,*" I replied with passionate sincerity.

"Shh. Not so loudly, Aurielle. That is a secret between us."

"A secret many know," I replied wryly. "Roxanne,

Ulysses, Ondine Chaille, Sebastien—you, Kincannon, and I."

"That is not so many, Aurielle," he replied cheerfully. "Surely all of us are trustworthy." Then smiling, "You and Roxanne have a great deal in common after all. Have you become friends?"

"Just civil enemies, Rodeur," I replied, joining in his laughter. "Are you really the captain's business partner now?"

"*Oui.* I put all my money into his importing firm. He has borrowed a great deal from the Dessaultes Bank, but then he has much collateral to borrow upon. I have moved into his house on Bourbon Street and I will help him manage his accounts—I am an old hand at that."

"He is lucky to have you! You must come to call on me. Oh, Antoinette is going to be so happy to learn you are alive!"

"Toinette has found a happy place as your maid, I hear."

"I owe her—so very much, and I shall repay her every cent and more," I said fervently, which brought to mind my wealthy suitor. I bubbled with sudden joy. "Oh, I am in love, Rodeur!"

"You are? Which of these men has caught your fancy?" he asked alertly.

"Valier Dessaultes."

His face fell and I felt my own heart lurch downward, obscurely frightened. "You do not approve?" I asked anxiously.

"You know of his—romance with Dolores Ysidro?"

"Oh, yes," I replied impatiently, relieved that it was no more than an old love affair.

"And that he called out and killed her four brothers and father after she was sent away to Savannah?"

Breath went out of me for a moment. "I knew about the father. But not that it was *four* brothers—" I rallied quickly, "They must have treated him intolerably!"

"Or Dessaultes is a vengeful, vindictive man," Rodeur whispered as the music came to a halt. We both saw Valier Dessaultes approaching purposefully and Rodeur murmured, "Dear Aurielle, I hope you will not be precipitous if he proposes. Give the man time to court you for a while—come to know him."

I brushed aside his cautioning and smiled invitingly at the advancing Valier. I loved Cheviot, but not as I loved Valier. When I went into his arms, I turned back, still smiling. "I hope to see you again very soon, M'sieu Cheviot."

"I thought you overly provocative with that new partner of Captain Kincannon," Valier said softly as we danced away.

"Are you jealous?" I asked artlessly.

He laughed. "I believe I am."

"You need not be. You are far more interesting, m'sieu," I replied as we swung about.

Suddenly I found my eyes seeking Ondine. She had been gone a very long time. The new servants must not be so competent as she had hoped. An unrepentant voice within me whispered, *I'm glad!* Perhaps she would let our own people serve the next party. They would enjoy seeing the festivities.

Valier and I continued to parry with words as I sought my benefactress without success. Two dances later, I was still looking for her, first from Gabriel Villiere's arms, then Eugene Poliet's. Kincannon then had the temerity to claim me for a dance and before I could summon up an excuse, he had whirled me out on the polished floor.

"Why are you so distracted, miss?" he asked with his customary impertinence.

But by now I was beginning to worry and I said without thought, "My aunt has been gone to the kitchen to see about the caterers for some time. I—"

"Yonder she comes, followed by her watchdog." His eyes narrowed and he added, "She looks very much like the cat who got the cream."

I glanced around and was startled by the beauty of her face. It was animated; color stained her flawless cheeks and her eyes were brilliant, her laughter quick and lovely. Indeed she was so radiant that the younger men crowded about, seeking her favors, her dances, her smiles.

"Why, she looks no older than Roxanne or I," I murmured.

"Quite true. Now what do you suppose has put her into such an exalted state?" His dark eyes gleamed and as they bent to mine, I drew a swift breath. He smiled slowly. "Your resemblance is only superficial, you know. Actually, you do not look at all like her."

I wanted dreadfully to slap him. I always wanted to slap him. He was the only man I knew who made my hand itch. "I *do* resemble her," I snapped. "I believe we are related."

He threw back his head and laughed loudly, causing others to look at us curiously. Then sobering, "Are you happy at last, Aurielle? Everyone fancies you great ladies, you and Roxanne. Yet you are peas from the same pod."

"Don't compare me with Roxanne," I replied irritably. "And you yourself are masquerading as an American. Even the governor thinks you an American, but he also knows you to be a former pirate and has no use for you."

"I *am* an American," he replied imperturbably. "I have made this country my home. As for the governor knowing me to be a former pirate, it is well known by everyone that I was a privateer and my wealth honorably acquired, according to the laws of the sea."

"That's a lie," I said heatedly. "You know you've sold slaves and that's against the law. And I'll wager you've taken many an *American* vessel in your piracy. Why, even the *Wind* was an American vessel and you took her."

"The *Wind* was a slaver out of Boston," he replied evenly. "I merely saved the American government the expense of taking her."

"And her cargo—you sold those people!"

"Not I. I took the ship for my trouble and Jean took the cargo." His mocking smile was full of cynicism. "Now I am even more respectably engaged as a merchant and landowner. I have never sold nor bought a slave."

"Then who will work that big sugar plantation of yours?" I asked triumphantly.

"Sugarhill? Anyone can work it for me who will accept the good wages I shall pay."

"They'll never accept *you* here in New Orleans," I said cruelly. "It was in the governor's voice. They think you're crude and vulgar as the Kaintucks."

"Perhaps you are right." His twinkling black eyes were unrepentant. "I haven't given my heart to New Orleans. Only to America. It's a big country."

I made a little face of disbelief, then said, "No matter. If you will keep my secrets, I shall keep yours."

"We are agreed," he said, his eyes crinkling at the corners. I noticed again the pervasive clean fragrance about him, like sunshine and fresh air. All the Creoles, even the men, wore perfume, some cloying and some overpowering, but Kincannon smelled of the out-of-doors. Only Valier had a *subdued* fragrance about him. I had found it quite delightful after Eugene Poliet's musky sweetness, and yet there was something about the scent of Kincannon that stirred me. I put it down to my love of cleanliness.

We suddenly faced Roxanne in the dance and from the arms of Pierre Denis LaRonde she sent Kincannon a sultry smile. He returned it and as we passed he said, "The next one is mine, Mademoiselle Deveret," and her face was suddenly ablaze with love and excitement.

It was at that moment I turned to see Ondine and Ulysses again leave the room. I was annoyed that the caterers would need so much supervision now. It seemed especially inexcusable in view of the fact that she was having such a wonderful time otherwise.

I noted the older men and women were cool to Kincannon, but their daughters looked at him with surreptitious longing. I was right—the old ones had no use for him, but the young ones could well defy their parents. And to give the devil his due, Kincannon was certainly a handsome man.

I floated from one pair of arms to another, and in the course of the next hour, I met Mr. Edward Livingston, that tall and impeccable Princeton gentleman who had practiced law in New York and was now practicing it for Jean Lafitte. After that, I met his good friend and the district attorney, John Grymes, who was also advising the Lafittes.

However, most of my dances were taken by Eugene Poliet, Gabriel Villere, and Valier Dessaultes. I did meet many others, among them the Montreuilles, the François Languilles, Edmond Macarte and his charming wife and their two pretty nieces, Belise and Marthe Macarte, the slightly stooped and distinguished Louis Chalmet, Philipe Rodriguez and his small dark wife, Luisa. All of these people were great planters from Pointe St. Antoine.

Another vivid personality was the dashing, though older, Colonel Pierre Denis LaRonde, who was completely captivated by Roxanne as she coquetted outrageously with him. There was one woman, a widow whose overbearing presence impressed me. She was Madame Emilie Broussard and, from the deference she was accorded, I knew she must be an arbiter of society. But I did not like her opinionated and flat remarks.

In less than an hour, I noted that Ondine had returned once more to the room, her exquisite face still aglow. I realized with sudden insight that parties were meat and drink to her. She sparkled and dazzled as she played the warm and charming hostess.

Toward one in the morning, the evening drew at last to a close. Guests began leaving reluctantly, two by two or in groups of three and four, each exclaiming that the ball had been magnificent and their pleasure unrestrained. They passed into the small front courtyard and out the gate to Chartres Street. Some had come by carriage and some on horseback. A few, from houses not too far distant, had walked in the warm night air.

Ondine stood in the foyer, flanked by Roxanne and me, making gracious good-byes. Ulysses and Sebastien, in their good black suits, were dark shadows behind us. Already we had received four invitations to afternoon coffees and two for galas in the evening.

Valier was last to leave. He waved his mother to the door. *"Maman,* I will join you in the carriage in a moment. I have a request to make of Mademoiselle Stuart."* His mother paused in the doorway, her black eyes glinting.

"I will wait inside here for you, Val——"

"No, Mother. You will please wait outside. I will not be long."

With a whirl of her skirts, Claudette Dessaultes flung herself out the door so hastily she stumbled, and Ulysses, who had moved forward, took her arm courteously.

I turned starry eyes to Valier. How he had set his mother back! Perhaps I would not have so much of a mother-in-law problem after all. Valier took my hand and brought it to his lips, ignoring the eyes of Roxanne and Ondine.

"Mademoiselle Aurielle, will you permit me to escort you to these coffees in the homes of our mutual friends and to the galas later?"

"I would be delighted, but I have promised Eugene Poliet that I will go with him to the Macarte coffee and with Gabriel Villere to the Languilles." I was glad I had thought to refuse their pleas to attend the galas with them.

Valier was frowning slightly. "But the other affairs —you will attend them with me?"

"Indeed," I replied, concealing my shining happiness under a faint smile, aware of Roxanne's cynical glance.

"And Madame Chaille—Ondine—you will permit me to call on Mademoiselle Stuart tomorrow afternoon?" His bow to Ondine was graceful and easy.

"I shall be happy to welcome you," she responded, smiling brilliantly.

After a few brief pleasantries he was gone and I turned to my companions excitedly. "Ah, is he not the most handsome man—and he likes me!"

Roxanne tossed her copper curls. "I know Quent would have asked me to all those affairs had he been invited."

Ondine shrugged. *"Chérie,* I cannot guarantee his social acceptance. Why not accept the invitations of Pierre LaRonde? He is immensely wealthy and so taken by you." Her affection for Roxanne was of long standing, and Ondine could not endure to see her disappointed. "Sebastien, you will remain to see the caterers out of the house and that all lamps and candles are extinguished."

Ulysses took up two candles from a nearby table, one in each strong brown hand, and lighted our way up the stairs. At each bedroom, he paused to light fresh candles for us, lingering in Roxanne's room where we could hear her light voice instructing him about some purchases for her at the shops the next day.

Later, as I began slowly to disrobe, Antoinette entered, carrying a candle. Her face was unusually pale in the flickering light and I asked with a touch of alarm, "Toinette, you are—all right?"

"*Certainement, chérie.* I have come to help you to bed and to hear of your triumph."

"But you are so pale—"

"It is nothing, little one. Only I have been uneasy in my room. I heard strange noises—but it amounts to nothing. I am given to great imaginings. Tell me, did the young Dessaultes ask to see you again?"

"Indeed he did! Except for a coffee with M'sieu Poliet and one with M'sieu Villere, I am going to all the coming social functions with Valier," and I launched into a detailed account of the evening.

When Toinette left, she snuffed my candle and took her own. I could see light lengthening and fading in the dark hall. Then the pale reflection from a full moon filtered in the long windows, which looked misty through the gauze folds of the *baire* that covered me.

I moved restlessly about, remembering Ondine's loving eyes when she looked at Roxanne. With stunning suddenness, I realized that I was jealous of her affection for the girl. After all, if she were *my mother,* I should come first! I sat up, flinging the *baire* aside, and put my feet over the side of the bed. Without waiting to reach the steps, I slid the full length to the floor; the hand-hooked rug was soft against my bare feet.

I stepped lightly to my door and into the hall. Just what I would say to Ondine when I reached her was unclear. I knew only that I must talk with her, learn what I could of her past, which was never mentioned.

As I reached her door, it opened before me and I stared up into the strange, eliptical eyes of Sebastien. He was fully clothed and held a candle in one dark hand; it did not waver as we stood looking at each other.

Then he bowed slightly, "You wish to see madame?"

"I—" I swallowed. "I wanted to—"

"Who is it?" Ondine called and I peered around Sebastien's huge bulk to see her in a floating chiffon peignoir, seated at her dressing table.

"It is Mademoiselle Aurielle, madame," he said and, without another word, made his way toward the stairs at the far end that wound up to the servants' quarters on the third floor. I watched him go, his rolling walk reminding me of the sailors I had seen aboard the *Wind.* Suddenly, I shivered uncontrollably. When he had disappeared up into the blackness, I turned to find Ondine had risen from her dressing table and was coming toward me.

Reaching out, she caught my hands in hers. "Why, my angel, your hands are cold as ice!"

"I—it is nothing. Nerves and excitement, I guess."

"What did you want, darling?" Her velvety voice was rich with affection.

"I—just wanted to thank you again. I cannot believe my good fortune yet."

"Ah, yes," she replied indulgently, pulling me into her perfumed room. "The young Dessaultes is very taken with you. But then we knew that, did we not?"

I was trying desperately to pull my thoughts together. Sebastien had been menacing in aspect, malevolent toward me. I knew it. I *knew*. And through it all, an incredible thought pushed to the surface. *Was Sebastien Ondine's lover?* They were so close, sometimes even seeming to anticipate each other's thoughts.

"I owe you so much," I murmured.

She looked at me keenly, *"Ma chérie,* you seem distressed. How can that be, when your evening has been such a triumph? I do believe the elusive Valier could be thinking of a lasting and legal commitment already. You have only to play your cards in the proper sequence."

"I know. I mean I feel sure you are right." Gone were my tentatively thought-out questions. Instead, there seemed to be lingering in this exquisite bedchamber a faint miasma and the delicate perfumes only compounded it. Suddenly I wanted to run, but I stood fast, both repelled by and irresistibly drawn to Ondine. I murmured, "Well

—I seem to have made a botch of my thanks, madame—Tante Ondine. I should not have disturbed you. It was only that I felt—" What did I feel? I felt more strongly than ever that she was my mother, yet I wanted to flee the thought at this moment.

She put her arms about me impulsively and drew me to her. Her perfume was like flowers in the air about us, ever more persuasive in her arms. "I know what you feel, Aurielle," she said warmly. "And you are a dear little girl." She laughed gaily and pointed to the mirror at the dressing table where we were reflected. "Look, Aurielle—" and I looked to see her glowing face next to mine, our hair tumbling about our shoulders in gleaming profusion, the blue eyes wide and clear, our white garments about us like a mist. "Do we not look alike?" She hugged me again, laughing harder. "Ah, I shall enjoy your triumph doubly for it."

"There *is* a resemblance. Do you think we might be —some distant relation to each other?"

She was instantly sober. "Who knows? *C'est possible.*"

I pulled from her embrace and looked searchingly into her eyes. "Did you—did you leave relatives in France? Or perhaps England?"

"No," she replied too swiftly. "No one."

I felt she was lying. It was in her voice, in the suddenly veiled eyes, and my heart, instead of leaping, sank slowly to a dull beat beneath my breast. "Ah, well, I am grateful for our resemblance, however little and however accidental it may be," I said, with an attempt at brightness. "I will leave you to sleep, Tante Ondine. We have had a most exciting evening." I moved toward the door.

She followed and put her soft hands gently on my cheeks, bending my head so she could brush my forehead lightly with tender pink lips. The exaltation I had observed earlier in the evening was still on her, as if she knew some secret source of power—even ecstasy. "Sleep late, darling," she said gently. "Skip breakfast, if you like. You will have callers tomorrow and you want to look your most beautiful."

194

The days spun by, halcyon and beautiful golden threads linking my life closer to that of Valier Dessaultes's. June became July and the heat was oppressive and moist, but I was unaware of it, for my relationship with Valier was deepening with each meeting.

He took me to places the *haut monde* frequented and I saw the spangled, glittering life of the elite of New Orleans. He introduced me to the opera and I drowned in the beauty of Mozart's *Così Fan Tutte* and *Don Giovanni*. Each week we saw a new production at the magnificent Theatre d'Orleans, which had very recently been opened by a Santo Domingo entrepreneur, John Davis, who had also built alongside it the even more ornate Salle d'Orleans, which had gaming rooms on the ground floor and a ballroom one flight up that was said to have the best dance floor in the United States.

Gabriel Villere and Eugene Poliet escorted me occasionally, but my heart was so taken by Valier that their desire for me turned to frustration and they finally took Roxanne out instead. But that fickle jade, still yearning after Kincannon, preferred her older suitors, Pierre Denis LaRonde foremost among them. She came home often from an evening out, wearing some new diamond bangle given to her by the doting LaRonde, which I felt sure was one reason she preferred the older man.

I saw Quentin Kincannon each time Valier took me to the Salle d'Orleans, that fabulous gambling house and ballroom, finished with hardwoods and hung with crystal chandeliers. I saw him mostly in the gambling rooms downstairs, where every form of card game from poker to *vingt-et-un* was in full sway. Except for Cheviot and the men with whom he did business, he was always alone, sitting at the tables, his black hair tumbled carelessly over his forehead as he squinted at his cards through the smoke of his small cheroot. Rodeur always flashed his lighthearted smile at me as Valier and I passed by.

Sometimes Kincannon would come up to the ballroom, and Roxanne would always leave her current escort to talk with him; occasionally he would dance with her. I tried not to look at him at all. Most of the time I was successful.

Looking back now, I can see I had encased myself in a kind of golden bubble which formed a transparent wall between me and the life that was going on about me. The constant callers at Ondine's now were dreamlike, for I saw them all through the eyes of romance.

I remember one hot, dark evening, Jean Lafitte called, bringing Ondine a jeweled Spanish medallion and Roxanne some diamond ear studs as a token of his esteem. He brought a length of sky-blue watered silk for me. He, Ondine, and Roxanne laughed like three children together, while I sipped at my tea and smiled sympathetically. I knew the medallion and studs were meant to grace the slender throat and delicate ears of a Spanish noblewoman, but I could not help thinking how much more effective they were against Ondine's and Roxanne's satin flesh.

Claudette Dessaultes was a frequent visitor, for she was fond of Ondine, though there was a good difference in their ages. She knew her son was seeing more and more of me, and, while she did not like me, I knew she was striving to hide her hostility before the woman who claimed me as niece.

Despite her many escorts, Roxanne was restless and unhappy, for, in the weeks since Ondine's ball for us, only Quentin Kincannon had not paid a call. We knew he had made no more efforts to host a soirée at his lovely house on Bourbon, where he and Cheviot resided, attended by a few paid servants.

Ulysses and Sebastien brought the news from the marketplace that the mothers and fathers of most of the eligible girls in town were annoyed because their daughters were so enamored of the man. The refusal of the aristocrats to accept him and his aura of lawlessness only added to his glamour and unattainability.

Then one hot July day, a small black boy came to the house and presented a note to Ondine. Roxanne and I were always attentive when the bell sounded because it usually heralded guests or invitations. At Ondine's frown, we moved to her side and looked at the note questioningly.

"It is from Captain Kincannon. He asks permission to call upon us tomorrow afternoon." She looked somberly at Roxanne, who seized the note and examined the bold black script. "Will we receive him, Roxanne?"

"Oh, yes, yes! *Tante,* he is coming to call on me at last. I knew he would!"

Ondine sat down at her desk and penned a restrained note in response, giving it to the youngster who waited patiently. "Roxanne, you know I do not approve of the captain. Pierre LaRonde can give you everything a woman could want."

"Everything but love—*my* kind of love," Roxanne replied flatly.

I retired to my room for a nap after lunch, but sleep would not come as I thought of Roxanne's obsessive love for Kincannon and his indifference to her. The memory of the night in Cheviot's cabin lay like a burning brand in my brain. How could I think of the man so often when I *loved* Valier, I thought angrily. I wished with a strange sort of desperation that he would marry Roxanne. Perhaps then I would be rid of them both.

197

The next day, Ondine marshaled us into the salon; we were each in summer frocks of silk, Roxanne in pale green, I in pale yellow. "Monsieur Kincannon is, ostensibly, calling on all three of us and we shall make him welcome for Roxanne's sake. Then"—Ondine paused delicately—"when the opportunity presents itself, Aurielle and I will ask to be excused and you two may have some privacy together, Roxanne."

Unfortunately for Roxanne, Kincannon was ushered in by Sebastien in the company of Rodeur Cheviot. Her face fell, but I was overjoyed. Only Ondine's hand on my arm restrained me from flinging myself into his arms. As it was, I cried, "Oh, Rodeur, you look wonderfully fit!" And he did, tanned from hours in the sun, probably at the site of Kincannon's new house out on Pointe St. Antoine. Only a litle scar, a memento of the fight that had almost killed him, gleamed white where it ran into the thick black hair beside his ear.

He took my hand and kissed it with courtly grace. "Mademoiselle, I can return the compliment. You are very beautiful," he said in his impeccable French.

But I continued to tell him how much I had missed him until Ondine stopped me with a gentle pressure on my shoulder. Then she said to Rodeur, "M'sieu, we are so glad to see *both* of you."

Chastened, I fell silent. I noted then that Kincannon carried an enormous box and as we entered the sitting room, he placed it on the low, marble table before one of the sofas. "It is for you, Madame Chaille—a gift by way of an English ship and Lafitte—with my deep thanks for admitting me to your home."

Ondine nodded coolly as we took seats. I sat on a sofa beside Rodeur, still smiling into his handsome face. Roxanne took a chair as near to Kincannon's as she could arrange and immediately engaged him in conversation while Ondine tore white paper away from the box and reached into its depths.

A breathy *Ohh* went up from us as she slowly lifted a sterling punchbowl with an intricate design of grapes and leaves about the lip and base. She set it down and pulled forth the ladle, which was solidly entwined with tiny, perfect bunches of grapes and leaves.

"Captain Kincannon, it is quite the loveliest gift I have ever received," Ondine said sincerely.

"'Tis only a small token in gratitude for your kindness to—all outsiders." His teeth flashed whitely in his bronzed face, but his black eyes flicked Roxanne and me with a touch of irony.

Ondine was aware of his double entendre, for her smile was cool as she murmured, "I shall ring for coffee, messieurs," and she took up the small silver bell beside her. Sebastien appeared at once and she said, "Coffee—and some of Selina's little tea cakes, please, Sebastien. Now, Captain," she said politely, "tell us how your magnificent new home at Pointe St. Antoine is progressing."

The black brows lifted and Kincannon drawled, "Indeed, madame, it is at a standstill. The British blockade is drawing tighter and the marble for the mantels, ordered from Italy months ago, has not arrived."

"Ah, that is dreadful. I had thought you would be in it by fall."

"Nay. I have closed down work on it. As a matter of fact, the warehouses in town are stacked high with barrels of sugar and my planter friends tell me they are making work for their slaves—cleaning canals, clearing land for planting and so forth. The blockade may yet bring us to our knees."

"*Alors,* Napoleon is keeping them too busy to invade New Orleans," Rodeur said with a kind of cynical cheer. "I hear he has reached Breslau."

"Quent," Roxanne said with sudden intensity, "please have another ball at your home on Bourbon. I know the ladies would come. *I know it!* For Ondine and I will send out the invitations for you."

Ondine gave her an inscrutable glance and Quentin Kincannon said dryly, "I do not think Madame Chaille would like to do that."

"Oh, please, Tante Ondine," Roxanne begged. "It has been so long that Quent has been in town and he is such a good citizen. Surely now they will begin to accept him."

Kincannon's eyes were veiled. "I do not know, Roxanne, if I wish to be accepted now. I have grown accustomed to my way of life here."

"Just try it—once more," Roxanne pleaded.

"I find I am no longer interested in whether the ladies accept me." Kincannon's smile was pure cynicism.

Roxanne's pretty face was a study in frustration and Ondine was expressionless. Then she said, "I think you are wise to wait a little longer, Captain." Her smile was wintry as she added, "I had thought you might have a ball at your new plantation home when it is finished."

He said with sudden coldness, "You know well, madame, it would be unattended but for my business associates. I am happy in my house on Bourbon. And my good friend, Monsieur Cheviot, is increasing my household staff even now."

Cheviot smiled. "Quent has scruples about owning slaves, ladies, which makes my task more difficult. I'm progressing, albeit somewhat slowly."

I rose abruptly and said, "I hope you will forgive me, but I am attending the opera this evening and I must make preparations for it."

Kincannon looked at me appraisingly. "Rumors are thick about you, mademoiselle—that you will soon be making an announcement."

I shrugged with elaborate nonchalance. "I was unaware of that."

His laugh was mocking. "No, you weren't. You know only too well that Dessaultes is very serious about you."

Ondine's tinkling laughter sounded. "Yes, he is and I feel sure I will be having another ball soon to celebrate."

I felt my cheeks burning. Quentin Kincannon still had the power to render me speechless with anger. How dare he bring up rumors? And his tone had been jeering, implying all sorts of things, mainly that he remembered the night we fought together in the darkness, that he knew my background and held me in a sort of contempt.

I lifted my chin, fanning myself rapidly. "I cannot

know your rumors, Captain, but, despite what my aunt says, I am not promised to anyone yet."

He and Cheviot had risen as I did and now Kincannon bowed to me, saying, "Love is the most beautiful of all emotions. I wish you much of it, in any case."

I left the room swiftly. Now if Ondine would make an excuse, Roxanne would be left alone with the two men, which, if not the ideal situation, was at least better than having two extra women about.

On the stairs, I encountered Bess Bonham, pale as usual with blue smudges beneath big dark eyes. She had her doll in her arms. I stooped and caught the child to me. "Ah, pretty little Bessie! I have saved more scraps and I have time now to make your doll another dress. Come with me and we will sew togther." I had more than enough time to prepare for my evening at the opera with Valier.

Bess was stiff in my arms at first, then as if a dam had broken, her little form flowed against me and she put her arms about my neck, murmuring, "I love ye, Ma'amselle Aurielle. Ye be so kind ter me," and we went hand in hand down the hall.

In my room, with happy chatter on my part, we cut out the cloth and I began to sew. I realized suddenly that Bess was very quiet, her little face pinched and drawn with hidden pain. I put down the needle and thread and said, "Bessie, are you growing ill again?"

"No, no, ma'am," she said hastily, fearfully, and the uneasiness with which I was so familiar swept me.

"What is the matter, dear? Can't you tell me?"

"I can't tell you nothin', ma'am. Sebastien—he would —he would—" She faltered and stopped.

"He would what?" I asked tensely, my fear growing.

"He would—nigh onto kill me." It was said with such simple sincerity it was irrefutable. "Don't ask me no more questions, Ma'amselle Aurielle. It'll only make it—worse."

I caught the child's warm little body to me, stunned. I had sensed evil in Sebastien and now I suspected he had been abusing this child. The thought was so repug-

201

nant I rejected it for a moment. I said low, "Madame must be told of this."

"Oh, no!" she broke in frantically. "Madame thinks Sebastien—is good. Oh, you mustn't say nothin' to madame!" Bess's whole appearance was one of wild agitation, and, holding her firmly, I murmured soothing words to her—anything to ease the terrible trembling in the small, thin body.

I sat her back down on the broad sofa beside me, talking now of the opera and how I loved the beautiful music, how excited I was over the prospect of this evening. With quick fingers I finished the small dress, continuing to talk in a low, gentle voice.

When at last we put the dress on the doll, I said, "Bessie, you must help me decide which of all my fine dresses I shall wear with M'sieu Dessaultes this evening."

The child had quieted under my soothing talk and after I showed her four or five dresses, she decided on an apricot gown with creamy lace inserts about the low-cut neck and in the short, puffed sleeves. The whole thing was a confection of gauze over thin silk.

Ondine came into the room as we were admiring it. "Ah, Aurielle, you are spoiling Bessie again, I see." Her gentian glance touched the little girl kindly and, without a word, the child took the doll and its clothes, curtsied stiffly, and departed.

"We chose this one for the opera tonight," I said, looking at this beautiful woman I had come to love so deeply. Yet I was forced to conclude that all of the servants were in deadly terror of her trusted and beloved Sebastien and it was a cloud over what should be complete happiness for me.

"That color is most becoming to you, *chérie*," Ondine said, touching the misty folds of the skirt. "You will be quite irresistible to Valier in that. I wouldn't be surprised if he proposed to you tonight—whirlwind courtship that it has been."

"Perhaps," I said thoughtfully, then added boldly, "Tante Ondine, does it not seem that the servants are uncommonly afraid of Sebastien?"

"Has Bessie been carrying tales about Sebastien?" she asked, smiling.

"No," I replied readily. "It is just a feeling I have that—"

"They have rather had their noses out of joint since the night of your debut, I must admit. They hate being usurped by the caterers, and if they were just a bit more polished, I would let them help," she said regretfully.

"But Sebastien—"

"Ah, my darling, Sebastien is the one who reprimands them. He must mete out any punishment for me. My heart is much too tender to punish them for their infractions. They hold it against him, I suppose." Her voice was sad. Then brightening, "Shall I send Pearl and Tressa up with hot water for your bath now, *mon ange?*"

"Yes," I replied slowly. "And I will need Toinette to help with my coiffure."

Ondine had not allayed my fears that Sebastien was cruel, more cruel than she knew.

I shall always remember that sweet, hot night of July sixth, for it was the night I was sure all my dreams had come true. I was like a greedy child at the opera, the vast array of musicians in the orchestra pit feeding a newly discovered hunger in my soul. I think I must have been a little drunk on the heart-stopping music, for when Valier and I reached the open carriage, I cried, "I don't want to go home! I may never go home again. I feel as though I were soaring like a—like a seagull in the wind!"

Valier laughed. "You liked our opera then?" He sounded amused and pleased by my childlike infatuation with the art.

"I loved it! I can hardly wait for the next one. When will it be shown?"

"This one will run for two weeks. By then, John Davis's company should have another one ready. I feared you might be bored, having seen better opera in England."

"I—led a very cloistered life. Seeing an opera performed is much different from practicing music with a tutor." I forced a laugh, hoping I had not revealed a glimpse of my low background.

203

He did not question me. "That is true." The carriage lamps shone on his dark face and gleaming eyes as he took my hand, enclosing it warmly in his own narrow steely one. A pulse within me leaped hotly to meet the current of feeling that was in his touch.

Leaning toward him involuntarily, I murmured, "Ah, Valier, you are so wonderful—"

Swiftly he took me into his arms and his lips came down on mine in a long, tender kiss. It was gentle at first, but as our mouths clung, it grew more heated, more intense, and I felt my trembling lips part under his as his hands slipped down my body and into the folds of cloth about my hips.

Fearing the onslaught of my own sensations, I began to withdraw and, for an instant, I thought Valier beyond restraint. My struggles increased and as they did, he loosened his hold on me, a muffled sigh escaping.

I leaned back against the carriage cushions and looked up into the starred vault above us, my joy evaporating like smoke. I had evoked passion but not love in the breast of the man beside me, I thought bitterly.

Then abruptly and with no preliminary, he said, "Aurielle, will you marry me?"

Though Ondine had told me it was surely coming and I had dreamed many times of the question, I was totally unprepared for it.

His voice was gentle. "You must surely have seen my hope in my eyes, Aurielle. You are the most beautiful woman I have ever seen—and no doubt the busy tongues of New Orleans have told you of my lost love, Dolores Ysidro. Believe me, that is over. Your beauty has wiped her from my mind."

"Oh, Valier," I cried, galvanized into action, "I do love you!" and I flung myself into his arms once more.

We kissed and clung a moment until he put me from him with a little laugh. "You haven't answered my question, Aurielle."

"Yes, yes," I whispered, winding my arms about the broad shoulders again, putting my head down on his chest where the solid thump of his heart could be heard, a slow drumbeat of security and happiness.

He held me in his arms all the way down Chartres Street and we kissed again with increasing passion before he saw me to the Chaille door.

Shortly after the announcement of our coming nuptials in September, there was an outbreak of Bronze John, the yellow fever which turned its victims an almost saffron color. Many people fell in the streets and had to be carried to their homes, where some rallied, but many died, vomiting the terrible black liquid that arose from their illness. Hosts of citizens fled the city to country homes of friends, but Ondine was almost casual about it.

"I have discovered that if we use the *baires,* it filters out the illness of Bronze John as well as various insects. I believe the disease is in the night air. Besides, we have far too many things to do to ready Aurielle for her marriage. It will be the social event of the year and we haven't time to run off to the country."

Roxanne, who had been uneasy about the yellow fever, *fièvre jaune* as she called it, responded, "It would be a sad wedding if the bride fell ill."

Ondine ignored her gloomy remark and said lightly, "I have even bought *baires* for all the servants. I'm sure we will all stay well." I knew fresh love and devotion for her. *She had given the servants* baires! She continued happily, "I shall have the wedding ball in the main salon and we shall celebrate all night—having breakfast at dawn!"

Despite my joyous heart, I slept restlessly these summer nights, for it was very hot and humid with frequent warm rains that kept water standing in the roads and ditches. Once I felt smothered by the *baire* and threw it off, to sleep spread-eagled, with the timid breeze touching me softly, until the plague of mosquitoes made it impossible and I had to creep back under the *baire.* Ondine was adamant about the *baires.* She said they not only kept the mosquitoes from us but kept out the unhealthy effluvia that filled the summer nights.

Two days later, Valier took me to dinner. I felt vaguely indisposed—nothing I could put my finger on, just a general feeling of fatigue which I charged up to excitement over the wedding next month. Due to the yellow fever scare, many of the entertainments, including the opera, had shut down. The restaurant, Café des Roses, was nearly empty and the waiters were uneasy and low-voiced. Valier, who had had the fever as a child and recovered, said that more and more of the citizens were leaving the city to stay with friends in the country. New ones were falling victim every day.

As we departed the café and were walking to the carriage that waited at the curb, an astonishing thing happened. My knees buckled and I sank to the ground. My head and neck were aching, but not enough to cause such weakness.

"My darling!" Valier cried, as he picked me up in his arms. "Are you ill?"

I was puzzled. "My head aches, but not nearly enough for such weakness," I responded as he carried me to the carriage and deposited me gently on the seat. Valier bade Jacques drive swiftly homeward and we rattled down the street at a fast clip.

He insisted on carrying me to my room, where the concerned Antoinette and Ondine helped me disrobe after he had left. I was beginning to feel worse and worse, with sharp pains in my head, neck, and now in my abdomen. I did not sleep well and woke with a raging thirst, which kept Antoinette bringing pitchers full of water to my room where I lay miserably in the middle of the bed. It was the first time I had been ill since I was a child and my impatience added to my misery. The malaise seemed to affect my eyes and nose, and my wild craving for water could not be slaked.

By the second day, I was alternating between chills and rising fever, and my thirst was unquenchable.

Roxanne came into my room and looked at my face. "You have *la fièvre jaune*, Aurielle—I warned Ondine that we should leave! Already you are turning yellow!" She kept well away from the bed and her face was the picture of revulsion and fear.

My heart sank. So many died of the yellow fever!

Surely with my fulfilled dream only a little more than a month away, I could not die!

But Roxanne proved correct. The next day found me thrashing about in the bed, suffering horribly with sharp pains in my stomach, which radiated to every bone in my body; my fever was rising astronomically. I knew with despair that already I was drifting in and out of delirium.

Ondine came to my room early those days and bathed my face with cool water with her own hands. When I protested feebly that she might catch my disease, she replied calmly, "I had this fever when I stopped off at Santo Domingo on my way here from Paris." There was a slight evasiveness in her words. "But I recovered and I have never feared it since. I will nurse you myself, *ma pauvre petite.*"

Between bouts of delirium I was aware that Roxanne had left to spend the days with Belise and Marthe Macarte out in the country at Pointe St. Antoine. I couldn't blame her, I thought in my agony. The disease was enough to make one wish to die, so virulently painful was it.

Dimly I heard Ondine telling me that Valier came to see about me every day and my blurred vision rested on the great vases of roses he sent. Ondine was faithful, leaving me scarcely at all and then only to eat. She kept me packed with cool, damp towels, and when at last the dread crisis came, she held the bowl while I vomited up the vile, odorous black liquid that was the nadir of yellow fever. I retched miserably at the bitter, nauseous taste.

At last, I lay back weakly in the bed and looked up into Ondine's tenderly concerned face. Behind her floated the drawn features of Antoinette, her heart in her eyes. Then both women swam before me and I closed my eyes exhaustedly.

I heard Ondine say, "She is passing the crisis—I believe we are going to save her."

And then came Antoinette's fervent French, "Thanks be to the good God that watches over us all."

But sounds faded and I thought I was dying, for

I sank into a whirling blackness that drowned consciousness. I had fallen into a deep sleep, during which my ravaged body began to heal itself. I had come very near death, but my youthful strength and vitality had pulled me through—that and Ondine's tireless and expert care.

When I woke at last after nearly twenty-four hours of sleep, I was ravenous, but Ondine fed me only bouillon and fruit juices. My recovery had begun. For such a devastating disease, yellow fever had a remarkably short recovery period. By the end of the week, I was chafing to get up and I was eating all the soft and bland foods put before me like a starving orphan.

Ondine sat by my bed, smiling and talking with me, telling me of Valier's devotion. Antoinette bathed me each morning as I lay in the bed, and I felt strength flowing into my limbs as my spirits lifted miraculously. I had had the dread *fièvre jaune* and I had survived.

"All of our citizens who have fled to the country, Aurielle," Ondine said conversationally, "will soon return, for the epidemic is on the wane."

And she was proved right, for Roxanne came back, petulant that Kincannon had not called in her absence, but she looked at me and said with disgust, "You look very pale and even *that* becomes you. Do you feel well?"

"Weak, but gaining each day," I responded tartly.

We did not put off the wedding due to my illness, for my recovery was rapid and complete. And each day when I saw my handsome fiancé, I was more and more impressed with his virility and intense masculinity. It stimulated me and I found myself visualizing the children we would have. They would be beautiful and highly intelligent.

My love for Ondine had grown even more for her kindness during my illness. During these days, I reflected that not even a mother could have been more careful of me, more gentle and more effective in fighting off what could have been a killing disease. I owed her my life, and my worship of her was now bone deep.

Each Sunday, we went to the St. Louis Cathedral

where the banns were read for Valier's and my approaching marriage. This caused me great uneasiness. When the priest asked if there were any who knew cause why we should not be wed, I thought of my origins and the masquerade I was perpetrating. I spent some sleepless nights in worry and in fervent prayer that no one would let slip the truth about me. I was greatly relieved when the weeks of announcing the banns were past and no one had come forth with the truth.

Another of the few flaws in my perfect happiness was the fact that Claudette Dessaultes had not reconciled herself to her son's choice and was cold to me. She made it plain she had hoped Valier would marry the Poliet girl or Solange Villere, for their families were as old and patrician as the Dessaultes. I was sure Valier and his mother quarreled about it when they reached home. It was in Valier's eyes, the set of his mouth when he mentioned his mother. But Claudette's love and pride in her son were enormous and I had qualms that I determinedly ignored.

Still, Claudette would live with us after our marriage, which sat poorly with me. The Dessaultes were more than able to afford a luxurious separate establishment for her. But she remarked, and often, that she could not bear to be away from her darling son and must see him every day. Her overriding ambition, Valier confided, was for grandchildren, and I think that alone made my coming marriage to her son bearable.

As usual, Ondine spent a fortune on clothing for me and I assuaged my sore conscience by telling her repeatedly I would repay every penny.

I told Antoinette the same. "You will come with me and live in the big Dessaultes house. I could not get along without you, Toinette. And I shall pay you back *five* thousand dollars for your three, as well as a ten-dollar gold piece every month!"

Occasionally, I would suffer further apprehension over the sums of money I would soon be asking Valier to give me for my debts, but I reassured myself that he was so much in love with me it would be of small moment. Certainly the Dessaultes were one of the wealthiest families in all of Louisiana. Proof of that came in the wedding gifts, luxurious and expensive, that flowed into the house, each day bringing more.

The Chaille household was the happiest I had ever seen it during those days before my marriage. All the servants were cautiously excited over my coming nuptials and, in their subdued and cowed way, made known to me they wished me every joy. I was so in love, I was able to laugh at my worry about them and their fearful demeanor. I saw the whole of the world through a rosy enchantment.

Though I thought it would never come, my wedding day finally arrived. I was still a touch pale from my illness, but it gave me a fragile, translucent appearance, which Ondine said was the most attractive. I was cosseted, pampered, bathed, and perfumed. Even Roxanne came into the room as I donned my white wedding dress, leaning against the doorway in her old pose from the days at Barataria when she wore a sword at her side.

"It has all gone as you planned, Aurielle," she said moodily. "But I can get no declaration from Quent. Christ! He is so absorbed in his business now." She paused, then added angrily, "And I suspect that he has some idea of marrying one of these bloodless aristocrats. What a fool he is!" Then glumly, "But no more than I."

"Give him more time, Roxanne," I said, but there was no real conviction in my heart.

She strode in and flung herself on the sofa. "Sometimes, I have the absurd desire to run him through with my sword—and I *miss* my sword!"

"Sometimes I wish I could carry my poniard again. But we cannot do such and be true ladies, Roxanne."

"I am not sure I like being a lady," she replied sullenly. "I have beautiful clothes and polished manners—but I have nothing of *freedom*."

"We all pay a price for what we want."

"I have paid the price, but I do not have what I want." She looked into my eyes and an instant of real communication flashed between us.

I said slowly, "I do not—I cannot be sure that I am getting what I want—until I have it." Then with intuitive dread, "And then it will be too late." With the spoken words my heart rose up in rebellion. *It would be what I wanted—it would!*"

Roxanne's smile was ironic. "It is even too late for that kind of talk. The priests at St. Louis Cathedral are ready. The church is decorated and God knows all of New Orleans will witness this wedding."

Ondine appeared at the door. "Ah, *mon ange,* you are a vision! Valier will be beside himself tonight—all those transparent nightdresses and peignoirs," she laughed wickedly. "You will be pregnant before the sun rises tomorrow. A pity, really."

I suddenly wished they would all go away, even Antoinette who was fussing busily with the pearl-encrusted bodice of my wedding dress and adjusting the heavy satin folds of the skirt. I wore a tiara of pearls in my shining hair and on my wrists two lustrous pearl bracelets belonging to Ondine's fabulous collection.

I wondered briefly if Valier Dessaultes's mother would see us to our bedroom, and I smiled faintly.

Chapter 11

When at last I sat in the Chaille carriage, Ondine, Roxanne, and Ulysses about me, and Sebastien driving, I was filled with fresh joy. It was all as elegant as I had so often envisioned. Passersby stared at the open carriage as we made our way down the rutted dirt streets and I thought once more how lucky I was.

We drew up before the great cathedral, flowers banking even the broad open doors. In the church itself, flowers were everywhere, the delicious scent of them almost overpowering. It was the hour of dusk and in the golden interior of the cathedral, candles twinkled from tall, silver candelabra, imparting a fairy glow over the great crowd that filled every pew.

I saw Valier just inside, watching eagerly as Ondine and Roxanne fell behind when I entered the large foyer. Ulysses now stood impassive as a statue opposite Sebastien at the doors. Madame Dessaultes was just about to traverse the long aisle to her seat. Her high, thin-bridged nose was pinched at the nostrils and it seemed to me her snapping eyes held a wealth

212

of malevolence as they rested on me. For an instant, a premonition of horror gripped me, but I looked at Valier and saw the tenderness in his face, and my fear melted away.

In the flurry that surrounded us, he took my arm and in moments, we were walking with slow and stately tread down the center aisle of the cathedral. The altar was a glittering blur of gold and silver statues. Suddenly I was sure all my misgivings were false and a shining future waited.

It was a moving ceremony and the words touched me deeply. I would be this man's wife all my life and our children would carry on for us when we grew old and full of years. Complete happiness was mine as we were joined one to the other and made our way slowly back up the aisle. I was a good Catholic now, I told myself, and I promised God silently that I would come to mass every Sunday and often during the week. Only the thought of confession marred the moment. How could I confess to a priest my background? I could not. God would surely understand and forgive me.

It was at this precise moment I looked to my left and directly into the black eyes of Quentin Kincannon. He had sent as a wedding gift an ornate set of crystal goblets. Now there was something so intense, so piercing in his eyes that my own were held, despite my desire to tear them away. I even turned my head slightly, clinging to those dark depths where all my previous doubts were mirrored. I felt suddenly sick with fear, but I tore myself from his gaze and smiled brightly into the quizzical face of my husband as we hurried the last few steps to the foyer and through to the carriage waiting outside.

At the Chaille house, we found the caterers were busy about their duties. An orchestra was playing softly in the main salon. It would be an evening to remember always, I vowed silently. I saw none of the regular servants. Only Antoinette was in my room, helping me readjust my hair and gown.

"I had so hoped Bonnie, Catherine, Bess, and

all could have celebrated with me. I mentioned it to Ondine," I said, half to myself.

"You know well madame will not let them be seen at her entertainments, Aurielle."

"I hate that," I said sharply. "I told her I wanted them all to *see* the festivities, but she merely smiled and said perhaps. And what can I do? I am here myself only thanks to her kindness of heart."

"We will be gone from here tonight," Antoinette said, relief undeniable in her voice. "Then what Madame Chaille does with her servants will be none of our affair."

Still, it rankled as I took the stairs and made my way to the salon where I was engulfed by well-wishing friends. Eugene Poliet seized my hand and claimed the right to kiss the bride. He did this rather wetly, before handing me to my husband. As the guests swarmed about, I saw they were all there—the great landowners of Pointe St. Antoine, the wealthy merchants, the Creoles who had inherited immense fortunes. They congratulated us, complimented our appearance, the wedding, Ondine's flower-decked mansion, and the beauty of the bride.

I glanced into the dining salon to see the caterers busily setting out the enormous buffet. Both black and white servants were carrying steaming dishes and great glazed birds, hams, and turkeys with every bread and side dish I had ever seen and some I had not. The table was covered with smoking platters.

Everyone stood in little groups conversing animatedly while the orchestra played. When Sebastien announced the buffet was served, the guests streamed into the great room, each taking up a plate and being served by the elegantly clad waiters. Even the governor, accompanied by his lovely, dark-haired wife, stopped to chat with Valier and me in the main salon where we had seated ourselves after being served.

"I shall be glad when our part in this is over and we can go home, my little love," Valier whispered as the governor and his lady left us.

I gave him an intimate smile. My own impatience

was hard to contain. Looking up into his shining dark eyes, I thought, *I am Madame Valier Dessaultes!*

Ondine swooped down upon me, handing my half-touched plate to a waiter. "Come, my darling, you must go with us up to my room to freshen up a bit," and she took my hand, pulling me with her and half-a-dozen girls including Roxanne. Their eyes were bright and their faces rosy with excitement and envy. "The girls want a chance to talk to you." She smiled warmly at Marthe and Belise Macarte, Lille Chalmet and Solange Villere. I noted that even Tollie Broussard was with them, hanging back a little, for her imperious mother had rather intimidated the girl. We scampered up the long staircase and down the hall to Ondine's chamber.

She had arranged several bowls and pitchers for those who would wash their fingertips. Behind an ornate screen stood a row of fine porcelain *pots de chambre*. This latter necessity was relievedly used by most of the girls who had made free with the champagne.

Lisette Poliet, whom I had never liked since the moment I first saw her hanging on Valier's arm at the Temple, was bursting with news. She did not like my being the center of attention. She clutched Ondine's hand, glancing around at those of us chatting, and said, "My dears, have you heard about the hideous massacre at Fort Mims in Alabama? Everyone in the Mississippi Territory is terrified now, they say."

"Would you like to tell us about it, Lisette?" Ondine asked quietly, her shining eyes on Lisette's face.

"Well—it happened last month and word is just now reaching the rest of the country. But the fact is that more than a thousand Creek Indians stormed the fort just at the dinner hour and massacred over three hundred men, women, and children."

"Terrible!" Ondine whispered, her face paling. "How were they—"

"Awfully!" Lisette was obviously enjoying the rapt attention that was now focused on her. "The Indians mutilated them horribly. Papa says they scalped them all!

Blood was everywhere. Some of the women had their breasts cut—"

"Stop!" cried Solange Vilere. Her face was as pale as Ondine's. One of the girls made a retching sound.

Lisette surveyed the mesmerized faces and said slowly, "Papa says they didn't scalp the babies. They took them by their little feet and smashed their brains ous against the trees. Papa talked to one of the men who found them a few days after the massacre. It happened in August during a hot, dry spell, and Papa says the man told him the stench was awful. He couldn't stop vomiting."

"Lisette," I said coldly, "you should not peddle atrocities. Look, your friends are ill from your tale."

"They're interested," Lisette said defensively.

"You must choose a harder audience after this," Ondine said in a deceptively, gentle voice. Her lovely face was expressionless but her eyes were brilliant and her whole body was tense. I had the feeling her nerves were strung as tightly as stretched wire. Lisette's story had struck some deep chord within Ondine Chaille, and for a moment I thought she might faint. Had she, during the French Revolution, known a paralyzing moment of horror comparable to the one so blithely described by this empty-headed girl?

"Come, Lisette," I said with ill-concealed anger. "You have upset us all. Let's hear no more of this massacre. This is to be a night for pleasure."

Lisette was sullen as we began leaving. Hilarity, gaiety, and merriment were at a peak as we reached the salon. My eyes found Valier engaged in conversation with his mother across the room. With their profiles to me, I was struck by the perfect resemblance. For the first time, I reluctantly conceded that Claudette Dessaultes was a very handsome woman. Still, I was glad their likeness was less when she turned her full face toward me.

"I see yours across the room," Roxanne whispered to me, then added joyfully, "and here comes mine!"

Kincannon was approaching purposefully and before

Roxanne or I could speak, he took my hands. "I claim a dance with the bride, Madame Dessaultes." It was the first time anyone had spoken my new title and I felt a flush of pride. "Save one for me, Roxanne," he added carelessly. "I've news from Barataria that will interest you."

The mulatto orchestra was excellent as always and we stepped in rhythm to the gay little tune. "You are extraordinarily beautiful tonight, madame," he said with a half smile.

"All brides are beautiful," I retorted. Why didn't Valier see and rescue me?

"That is true, but it seems you overdo the privilege."

"How is it that you can make even a compliment a slap in the face?"

He laughed silently as his eyes fixed on Ondine some distance away. Then, "The ubiquitous Sebastien has approached your aunt. For so competent a man, it seems to me he must call her away from her guests frequently."

I turned to see them vanish into the foyer together. "It is very hard to oversee a ball as large as this," I said defensively. Still, he was speaking my own thoughts.

"There is much about your—ah, fairy godmother —that puzzles me," he murmured.

"What do you mean?" I asked sharply.

"It is only that I would know more about her. Did you know that none of these who think her such a social arbiter know anything of her deceased husband in Paris, or the source of her wealth?"

"She inherited her wealth—from her husband and father!" I said heatedly. "What are you suggesting?"

"Only that she is something of a mystery," he said somewhat absently as the music stopped. I realized he was looking directly down into my greatly exposed bosom. I restrained a desire to put my hands over it.

"You are the only man I ever met who deserves to be slapped regularly," I said angrily.

This time he laughed aloud. "I wouldn't advise you to give me my desserts now or later, madame." He bowed, murmuring, "Unless you care to risk the consequences."

"May I have the next dance, mademois—madame?" It was Rodeur Cheviot at my side, his winning smile white and the blue eyes vivid in his dark countenance.

"Of course," I said with a glad little laugh. I went to his arms without acknowledging Kincannon's departure. Across the room I saw Valier frowning in my direction. I had not yet danced with my husband; still he had been deep in conversation with his mother when he should have claimed me.

"You looked rather unhappy just now, *chérie,*" and though he still smiled, Rodeur's voice was troubled. "Surely this marriage is what you wanted?"

"Oh, yes, Rodeur," I replied. "It is only the captain who makes me unhappy. He is—he has a sharp tongue and he will not hold it. Besides, he is not responsive to Roxanne and she loves him very much."

"Why this sudden concern for Roxanne?" he asked in French. "I thought you'd rejoice to see that one unhappy." His grin was mischievous.

"I want everyone to be happy tonight!"

"Ah, Valier Dessaultes is indeed a fortunate man."

"And I am a fortunate girl." My voice lowered and I said, "Rodeur, Moll at the Boar's Head in Portsmouth always counted my birthdays in April because that was when my father brought me there. So I think I am seventeen now. Did he—never tell you—when I was born?"

"You promised never again to ask me about my life in France," he replied roughly.

"That is a very hard promise to keep, dear friend. You must forgive me when I break it," I said low.

"If you can forgive me when I do not answer," he said and it seemed to me there was anguish in his voice.

I looked at him, startled. "Rodeur, I did not mean to hurt you," I said quickly. "I know you must—grieve over your lost place in France."

He was silent as we danced, then said slowly, "I grieve for many, little Aurielle. I dare not look back."

After that, neither of us spoke and I was near tears.

There was something about Rodeur that made me want to comfort him, to take his hands and tell him that everything would be all right. It was a strange emotion, for he was a strong and courageous man, well able to take care of himself in any circumstance.

The dance drew to a close and Valier was there to claim me this time.

"I enjoyed the dance, m'sieu," I said in response to Rodeur's courtly thanks.

Then as the music took up a new beat, Valier said, "I thought it was customary for the bride to dance first with her husband," but he smiled when he said it.

"So did I, Valier, but I couldn't catch your eye."

"But you caught the affluent captain's," he teased. "You made quite a handsome couple."

"I can scarcely believe that," I responded coolly. "The captain and I do not get along well together."

"Now why is that?"

"He is an—extremely conceited and arrogant man. And he is *nouveau riche*."

Valier laughed tolerantly, "There are a great many *nouveaux riches* in New Orleans, *chérie*. It is not considered bad manners to make a fortune here. Besides, the good captain banks his dollars with me—and borrows more."

"In that case, I shall be civil to him, but civil only." I glanced at the foyer door, concerned once more that Ondine was so taken up with the caterers.

"You are distracted, my love. What is it?" Valier asked with a keen look.

"*Un rien*," I murmured. "Isn't a bride permitted to dream a little?"

He swept me to him to the beat of the music and for a moment, the long length of him was pressed against me. "Of course you are, my love!"

We danced in silent enjoyment until the music trailed away. Then I looked up to see the slender-hipped and eager-eyed Eugene Poliet waiting to claim a dance.

I do not know how many more dances there were before Ondine and Sebastien returned at last, but I saw them as they came back. Sebastien took his customary place beside the door and Ondine swept into the room. As had been the case before, her eyes were lustrous, her pearly skin luminescent, and she seemed to float into Kincannon's arms.

Another hour went by before it happened. A piercing, terrified scream floated in through the open French doors to the courtyard. It reverberated in the high-ceilinged room, shrill above the music before it was cut off abruptly. Everyone froze into immobility. The orchestra stopped in mid-song and each of us looked from one to another.

"It's from the side of the courtyard," I heard Kincannon's deep, authoritative voice clearly. Then he was sprinting to the doors opening on the rear courtyard where he disappeared into the night beyond.

I tore myself from Valier's arms and ran to the doors. A rising wind whipped the trees as I took the steps and strained to see in the darkness. Looking back, I saw Valier and the guests crowding behind him. Some had taken up candles in crystal chimneys so the wind would not blow them out. I could see in the gloom that Kincannon had not stopped in the empty courtyard but had taken the path through an open wrought-iron gate to the side yard. I could not see him, but a terrible premonition of tragedy filled me.

Hastening through the gate in the dim light, I saw them—two figures, one large, one small, lying very still on the great flagstones that covered the side yard. I ran forward and, in the moonless night I could not at first discern who they were. Then as the others flooded about with candles and lanterns, I saw it was Bess; she lay in the curve of Selina's arms. There was a trickle of blood from the child's mouth, but her pale little face was serene and unscarred, as if she were sleeping.

"Ah, God," I whispered, "let them be alive!"

The others swarmed around us and I stooped to take Bess's head in my lap. The blood trickled down onto my pearl-encrusted satin dress, but I paid it no heed. I rocked her back and forth, crying, "Bessie, Bessie darling, open your eyes!"

There was a babble of many voices about us, before Kincannon's rose commandingly. "Here, madame, let me see. Perhaps they are not dead—though they must have fallen from the third floor." He knelt and put his hand to Selina's breast. The black woman was so still I despaired of her life.

Ondine suddenly gave a great cry of distress and wailed, "Bessie has always been a sleepwalker and her mother sleeps so soundly!" She caught her breath and continued in a lowered voice, "Selina must have followed and tried to save her—she has done so before. Ah, how terrible!" Great tears rolled down her cheeks, glittering like diamonds in the pale candlelight. The guests were murmuring sympathetically. Claudette Dessaultes and Rodeur Cheviot came to put their arms about her and hold her upright. She looked as if she would collapse at any moment.

"They are both dead," Kincannon said, rising to his feet. His voice was noncommittal and his eyes on Ondine darkly alert. I sat rocking little Bess's head in my lap, my fine gown completely forgotten, dragging on the flagstones and soaking up the child's blood.

Kincannon said gently, "You must send for the authorities, Madame Chaille, and explain the circumstances to them. The child's mother should be roused and informed as well."

"I know, I know," Ondine wept. Then turning, "Sebastien, you will go to the Cabildo and ask for the inspector and the coroner immediately. Oh, first go waken—poor Catherine. Tell her what has happened before you send her down to me."

I noted then that Governor Claiborne had taken Rodeur's place at Ondine's side and was comforting her as she again wiped her eyes.

Sebastien turned silently as a cat and made his way to the house. The guests were talking among themselves, several of them stepping up to touch Ondine's shoulder, to make comforting sounds to her. She appeared beside herself with grief and repeated, "I have so often told Catherine something should be done about Bess's sleepwalking. The child has done it so often—" She broke off with a sob, then whispered, "Ah, *le bon Dieu* bless her and poor Selina."

Roxanne's face was a study in puzzled regret. She turned. "Ulysses, will you pick them up and take them inside—Will the sitting room be all right, Tante Ondine?"

Ondine nodded wordlessly, wiping her eyes with a dainty, scented handkerchief. "What a terrible thing to happen—on Aurielle's wedding night and during her ball!"

Valier put a hand under her elbow as Governor Claiborne went to his wife, who was weeping in sympathy. He said soothingly, "Do no cry so, dear Ondine. Tragedy strikes when least expected. This will pass, sad though it may be now."

Kincannon stooped and caught the child up in his arms. "Here. I will carry the little one," he said to Ulysses, who had picked up the fallen Selina with effortless ease.

The guests began to make their way back into the house and I followed wordlessly at Valier's side. He had my cold hand in his warm one and was saying quietly, "My darling, do not be so sad. It was over quickly for the child. She did not suffer."

Tears ran unheeded down my cheeks as we paused on the steps to the French doors, where he took out his big, clean handkerchief and began to wipe my eyes with a surprisingly light touch. "Do not let this ruin your wedding night, my love."

I still could not speak. Swallowing, I nodded silently and Valier added, "It has put a great damper on our ball. Look, the guests are going to leave. There will be no breakfast." He laughed wryly. "It is just as well. There will be fewer aching heads in New Orleans in the morning."

I looked after Kincannon's tall form as he made his way through the departing guests toward the sitting room, Bess limp in his arms. My tears were still flowing as people about me bade us good evening in low voices.

I was unable to answer. Ondine was at the door, seeing her guests; she was able to converse with them composedly now.

Again Valier put his damp handkerchief to my eyes and said firmly, "You must not grieve like this, beloved. Such accidents do happen and we must be brave."

"I loved Bessie," I said thickly, speaking for the first time.

"I know, *chérie*. But I will help you forget your grief—tonight."

"And Selina was kind to me," I went on. Selina's kindness was innate despite her timidity. I could easily understand her plunging to her death in an effort to save Bess. I looked down at my dress where the red blood of the child had soaked into it in a great scarlet blemish on the virginal white. The dress was forever ruined.

"Poor Ondine." Valier was looking at her saddened face. "She is devastated."

Only Kincannon and Cheviot remained in the sitting room with Roxanne, Ulysses, and the bodies. I moved away from the door to Ondine's side. She was beautiful in her grief. Her lovely face was not blotched as I felt mine was. And the tears on her lashes only enhanced her clear eyes.

As the last guests departed, she turned to Valier's tall mother, who had come in a separate carriage, and said, "I am so sorry this tragedy happened on Aurielle's wedding night—" She glanced around and caught me in her arms. "Ah, *mon ange,* your dress is ruined! But no matter. You must go with Valier now and do not look back. Do not think of our poor little Bess and Selina—think only of your own hapiness."

"I feel as though I shall never be happy again," I murmured, remembering Bess's great sad eyes and small, trembling mouth breaking into a smile at the sight of the doll. I had the ghastly notion that something evil hovered over my marriage now and that happiness was not to be mine after all. Was I to be repaid thus for overweening ambition, ambition I had clung to against all odds?

I had noted it when Catherine Bonham came down the stairs fully clothed. She was so quiet that none of the departing guests had seen her as she flitted like a shadow into the sitting room. Now I went in to comfort her. She was bent over Bess's body, which had been laid on one of the sofas in the room.

Fresh tears welled up as I took her thin hand and murmured my consolations to her. She did not look at me but kept her face averted and only the crouching pose bespoke her sorrow. I knew her grief was too deep for tears.

It was not long before the authorities arrived, took note of the sleepwalking disaster, and carried the two bodies away in a great black carriage. They would take them to the Cabildo where there was a special room for those killed by accident. Cheviot, Kincannon, and Claudette Dessaultes took their departure along with the coroner and his men.

Valier and I made our adieux after that, and Ondine kissed me tenderly at the door. "My angel, I repeat, do not let this—sadness spoil your wedding night. Remember, Valier did not know Bess and you can scarcely expect him to be broken up over it. Forget it"—she smiled mischievously, leaning forward to whisper in my ear—"when you get into bed with your beloved."

I looked at her without smiling. "I shall try to make my husband happy."

The fountain gave forth its musical and subdued splash as Valier and I passed it. Sebastien, who had followed us, opened the gate to permit us exit and he said quietly, "Good night, madame—Monsieur Dessaultes."

But Valier and I did not speak as we mounted the carriage. Once inside, Valier took me into his arms and, murmuring endearments, began to kiss my brow, my cheek, then lingeringly my lips.

"You are so brave, my darling—my dearest darling." He spoke softly in French. "You shall forget your sorrow. I shall make it my duty to see that you do."

And my tears dried. It did not occur to me to think that Valier had never once said *I love you.*

Chapter
12

As we drew up before the Dessaultes house, I saw there were many candles alight within it. The door was flung wide by the Dessaultes's second man, a tall, slender black named Pointer. Madame Claudette Dessaultes was conspicuous by her absence, and I felt sure Valier had commanded her not to intrude on our wedding night.

The house, which I had been in but once when Ondine and I called on Claudette, was beautifully French, with the mandatory winding and unsupported stair. As I entered, the servants seemed to be everywhere. Some I knew, but most I did not. They congratulated us and slipped away as Pointer decorously lighted our way to Valier's bedroom.

When I stood in the doorway to that room, I drew a long breath. It was bigger than Ondine's and there was a strong masculinity in the massive rosewood sofas and chairs. The bed was enormous, testered and with curtains at the four sides to insure privacy. A mist-like *baire* was suspended from the tester in gathered folds.

I said fervently, "Valier, this is a beautiful room!" Mirrors were predominant. One, gold-framed, stood at the end of the room, covering the entire wall and making the spacious room seem twice its size. On the other walls were crossed swords and other weaponry, as well as a rack containing several dueling pistols. Impulsively, I turned and caught Valier in my arms, pulling his tallness down to me and covering his face with little kisses. "You are so good, my darling, and I love you very much!" For a brief moment, I forgot the bloodstained little head that had lain in my lap such a short time ago.

I left him then and went into the adjoining room, which was to be Antoinette's, to find she had already arrived and was waiting to help me disrobe. She was so excited she spoke in French. "Ah, my little one—look at this lovely room that is mine! I have put all your clothes into that big armoire over there. See the bed, so big! It was the room of M'sieu Dessaultes's valet once."

Her room was a smaller replica of Valier's, complete with crossed rapiers on the walls and a rack of dueling pistols. I agreed with her that it was a fine room. As she unhooked my satin dress, she murmured sadly over the blood that marred the front.

The grief and horror in Ondine's courtyard earlier faded still more as Antoinette slipped over my head my frothiest, most beribboned nightdress. She pulled me to the tall mirror beside the pitcher and bowl and slipped the pins from my hair, brushing its long, shining length. I told myself firmly I must put death from my mind. Valier deserved better than a weeping bride on his wedding night.

When I stepped back into our bedroom, Valier sat waiting on a sofa before the empty fireplace, his eyes alert. The night was warm and a faint breeze belled the curtains inward. He wore a dark green robe, and those impenetrable eyes, which had always intrigued me, had a faintly menacing look.

"How beautiful you are," he said slowly, "and how I have wanted you for my own."

I came to him, putting my hands to his cheeks and

looking deep into the veiled eyes. "And I have wanted you, *mon cher*. More than you dream." I leaned forward and my thick fragrant hair swung about us as we kissed deeply, slowly. He reached out and took me in his arms and I sat in his lap, our kisses growing more fervent and exciting. He was so virile he accentuated my femininity and the desire to surrender.

"You see," he gestured, "I sent for champagne, my love. We will toast each other before we retire." On the table nearby stood a silver bucket on a tray. From its bed of ice, that precious gift of the north, there protruded the neck of a bottle of champagne. Beside it were two slender glasses.

"How lovely!" I nestled against his shoulder. I could sense a force within him that was tightly in check and an odd uneasiness crept into me. There was no need to hold back our desires now. We were free to indulge our wildest and sweetest fantasies together.

But Valier opened the bottle with a resounding pop and, without speaking, filled the glasses to the brim. Silently he handed one to me, then touched his glass to mine. When I saw he was going to say nothing, I spoke up boldly. "To us, Valier—and to our children."

He smiled faintly, saying, "To our children, Aurielle," and we sipped without words. When we had finished, he asked, "Would you like another?" and, without waiting for my reply, took up the bottle and refilled my glass.

I would have said, *No, I am already excited enough despite the death of my friends,* but Valier seemed to want to draw the moments out. He looked broodingly at me over the rim of his glass with each sip he took.

"You are so silent, my love," I said hesitantly.

"I am thinking perhaps you have had enough of shock and surprise tonight. I am worried about you, Aurielle. You are flushed one moment and pale the next."

I looked away. What he said was true. Suddenly I was once again in the cool courtyard, the head of little Bess so terribly still in my lap. I thought of the bloodstained wedding gown Antoinette had flung over a chair in the adjoining room. I swayed, spilling the wine upon my wrist.

Valier put down his glass swiftly and took me into his arms, lifting my own glass from trembling fingers. "My poor little one," he whispered against my tumbling hair. I could feel the warmth, the strength of him against me, but it did not comfort me as it should. Instead, a vague sense of fresh disaster welled up.

"Valier, I—"

"I saw your face when you cradled the child," he said softly. "You need say nothing. I feel your distress intensely." He swung me up into his arms and strode across to the great soft bed, where he put me down. He turned and snuffed out the candles about the bedchamber.

The vagrant breeze stirred the light curtains once more, carrying the September scents of late honeysuckle and jasmine. When Valier entered the bed, he swept the gauzy *baire* about us and we lay uncovered in the warm air.

I turned to him and he caught me in his arms and kissed me, once on the forehead and then hungrily on my mouth. All the manhood in him was leashed, reined tight, and I knew suddenly that he would not take me this night. I fought against a knife thrust of disappointment. *I am thinking perhaps that you have had enough of shock and surprise tonight.* How kind he was, I told myself, how thoughtful!

Even as he held me, I relaxed and drifted into exhausted sleep. But my sleep was fitful and I dreamed. Not of Selina and Bess, but that Roxanne and I were back at the Temple and the shells gleamed ghostly white, casting their shroudlike reflection on the thick leaves in the trees above us. Ondine Chaille swept up before us, splendidly beautiful in her sumptuous brocaded silk. Her face was tenderly benign, warm with love for the two of us. She took my hand in hers, but as she held it, her hand became a dead thing, cold and clammy. When I looked up from it in horror, her eyes were staring, distended and blank.

I arose with a wild cry and Valier reached up to pull me back into his arms as I wept uncontrollably. I loved Ondine with all my heart and she had been *dead*—dead as little Bess in my lap. Sobs shook me. All the caresses and endearments Valier murmured against my wet cheeks could not console me. It was a long time before I slept again, for I was fearful of sleep and of seeing Ondine dead before me.

When I awoke, it was to find Valier gone. I lay there for several minutes reflecting on the disappointment my marriage—no, my wedding night—was to me. Valier could not be blamed for this. He had done a very noble thing in comforting and consoling me to the best of his ability. His restraint in making no demands on me was honorable in every way. Nevertheless, I was lethargic as I rose to a sitting position and pushed aside the *baire*.

There was little breeze from the open windows. I looked down at my fine silk nightdress, remembering how Ondine had advised the dressmakers regarding it, taking care that it should be most seductive, even sensual in its half-revealing draperies. An ironic smile crossed my lips. Little good it had done me!

I slipped quickly from the bed and, going to the washstand, bathed myself in cool water from the pitcher. I assumed Antoinette had gone to breakfast when I did not find her in her room as I entered. The tall mahogany chest of drawers was filled with my delicately embroidered lingerie and nightdresses. My spirits lifted slightly at the sight of all my dresses in the armoire.

They lifted more when I put on a pale yellow morning dress with little ruffles about the neck and shoulders. There was a pelisse that matched it but the day was too warm for that.

A firm rap sounded and I heard the door open behind me. I looked around quickly as Claudette Dessaultes stepped in, closing the door behind her. There was something menacing in her stance. It was fitting that two of the crossed rapiers should form a background for her.

I summoned a smile for my grim mother-in-law. "Good morning, madame." I made a little gesture of welcome. "How are you?"

"You are late rising, Aurielle."

"I am sorry. I—was much distressed by the deaths of my friends, Selina and Bess."

"Servants," she said, dismissing them. "You should not allow your affections to be so loosely given."

"My affections are never loosely given," I replied, checking my rising temper.

"Hmmn. I warned Valier you are very young and foolish, insisting that we hire that stiff-necked Antoinette Desmottes. I hope you will develop no such attachments among the servants here."

"I probably shall—as well as hiring some to my own liking."

"You certainly shall not," she replied icily. "You are too young to know what to look for when hiring servants."

"My dear *maman*—may I call you *maman*? No? Madame, then. Valier will tell me what I may and may not do, and I expect to do very much as I please."

Her sharp face softened suddenly, not with warmth but with craftiness as the black eyes went to my narrow waist. "When you give me a grandson, I shall give you five new servants of your own."

"How generous you are, madame. And if it is a granddaughter?"

"The same—for each new child."

"La! I shall be swamped with servants."

"We shall see. Come now. Valier wants to breakfast with you in the courtyard."

It was lovely in the sun-dappled courtyard. Valier rose at once and said in French, "Good morning, my love." He pulled a chair out for me. "Are you not hungry?"

"Yes," I replied, suddenly realizing as his mother left us, how empty I was.

"Then you shall have a glass of Chablis before Trudi serves your egg and toast. A breakfast without wine is like a gloomy day, and this day has faired off beautifully."

He was right. The Chablis increased my sense of well-being and I ate all that was put before me. It was especially pleasant since my dour mother-in-law did not return to join us.

After I finished, I put the fine linen napkin to my lips and said daringly, "Tonight I will not be so upset,

Valier, dear. *This* shall be our wedding night." My eyes on his spoke the other words I was thinking and his slow smile made my fingertips tingle. I continued somewhat breathlessly, "And now I would like to call on Tante Ondine—I want to attend the funeral of Bessie and Selina—put flowers on their graves."

"It is sad for Ondine, my Aurielle. You must be kind to her—as I know you will."

"I shall." A warm flood of affection for Ondine suffused me. Then, as my husband rose to his feet, I asked, "You are going to the bank?"

"*Oui.* Our crude Yankee friend Kincannon is going to make a deposit in gold today and I must arrange to invest it wisely for him."

"You are so fine—so very astute, Valier," I said impulsively, standing on tiptoe to kiss his mouth. Suddenly his arms went about me so tightly I caught my breath and said, laughing, "You are very strong, too, darling. I vow you cracked my ribs."

He released me and said soberly, "My dear, you are far the fairest woman I have ever known, bar none. Remember that, Aurielle, no matter what the future holds, no matter the way things are—that I found you fairest of all." There was something so sad in his voice, so full of dreadful portent that my heart lurched downward.

I caught him to me again. "Why do you say such strange, sad things?"

"They are not strange." He smiled a touch cynically. "They are complimentary."

"But you *sound* so sad. Aren't you happy?" It flashed through my mind how happy I should be. I had everything I had longed for through the years. I was married to a rich and handsome man. My place in society was secure.

"Life is sometimes sad, *ma petite.* You will learn that as you grow older. We cannot have it all our way all the time."

"I'll settle for part of the time—and *now* is part of the time." But as I said it, I realized that something leaden and heavy had come to rest in my heart and it dimmed the sunlight, made the fragrances in the air tran-

231

sient and passing. I could not understand it and put it from me forcefully. My husband kissed me lightly and was gone.

In my room, I found Antoinette tidying up. "I see you have made the bed, Toinette," I said, hugging her thin shoulders lightly.

"I didn't make the bed. A young black girl named Pansy came up here and did it. I had my hands full, keeping her from your dressing table, so fascinated was she." Antoinette sounded exasperated. "There are two more maids, Esther and Helen—both black, and the cook, Trudi. Then there's Pointer, a butler, coachman, and jack-of-all-trades, and Jacques Voudreaux, the only paid employee besides me. There are six servants here and I make seven."

"I have never considered you a servant, Toinette. You are my dear friend—who helps me. Soon I shall repay your loan, too."

"You have worried more about my money than I have, Aurielle," she said with a little smile. "Do not press your husband too soon, little one. I can wait."

When I called for the carriage I had a brief exchange with my mother-in-law, who had not known of my determination to attend the funeral services.

"I had thought to call on Ondine today, myself," she said peevishly.

"Then you are welcome to come with me," I replied courteously.

"No—I had forgotten about the servants' deaths. I had rather not go now. No doubt the house is still under a miserable pall."

"I imagine so," I said, carefully bland. I masked my contempt for this unfeeling woman who worried only about the discomfort of being under a pall.

Later, when Ondine swept into her parlor to greet me, she was clad in a simple and subdued gray silk that showed her lovely breasts demurely cupped in the tiny stitched pleats that molded the bodice to her slender form. There were pale blue shadows under her big eyes and she appeared a little drawn. A sudden surge of pity welled up. She was suffering and it increased my own sorrow.

I embraced her, kissing the silky cheek briefly. "Dear Tante Ondine, it will soon be over."

"I shall be long in forgetting this sadness," she replied, putting a scented handkerchief to ready tears that glistened in her eyes. "Do sit down, *mon ange*—ah, Roxanne! I am glad you have come down at last. I missed you at breakfast."

"I overslept, *tante*," she said, then turned to me and added, with her customary impudence, "How is the great lady?"

"Grieving. I had thought you might be, too."

"I *am* sorry," she said lightly, "but I was not as close to Bessie and Selina as you were."

"The funeral will be in an hour," Ondine said, again blotting her eyes. "I have arranged for them to be buried in the Chaille family plot in the St. Louis Cemetery. Would you care to attend with Roxanne and me, Aurielle?"

"That is why I came. Catherine and the others are going as well?"

"Indeed yes. Sebastien will drive them in the big barouche. Ulysses will take us in the carriage. Father Doumergne will conduct the services—Ohhh!" At her shrill scream, Roxanne and I started from our seats and Sebastien and Ulysses were in the room in an instant.

I saw her staring fixedly and with horror at her little gray shoe, now thrust from beneath her silken skirts. My own eyes widened as I saw a scarlet thread of blood across the shoe. Sebastien was on her in a flash, and before my astonished gaze he flipped up the edge of her skirt and ripped a small bag from it, pulling loose the threads with which it had been sewn.

He muttered an oath, then said protectively in French, "Have no fear, little one. I will burn away the power!"

"What is it?" I asked, bewildered.

Ondine was looking furiously at the two servants. "Call the others in here at once!" Her face was white and her eyes hard and sparkling dangerously.

Swiftly Sebastien stepped from the room to disappear in the foyer. No one spoke. Roxanne was looking at Ondine with speculative concern. Then she said softly, "Do

233

not fear, *tante*. Sebastien will burn it. It will have no effect."

Now Ondine looked wildly at Ulysses who towered in the doorway, his face impenetrable. "You're from Santo Domingo, too, Ulysses—you know all about voodoo! It has been brought to Louisiana by you people! What kind of charm was that thing? I know it was evil."

"It depends upon what was in it, madame," he replied as the servants began to file into the room, appearing drawn and frightened.

Ondine's face was still bloodless and now she turned the full force of her rage and fear on the hapless servants before her. Sebestien was not with them and I assumed he was burning the bloody bag.

Ondine held up the hem of her skirt, exposing the broader bloodstains, and thrust out her ruined faille shoe. "Which of you did this? Tell me this instant!"

"I ain't no voodoo—" Tressa began, shrinking.

"I ain't know nothin' 'bout that blood, madame," Pearl said, retreating.

"Some one of you sewed that in my skirt and only this morning! The blood is"—she shuddered—"fresh."

Bonnie was plainly ignorant, but her terror was genuine. "I ain't never heard o' voodoo til I come here," she said, gulping. "I—I think it's a lot o' twaddle."

Ondine's sudden burst of laughter held a touch of hysteria. "There! That's the only sensible thing that's been said. It's a lot of twaddle." But her shrill voice held no conviction as her eyes went to Catherine. "You've been here long enough to absorb some of this—this superstition, Catherine. Did you, by some tortured reasoning, do this to me because of Bessie's death?"

"No, madame," Catherine replied, her grief-ravaged face impassive. "Where or how would I be gettin' such a thing? I never leave th' house—no more do any of us. It ain't my doin'."

Sebastien reentered the room, an angry scowl on his face. "I burned it in hamfat, madame. It was entrails and bits of bone, a twist of hair, and the cloth may or may not have been from one of your dresses. You will have to make sure of that yourself. See if any are cut."

234

I did not think it possible, but Ondine's face grew whiter still and she whispered, "It is worse than I feared." Then with heroic effort, she pulled herself up, and composure took hold. She said firmly, "Sebastien, you will see that the servants get to the barouche and to the cemetery. Jasper—Couri, you will get out the two carriages and go with the others. Ulysses will drive us."

The graveside services were simple. It was depressing despite the bright sunlight, for all of us were uneasy over the two-inch square of bloody scraps sewn to Ondine's skirts.

We were back at the house before noon, where Ondine insisted I stay for the noon meal. It was an unhappy affair, made more so by the fact that Tressa was an inept cook.

Afterward in the sitting room, while serving the café royale, Sebastien said, "Madame, I will take you this very afternoon to the auction block and you can secure a new and more experienced cook."

"Sebastien—whatever would I do without you?" Her eyes on him gleamed with warm intimacy and he bowed impassively.

Later, when I reached the Dessaultes mansion, I found my mother-in-law had discovered Antoinette's talents with coiffures and was closeted with her in her own bedroom. It was just as well, for I did not think I could be civil in my response to her acidulous comments. I went to Valier's and my bedroom.

My spirits had picked up somewhat by the time Valier returned home shortly before dinner was served, and I stayed in the bedroom with him while he washed up. I told him of the events of the day, ending with the strange story of the bag of voodoo mixtures sewn to the hem of Ondine's dress.

"That is not good," he said seriously, wiping his hands on a towel at the washstand. "Voodoo is a powerful force among the blacks—and a great many whites. And make no mistake, it is effective."

"Then my—aunt is in danger?"

"I would say she is," he replied thoughtfully. "But

235

she has Sebastien to look after her. I imagine he is as conversant with voodoo and its antidotes as any man in town. He will protect her."

"I cannot imagine why anyone would wish evil to a woman as kind and good as Tante Ondine. Tell me some of the practices of this voodoo," I invited.

He smiled obliquely. "Get our Trudi to tell you—if you can. Much of it is secret. When you have been in New Orleans a little longer, the tales will reach you, *ma petite.*"

When night came at last, I was in a turmoil of excitement. With Antoinette's help, I donned my loveliest nightdress and touched my wrists and my temples with the lightest of perfumes.

Antoinette sent me into the next room with a whispered *"Tiens!* You are a dream of loveliness—"

When finally I lay in the bed, I was in a fever of anticipation as Valier made himself ready to join me. Only a faint uneasiness was mine as I unwillingly thought of those frenzied moments of struggle in Quentin Kincannon's arms more than a year ago. The unexpected rush of desire, the stinging sweetness of his lips on mine had haunted all my dreams of love. Surely, after tonight, they would at last become only a vague memory, for I loved Valier Dessaultes. I was perfectly confident that I would awaken in the morning with Valier's son under my heart.

When at last he came to slip under the *baire* with me, we clasped each other and I gave a great sigh of sheer happiness. He had left a candle gleaming on the table beside the bed and we could see each other as he began to make love to me. He caressed and fondled me with slow expertise and the sensations he evoked were delightful. His breath was growing short when suddenly, with powerful strength, he crushed me to him, taking my breath away. I kissed him with deep fervor and his return kiss was equally passionate.

He murmured, "You are so beautiful, Aurielle," and the words opened a wealth of tenderness with me. I clung to him in a sweet agony of desire, but he continued only to stroke, to fondle me until I reached a sudden peak of excitement.

I whispered helplessly, "Oh, my dear—please—please—"

I was stunned when an agonized groan burst from my husband and he flung away from me. An intuitive panic struck. I reached out and put my hands on his shoulders, murmuring, "Valier, what is it? You are in pain?"

"Yes—a constant pain, for which there is no cure."

Bewildered and frightened, I asked, "But *mon cher,* where is it? Surely the doctors can—"

"Doctors can do nothing for me, Aurielle. I am a man who wants you violently and is unable to consummate that desire."

More bewildered than ever, I cried, "I don't understand!"

There was a long silence between us and then he said slowly and heavily, "You have heard of gelded stallions?"

Half-forgotten tales I had heard of such operations flooded back. "Yes," I murmured, "I—think so."

"I have been not quite—but *almost* gelded, Aurielle."

"Oh! *Why—how?*"

"It was a botched-up job by four of my peers, none of whom was a doctor." He spoke with bitter venom. "I had been paying court to Don Alexander Ysidro's daughter, Dolores—I loved her deeply. *I still do!* I wanted to marry her, God damn the old man's soul! He hated my father and he hated me, swore I wasn't good enough for her—*I,* with everything I had to offer Dolores!" He broke off, his breathing labored under the onslaught of his passions. "But she slipped out, lay with me and became pregnant with my child. We went to the Don, sure that he would let us wed when he knew she carried my child. The old devil cursed me, threw me out, and sent Dolores to Savannah, where she married a cousin." A groan was torn from him as he whispered, "She died, bearing my son—they both died and the Don blamed me. He had his four sons waylay me on a dark night near the alley at Conti and Dauphine. They performed a half-effective operation, leaving me with all my passions but mutilating me so that I can no longer hold an erection—cannot quite function as a whole man." He took my hands, kissed them and

237

murmured, "Yet I have all the old desires—*all!* You must believe me when I say that."

I was silent as the full import of all he had said hit me. There would be no children for me and Valier, ever. A great wave of pity washed over me. We had risen to a sitting position in the deep featherbed and now I pulled my hands from his to put my arms about him, murmuring over and over, "Oh, my dear, my poor dear." Then with sudden rage, "They should all have been put to death for such a deed!"

"They were," he said dryly. "I went to a friend's plantation farther up the Mississippi to recover and when I was myself again, I called each of them out beneath the oaks and killed them one by one. I killed Don Alexander last. My prowess on the field of honor was little comfort to me, my dear." Then seizing my arms in a fierce grasp, he said low, "No one but you knows of this. Not even *ma mère*—she least of all, so determined on grandchildren is she. It would break her heart."

I sat still, staring down the long corridor of the years when I might reign as New Orleans finest lady, but barren, childless and lonely. It seemed more than I could bear. How could I lie in bed, caressing and being caressed by my husband without ever knowing the sweet fulfillment of love? A slow bud of revulsion began flowering in my breast. And he still loved Dolores Ysidro. He had said so. Why in the name of God had he married me if he did not love me? I remembered now—too late—he had never said *I love you.*

He spoke suddenly. "I know you will come to feel that I have deceived you and you may even come to hate me for it. I have thought of this and I feel you will approve of the plans I have made."

I looked at him in the light of the single flickering candle beside the bed, wondering what sort of plans he could possibly devise that would in any way alleviate the situation. "What are your plans?"

"My dear, I propose you take a lover, long enough to become pregnant—a child we will claim as our own. I have thought of this for a long time and I have many friends. It would be easy enough to arrange. You are a fine, strong girl and you love me—I know you love me! Enough to give me what I most want in the world—a son."

I recoiled. "Valier—I cannot do that! I am bound to you by my sacred vows. I could not do—that—with a stranger."

His voice took on an edge, "Aurielle, he will be no stranger. I will arrange that you may take your pick of them. Remember, you will be doing it for *me*." Then quickly, "And for yourself, of course. The Dessaultes name must not stop after so many generations. Perhaps you could bring yourself to do it twice—with two different men, of course—so we could have at least two children."

His calm, reasonable voice, laced with steel, was filling me now with deep repulsion. "And this man—he will know it is his child. How could he keep such a secret?"

Valier's face in the candlelight wore a wintry smile. "I plan to challenge the man you choose—afterward. And there will be no one, then, who knows but you and your husband."

"I cannot do this thing, Valier. I would be the scandal of New Orleans should a whisper of such promiscuity escape!"

"You must think of it awhile, *chérie*, and the wisdom of it will come to you in time. I do not plan to give up my right to caress you. That brings me great pleasure despite the frustration that follows it."

"I cannot," I reiterated, not really knowing whether I was referring to his plans or to his caresses.

He looked at me steadily, his black eyes glittering in the flickering light. His voice was that of a stranger as he said slowly, "After all, Aurielle Stuart *Dessaultes,* we both have dark secrets to keep, have we not? My lawyers found two fishermen at Barataria. They talked earnestly and long for a hundred gold pieces. You see, my investigation before I enter into any agreement is extensive. But I am most willing to bargain with you."

I was numb. Valier had known what I was all along and had married me despite it. And he was giving me what I most wanted—except the delights of true marriage and, worse, no children.

"You are threatening me with exposure—of my past?"

"Of course I am," he smiled.

"And you never once said you loved *me*—"

"I can never love another woman as I loved Dolores." Then he added gently, "But I am very fond of you, Aurielle. You excite me greatly, though I can do nothing but enjoy the momentary excitement. I chose you because you are beautiful and strong and because you have no *papa* and *maman* to run to, carrying the story of my inability to perform." He reached out and put a thumb over the wick of the candle and we were plunged into darkness. His voice, rich and soothing, came to me. "Now we will sleep on this, little one. You will see the wisdom of our arrangement in the morning."

I said nothing. In the bed, I tried to avoid touching him, for he had become repellent to me in the short time since I had so joyously laid myself on this travesty of a marriage bed. I did not sleep. I lay all through the night, frantically trying to find a way out of this cul-de-sac.

In the morning, Claudette Dessaultes remarked, "You look very hollow-eyed, Aurielle. Did you not sleep well?"

"I slept very well, madame," I lied. "I suppose I am showing the results of the long preparations for my marriage." I lowered my thick lashes and did not look at her as I sipped my morning coffee.

"*Maman,* you should not question a bride about her nights," Valier said with a light laugh. "I thought you much too tactful to do so."

The older woman's face actually reddened and she said quite humbly, "I did not mean to embarrass *you,* my dear." It was coming to me that this woman's love for her son was truly a towering obsession. She lived for and through him. Her eyes on him now were as reverent as any penitent's at mass.

"I'm not embarrassed," Valier said cheerfully. "It is only that I feel our nights are between Aurielle and me alone."

"Of course, my love. I was thoughtless," she murmured.

Valier's eyes on mine were amused. I knew he was

thinking of our separate dark secrets, and distaste swelled in my breast. In some unfathomable way, I felt soiled, almost abnormal, and suddenly the prospect of lying in his arms again tonight was repugnant to me. *He should have told me before,* I thought with sudden fire. *He should have let me make my own decision whether to marry him or not under the circumstances.* He had done to me what he had not dared to do to a girl of fine family, with a father and mother to whom she could run.

And what would my answer have been, welling up out of the driving ambition that had filled my soul for so many years? I would never know now. And the seed of a lover that he had planted bore strange and ugly fruit in my mind. Now I even wondered if I had ever loved Valier. His power in New Orleans, his position, the material wealth and prestige that was his had blinded me.

As I sat there silently, while Claudette and her son carried on light conversation, my thoughts were burning and chaotic. For the first time in months, I faced the future squarely and the results were not reassuring. I was powerless to prevent disgust for Valier from sweeping over me.

We finished breakfast at last and he came around to kiss me briefly. "I must go to the bank now, my love. I will be home for the evening meal."

In a moment he was gone and I was left with the hostile woman who was my mother-in-law. I realized anew that Valier had been hers, all hers, until I came into his life, and she would never forgive me for it. I groaned silently as I followed her into a hallway, wishing with all my heart that he was hers entirely once more.

As the day wore on, the yoke of marriage settled more firmly about my slender shoulders and I realized that a crushingly heavy burden was mine as Claudette enumerated the duties in running the household. I was a lady at last, a lonely, frustrated, and miserable lady, caught in a web of her own making. And I dreaded the coming night when I must endure the caresses of the poor, mutilated man I had married.

The only bright moment came late in the afternoon when the knocker sounded and Roxanne Deveret was ushered into the salon. When Claudette stalked to meet her, I followed in her wake and was so glad to see the outrageous little pirate I almost kissed her cheek.

"I had to be your first caller, *cousine*," she said, with her irrepressible grin as we embraced lightly. "Tante Ondine would have accompanied me, but the poor thing is so engaged with the new cook and maid that she and Sebastien are as busy as bluetail flies."

Madame Dessaultes frowned at the lèse majesté and spoke sharply. "I cannot understand why Ondine made such a to-do over the loss of a servant and a mere child. I think she indulges you two girls in foolish sentimentality."

"*Zut!*" Roxanne said merrily. "Aunt can deny us nothing. Our dear Aurielle had become so attached to the staff she would have taken them all with her had Ondine agreed to part with them."

Claudette said angrily, "Ha! We have no need of more servants. Thank *le bon Dieu* that ours are slaves with no need of pay, except for Jacques Voudreaux and now this Antoinette."

Roxanne shrugged eloquently. "Aurielle does not approve of slavery." Then with a sly smile at me, "*Or* redemptioners and indentured servants."

Claudette looked at me down her long, straight nose. "Aurielle is a fool."

"Madame, I admit to being foolish on occasion"—I paused, reflecting on what a fool I had been to marry into this house—"but I am right about slaves and redemptioners. They are human and therefore have the right to pursue employment honorably."

Claudette was plainly annoyed beyond measure. Swallowing her annoyance, she said coldly, "I shall go see that refreshments are served. I'm sure you two young people have much to talk of together." With a swish and rustle of fine muslin, she was gone. I knew it was but an excuse to get away from me for a while, for she had only to ring the silver bell on a side table to bring half the household to do her bidding.

"How is it with you, *cousine?*" Roxanne asked with a lifted brow. "You do not look happy. In fact, you look

242

as miserable as the day I first laid eyes on you, but for that fine dress."

"You are mistaken, Roxanne. I am very happy," I lied. "Now tell me how—our aunt is. I have been most concerned since her experience with that horrid voodoo sewn to her skirts."

Roxanne's gaze shifted uneasily. "She's all right, I think. But Ulysses told me privately that the voodoo's after her. Why, I cannot guess. He says the voodoo queen, Clothilde LaVaux, knows Ondine from somewhere. Perhaps it was when Ondine came from Paris by way of Santo Domingo." She laughed suddenly. "I am from the islands myself, you know, but I remember nothing of it."

"Can you tell me more about voodoo, Roxanne? It is such a mystery to me."

Roxanne looked warily over her shoulder at the door Claudette had taken. Then she said in a low voice, "Once, when I was but a child, we visited New Orleans from Barataria. I stole after Ulysses when he went to a meeting. It was out near Bayou St. John. They—all the blacks and oddly enough, two whites—sat in a circle about the queen, Clothilde LaVaux. Fires were all about and I could see plainly that she held a living snake in her hands." An uncharacteristic shudder swept Roxanne and her green eyes deepened. "Then after a while, they all rose up and began chanting as they danced around the queen, who stood up, winding the snake about her arms. The dancing grew wilder and wilder and oh! Aurielle, she would let that forked tongue flick out against her cheek! And then all of them tore off their clothes until they were dancing naked as jaybirds. Then they darted out and brought a little goat into the circle and cut its throat, letting the blood gush into a pan. They each drank some of its blood and that's when they began to get the *power!*" Her voice fell. "I was scared to death by then and sort of sick from watching them drink—and I made such a noise leaving they caught me."

"My God, Roxanne! What did they do to you?"

"Ulysses had to talk fast to get me out of there—I was no more than thirteen. All the way back to the city, he lectured me. He didn't know I knew about him being in the voodoo and I guess I wasn't sure until that night." She swallowed, her voice suddenly that of a chastened child. "He was in a fury. He said voodoo can *kill* you with just potions and gris-gris. After watching them, I believe it. It's terribly—frightening." She broke off and we were both silent, contemplating the scene she had so vividly brought to life.

At last, with an attempt at courage, I said, "I don't believe their potions can do anything."

Roxanne's eyes were inscrutable. "But what do you think *they* can *do?*"

I paused, then said, "That's why I fear for Ondine— for the things they are capable of doing themselves."

"You shouldn't," she said. "Sebastien has plenty of power himself. Ulysses says Sebastien'll die before he lets anyone—or *anything*—touch her." Then dismissing the subject, she looked about the salon. "I've always thought this place far grander than even Ondine's. It's a pity old Claudette doesn't entertain more." She laughed shortly, "You must change that, *cousine.*"

Antoinette appeared suddenly from the foyer carrying refreshments. She nodded and smiled at Roxanne.

"Toinette, it's good to see you looking so happy." She grinned impudently. "How do you like your new home?"

"*Très bien,*" she replied, placing the tray on a low table.

"You look better than Aurielle," Roxanne said lazily, reaching for a nut-filled sweet as I poured coffee. "Poor Aurielle looks as though she's run through a mangrove thicket."

"I did not prepare her coiffure this morning," Antoinette said in quick defense. "I will repair it before m'sieur returns this evening, little one," she said to me reassuringly and made her way from the room.

"I'd swear living in the grandest house in New Orleans didn't agree with you." Roxanne gave me a penetrating stare.

"I thought all brides looked this way after their first and second nights," I retorted lightly. "No doubt you will, too, when you and Kincannon are wed."

Her brows drew together. "I wonder if that day will ever come."

"Don't tell me you're giving up!" I mocked.

She smiled faintly. "Not yet, anyway." Then abruptly, "We talked once of getting what we most wanted. Has it made you happy, Aurielle?"

"No," I spoke involuntarily and my hand shook so that I was forced to put my cup down in order not to spill the liquid. "I mean—that is to say, not yet."

"Is it the old one?" she asked, eyes narrowed. "I saw that stone face. She must be hell to have in the house."

"Yes," I replied relievedly. "Madame Dessaultes does not like me."

"Humph. She wouldn't like anyone who took any part of her darling boy away from her." Roxanne took up another sweet and munched on it as she studied my face. "*I* wouldn't take any nonsense from her, Aurielle. The only way to handle one like that is to give as good as you take."

"I shall be firmer," I replied, wondering what Roxanne would say if I blurted out the truth, that for all his beautiful body and charming ways, my husband was a sexual cripple. And further, I somehow sensed at last that it had not only deformed him genitally but mentally as well. Knowing Roxanne, she might even laugh after her initial surprise. But no, my husband's secret was mine and I must guard it well. I added idly, "I have thought it would be pleasant if we invited Captain Kincannon to dinner one night soon—and you as well."

She flashed me a brief, astonished glance. "That's uncommonly nice of you, Aurielle, considering how you feel about me."

"I find my feelings for you have undergone a change —since *you* are no longer the swaggering, insolent little pirate you were."

She laughed cynically. "Ah, but underneath this veneer of ladyism I *am* a swaggering, insolent pirate. Perhaps it is that you have forgiven me for being so—even as I have forgiven you for being more beautiful than I. You are even more beautiful than Ondine and I had thought her the loveliest woman alive."

I was astonished by her candor and said cautiously, "You have restored the confidence you destroyed earlier when you remarked on my unhappy appearance."

"I shan't ever pay you such a compliment again," she retorted, scowling. "Indeed, I already regret—" She broke off as the sharp-faced Claudette Dessaultes returned.

"Ah, you cousins are having a fine visit, I see. May I join you for a cup of coffee and a sweetmeat?" she asked with a smile that was as false as the color in her cheeks.

We both murmured assent and the conversation then veered to Valier, with his mother singing his praises and inevitably leading coyly to the promise of grandchildren. "I can hardly wait to fill the house with them," she sighed. "Valier is so handsome. His children will be beautiful and brilliant just like their papa."

She went on for several minutes and Roxanne concealed a yawn. At the first break in Claudette's litany, she said, "I must leave. It has been delightful and you must come and see us soon, Aurielle." She looked at me with a grimace on the way out and whispered, "Old nannygoat —what a bore!"

I almost laughed despite my gloom.

That night after dinner, I sat in the drawing room with Valier, who smoked his pipe, and his mother, who was needle-pointing. We spoke desultorily of the day, with Claudette first regaling him about showing me the duties I was expected to perform. Valier in turn discussed his day at the bank. Claudette ignored me so expertly that I had only to murmur occasionally as my part in the conversation.

"Captain Kincannon has persuaded his associate, Rodeur Cheviot, to put his money in our bank instead of the Bank of Louisiana, *maman*," Valier said, tamping his pipe with fresh tobacco. "Kincannon now owns considerable shares of stock in the bank and I do not propose to sell him more or he would own more than I." He laughed, putting a candle to the pipe and drawing strongly before adding, "And here is a further note of interest. Kincannon's new plantation home is over half finished, but he must stop construction. The blockade has prevented delivery of marble and mahogany."

"Very domestic plans for a single man—and one who is not accepted," his mother sniffed.

"I would like to invite him and Monsieur Cheviot to dinner soon," I said quietly, "along with my cousin Roxanne and Tante Ondine."

"I suppose *you* plan to help him break into our society, since your dear aunt was charitable enough to let him call at her house," Claudette said with a chilly smile.

"I think she's a bit of a matchmaker, *maman*," Valier said indulgently.

"I think possibly I am," I replied, uncomfortably aware that I was thinking more about seeing Kincannon again than any of the others.

"You plan to pair Roxanne and the captain—Madame Chaille and M'sieu Cheviot?" Claudette lifted her brows.

"That would be nice," I admitted.

"It is dangerous to manipulate lives, Aurielle," she said acidly. "Take care lest you perform a disservice."

"I propose only to put the opportunity before each of them, madame," I replied coldly.

Valier laughed easily. "And at this dinner I would like to also invite my good friends Eugene Poliet and Gabriel Villere. Both are fine Creoles—and Mother can find no fault with them." He looked at me with inescapable meaning. Opportunity was being put before me as well.

I shrank inwardly. He would parade these men for me, making it simple and discreet to take a lover—with cold murder in his heart.

"That would be lovely," I said, smooth-faced while fresh panic took me as he rose and tapped out his pipe. How could I go up into that beautiful bedroom with this twisted man who proposed I take a lover to provide him with children?

He stretched his arms above his head and said, "We will retire, *ma mère*. The hour grows late and I am sure Aurielle has had a long, hard day. I do not wish her to grow too tired with her household duties."

I was aware of Madame Dessaultes's resentful eyes as we left together.

In the bedroom, Valier closed the door firmly and as

firmly took me into his arms, kissing and caressing me. It was at that moment I realized I could not endure it. No matter the pity I felt for this man who had lost the love of his life and the son he hoped for—and had been robbed of his manhood as well. Suddenly I could not tolerate his futile lovemaking. I was passive in his arms, for I wanted to tear out of them and run screaming through the night.

"You are cool, *chérie*. Can you not put a little passion into your kiss? Come, make love to me—"

I turned my head. "I am very tired, Valier. It has been a long day. Your mother spent most of it giving me instructions."

"I shall have a chat with my mother, then. You are not to tire yourself. I want you fresh and ready for *me* when I come home of evenings," he said thickly.

Suddenly the distant roll of thunder came to our ears and he said, "Ah, a storm is brewing. A good night for making love." He began slowly unbuttoning my bodice and still I did not move. He slipped it from my shoulders, stroking my arms and back as he did so. I could bear it no longer!

I pulled away. "I will disrobe myself, Valier."

"Let me watch you then." His voice was unsteady with frustration and all at once, I felt my disrobing before him was somehow obscene. All my feelings for Valier Dessaultes had undergone a powerful change. I sensed that he was dimly aware of this and it only increased his frustrations. I wanted desperately to flee the room, and if I had had any other house to run to, I should have done so.

Instead, I went about the business of disrobing before him like an automaton. If I had attempted to go into Antoinette's room, I felt sure he would have struck me. Violence was in his clenched jaw, his glittering eyes, and the little vein that pulsated so furiously in his forehead. Finally, as I stood nude, ready to don the foamy lace and silk nightdress, he caught it from my hands and said, "No. You will sleep nude tonight."

By now the thunder was incessant and flares of lightning flickered in the candlelit room. All at once the storm broke and rain drummed a heavy beat against the windows and house. I sat naked on the bed, shivering while Valier disrobed. He did not remain nude, nor did he permit me to see his mutilated parts. He donned a nightshirt and came to me with arms outstretched. I longed to duck away, but sat immobile while he fondled me.

Suddenly he threw me fiercely to the bed, his body over mine, his sinewy hands wound into my thick hair. "You *are* changed! What has changed you? My God-damned mutilation, isn't it? You thought you married a *man*, didn't you? By God, you did, you fool! I can give you everything you desire—including fulfillment, *and you shall have it.* But you must love me—*only me,* you understand? I know your background well and I have lifted you high above it. You *owe* me, Aurielle Stuart Dessaultes—and you will pay in proper coin!"

Abruptly I was swept by fury that he should threaten me again. I writhed out of his grasp, crying hoarsely. "No, Valier, no! This is a travesty of love. I cannot share your bed with you. *I cannot!"*

He rolled away, breathing heavily, and we lay stiffly side by side until he spoke in a cold, controlled voice. "What do you propose to do?"

"We must have separate bedrooms. I feel—I feel warped and twisted when we touch. I cannot bear it. If you do not give me a separate room, I shall run away. I swear it."

"And I could have our marriage annulled. Once your background is known, you would wind up on Rampart Street in a little house with a dozen illegitimate children. Can you not see what I offer is far better than that?"

"I know you plan to parade a series of potential lovers before me with the object of pregnancy—then murder. I cannot do that either."

"Yes, you can." His voice was hard as iron. "I chose you deliberately because you are strong and beautiful. You were born for love, for the bearing of strong, fine sons, and you shall bear them—and they will be Des-saultes sons."

Where would I be if Valier denounced me, claimed he was defrauded, that his bride had false credentials? Ondine could not take me back. I would truly be cast out into the streets. I said huskily, "Then at least spare me this—this pretense of physical love. Please let me have my own bedroom and refrain from—these caresses."

He laughed harshly. "And I thought because you were from the gutters, you would be ready for any lover, despite your beauty. You are full of surprises, my little tart. Ah, well—unlike these New Orleans ladies of blood, when the bargain is not to your liking, you cannot run home."

I was silent for a long moment, then said quietly, "You are wrong about me, Valier. When I give my heart to a man, it will be forever."

"I *am* a man—you *gave* your heart to me!" There was a catch in his voice.

"I only thought I loved you and I cannot face this empty act of passion that leads to nothing." My voice grew muffled. "I was—wrong. Oh, I am so sorry for you—"

Suddenly he gripped me with hands of steel and I cried out with pain. He spoke between his teeth, *"Never* say you are sorry for me! I want no pity. I will kill the man or woman who pities me. I am strong and my body is tough and I *am* a man, despite what happened to me."

"You must forgive me," I whispered, biting my lip to control tears of pain. "You must try to understand my feelings, Valier." A sob caught in my throat.

He was silent. He did not loosen his grip and I bit back a scream. Then he said slowly, "We will go on as planned except I will grant your wish for a separate bedroom—we will arrange it in the morning. You will choose a lover and bear a baby for me. *That must be."* He released me at last and rolled to the far side of the bed.

I lay quivering in a tide of repulsion, disillusion, sorrow and pity. Toward dawn I slept.

Chapter

13

Antoinette was puzzled, but without voicing the questions in her eyes, she moved to a small room on the third floor with the rest of the servants and I moved into the room adjoining Valier's larger one. The decor, the crossed swords and pistols, made it hard for me to forget my experience in Valier's arms and I did not look at them when I could avoid it.

Claudette was aghast at our separate bedrooms. However, Valier pointed out to her that there was a door between and it was easy for us to join in one room. And her promise to put the house under my authority proved false. She kept a stranglehold on all decisions, leaving me with much time on my hands. Thus it was that Valier arranged for me to continue my music lessons with the fever-eyed and gently spoken Belle Fontaine. However, most of my spare time I spent among the hundreds of books to be found in the Dessaultes library.

My husband and I went to many galas and balls during October and the days slipped by as winter drew on. Claudette Dessaultes went with us to every social function and I was constantly aware of her silent reproof that I was not pregnant. I wondered how long it would be before her disappointment and anger became vocal. These days my husband watched me with a terrible kind of patience and his mother was worse. Her eyes went to my waist every morning, as if by watching she could *will* a child within me.

Nearly every evening, Valier would bring home one or two male friends. To please him, I would look at them appraisingly and sometimes I would almost play the coquette with them.

At our dinner parties, Valier would always insist there be at least two extra men. Because he thought I liked them better than the others, it was usually Gabriel Villere and Eugene Poliet. Thus they were present at another of the parties I had promised Roxanne and so were Kincannon and Chevoit.

When dinner was served, I found myself observing Kincannon surreptitiously with a keen and unexpected awareness. Unbidden in my mind, his powerful figure arose as I had first seen him, his shirt open to the waist with the curling black hair that grew so thickly on his chest he must shave it off his throat. *He* could sire sons by the dozens!

Sudden guilt took hold of me. I had not invited him for Roxanne. I had invited him because *I* was drawn to him. I paled and my mouth went dry. I felt my husband's cynical eyes on me. I looked steadily at my plate through the main course and I did not look again at Kincannon.

Cheviot was charming to all the ladies present, these social events bringing out a nobility and aristocratic gallantry that I had always recognized in him, even at Barataria.

Ondine sparkled in bright conversation. Her pearlescent skin glowed as she talked merrily of her new servants and how well they were adapting to her household. Once our glances met and she nodded imperceptibly as if to say she was glad to see that I was so well situated. I hid a hysterical laugh behind a cough.

Later, over after-dinner liqueurs in the drawing room, Ondine clapped her little hands and said, "I am going to have a great ball on January fifteenth, *mes amis*. And you must all come! It will be a sort of pre-Shrove Tuesday celebration, a *mardi gras,* you might say. I have already begun arrangements with the carterers. There will be food to make your mouth water and I shall simply flood the house with champagnes and liquors!"

Everyone spoke at once, expressing pleasure and excitement over the prospect of one of Ondine's sumptuous parties. Talk swirled among us and the evening was a great success. Valier was quite winning, the perfect host, and Claudette was fatuously pleasant. I flirted innocently with Gabriel and Eugene, so innocently I was sure they would not follow up on my smiles and twinkling eyes.

Roxanne, like some brilliant and fluttering bird, spent her charms on Kincannon, while Cheviot devoted himself to Ondine. But at the end, Roxanne and the captain departed separately after a friendly good-bye, and I was secretly glad.

The following morning I took my courage in my hands and entered Valier's room after rapping on the adjoining door. I had been building up to this moment for weeks, but now I discarded all the well-chosen phrases I had prepared during sleepless nights.

Without preamble, I said, "I owe a great deal of money to Antoinette Desmottes and to Ondine Chaille, as you probably know. I would appreciate your making it possible to repay them."

He smiled coldly. "You are not the warm-blooded woman I had hoped would be my wife. Why should I repay your debts?"

"Because I *am* your wife and I shall keep your secret from others, even as I discharge my duties"—I paused, swallowed, and concluded—"as you wish."

"Then you will choose from among the men I have brought before you?"

"You have not yet brought one I would submit to, Valier. When you do, I shall—make my choice."

He smiled obliquely. "That is good enough. How much do you need for each?"

"Five thousand for Antoinette, five for Ondine."

"Ten thousand. You come high, my dear, for a guttersnipe."

"And you will never refer to me by that epithet again," I responded coldly, "if you expect my cooperation."

Within a week, I had repaid the old debts that had harassed me for so many long months.

During the Christmas season, Valier took me shopping, which he seemed to enjoy thoroughly, and he denied me nothing. He even managed to prevent his mother from accompanying us most of the time. As we made our way through town on these shopping excursions, he often stopped to introduce me to some handsome Creole cavalier, which always disheartened me, for I knew I had not yet prepared myself to accept a lover. But the dress that he chose for me to wear to Ondine's ball was another indication that my time for choosing was growing short.

It was an exquisite gown of deep rose that revealed more than it concealed. It clung to my breasts and fell gracefully over my thighs, showing their curved and slender shapes when I moved.

And on the evening of Ondine's celebration, Valier and his ubiquitous mother and I left in our carriage at around nine in the evening. It was Valier's casual way never to be directly on time. It was one of his vanities to create an entrance and I had long ago adjusted to it.

By the time we arrived, the festivities were in full swing. Ondine Chaille greeted us and I admitted to myself that I had never seen her appear more beautiful. There was a glow about her, an incandescence that made the three-tiered crystal chandelier above the salon pale by comparison.

"Good evening, my dears," she cried, with a dazzling smile. "Here, give your wraps to Sebastien. Do come in. Ah, my angel," she whispered in rapid French, "you look ravishing." Then, "I'm sure you know everyone here. Eugene has never recovered from your marrying Valier, Aurielle!" She bent a roguish eye on Valier as she added, "He is waiting your arrival even now, *ma petite*."

Only when we were safely launched in the great salon did she turn her charms elsewhere. As Valier took me in his arms for the dance, he murmured, "I see the estimable Captain Kincannon dancing with Solange Villere, despite the scowls of her father."

"You would think the people of this city would accept the man," I said with asperity, "after so long a time."

"It is the wives and mothers, my love. They keep the men incensed and I do not expect them to ever accept him because of his——"

"Baratarian background," I interrupted with sarcasm. "I'm sure I would suffer the same treatment but for your name, Valier."

"My name and your pleasant fiction about a lord's daughter," he agreed. "Ah—Poliet has spotted you. He is not exactly what I had in mind to father my son—Villere is much more the man—but he will do if you choose him."

"I do not choose him," I said remotely.

"You must choose one of them and soon," he said, his voice growing rough. "*Maman* is more and more anxious to become a grandmother."

I made no answer as I observed Ondine motion to Sebastien and the two of them left the room together. I thought for the dozenth time, *Poor Ondine isn't free of her duties even with a fleet of caterers to serve her parties.*

As I floated from one pair of arms to another, flattering with my eyes, making inconsequential chatter, I was not aware how long she and her servant had been gone until they reappeared, first Sebastien, then a little later, Ondine. Her face was flushed and she appeared no older than eighteen, causing me to marvel anew at her inexhaustible joy in living. Once again, I thought with wistful longing, *Ah, you could be my mother. You could!*

I laughed aloud at my foolishness, causing my partner, Gabriel Villere, to say alertly, "Something amuses you, Aurielle? Such a sad little laugh, so full of longing."

"I was laughing at my own foolishness, Gabriel. You cannot expect me to reveal such a thought," I returned flippantly.

"Everything about you is *charmante,* dear, dear

Aurielle. I long to know your innermost thoughts, even those contemplating your—foolishness. I wish I could be part of your foolishness." He spoke in a low, intimate tone and once again I had the sensation that my husband had somehow conveyed to all his friends that my life was my own and he was an indulgent husband.

It was a situation I was to encounter many times during the evening, that of finding myself with a man prepared to take liberties with me. Indeed, the bachelors —and some of the husbands—sought me out with disturbing regularity. My husband left me much to myself, dancing all too frequently with wives as well as single girls. And my popularity, while rising with the men, was sinking correspondingly with the women of my acquaintance.

My last would-be partner was the persistent Eugene Poliet and I sent him to fetch a glass of wine for me. While I sat on a sofa at the side of the big salon idly fanning my flushed face, I noted Ondine, wearing an expression of intense concentration, leave the room once more in the company of Sebastien. This time I rose involuntarily and went to the door where I observed them mount the stairs in the rear of the foyer.

Surprise spread through me slowly as I watched them hurry up the flight and disappear into the shadows above. Candles in the wall sconces flickered at their swift passage and steadied. I turned back to take my seat as the other ladies observed me with varying expressions. The young ones wore poorly concealed envy and the older ones were reproving.

I frowned. *Where* were the two of them going? I remembered my conjecture that Sebastien and Ondine might be lovers. No, they would have betrayed themselves in a dozen ways—but would they? I was suddenly consumed with curiosity. I gazed unseeingly at the dancers before me.

My glance was caught by Kincannon as he looked out over the bright head of Roxanne and he smiled briefly. As they turned, I saw she was talking and her expression was angry. Eugene Poliet drew up before me, two glasses in his hands. He gave me the wine, retaining the brandy for himself and made ready to seat himself beside me.

We had again returned to the sofa when Ondine and Sebastien entered the room forty minutes later. Again she wore beauty like a cloak about her. Her lovely hair was untouched, her dress exquisite. *No,* I thought—*she and Sebastien have done nothing together that would disturb her appearance, yet she has drunk of some marvelous mixture that has rejuvenated and refreshed her.* Sebastien was impassive, but his eyes were brilliant. What was upstairs? The servants were in their rooms on the third floor, but Ondine, herself, and Roxanne were the only ones who occupied the second floor.

"—and we could take a long drive before," Eugene was saying in a low, enticing voice. "Then you might stop off at my home. We could—"

"What are you saying, Eugene?" I broke in with astonishment. "I can go for no ride with you. I am a married woman."

He flushed a dull red and said stiffly, "I beg your pardon, Aurielle, but Valier himself said you grew bored and lonely during your long days at home. I thought to ease your boredom."

"That is most kind of you, Eugene. Will you excuse me, please? I must go upstairs to—fix my coiffure." I left abruptly and went into the foyer.

Hesitating but a moment, I took the stairs and quietly made my way up them. At the second floor, I looked down the familiar hall and paused. Instinct was loud in me. The two did not stop here. One candle burned in the wall sconce beside Ondine's door. Had she gone up to confer with her own servants? It seemed uncharacteristic that she would have gone up to reassure them for any reason whatsoever.

Still, my feet continued to mount the stairs. Up on the third floor, the darkness was smothering and I knew a moment of panic. I paused again, peering upward into the stygian gloom that was the attics. I descended to the second floor once more.

For some inexplicable reason, I felt impelled to take those unseen steps to the attics. If only I had a candle! I looked once more down the hall at the single candle glimmering on the wall beside Ondine's door. It was late and the candle was almost spent. I walked swiftly to it, lifting it from the sconce, and retraced my steps to the attic stairs.

It was the first time I had ever gone up those stairs, but I climbed the steps steadily. It was cold and damp up here and a faintly repulsive odor smote my nostrils. I halted momentarily. I was treading loose boards which were laid across the beams that supported the house. In that instant, a muffled groan came to my ears and suddenly my heart gave a wild bound of unnameable fear. Still, some spectral force drew me along the narrow passage that had opened where the stairs ended.

It was then I saw the thin thread of light beneath a door where the passage branched off. Standing perfectly still, I waited. The hard thump of my heart seemed almost audible, but it was my own pulses I heard singing in my ears. The sounds from below were faint and the whisper of music from the orchestra was like the sound of wind above the eaves. It was lonely and terrifying up in this thick darkness.

Drawn to the door with the faint light beneath it, I moved like a person in the grip of a nightmare. I was unable to help myself. Some force greater than I drove me onward. Reaching the door, I touched the knob, realizing that my hands were cold and wet with perspiration as I slowly turned it.

The sight that met my eyes made my brain reel. One dim candle burned on the single piece of furniture in the room, an old table. There were chains embedded in the rough timbers that framed the unfinished chamber. Pearl and Tressa were held upright by them. Their naked bodies were covered with dark weals from the slashes of a whip, which lay across the candlelit table. Bonnie Trelawney lay prone upon the floor beside Catherine Bonham. Only Jasper, Couri, and the two new servants were missing. Both Catherine and Bonnie also bore marks of the whip, but their breasts appeared burned, as if by hot coals. It was then I noted a brazier full of rose-red embers beside the table.

The stench of sweat and blood and seared human flesh in the room was overpowering. Excrement, released in their agonies, added to the nauseating smell. They stared at me with dull eyes which widened slowly.

"God and the devil!" I burst out. "I cannot believe my eyes!" I rushed to the single window and threw it open to the cold winter wind. It opened on the side roof and I suddenly realized it was probably the window through which Selina and Bess had plunged to their deaths. *And Ondine had said Bess was sleepwalking—that they fell from the second floor!*

I began with Catherine, swiftly untying her hands and feet while I asked, "Catherine, what is the meaning of this? Why in God's name are you in this chamber of horrors?"

From her place beside Catherine, Bonnie Trelawney moaned softly, "Ah, now Sebastien'll true kill us—"

Catherine's dark eyes were wide with terror. "Mistress, ye won't tell ye've discovered—"

"Aurielle," the voice behind her was low, hard, and cold. "Get up from there immediately and get back down to the guests."

I turned to see Ondine Chaille in the door. Behind her loomed the black bulk of Sebastien. As I stared at the two, he moved her aside and stepped into the room, picking up the long black whip from the little table and said, "I told you, madame, no good would come of taking this one into your home."

"Fer God's sake, Madame Aurielle," Pearl whispered in agony, her dark skin gleaming with sweat, "do as she says er we'll all die."

Sebastien lifted the whip and, with an expert flick, drew blood from Pearl's shoulder with the tip of it.

I screamed, "Stop it—" and Ondine was on me, her smooth hand across my mouth.

"Sebastien, you will do as I command!" she said huskily. "Get their bonds off—hand them their clothes and get them out of here to their rooms. I will take care of Aurielle. *Vite, vite!*"

Before she had finished speaking, Sebastien was moving lithely among the servants, unlocking their chains, untying their bonds. Then with a speed that was amazing, he quietly closed the window I had opened. From a darkened corner, he flung the clothes at the women and they began scuttling into them.

Ondine had not released my arm and her fingernails were cutting into my flesh. I tore from her grasp and panted, "Madame—Ondine, what do you mean by this? Why are you punishing them so horribly?"

Sebastien herded the women into the passageway and I could hear him. "If you think you have suffered, beasts, you have much to learn. If you utter a word against madame or me, I swear you will die in ways much more painful than you have known." His voice faded.

Ondine snuffed the candle on the table and then the one I held, and we stood in utter blackness. The evil odor of sweat and excrement gagged me. I swallowed down a desire to retch.

Her hand was soft now as it sought mine in the darkness. "You will be missed, Aurielle—by your husband and by others if you do not return soon."

I jerked from her light grasp as she led me into the long, narrow passageway. I heard the click as Ondine closed the door to the foul and fetid room. I stumbled in the darkness and felt her hand catch me.

"Come," she murmured, "we will go to my room and talk a moment while you collect yourself. Whatever made you do such a foolish thing as to come to the attics —the last place *you* should be."

I made no reply and she led me firmly down the stairs where light bloomed slowly about us. Sebastien before us had lighted six fresh candles in wall sconces. Dimly, I marveled at the big man's ability to move with such rapidity.

She said softly, "I do hope no one comes seeking you before you can present a reasonable appearance. You look wild, my dear."

"Then you would be uncovered—for the monster you are," I said thickly. How could *my mother* be guilty of such barbarity? A wave of nausea swept me and I leaned weakly against the wall, gagging miserably.

"Ah, Aurielle," Ondine said soothingly, "we will soon

be in my room and I will bathe your face with cool water, my angel."

"I'm not your angel—you are *not* my mother. I couldn't bear it!"

In the dim light I saw her eyes narrow swiftly. *"Chérie,* you do not know what you are saying." She opened the door and pulled me into her room.

"I know exactly what I am saying. You are a monster." My voice was choked. I had loved this woman with all my heart and she had, in one horrible instant, violated that love.

In the glowing warmth of her beautiful room, she faced me, her white face blazing, red lips quivering. Incredibly, two diamond teardrops hung on the long, thick lashes. "Aurielle, I love you—my own. How can you call me a monster?"

I backed away from her, outlined by the light of the oil lamp on her dressing table. What did she mean, *my own?* Was she at last ready to admit that I was her daughter? Oh, God, don't let it be so! I whispered, "Because you drove that child and Selina to their deaths. My God, Ondine, I could forgive you nearly anything but abusing—driving that child to her death!"

"But I didn't! I left Selina to care for her while we—while I—"

"While you came down to my wedding ball and danced and *laughed,*" I cried. "I know now why they died. It was suicide, to escape this house of horrors! Under my breath I muttered, "I think you are insane."

"But I am not insane, *chérie.*" Tears fell upon her cheeks and slowly rolled down. Like a bird fascinated by a snake, I watched her in the lamplight. She was so beautiful—*and so evil.* "You cannot know the—emotion—the feelings that drive me." She put her scented handkerchief to her eyes, then added piteously, "You must not tell what you have seen. It would ruin me in New Orleans. Have you no pity?"

"Pity?" I cried. "You speak of pity? You who had none for those poor people you torture? How long—how many have you killed doing this?"

"I do it only when we have an entertainment. It is

then I am stimulated." Her voice fell to sudden pleading. "Ah, Aurielle, you cannot imagine the exhilaration, the joy, the excitement that Sebastien and I know when he lays on the whip—or I handle the brand in the tongs. You must try it, my love, to know it. The ecstasy is unimaginable." Her face was alight with a kind of glory and I realized all at once that she was under a vast sexual stimulus. She flushed with pleasure in remembrance, then caught herself. "Aurielle, I have not done it so much—since you came into my life."

"I shall expose you for what you are," I said huskily.

"You cannot do that," she replied with sudden calm certainty. "You owe me a debt besides the five thousand, Madame Valier Dessaultes, a debt you have sworn to pay. I am calling on you now for payment."

I put a hand out and caught at the edge of the armoire as realization washed over me. It was true. I had sworn to repay Ondine for all she had done for me. The very clothing I had worn, bloodstained though it had been in September as I held Bessie's head in my lap, had been bought by Ondine. For all those long months, this woman had bought my food, supplied my every wish, educated and cared for me. More, she had nursed me back to life when I had nearly died of yellow fever—I would have died but for her. Having repaid her in money, I still had a debt of the spirit, an intangible debt.

"I knew you were not a bastard. I had faith in you and I have taught you everything of honor that you know—"

"Honor?" I swung on her in a rage. "What do you know of honor? Beating, burning, torturing innocents who are threatened with death if they speak of it—and all to satiate a twisted and perverted desire in yourself!"

"Does this mean you will not honor your debt to me?" Those incredible tears were glistening in the azure eyes once more, but her head was held high, lamplight gleaming on burnished curls.

I hesitated, my eyes narrowing. "I will honor it only if you give freedom to your servants. If you hire free men and women—if you will swear never to torture another living creature."

She was silent, then said, "You drive a hard bargain. If I free Tressa, Pearl, Jasper—all of them, where will they go? They are used to life here—"

"What a lie! No one could become used to such a life. They will come with me. I will hire them to serve in the Dessaultes house."

"You are taking away all the joy in life for me. You know that, do you not?" she said lifelessly.

"I will not argue with you, Ondine. If you do not promise, I shall go downstairs and tell the governor himself. I will ask the authorities at the Cabildo, the judges, the lawyers, the police, to come and see the room for themselves. It is against the law to abuse a slave."

"No, no! I promise. You may take them with you!"

"And have I your promise to hire free men and women? That you will never torture another?"

"Yes—and you will say nothing?"

"I will say nothing," I agreed. "And we are even. I paid you back the money you spent on me and now I am paying with loyalty."

"When do you want the servants to come to the Dessaultes?" Her voice was full of hopelessness. The lovely face was white and drained.

"I will come tomorrow with two carriages. Have them pack their belongings, for I shall take them home with me in the morning." I thought fleetingly of facing my mother-in-law and put it aside. I would talk with Valier this very night, persuade him to let me hire the Chaille servants en masse. *Oh, I am getting deeper in his debt each day,* I thought uneasily. But I pushed away the thought of eventual payment to *him.* "I have your word, Ondine?" I asked once more.

She looked up, eyes glittering. "On *my* honor. Which is better than you imagine."

There was a soft laugh from the door and both of us whirled to see Roxanne leaning there, her turquoise dress shimmering against her bare white shoulders, her copper hair agleam.

"How long have you been there?" Ondine asked in rapid French.

"Since you began your fascinating conversation. Indeed, *tante*"—she came down hard on the word—"when I saw Aurielle was not to be seen, I came looking for her—very discreetly, of course."

"You should have made your presence known," Ondine reproved.

"And missed your argument with all the interesting details it revealed? Ah, Ondine, you are a woman of many facets, while you, Aurielle, are like a glass of clear water."

"That means, I suppose, that you do not condemn Ondine's—perversions?"

"I condemn them, *cousine,* but I, even as you, owe her a debt and I am willing to settle for the promises you have extracted from her." Again she laughed softly, but there was biting contempt in her eyes.

"What is to keep my servants from talking, Aurielle?" Ondine asked, a tremor in the calm voice.

"I'm sure Sebastien will think of something to tell them that will make them hold their tongues. Certainly they have held them all these months. I'm sure they will be only too glad to escape with their lives."

"Ah, but when they are free—" Ondine's great blue eyes were tragic.

I knew I should pity this deformed mind, but I could not. "I will tell them," I said, "that the price of their freedom is their silence."

She looked down at the glittering bottles of perfume that lined her dressing table. "My life is empty and my Sebastien's as well," she said sadly.

I turned to leave. Roxanne fell in step beside me. "Are you really going to remain silent?" she asked curiously.

"If she keeps her promise to me, I shall."

We began descending the stairs. "And if she does not, Aurielle, how will you know?"

I halted and turned to her. "Roxanne, you and Ulysses could observe her actions. You would know."

"Spy, you mean?" she asked coldly.

"I thought you were as repelled as I by such practices," I said with equal coldness.

"I am repelled by spying, too."

"Very well. I shall have to observe her myself, when I can."

"I will watch her," she said grudgingly as we took the stairs again. "She is very smooth—all these months and we didn't suspect."

"You will know," I replied as we reached the bottom step and then entered the salon. "She will wear that *look* —young and beautiful and transported."

The dance was in full sway. I glimpsed my husband with Lisette Poliet and remembered her conversation about the massacre at Fort Mims. How fascinated, how rapt Ondine Chaille had been at her graphic descriptions of the grisly details! I went directly to one of the waiters who was serving wine and took a glass from his tray. I still felt nauseous and faint. I stood near the dining-room door with my head averted from the succulent foods that were spread on the table. The room was crowded and I saw Kincannon among the others. He was looking at me; with a word to his two male companions, he left and approached me.

"You are extraordinarily pale, Madame Dessaultes," he said with a faint smile. "Does this presage another happy announcement?"

"You are insufferable," I whispered, growing paler with anger.

"I meant only to offer my congratulations." His black eyes were alert and curious and contained something else I could not name. "I am concerned for you. You appear to have suffered some—shock?"

I had not suspected him of such perception. "I have had a shock," I murmured, leaning weakly against the wall.

"Is there something I can do?" he asked swiftly.

"No."

"Can you tell me what has so—distressed you?"

"No."

"Then let me fetch you another glass of champagne." He went to the sideboard, where he was met by a waiter with a tray of fresh-filled glasses. Returning, he handed one to me, saying, "We will go into the sitting room where you may collect yourself. You look ready to faint."

Silently, I let him take my arm and steer me into the foyer and beyond to the empty sitting room. There I sank down upon a sofa and took a deep swallow of wine. For some minutes we sat together without speaking.

Then he said slowly, "I have been observing you at the various social functions we have attended and I have come to the conclusion that your marriage is not a happy one, Aurielle."

"I should think that would afford you some amusement," I replied bitterly. I could not get the stench of the attic room out of my lungs and I felt ill with it.

He said bluntly, "I have never had much use for Dessaultes. He is a reckless, hot-headed man." He paused. "And lately, I have wondered if he is as good a businessman as I previously thought."

"It is too late for me to wonder about any of those things," I blurted and immediately regretted what the remark revealed.

"Then you are *not* happy."

"I am miserable," I responded, heedless of what I was revealing and to whom. I was full to bursting with my misery and the opportunity to pour it out was more than I could resist. "Nothing has gone as I planned." To my disgust, two great hot tears welled up in my eyes and I put the empty wineglass down on a nearby table and dashed the tears from my eyes. I felt better than I had in days, just for blurting out the truth about my marriage. It seemed to ease some of the pressure of Ondine's diabolic cruelties as well.

With curious tenderness, Kincannon drew a large linen handkerchief from his pocket and began blotting my tears, which only increased with his unexpected kindness. "There," he murmured as to a distraught child, "it cannot be as bad as you think. Tell me about it," and he put his arm about my shoulders and drew me to him.

I think I might have poured it all out at that moment, despite my firm intention to keep the terrible secrets that were mine, but I was forestalled. I had no sooner melted into those strong arms than I moved my head a fraction and found myself looking at the door to the foyer where Valier Dessaultes suddenly materialized.

His face was white and his eyes were blazing with fury. I stiffened in Kincannon's arms as the blood left my own face.

"What is it, Aurielle?" Kincannon was puzzled as he took my shoulders in his hands and held me from him. Then he followed my frozen glance and turned to face Valier. "Good evening, Valier," he said imperturbably. "Your wife—"

"I am not feeling well," I babbled hastily. "I have a terrible headache, Valier, dear."

"So it appears. Thank you, Quentin, for seeing to her," he said quietly, coming into the room and taking Kincannon's handkerchief from me to wipe the last traces of tears from my eyes.

I was weak with terror. Would Valier strike Kincannon and challenge him before my eyes? A brief vision of the two of them exchanging blows on the spot swept past. They did neither.

"You are most gallant to lend her your handkerchief, Quentin," Valier said, "It must be a very painful headache to bring tears. Here you are." He handed the square back to Kincannon, who took it silently. "I will give her mine."

"I—I no longer need one," I murmured. "I would really like very much to go home."

"What? And ruin your evening?" Valier chided gently. "You will offend your aunt as well, my dear."

Some of my poise was returning. "I think my aunt would be the first to recommend I go home."

Kincannon was observing us narrowly, but he was silent.

"The evening is young yet," Valier said lightly. "Do you not think you might feel better if I fetched you some wine?"

"I have just had some wine."

"Then come. I have had but one dance with you, my love. I feel slighted."

That was his doing, I thought angrily, for he had danced with every woman in the room during the evening. Kincannon was still, wariness in every line of his big, graceful body. I knew that he fully expected Valier to challenge him for having held me in his arms, but Valier seemed inclined to be companionable despite the rage that had been in his black eyes.

I said coldly, "Valier, would you keep me here when I am unwell?"

"Of course not," he said regretfully. "It is only that the night has been such a success and you never looked lovelier. We will leave at once." He turned courteously to Kincannon with a slight bow. "You will excuse us, Quentin, my good friend?"

"Of course. I hope Madame Dessaultes recovers soon," he said evenly and with a nod of his head he left us.

Later in the Dessaultes carriage with Valier, I leaned back against the leather seat and drew a ragged breath. What had moved my husband to accept the scene so calmly? I knew he had been in a killing rage the instant he saw me in Kincannon's arms.

His mother had elected to stay the balance of the evening at Ondine's and we were alone in the carriage as Valier turned on me. In a low, cutting tone he said, "I am glad you have made your choice at last. It is not the one I would have you choose, but I accept it."

"What do you mean?" I asked, my heart taking a great bound.

"That you have settled on Kincannon to sire our child, of course," he spoke in a rush. "I have no use for him, a pirate—a man with a shady background, no matter the rumors of his noble birth." He turned and his arms shot out to grip me in a vise, jerking me to him. He brought his mouth down on mine in a long, angry kiss in which he forced my lips apart and attempted to thrust his tongue between my teeth. Instinctively I recoiled and twisted in his grasp.

This seemed to bring his rage to a new high and with cruel strength he forced me back against the cushions, throwing his leg over me to hold me immovable while his kisses grew more savage, more bruising. I was suddenly still as death, neither resisting nor responding, and it had the desired effect, for slowly his passion faded. He kissed my cold, unresponsive lips one last time, then drew away, muttering, "Damn your soul to hell, Aurielle. Damn you for the cold, unfeeling woman you are with me."

We were silent until we reached the house. But on our way to our adjoining rooms, he caught my wrist in steel fingers and hissed, "I'll wager you were not so cold to Kincannon before I came upon you!"

"He was trying to—comfort me."

"Comfort you?" He swung me hard around to face him. "For what? Did you tell him about me?" He caught my other arm, his fingers digging into the soft flesh. "Did you?"

"No, I did not," I blazed suddenly, "and you're a fool, Valier." I began to lie. "I cannot stand the man. I have hated him from the day we met. I have not chosen him—I wouldn't let him touch me!"

He burst into laughter. "My dear, you are the fool, not I. He was touching you and you were willing—more than that! I saw your faces." He released me suddenly. "You have chosen indeed, despite your protestations. And I shall make it easy for you. Tomorrow night we will have dinner together."

"I shall be ill again, then," I retorted.

He looked at me through slitted eyes and rocked a little on the balls of his feet. "I have never beaten a woman," he murmured with a thin smile. "I might even enjoy beating you, Aurielle. You tempt me."

I drew a quick breath. "You wouldn't dare!"

"Try me. I could do it very silently, in such a way as to leave you unmarked but in severe pain, *ma petite*." He paused, reaching out to take my shrinking shoulders in his hands, gently this time. "Do not misjudge me. I am quite capable of killing you—by means that would never be discovered. And I will do that, my love, if you fail to provide me with a son." His hands dropped and he turned away to enter his room.

I stood frozen for a long moment. *My husband had just threatened me with death.* Now indeed was I caught in a crossfire from which there was no escape. Where could I turn? Realization crept in upon me. There was nowhere I could turn, nowhere to run.

It did not occur to me that I would be going to fetch

Ondine's freed servants the following morning until I crept into my bed. One more tie among the many that bound me to Valier. Quietly I struck the flint beside my bed and the candle bloomed into light. I took it in an unsteady hand and made my way to the adjoining door and rapped lightly. There was an instant answer.

"Come in, Aurielle. It isn't locked."

I opened it to see Valier sitting in a large chair beside the dying fire, a glass of brandy beside the candle on the table. "You see, you have driven me to drink." His laugh was low and ugly.

"Valier, I—I want to hire Ondine's servants to-morrow morning. I have persuaded her to free them in order that I might bring them with me. I—I am so very fond of them all."

"What did you say?" He looked at me dumbfounded and I repeated my words. "My God," he ejaculated, "what an anticlimax! I've threatened you with death and you tell me you want to hire your aunt's servants. They must indeed mean a great deal to you."

"Yes. I had great—difficulty in persuading Ondine to part with them, but because of her deep fondness for me, she is willing to let me have them." I hesitated. "You wil let me hire them, will you not?"

He was suddenly crafty. "I would let an *obedient* wife hire them. But alas, I have a most recalcitrant wife." I was silent. "Is it not true, Aurielle? Aren't you reluctant to give me what I most want? Haven't I, over the last months, given you every opportunity to do as I ask?"

"Yes," I replied in a whisper.

"I want very much to make you happy, but that is a two-way street, isn't it?" When I did not answer, he repeated the question and again I whispered, "Yes." "Then surely, in all fairness, you wouldn't expect me to go on being so generous. After all, my dear, I have paid your debts, bought you everything you desire. And now you want me to *pay* for a whole fleet of servants we do not need." He took up the brandy glass and drained the contents in a single swallow. *"Vraiment,* Aurielle, I must have your promise for the one thing I want in exchange for my generosity." He took up the decanter and poured a fresh glass of brandy. "Do I have it?"

Again I whispered, "Yes."

He laughed low and mockingly. "Then you will dress in your finest and have dinner tomorrow at the Café des Roses with Kincannon and me—and you will be your most charming with that questionable gentleman. I've no doubt that will come easily."

"Yes," I replied, turning back.

His voice cracked like a pistol shot. "Wait!"

I faced him.

"Come here, madame. We will have a drink to that!" He strode to the cabinet beside the fireplace and removed another brandy glass, filling it to the brim. He thrust it toward me. "Drink up, Aurielle. That should ease your headache and the tears that put you in Kincannon's arms."

I took the glass and my hand shook slightly, spilling a drop or two of the liquid; his little laugh was malevolent. "So you're afraid of me. That's good, madame, for I meant it when I said I would kill you. Now let me hear your promise."

"I promise to do as you—ask."

"You will have Kincannon's child and we will tell all New Orleans that it is mine, for I shall kill him as soon as your pregnancy is confirmed. Is that correct?"

"Yes." I put the glass to my lips and sipped the fiery drink.

"Drink it all, Aurielle. That will bind our pact."

I suddenly tossed it all down and, coughing, eyes watering, I handed the empty glass to Valier, who took it with a light laugh.

"Now," he said coldly, "we have a bargain. Bring your servants tomorrow. I will tell *maman* in the morning that I expect them."

Chapter
14

The following morning found me at the Chaille house, where Roxanne greeted me. "The house is in a ferment, *cousine*," she said cheerfully. "*Tante* and Sebastien are both organizing the servants—or at least Sebastien is. *Tante* is in the library at her desk, writing out the papers freeing the slaves and releasing those who are indentured. She was wondering if you expected to take the new cook and maid, after all."

"No. They are covered by her promise to me. It is only my *friends*—the ones she treated so cruelly that I will take."

"I cannot offer you coffee, Aurielle, unless I serve you myself. "Roxanne laughed.

"I wouldn't expect that, Roxanne," I retorted dryly. "Now that we are such ladies, serving others is beneath us, of course."

"You do not sound as if that agrees with you, *cousine*."

"I sometimes wonder if true happiness is not to be found only through serving others."

"*La,* what a profound statement!" she said merrily.

"It is one fit only for the very old who can do none other but serve—or for the very poor who have no choice."

"There is something in what you say," I sighed. "Where are the servants?"

"They are all in the kitchen with their bundles and bags. Ah, Tante Ondine, here you are!"

Ondine Chaille entered the sitting room, pale blue shadows beneath her blue eyes. Other than that, she bore no signs of the long evening just past. "Aurielle, here are the papers, showing all of my dear servants are free. When I told them, they did not know what to do—but then I informed them you were going to hire them at wages." She smiled sadly. "They were overjoyed, of course." Then turning at the sound behind her, she said, "Sebastien, will you have the servants come in and greet their new employer? I hope they will give you no trouble, Aurielle," she finished as the powerful black man bowed impassively and disappeared.

"I don't anticipate they will," I replied coolly. "Are you feeling well, Ondine?"

"I am tired, *chérie,* but it will pass. I regret I can offer you no refreshments due to the disarray—"

"I know," I put in ironically. "Roxanne has pointed out the disarray I have caused."

"Sebastien and I will go to the auction block today and possibly to the docks where I shall secure some likely bondswomen."

"But you promised to *hire* servants!" I said accusingly.

"Aurielle, my angel, you know how impossible that is. Look at the trouble Captain Kincannon is having. He cannot keep them. I swear to you I shall be kind to them and more—I shall soon free them."

"You will keep your word, Ondine,"—my voice was hard—"if I am to keep mine."

"Oh, to be sure, *chérie.* You may bank upon it." She smiled at me then, that angelic and warm smile that was so much a part of her.

Still, I was curiously uncomfortable as the servants filed in. Tressa and Pearl were grinning broadly, as were Jasper and Couri. Bonnie Trelawney's face was white and

273

drawn, as was Catherine's, although their eyes were dancing.

"Are you ready to go?" I asked, smiling myself.

"Yes, madame," they chorused, clutching the cloth bags and sacks containing their meager belongings.

"Then you will all go in the big Dessaultes barouche. Jasper, you and Couri see that the ladies mount safely. I shall be along in a moment."

After they were gone, I made my good-byes and went out to mount the carriage with Jasper's eager assistance. Jacques, Valier's little brown French driver, looked disapproving, no doubt a reflection of Claudette Dessaultes's attitude. Earlier, at a breakfast which we shared alone, Claudette had been sharp with me. Valier had gone some time before and she felt free to speak her mind. She could not understand my *hiring* the Chaille servants. My reasons carried no importance with her.

"If she had *given* them to you, it might be better. But for Valier to have to pay them wages—slaves and bondswomen—how ridiculous!"

We had parted then with ill will between us, as usual, and now, when I arrived home with my new employees, she displayed little grace as she had Helen show them up to their rooms. Antoinette followed and I was sure she made them welcome.

I went directly to my room to avoid further conversation with my surly mother-in-law. The day was growing colder and a chill wind blew in off the river. I went to the window and peered out at the darkening sky. I suddenly wished it would pour rain. It might cause Valier to call off our dinner engagement with Quentin Kincannon.

Antoinette rapped on my door and entered almost simultaneously. "Ah, Aurielle, such happy people! How did you ever persuade Madame Chaille to part with them, you clever girl?"

"It was easy," I replied cheerfully. This was one more promise I must keep, the promise never to reveal Ondine's perversion. "When I told her last night how lonely it was for you and me in this great house with so few servants—and those strange to us—she kindly offered to free them."

274

"That is what so astonishes me, little one. I sadly misjudged madame. I never dreamed she would *free* them." She took up the dress I had just removed, straightened it, and hung it in the armoire. "What will you wear to dinner with monsieur tonight?"

"The rose taffeta, I think." That was the one Valier had chosen himself when we were last shopping together. It was a favorite of his.

Antoinette took the dress out from among the many others and shook it, spreading it across a chaise longue. "*Très belle!* Truly, it is the most beautiful gown you have Now, do you wish to bathe and wash your hair, *chérie?* It would be well to do so in order that your hair may dry in time for me to prepare your coiffure."

That evening, due to the heavy rains, the streets were a sea of mud as Valier and I sat in the carriage on our way to the Café des Roses. I could feel the wheels slip in the quagmire as we made our way to the heart of the city.

"I'm glad you are going to be reasonable about this, my love," Valier said calmly. "Despite what you say about animosity, I know there is an attraction—oh, yes, it may be only physical—between you and the captain. I urge you to nurture that." He laughed unpleasantly. "And I will make it easy for you to meet. I have the feeling this man is shrewd and will be most discreet."

"And in the end, you will kill him."

"But of course," he said matter-of-factly. "You do not love him. Why should his death worry you?"

"Being a party to murder worries me."

"But I will kill him fairly on the field of honor. He shall have a chance to strike at me as well."

"But you know there is no swordsman in Louisiana who is your equal. It will be murder."

"You are, as *maman* says, squeamish," he replied impatiently.

I was silent. I hoped desperately that this scheme of Valier's would fail, despite our agreement.

When we reached the Café des Roses, Jacques pulled the carriage close to the banquette and Valier lifted me carefully to the wooden walk. When we entered, we found the captain had arrived before us. The room was crowded and the scent of savory foods floated delicately on the air. The snowy tables were set with bone china and crystal, with the warm gleam of old sterling at the places. All about the room were potted ferns and lacy palms, giving it the appearance of an indoor garden. A velvety red rose centered each table.

I gave my cloak to the waiting servant and Valier looked at the rose taffeta dress with approval. The neck was cut very low, exposing much cleavage, and my shoulders rose whitely from the little cap sleeves. I wore a single strand of pearls and small pearl earrings, both gifts from Valier.

"You are beautiful—too beautiful," he said thickly, his hand tightening on my arm until I gasped.

"There will be a bruise there in the morning," I said coldly, and he released me at once.

We made our way to the table across the room, where the captain had risen at the sight of us. He was impeccably clad in black broadcloth, his cravat a small frill of white at the dark throat. He bowed as we approached, pulling out a chair for me.

I looked at his clean, shining dark hair and it seemed to me the fragrance of soap and fresh linen emanated from him. With an intensity that was new to me, I noted his tanned hand on the back of the chair and his broad, muscled shoulders. Fear struck at me. *Valier had done this to me!* He had planted the seed of possibility in my torn and furrowed mind and it had taken root.

"I have taken the liberty of ordering wine. Champagne for madame and Madeira for the two of us, Valier," Kincannon said pleasantly. I could feel those polished black eyes on my face and my heavy lashes hid downcast eyes.

"That is most thoughtful of you, Quentin. Here is the waiter with the wine now—" and at the swarthy waiter's warm greeting, my husband said, *"Bon soir,* Voltec."

As the wine was being poured, Kincannon said, "Madame Dessaultes, may I congratulate you and your husband on your unusual and belated wedding gift from your aunt?"

"What is that?" I asked, startled.

"I heard today that she has made you a present of all the Chaille servants."

"Not quite all," Valier said, smiling. "She kept Sebastien, of course, and the new cook who took Selina's place, as well as the new maid."

"A most uncommonly kind gift," Kincannon reiterated, looking at me keenly.

"I had become very fond of them"—I was cool—"and Aunt Ondine thought they might comfort me in my new home." How fast news traveled in New Orleans! "No doubt by now she has a new staff. She and Sebastien were going to secure more this very day."

"I know." Kincannon was dry. "I was at the auction block when she and Sebastien were bidding for them. It was then she told me of her generous gesture."

"My aunt is a very kind person." My voice was somewhat muffled.

"Indeed she is. I owe her myself for some very pleasant evenings as a guest in her home." Kincannon smiled.

Valier asked pleasantly, "Now what shall we order for dinner?" and the two men began a discussion of the merits of fried softshell crabs as opposed to lobster and drawn butter, with *légumes* and assorted hot breads. They finally settled on portions of both seafoods after consulting me. I was finding it very difficult to keep my eyes off Kincannon's darkly handsome face as he ordered from the waiter, Voltec. I looked around the room to see the Poliet family at another table and I nodded to Eugene and his sister, Lisette, and their parents.

My husband was now discussing properties in and about the city and advising Kincannon to invest heavily in parcels of land just beyond the city itself. "New Orleans is growing. One day it will be the leading port city in your—our nation for this part of the country," he said seriously.

"If the British do not eventually capture it," Kincannon replied. "Things are not going well. The east is bottled up as tightly as a bee in a jug. Napoleon's number is up and I am certain they will strike New Orleans—and fairly soon."

Valier shrugged. "New Orleans is a long way from

Washington and New York. The British will try to take the seat of government first."

"I'm sure they will, and if they are turned back, New Orleans is a ripe plum for their picking."

"I feel you are borrowing trouble, *mon vieux*." When Valier turned to French in his speech, I knew he was irritated.

Kincannon appeared about to say more but changed his mind. He looked at me again and said gallantly, "That gown is most becoming, madame. I envy my friend Valier."

"You are most kind, Captain," I replied with a faint smile which faded as I looked into Valier's eyes. There was a depth of ferocity there, an eagerness too, and I thought with renewed fear, *You are signing your death warrant, Quentin Kincannon.*

"Ah," Valier said with a good-humored laugh, "I appreciate your compliment, too. Possibly more than my wife does, for it means you perceive my good taste."

"In truth, I do admire your good taste," Kincannon said with an oblique smile, "as well as your business acumen."

I hid surprise. That was not what he had said about my husband's business acumen last night. So Valier was not the only one practicing hypocrisy tonight.

"Bien!" My husband's voice was troubled, as a small black man approached our table somewhat hesitantly. "What have we here? You want something?"

"Yes, sir. You, sir. Mr. Molieve sent me ter find you —they told me at the house you be here." The man appeared extremely nervous.

"Well, out with it, man." Valier was impatient.

"Mr. Molieve say he need ter see you right away. Somethin' 'bout a cargo on the *Carrie Belle*. He at his office, Mr. Dessaultes. He say you'll know what he mean."

"Alors!" Valier spoke with apparent disappointment, but I sensed he had been expecting this. "I must go see Molieve. Something must have gone wrong. No doubt I will have to make some decisions." Regret filled his voice as he added, "Here, man, is a dollar for your trouble." The black pocketed the bill and hastened away. Rising,

Valier continued, *"Mon vieux,* will you see that my wife gets her dinner and take her home afterward?"

"Of course," Kincannon said, as Valier motioned for his cloak and the waiter hastened over to drape it about his wide shoulders.

"I will go with you," I said at once, rising so swiftly I overturned the slender-stemmed glass of champagne before me. I looked down with dismay as the liquid splashed the rose taffeta, making a darker rose stain.

"Indeed no, *chérie,"* Valier said quickly. He bent and kissed my cheek lightly. "I will not spoil the evening entirely for both of us. You must dine—they have already prepared it."

I wanted to rush out with him but I could not do so without creating a scene, for Valier was determined that I should remain with Kincannon. I knew unerringly now that he had arranged this. The waiter was approaching with a tray of steaming food even now.

"Monsieur Dessaultes was called away on business," Kincannon said, answering the waiter's question as he set the food about the table.

I did not speak as the servant placed portions on the plate before me and after he had finished serving us, I felt I could not eat any of the savory food. I was uncomfortably aware of my companion's quizzical eyes. He appeared about to smile and the fact that he was amused irritated me beyond measure. The man had put me in a flutter, right enough, and I blamed that upon my husband and his machinations.

The silence drew out after the waiter left and Kincannon quietly refilled the empty champagne glass that Valier had set upright.

"I do not care for any more," I spoke with low violence. I felt that all the blood had drained from my face and Kincannon confirmed it.

"You are ill?" he asked with concern.

"No."

He sipped his Madeira slowly. Then speaking quietly, he said, "Collect yourself, madame. I am not a stupid man. I know what your husband is conspiring to do."

I turned astonished eyes directly on him. "You do?" I was bewildered by his acuteness.

"It's not very flattering that both of you should think me such a dullard," he replied dryly.

Blood returned burning in my face. "Who told you— of my husband's—"

"Of your husband's what?" he asked alertly.

"Then you do *not* know."

"Ah, but I do. I know he intends me to seduce you. The only question is why. He could easily find another reason to challenge me."

"Then you really do not know—the reason."

He downed the last of the Madeira before answering. "But I will. Before the evening's over."

I pushed the plate of seafood back. "I cannot eat this." I averted my head.

"You must," he said calmly. "People are observing us."

I turned my head and saw that General Villere and his wife and daughter had joined the Poliets. They nodded, smiling at me. I returned their greeting mechanically.

"And not only the Villeres and Poliets,"—my dinner companion smiled—"but Mr. Edward Grymes and two friends." He nodded toward them.

I felt almost unclothed in so public a place with this man who stimulated me with such a wild variety of emotions. I picked up a heavy silver fork and began eating mechanically. It could well have been sawdust. "Let me know when you think it sufficient," I said between my teeth. "I am anxious to be gone."

He grinned with sudden mockery. "We will take the long way home, eh Aurielle? I believe your husband expects that."

"Don't be a fool!" I whispered fiercely and took a gulp of champagne. Already what I had downed was making itself felt in a certain lightheadedness. The sooner I was out of Quentin Kincannon's company the better.

But he kept up a light conversation regarding everything from the latest Paris fashions to the Catholic religion in New Orleans, he being a casual Protestant. His religion was another source of disapproval among the Creoles.

Over dessert, he said, "You have certainly made me carry on the amenities alone, Aurielle."

"I regret that. But you must understand I am somewhat disturbed over my husband's—plot."

"Yes. We will discuss that in the privacy of my carriage."

I made no reply, and shortly after, he was draping the velvet cloak about my shoulders. When his hard brown hands touched me I could not restrain a shiver that was compounded of many things, not the least of which was guilty pleasure.

I looked up into his eyes, so very dark in that enigmatic countenance. The look of a bird of prey was more pronounced than ever as he caught my glance. I looked away quickly.

Later in the carriage, Kincannon said softly, "Now, Aurielle, tell me why your estimable Creole wishes me to become your lover."

"I—cannot." My voice was muffled.

"Come now. We are old friends, Aurielle. I know all about you and your past. Surely you can confide in me."

"I can only tell you that any relationship between us would end in your death."

His sudden laugh was rollicking. "He has already marked me, this I know. But I cannot understand why he should grant me such a pleasure before calling me out."

Pleasure! With a sudden throbbing I knew it would be that—not only for Kincannon but for me as well. Helplessly I lived again the moments I had shared in those strong arms.

He went on reflectively as we bumped over the potholed, muddy street, "And why not, Aurielle? I have thought of you often since that night in Rodeur's cabin, and with desire. Since I am to duel with your husband, why not give him good cause?" There was hidden laughter in the deep voice.

"You would break Roxanne Deveret's heart," I said with quick rage, more at my own desires than at him.

"I do not love Roxanne—"

"But you made love to her. You made her love you."

He shrugged. "I did nothing that Roxanne did not want. You were different," he chuckled deeply. "You

281

were much more of a challenge. You still are. Roxanne has nothing to do with us, Aurielle."

"I *told* her months ago I wanted none of you and I—"

"Nonsense." Then audaciously, he added, "Will you visit with me in my house on Bourbon now? I can promise you a good wine, the like of which is hard to find. Jean Lafitte brought it to me the last time he slipped into the city."

"No," I retorted. "I wish to go home immediately."

But he leaned forward and spoke to the driver, telling him to go to the house on Bourbon. He turned to me. "You will do me at least the courtesy of inspecting my house. With your newfound taste and culture, you can tell me if it is all a rich man's house in town should be— until he can build a better."

"I have seen your house from the outside and you are giving my husband much to build his suspicions on. Why are you falling right into his hands?" A sudden jolt of the carriage threw me against him and I drew back swiftly.

In the dim light of the lantern swinging beside us, he turned his black eyes on me. "My dear Aurielle, your husband does not frighten me." His voice was cold and even. "Has it occurred to you that I am more than willing to fight him?"

My throat went dry and I swallowed before I could respond. "He has done nothing to anger you—"

"Everything about that supercilious Creole angers me, and what he is doing to you angers me most especially. I've seen that look in your eyes. Trapped, fearful."

"And why should you care if I am trapped and frightened?" I asked bitterly.

"I have wondered about that myself." Frustration mingled with annoyance in his voice. Then he said with abrupt amusement, "I am not a particularly celibate man, as I am sure you know. But I must confess you are the first woman who ever aroused any sort of protective instinct in me, with the single exception of my mother."

I looked quickly into the dark face above me. "If that be so, how can you suggest that we become lovers?"

"Because we would both enjoy it. We would have

enjoyed it that first time, but for your copious tears. I've never been able to get you out of my mind since that night." His laughter grew. "You occur at the oddest times and, odder still, protectiveness is part of it."

I refused to be deflected. "And it would fall right in with Valier's plans. In fact, you couldn't please him more."

He captured my hand in a tight grip. "And you will tell me why that is so before this evening is over."

"I cannot."

"Then you will spend the night in my home."

"You would force me?" I cried in consternation.

"I will have the truth from you."

"You'll never get it by forcing me to your will."

"You talk like an ignorant schoolgirl," he said in exasperation. "After all, you are a married woman now and have been for over four months."

"I am not—" I bit my tongue but it was too late.

He was on me like a striking hawk, catching my elbows, pulling me against him. "So that's it! Something ails the estimable Creole—he does not function as a man and you have known none other than the abortive moments with me aboard the *Wind*. Does he know of our— long-past alliance?"

"He knows—my background." To my mortification, I began to weep. I was able to choke back sobs and hold my face smooth, but I could not stem the great, hot tears that welled out of my eyes.

With sudden gentleness his arms closed about me and my face was pressed against the smooth black broad-cloth of his coat. The cleanliness of him filled my lungs as I drew a long, shivering breath of it. I wanted desperately to twine my arms about him, pull that hard face to mine, loosing the torrent of desire I was trying so hard to check.

He put a big hand beneath my chin and slowly tipped my face upward. My lips were wet with tears and when his mouth came down on mine, their moisture intensified the electric shock of his touch. I clung to him, drowning in the tide of my own sensations. It was a long, thirsty kiss, one that had been waited for, I knew now, since that night aboard the *Wind,* since that last time by the levee when he had kissed me while spring burst about us.

283

When at last he took his lips from mine, it was only to bury his face in the hollow of my throat. His breath was hot against my flesh and I put my face down against his dark head.

"Quentin," I said huskily, "we are falling into Valier's trap." My voice broke suddenly. "He knew this would happen. God and the devil! What did I do or say that made him know?"

Kincannon lifted his head. "Perhaps he knew it when I looked at you, Aurielle." Then he added dryly, "And I always fancied myself a subtle man."

"No, it was *I*. Something I said or did—"

"No matter. He knew it. A shrewd man—is he impotent, Aurielle? Our Creole gentleman?"

I winced. "Don't say that! I felt so sorry for him in the beginning, when I first discovered—" I could not go on.

He said musingly, "It must have come upon him suddenly, for this city still talks of his way with women. For years he played the field, so it's said. It must have been Don Ysidro's daughter, the famous Spanish beauty, who caused his downfall. In the coffee houses it's whispered that she was pregnant when her father sent her to marry her cousin in Savannah."

I shuddered. "And Valier called out all four of her brothers, one by one, and killed them. Then at last, their father. He wiped out a whole family—but they did a terrible thing to him—"

Once again that piercing glance was bent upon me. "They did? What?"

I shook my head wordlessly. I had almost revealed the secret I was sworn to keep! His next words confirmed my fears.

"So he killed them all for something they did. Ah— it could be but one thing. They castrated him."

"They mutilated him!" I burst out. "It was no ordinary cruelty they inflicted. And he killed them for it."

"That he did. All very proper, with insults exchanged and followed by duels *sous les chênes*."

The carriage rolled to a halt and the driver, a tall stoop-shouldered white man of indeterminate years, opened the carriage door. He assisted me down the step and Kincannon followed, saying, "Durward, keep the carriage waiting here. Madame will visit awhile and then we will return her to the Dessaultes."

At the door, we were met by a dignified black butler. Kincannon introduced him as Julius, adding, "My turn-over in servants is amazing. Julius is new and so excellent I fear I may lose him."

We proceeded into the exquisitely furnished salon. Then turning to the butler, Kincannon said, "Julius, serve some of that wine Monsieur Lafitte brought me before Christmas." Then to me, "Will you actually inspect my house?"

I smiled. "It was you who said I should. Not I."

"Very well—we will do what I intended all along—sit together and talk before the fire."

"Only for a few minutes. I don't want Valier to assume his purpose is accomplished."

"Why not let him think I have sowed seed for him? I presume he intends to claim the child as his own?"

"Of course, and it doesn't matter to him who the father is," I said wearily, glad that the ugly secret was mine alone no longer. There was great relief in knowing that Quentin Kincannon was aware of my trap. Julius entered silently, put the decanter upon a table, served us each a glass, and departed.

I took a sip of the wine and said, "His mother hates me for having married her son, but she endures me for the promise of grandchildren." I laughed without humor. "I imagine, as the months go by and she is cheated of that, she will hate me even more."

He rose up from his chair and came to sit beside me on the sofa, his hard-muscled thigh pressing against mine. A tremor of excitement went through me as he caught my free hand, enveloping it in his big, rough one. Putting his glass down carefully on a long table behind the sofa, he took mine and did the same with it. Then, very deliberately, he took me in his arms and began to kiss me. At first I was unresisting, for I was filled with yearning for him. The hunger I had been living with since the night aboard the *Wind* returned fourfold and it seemed to be insatiable as my lips clung to his. Into the heat of the moment came Valier's cold voice: *You will bear a son and I shall kill the man who sires him.*

I twisted violently in Kincannon's embrace. "Let me —go!"

His grip tightened and suddenly he pushed me down upon the cushions, his big, hard body covering mine. Anger exploded in me and I fought like a cornered cat, my breath coming in labored gasps. Our legs became entangled in my skirts and I heard the taffeta rip along my side.

"There!" I cried. "You've torn my dress! Valier will know I am pregnant."

"Let's give him good cause to call me out." Kincannon laughed, trying to hold my head still so he could bring his lips to mine once more. He was not holding me so tightly and I knew he was amused by the entanglement of my garments. They were hindering him more than my struggles.

"He'll kill you!" I said despairingly.

"That's possible," he agreed, still laughing.

I struggled to sit upright. My hair had tumbled from the pins Antoinette had so carefully put into it. I began breathlessly, "Anything is possible with a man like Valier—"

"Except pregnancy," he inserted smoothly, observing me with narrowed, twinkling eyes.

"Quentin, you are a fool to make light of it! It has warped him—to the extent of at least five murders."

"Every duel that ends in death is murder," he said, his husky voice still full of amusement. "Someday it will be outlawed."

We had half risen on the sofa, his arms still about me as I struggled. But it was his laughter, his endearing laughter that was my undoing. Quentin Kincannon's laughter was like an invitation to all things delightful. Looking up into his dark eyes, an abrupt gust of passion shook me so forcibly I trembled and sank back on the cushions. My hands clung to his shoulders and I groaned, "My God—Quent! I can't—I have no strength against you."

Thrusting my body upward to press against his, a

torrent of raw desire coursed through me as I met his mouth with mine. His lips lost their gentleness, became voracious and insatiable. The candlelit room reeled and I closed my eyes against its spinning, only to sink drowning in wave after wave of rapture so exquisite it was near to pain.

I turned my head seeking his mouth once more, but he had pulled my low-cut dress away from my breasts and was placing his warm, tender lips to them.

Blindly, willingly—nay, eagerly, I gave myself up to him, his hands on my bare flesh a narcotic against the thought of my husband's deadly plot. His gentle but strong easing of himself upon me was a wall against the thought of the price we both must pay for the ecstasy of this moment of coming together.

Soaring upward like a flame, I met his ardor with my own and realized a sweetness, a poignancy that was totally new to me. I was wholly unprepared for such a shattering experience and I cried out in abandonment to it. I knew I had waited all my life for this, but it was sweeter by far than in my dreams.

It was then his lips found mine once more and the afterglow spread a delicious, languorous weakness through my limbs and I wanted to lie forever beneath him, with the hard feel of his flesh against mine. And we did lie so for a few moments, my head still spinning, slowly steadying. But it was of short duration, for, unbidden, Valier's cold, aristocratic face rose up behind my closed lids.

"God and the devil," I whispered in sudden terror. "We have fallen into Valier's snare. He knew it would happen. He *knew* it! I must surely be carrying your child this very moment."

He pulled himself upright, readjusting his fitted breeches as I pulled at my disarranged dress. He laughed again, softly. "Not likely, Aurielle—the first time. And I know it was your first time, sweet innocent. It would take more evenings like this to find you with child."

"You can't be sure! It happened to Marianne the first time," I said my terror growing.

"I don't know Marianne, but I suspect it wasn't her first time." He reached over the sofa and took up the wineglasses, handing mine to me. "Drink your wine, Aurielle." He glanced at the golden clock on the mantel. "I am sure Valier expects you to stay much longer than this. You will disappoint him."

"That's exactly what I mean to do." I took a deep swallow of wine.

He looked at me thoughtfully. "I don't think that's a safe course of action for you, my dear."

"You mean I should tell him you—I—we—" I broke off explosively. "I do not mean to become a brood mare for him!"

"You think your husband would be pleased to have you carrying *my* child?"

"Yes."

"Nay. For all his plans, he would not. You can be sure he's eaten up with jealousy at this moment. For all that the Ysidros put an end to his potency, they've not put an end to his jealousy."

I put the wineglass down hastily. What Kincannon was saying was undoubtedly true. "All the more reason I must return home immediately."

Kincannon rose and took up the decanter, refilling both our glasses. He handed mine to me and said speculatively, "I have a distinct feeling, Aurielle, that your life depends on conception."

My eyes widened as I remembered Valier's white, implacable face as he outlined his plan to me. He had killed many men, I thought now. Why not a woman—a stubborn, arbitrary young woman?

"Tell me," Kincannon asked softly, "does anyone other than you and I know of Valier Dessaultes's unhappy condition?"

"No," I said slowly, "and I swore I would tell no one. I did not tell you—you guessed."

"So I did. Still, Aurielle, do you realize that no one who has known of it has been permitted to live?"

Silence fell. The words slid through my mind like oil, clinging, sinking into me. There was nothing to keep Valier from disposing of me after a baby was born—or before, if I failed to conceive. Indeed, his words so cold, so sure came back to me. *Do not misjudge me. I am quite capable of killing you—by means that would never be discovered. And I will do that, my love, if you fail to provide me with a son.*

I whispered, "He has already threatened to kill me." Then with uncertainty, "But it was just angry talk. Surely he didn't mean it."

"Didn't he?" Taking my cold hand into his big warm one, Kincannon opened it and bent his head. In silence he pressed his mouth to my inner palm. A thrill sharp as a knife blade slashed my heart. Lifting his head he said, "Patience is not one of my virtues, my dear."

My pulse, already racing, beat more swiftly.

"You have the look of a little bird caught in the hunter's net, Aurielle—and I find I do not like the idea of Valier Dessaultes as stepfather to any child of mine."

"I *am* caught," I said desperately. "He would never countenance a divorce. His religion, his position in New Orleans, forbids such. I—" I hesitated, my mind recoiling from the thought. "My only escape is to run away. But to where?"

"The coward's out, eh?" He was ironic.

"Then what would be your way?" I asked sharply.

"I intend to make it my way, madame, as you will soon see." He rose to his feet, pulling me up with him. "Come, put on your cloak." He went to the chair where it lay and handed it to me. "I shall see you home and take the first step to freeing you."

I wanted to ask him how but could not bring myself to do so, half guessing the course he was taking.

Later in the carriage, he turned to me and said, "Aurielle, I have never been a man with many pretty speeches for women. I make none to you now. I tell you only this. I want you. I have wanted you over a year now, while I dallied with the pretty ladies of New Orleans. Yet I do not savor the idea of your being offered up to me by your—husband. I find it a very unsatisfactory arrangement."

"I know." My voice was muffled and my hands intensely cold. I could not burst out with the truth, that I loved him with a fury of passion. Yet no words of love between us had been spoken. I knew only that he desired me and it had been wonderful.

Now I looked up at him beside me, and in the pale

glow of the carriage lantern he turned his predatory face toward me and smiled a slow, frightening smile. There was such promise of deadly violence in it I shivered and tucked my hands into my heavy velvet cape.

We did not speak again. The light rain that had fallen earlier had resumed and pattered against the carriage. The air was cold and damp against my face. Kincannon made no attempt to touch me again, and when we drew up in the porte cochere beside the Dessaultes mansion, he took my hand only to assist me to the steps after Durward had opened the carriage door.

"Come," he said, "I shall make it easy for Dessaultes to challenge me."

I stifled a groan. "You will throw away your life—"

"Ah, but it shall be for a gallant cause," he said with the laughter I had come to love so well.

Jasper opened the broad door at Kincannon's light knock. He had become butler for the Dessaultes, being better educated in the social niceties than Couri and Pointer. There was a candle in a crystal chimney in his hand and behind him I saw Valier striding forward. His face was pale and strained but his voice was all warmth and cordiality.

"Ah, Quentin! I see you have brought Aurielle home in good order. *Alors,* Aurielle, did you not enjoy that delicious dinner at the Café des Roses?"

"Very much, but I missed you sorely," I lied with a trembling smile.

"And I persuaded her to come by my house on Bourbon for a glass of wine. Two in fact," Kincannon said arrogantly. "Your wife has many charms, all of them delightful."

Valier's face paled further and his eyes flickered like lightning, but he smiled fixedly. He had not planned to kill Kincannon so soon and I could see the black thoughts that were careering through his mind even now. "You will have a final brandy with us, Quentin? It is a cold and ugly night." He was courteous as his regal mother, clad in rich wine velvet, approached.

"Good evening, sir," she said with chill politeness.

Kincannon grinned. "Valier, your mother's coldness

after your wife's—er—warmth does not invite me to your hospitality."

A little vein in Valier's head distended itself and began to pulse rapidly. I put in quickly, "Let us speak no more of my charms or warmth, Captain. Let us instead go into the drawing room and share a good-night glass of spirits." My own heart was a drumbeat in my breast and I was terrified by the emotion that swirled between my husband and this man who had come to mean more to me than I had ever intended.

"Gladly, Aurielle." Kincannon smiled at me intimately and I saw Valier's hands clench into fists.

There was an awkward silence in the room after Claudette sent Jasper for brandy and wine. Kincannon did nothing to ease the situation, drumming his fingers on the arm of his chair, his black eyes roving restlessly about the room. But when he took his brandy, he said, "Did you straighten out the—so fortunate for me—affair with Molieve?"

"Just a mixup over a cargo of cotton. With the blockade as it is, I had to order it stored—for the moment," Valier replied with icy politeness. Then, "Tell me, Quentin, about your partner Cheviot and the troop he has formed. I heard about it only the other day." I realized with intense relief that he was seeking less provocative subjects to discuss.

"My friend Rodeur is a true patriot. He fell out years ago with some of his countrymen when Napoleon first rose to power. Now he feels that his new country is in danger and he proposes to be ready for it."

"Are you part of his troop then?" Some of the color had come back into Valier's face as he drank and he looked more in control of himself.

"Naturally," Kincannon laughed. "Rodeur would not let me rest until I joined."

"I think he is mistaken," Madame Dessaultes said ponderously. "No one would dare touch New Orleans."

"The British would, madame. They are a very intelligent race of men and they know that with the city that controls the Mississippi at the bargaining table, our

291

fledgling republic would be reduced to an insignificant thorn in the British lion's hide."

"You make it sound very possible," Valier said with a faint smile, "when it is very unlikely."

"It is only men like you, Valier, who keep New Orleans dreaming the days away, unprepared and uncaring as danger approaches." Kincannon's drawling voice had become arrogant once more and I saw Valier's lips tighten. The silence between us all drew out.

"Sir, you are very uncivil as you partake of my hospitality," he said at last, his voice cold.

"You invite my comment, sir, with your attitude," Kincannon retorted.

I saw Claudette Dessaultes's face pale as she perceived the violence that hung in the air. Knowing it was part of the code that men did not extend the challenge before women, I kept my seat firmly. I realized with sick certainty that Kincannon meant to goad Valier into a duel and he meant to do it *now*.

"I do think we should talk of other things," Madame Dessaultes put in, her voice cracking perilously. "May I send for another brandy, Captain?"

"Nay, madame. I've not the stomach for another drink with those who are fearful and equivocate about the troubles we are suffering every day at the hands of the British."

Valier's head snapped around and his face was white with fury. He spoke in French. *"Maman, you and Aurielle will retire, please. I would have a few words with the captain in private."*

The last thing I saw as I left the room with my agitated mother-in-law was Kincannon's little half-smile.

In the hallway as we took the stairs, Claudette muttered, *"Mon Dieu, mon Dieu!* Another duel, I feel it in my bones. My darling son, how he risks his life! I *told* him this man Kincannon was an impudent newcomer and no good would come of his association." A little moan escaped her.

"Will they—arrange a duel, you think?" I asked as we reached the landing.

"Of course. My son will send his seconds to call on the man before the night is over. No doubt he will engage him in a duel before sun-up. Oh, what a crude, discourteous man he is. He was intolerable! An insult Valier could not bear and all because of *you*—staying to dine *alone* with him!"

I wanted to cry out, *Madame, it is only happening a little sooner than your son planned. He means to kill Kincannon—has always meant to.* And with the thought, the sick feeling in the pit of my stomach recurred. Madame Dessaultes and I parted in the hall with no further words between us.

When I entered my room, Antoinette, who had been waiting for me, took one look and cried, *"Chérie,* you are so pale—so ill and frightened. What has happened?"

"Valier is going to challenge Captain Kincannon." I took off my cape and flung it over a chair and seated myself before the dressing table.

Antoinette's eyes rounded. Swallowing, she said, "You mean a duel? *Mon Dieu,* one will die surely."

"I know," I murmured. Then, "Toinette, I shall not undress. I shall wait to speak to my husband before I retire."

"What brought this thing on?" she asked.

"The captain was—insolent. He threw off on Valier's patriotism. In so many words he called him a fool and an arrant coward by implication." I did not mention *my* part in their conversation.

"Zut! Then he knew what he was doing."

"Oh, yes," I said bitterly. "He wanted Valier to challenge him. He is as great a fool as he thinks Valier to be. My husband's reputation as a duelist is awesome." Suddenly I began to cry, putting my hands before my face as a vision of Kincannon, carried white and bleeding from the desolate spot chosen for such affairs, filled my mind. "He will be killed, I *know* it," I whispered, still thinking of Kincannon.

"That is very likely, *chérie,"* she replied compassionately. "I once saw the captain in a sword fight with a Frenchman who challenged his authority among the crew of the *Wind.* He was a fine swordsman, that Frenchman, but the captain cut him to ribbons. He died at once with the captain's sword in his heart at the end."

I looked up at her through a blur of tears. "I meant the captain," I sobbed. "Valier has trained with the finest swordsmen in the academies here."

"Yes, I have heard how expert he is, but you must save your tears if they are for Captain Kincannon." She gave me an odd look. "I thought you were weeping for your husband."

"Antoinette, I must confess to you, I do not love my husband. He is a cruel and unkind man. He is not a moral man."

She did not give a flicker of surprise, nodding and saying, "I feared as much when I first came to this house with you." She put her hands on my shoulders and we both stared into the mirror. In the golden glow of lamplight our faces appeared pale, and mine was openly fearful. "I have watched you, little one, and seen you with a—cornered look in your lovely eyes. I have seen your face held tight against fear. I pray to the good God that the captain is the victor in this duel. When is it to be?"

"I don't know," I said despairingly. "His mother thinks by sun-up."

"It is late—past midnight now—to arrange a duel so soon."

"You didn't see Valier's face. If it were not for the code, I think he would have dueled with the captain in his own drawing room."

Without warning the door to my room flew open and Valier stood in the opening. He jerked his head at Antoinette and said, "Madame will send for you when she is ready to retire." The little Frenchwoman gave me a quick, enigmatic glance and made her way swiftly from the room. Valier closed the door firmly.

"And now that your lover has gone, you will tell me how the evening went. I assume Kincannon was a satisfactory partner in adultery?"

"Adultery?" I flashed. "Is it still called that when the husband arranges such an act?"

Valier's eyes were murderous and his mouth twisted in a strange smile. "Was it pleasant?"

"Nothing happened at all, Valier. You are rushing matters." I tried to sound cool but my voice shook.

"Rushing matters?" His short laugh was ugly. "Yet

you can stand there with your dress torn from arm to hip and tell me nothing happened at all?"

I gasped and put a hand to my waist where the seam had ripped as Kincannon and I struggled. I withdrew it as if I had touched a hot iron. My husband strode up to me, seizing my arms and pulling me upright from the dressing table bench. Catching me in a cruel grip, he bent my head back and brought his face close to mine.

"So nothing happened at all, eh? You are probably *enciente* at this very moment." Suddenly he kissed me, his lips hard and angry, bruising mine. Then drawing back with his breath still hot upon my cheek, he said "It must have been a wild romp, damn Kincannon's soul to hell—where it shall be this time tomorrow!"

"I tell you, it is far too soon to expect results."

"You are worried for the life of your lover already," he said, releasing me abruptly. "And well you might, Aurielle. I plan to take it tomorrow—no, this morning at dawn. I have sent Pointer to the Poliet house for Eugene. He and his father shall act as my seconds. Your lover has but hours to live."

I stood staring up into his face. Kincannon had implied my life was in danger with this man and suddenly I was certain of it. What had been a nebulous fear on my part was now a reality. I knew with unerring instinct that once Valier achieved his purpose I could be dispensed with in a hundred different ways. His mother would gladly help him—and I would die, leaving the two of them and the unhappy child that might be born, alone together in this big beautiful house.

"You are terrified," he said smiling cruelly. "Is it for that scoundrel Kincannon?"

I pulled away and averted my eyes. "Can you not wound him in his arm or leg—to satisfy your—honor?"

"And make another assignation between you?" He laughed shortly. "Ah, no, not *this* man. I mean to kill him, madame. Nothing you say can alter my determination."

I turned away, anxious to be rid of his castigations. "I am weary and I—"

"I imagine you *are* weary," he sneered.

"—and I wish to retire. I can only tell you it is much too soon."

"You lie," he said, suddenly dispassionate. "You will have no more chances with this lover." He paused, then in a muffled voice, "It was harder waiting—allowing you to —more than I thought it would be." He wheeled and left me without closing the door behind him.

I stood shivering as his footsteps died away down the hall. The candlelight gleamed on the crossed swords on the walls beside the door and I wondered, *How many has my husband killed with these particular rapiers?*

Antoinette came around the door and into the room. She was clad in a wrapper now. "I heard m'sieu say he was going to kill the captain this morning. And I heard him say you have been—he implied you have the desire for the captain, Aurielle, *c'est vrai?*"

"You must have been listening closely, Toinette."

She laughed suddenly. "I told you once before, I always listen closely." She began to unhook my basque swiftly.

"Yes, it is true that he plans to kill Kincannon. I told you earlier I feared he would. He is jealous and frustrated and so he is evil. You know I have no desire for the captain."

Antoinette observed me narrowly. "You and the captain have long had the great hatred for each other. That is blood brother to love. Even at your tender age, you should know that." I was silent so long she asked, "Aurielle, are you in love with the captain?"

I whirled to face her. "I am not! He is Roxanne's choice!"

"Her choice, but not her conquest, little one." Then shrewdly, "There is something between your husband and you that you hide from me—but that is well. Perhaps I am happier not knowing, since you say he is evil."

I longed to blurt out the truth to her, that my husband had lost his manhood and there could never be anything between us, for I was married to a veritable eunuch, still filled with desires but unable to consummate them.

But I bit my tongue on the words. After hanging up my garments and brushing out my long, curling hair, Antoinette tucked me into bed like a child. Dropping a light kiss on my forehead, she took the candle and left me shivering with nerves despite the down comforter over me.

Chapter

15

I did not sleep. I lay wide-eyed in the blackness, wrestling with the newfound knowledge that I loved Kincannon. Valier had said he would be satisfied with nothing less than Kincannon's death and he had spoken with cold certainty. Behind my tightly closed lids I could see Kincannon, his crisp, clean black hair always a little disheveled above those piercing black eyes. I saw him laughing, I saw him scowling, and with each vision, my heart turned over and I knew that with his death my life and my chance for happiness would end, too.

And there was Roxanne. Roxanne could well kill me herself if she knew!

I groaned and twisted restlessly. The hours ticked by and I was alert and quivering with tension when I heard the sound of the carriage rattling on the drive beside the house. Rising swiftly in the chill darkness, I ran to the window and looked out in time to see the winking carriage lamps disappear down the street. Valier Dessaultes was on his way to the place they had chosen for the duel and somewhere, Quentin Kincannon was going to meet his own destiny there.

I abandoned further thought of sleep. Instead I slowly bathed my face in the icy water in the bowl on the washstand. When I finished my toilette, I opened the door and stepped into the hall in a pale blue silk and wool dress. The gray light of dawn was spreading slowly over the city, and as I took the stairs, I could visualize the two men and their seconds standing in the misty morning light with drawn swords.

Turning at the foot of the dark stairs, I made my way to the kitchen. Trudi might be up, building the fires and making preparations for breakfast. A warm glow of light emanated from the door and when I entered, I saw that Trudi had indeed stirred up the fire and lit two candles. She was putting the coffee pot back on the rack over the fire as I stepped in and said good morning.

It was then I saw Claudette and Antoinette seated at the kitchen table, cups beside them. Claudette sent me a lightning glance from her jet eyes, so like her son's, and said, "Come in, Aurielle. Since you are responsible for this duel, you may as well await the outcome with me."

"But I—"

"Do you think I did not hear the remark the captain made about your charms? You think my son would let anyone slur you? God knows, you are not worth it, but he is risking his life for you this morning."

"They quarreled about the war between Britain and America!"

"They quarreled about you, and you know it."

"Come sit down," Antoinette said soothingly. "You are so pale, *ma petite*. Did you not sleep well?"

"I did not sleep at all."

"For worrying about my son or the captain?" Claudette sneered. She lifted her long, straight nose and stared at me with open hatred.

"For both," I said tiredly. "Both are fine men."

"They won't *both* come back from this, Madame Aurielle. Your friend, the captain, will likely lose his life unless my son takes pity on him and allows him to live after the first blood is drawn."

"This here coffee's good an' hot, ma'am. Does you want a cup?" Trudi murmured discreetly.

"I would very much like a cup, Trudi," I responded. Then looking squarely at my mother-in-law, I said, "Madame, how long do you think it will be before we know?"

"Another hour. I expect the whole of New Orleans knows about this by now. You should never have had dinner with the man alone as you did, you little fool. It was enough to drive any man to a challenge."

"But I didn't want to! It was Valier who insisted I stay with—"

"What a liar you are! Valier himself told me last night that he wanted you to go with him, but you insisted on staying for dinner with the captain. And *then* you had the audacity to stop at his house on the way home—and arrived so *late*." She took a sip of coffee, staring at me malevolently over the rim. "I warned Valier before he married you."

I took my cup, forcing my trembling fingers to be steady as I lifted it to my lips. "Madame Dessaultes, this sort of talk is of no use."

But she seemed unable to stem the flow of bitter words. "Even now they are probably dueling—Ah, but my son has killed many men before. He will kill this insolent captain. And *you*"—she looked at me again with renewed fury in her black eyes—"you are sitting there so placidly when you should be weeping in your bed for the trouble you've caused. And all these months, you've been in my house with still no promise of a grandchild."

"Come, Antoinette," I said with sudden coldness, "we will go into the drawing room to wait." Antoinette picked up a candle and her cup swiftly.

As we were leaving, Claudette said with quiet rage, "If he is wounded, I shall see you pay for it, Aurielle, in many ways."

Antoinette and I did not speak until we were seated, side by side on a sofa. "Do not listen to the old dragon's ranting, *chérie*," she said gently. "She is too mad about her son to see anything clearly."

"But I *am* responsible for this duel, Toinette."

"You are not. M'sieur and the captain were destined for this duel since first they met. I remember that day on the road at Pointe St. Antoine when m'sieu first took you for a drive and we met the captain by chance. I think he determined in that moment to kill the captain if he could."

"I remember. But if only I had insisted on going with Valier last night! I should have done it even if I caused a scene—which I certainly would have, as Valier was determined to make me stay."

"You see—you were a pawn, used by m'sieu to bring about the duel," she said comfortingly.

I was silent, realizing that I was indeed a pawn, though not in the way Antoinette said. Thus we sat, silently drinking our coffee as the sun lifted itself over the city. A pale gold light was filtering in through the velvet drapes at the windows now. I rose and went to look out at the chill front courtyard. Rodeur would be one of Kincannon's seconds. And who would be the other?

"How much longer, do you think, Toinette?"

"I do not know. We can only wait."

"What do they do—with the one who is defeated?" I could not bring myself to say "killed." I could not think of Quentin Kincannon as killed.

"They bring him to his home, where he either recovers, or the burial rites are conducted."

"I would like another cup of coffee," I said, returning to the sofa and picking up my cup from the table. "But I cannot go back where that termagant is."

"I will get it, little one."

I sat dejectedly on the sofa until Antoinette returned with the full cup. By now the sun was well up and the garden and courtyard in the front looked fresh and clean from the previous night's rain. *Was it only last night?* I thought in wonder. It seemed aeons ago.

Antoinette had taken the cups back to the kitchen when I heard a carriage rattle up and turn toward the porte cochere at the side of the house. I leaped to my feet and ran to the door, but no one was there. I realized then that they had driven past and would enter through the rear courtyard.

When I reached the kitchen, Claudette had the rear door flung open. I could see the carriage in the courtyard beyond her. Her face was pale and strained as I drew up.

The carriage door opened and Eugene Poliet descended. In a moment, his brother Philip and their father, Etienne Poliet, passed the limp form of Valier Dessaultes down between them. I bit back a cry. I could see the red blood staining his white shirt just inside his fine coat. As Jacques, the driver, descended, he too took up the long form and the four of them carried Valier tenderly toward the doorway where we stood.

"Ah—*Dieu* help me. He is wounded! Surely that is all, just wounded! That renegade, that beast, the captain—" Claudette was weeping hard. "I curse the day you came into our lives, Aurielle!"

I drew away from her as they brought my husband in through the open door. "He is only wounded, isn't he?" Claudette implored.

"No, Madame," Eugene said compassionately, "he was thrust cleanly through the heart."

"Ahhhh—I shall die of grief!" Claudette moaned. "Bring him into the drawing room and put him on the sofa." Then as they followed her, she added, "I hope he killed Kincannon as well." Antoinette and I brought up the rear of the cortege.

Etienne Poliet replied in a troubled voice, "The captain—is a master with the rapier, Claudette. I have never in my life seen such swordplay before poor Valier received the final wound. I did not know there was one in the world with such lightning speed, such dexterity. I would sooner be posted than fight him."

"Truly," Eugene added sorrowfully, "Kincannon has established himself as the foremost swordsman in Louisiana today."

"Did my darling not prick him at all?" she wept.

Eugene looked uncomfortable, then clearing his throat, said, "No, madame, not one slash that brought blood. It was dreadful to watch."

Tears were streaming down the seamed brown face of Jacques, who turned and stumbled blindly from the room. I stood silent. Kincannon had known, had implied as much to me on more than one occasion. *I* should have known. Years as an adventurer and privateer had skilled him with many opponents. I was torn with pity for Madame Dessaultes and with a kind of grief for my poor mutilated husband, with whom I had so hoped to find happiness.

But as I looked down at his chill and imperious face, I remembered suddenly the look on it when he had threatened me with death. I could not stem the tide of relief that slowly filled me. I did not, at that moment, think of what it would mean to live in this house with the venomous woman who was my mother-in-law. But I was to learn; my education beginning as they laid Valier on the sofa in the drawing room.

"I will want the finest coffin at Bouvier's for him and his tomb shall be of solid marble, high above the ground," Madame Dessaultes said thickly as she knelt to look into the still features of her son. "And you, Aurielle," she rose to her feet and looked into my eyes, "will stay in this house with me, for I shall send out and have our mourning clothes brought to us. You shall go nowhere except to church—for a year, possibly two." She half-turned, then with a snakelike twist of her neck, she looked back and added, "We shall mourn. *You* shall mourn and love him in death as you failed to in life."

Eugene was looking at her in open astonishment, and when she stopped speaking, he and his brother Philip exchanged glances with their father. I must have been stunned in appearance, for Eugene said quickly, "Madame, your grief has deluded you. Young Madame Dessaultes loved Valier devotedly. *I know,* for I sought her favor and she told me."

But Claudette had sunk to her knees once more and put her arms about the stiffening body, her shoulders heaving as she sobbed dryly and silently.

I turned to Eugene. "Come, Eugene—Philip and M'sieu Poliet. Let us leave her to mourn in private."

I led them to the sitting room across the foyer and rang the silver bell for the maid. Instead, Antoinette came in, her face pale. With a glance at the men seated on the sofa, she said, "Madame, the servants are in an uproar over this tragedy. May I serve you?"

"You may bring brandy for the gentlemen." When she had left, I turned to the men. "You must forgive madame, messieurs. Her grief is such that it has deranged her for the moment."

"I do not know if she can find a proper crypt, Madame Aurielle, for the blockade has shut off all shipments of marble from France and Italy," Etienne Poliet said gently. "We are so sorry."

"That man, Kincannon," Philip's voice was hard, "has completely ostracized himself among us now. Though Valier told us it was he who challenged Kincannon, what has turned me from him was his choice of Lafitte for one of his seconds."

"Jean Lafitte acted as one of his seconds?" I asked quickly.

"*Oui*, madame. As insolent a blackguard as ever drew breath."

I looked at Philip coolly. "I thought New Orleans admired M'sieu Lafitte."

"M'sieu Cheviot was acceptable, but M'sieu Lafitte has spent time in jail."

"You are letting your affection for Valier color your feelings, brother." Eugene's tone was affectionate. "While Lafitte is no gentleman, there are those of us who accord him a certain respect."

"You say Captain Kincannon was unhurt?" I asked.

Eugene said grimly, "His sleeve was cut through and dangled about his arm, but his flesh was untouched. I have never seen such consummate skill—not even among the masters at the academies."

"The man is a smuggler—a pirate. What can you expect?" The elder Poliet spoke contemptuously. "He was probably schooled defending himself every day in plying his former trade."

"Best you say those things out of his hearing, Father. I would not care to act as one of your seconds in a duel with the man," Eugene said. Then he added, "I would not have your mother-in-law know, Aurielle, but Kincannon offered to settle this duel after he had pierced Valier's left shoulder, but Valier refused."

"He offered to settle?" I was astonished, for I had

thought Kincannon meant from the beginning to kill Valier. "Do you think he meant it?"

Eugene appeared uncomfortable. "I know he did, for he lowered his sword. That was when Valier cut his sleeve. If Kincannon had not been so swift in moving, Valier would have completely destroyed his sword arm. After that, it was terrible to watch." I saw him repress a shudder.

Philip and his father appeared silenced by the remembrance, and at that moment, Antoinette entered bearing the brandy and coffee on a tray. The men drank with little conversation.

Later, as they were rising to leave, Madame Dessaultes entered. Her face was pale but composed and she looked every year of her age. Even so, there was something unbroken in her, something evil and wild. She looked at me piercingly.

"Are you entertaining possible suitors already?" she asked icily.

"No, madame," I replied calmly. "I was extending hospitality to our guests while you composed yourself."

Eugene said hastily, "Madame Dessaultes, is there anything we can do?"

"My family and I are at your service," the father said kindly.

"Yes, you can tell our friends of the tragedy. I will see to the funeral personally." Her voice was bleak and cold. "And you can ask your wife, Eulalie, to call on me."

"Ah, she shall be here, madame, just as soon as I return home with the word of your sorrow," Etienne Poliet assured her. The three of them made a quick departure.

The rest of that day was a nightmare to me, for Claudette Dessaultes kept me close at her side while she ran the house as a general marshals an army. She made me stay while she supervised the preparation of the body. It was during this activity that I began to hope she would disrobe him and thus see the reason I had not conceived her grandchild, but she did not.

"He has fought nobly and honorably in this fine suit and we shall bury him in it. He shall not be subjected to our sight nude in death," she said to Helen, Esther, and Pansy, the three black women who had served the Dessaultes for years. She had chosen the three to help us prepare him for the coffin, which arrived within an hour of the departure of the Poliet men. It was, as Claudette had ordered, the finest Bouvier's had and it looked to be of hammered silver.

My mother-in-law bathed her son's face and hands herself and put a fine cambric shirt on him after the maids had bathed and bandaged his chest and shoulder wounds. After that, the mourners and old friends of the family began to pour in.

Ondine and Roxanne were there, but I had scarcely a word with them because of the great crush and Claudette's clawlike grip on my arm. She kept me by her side as mountains of food were brought in, and late that night, after all had departed, she said to me, "We shall sit up with Valier this night. We will keep vigil over him."

So I was forced to sit beside her in the oppressive gloom as she lit one candle from another before one could gutter out in the stygian drawing room where Valier lay in his coffin. It seemed forever to me before light began filtering in through the heavy drapes.

During the entire night, the woman had spoken not a word to me, but prayed incessantly and silently over the man who lay before us. I sat dry-eyed and sick at heart. Gone was my relief at having been released from Valier's threats and demands and in its place was the heavy burden of months ahead in this implacable woman's company. Too, there was the possibility of pregnancy. Despite Kincannon's reassurances, I was sure I carried his baby under my heart. It would be at least two weeks before I knew, and when I thought of it, fine beads of perspiration gathered on my upper lip.

Because the blockade was responsible for the lack of marble in the city, Madame Dessaultes had her son buried in the crypt with his father. There was barely room to put one coffin on top of the other, but she said that when the war was over, she would order an especially fine and ornate mausoleum for her son.

By the third day after the funeral, I could see that

Claudette meant to make grief her career for the rest of her life and she meant to see that I joined her in it.

Over my desperate protests, she fired all the Chaille servants I had hired. Bewildered and distraught, they left to seek other places of employment. Only Antoinette was allowed to remain. Further, Claudette's animosity for me grew with each passing day after we donned the funereal black garments of mourning. When anyone came to call, she sat like a burr at my side and steered the conversation into a litany of praise for her dead son.

I stood it for several days. Then, in the midst of one of her mournful diatribes to Eulalie Poliet, I set my coffee cup down hard enough to shatter it to bits and rose unceremoniously to leave the sitting room without a word.

"Aurielle! Come back here—" Claudette began. I did not even turn around, but I heard her say loudly, "Poor thing. You must forgive her. Valier's death has unhinged her and—"

I ran up the stairs, and Antoinette, who had been in the foyer listening as always, ran up after me. In my room, I flung myself down on the small sofa, my bosom heaving. "I cannot stand it another minute, Toinette!" I cried stormily. "Not another minute! I shall run away."

She came to put her arms about my shoulders, "No, no, my darling," she said in French. "You cannot throw away your inheritance—what is rightfully yours. Soon the lawyers—madame must give you a widow's portion of the estate."

"You know she told us that Valier left everything to her."

"That may not be so. The will should be probated soon. I heard her tell Madame Villere so only two days ago, when she was leaving."

I looked at her, startled. "You mean she may have been lying? I may yet receive something and—and find another house for us?"

"Yes, little one. It is worth biding our time. And besides, you do not want all the fine people who are your friends to think ill of you. Leaving his broken-hearted mother alone so soon? And where would we go, *chérie?*"

Suddenly the door flew open explosively and Madame Dessaultes stormed into the room, her face white with fury. "Antoinette, leave us! I must speak privately with my daughter-in-law."

Antoinette, with a warning look at me, took her departure. As the door closed, Claudette wheeled on me. "You little slut—leaving our guests so summarily—breaking one of my fine china cups! You will never do that again!"

"Madame," I blazed, "I will do that as often as I choose. You cannot stop me. I will *not* be treated as a half-witted prisoner. I will stay in this house because I shall mourn my husband's untimely death, but I am no puppet to be pulled about by you."

She came forward and her eyes were strikingly like Valier's when he had threatened me with death. "You will behave decorously—properly, *catin!*"

"Call me any names you like, madame," I responded in cold rage. "They are a measure of your mentality."

Her face contorted and she lifted her hand. As she swung it viciously, I was suddenly back at the Boar's Head and with the old agility I ducked. The force of her swing carried her forward and she fell over a chair to sprawl upon the floor. She scrambled to her feet, mouthing curses as foul as any I had ever heard. I was astonished. Her pretensions at aristocracy did not preclude a wide knowledge of gutter language.

As she faced me again, I saw her white face grow secretive and shuttered and she said softly, "There, there, my dear Aurielle—you are not well. I shall have the doctor come and examine you." Her rapid breathing slowed.

"I shall see no doctor. I am perfectly all right." I was vaguely alarmed.

"But you are not. It distresses me, Aurielle, that you will not admit your illness. But I suppose that is part of it." A strangely crafty smile curled the thin mouth. "Then I shall have a talk with him about your—peculiar behavior."

"Talk with him all you like, madame." I lifted my chin defiantly. "I shall see no doctor."

She contemplated me. Then pursing her lips and speaking in a voice of specious concern, "You must go to confession in the morning with me and ask forgiveness for your ugly behavior and unkind words."

"That is another thing, madame," I responded. "I shall not go to church with you—to pray for Valier's soul or anything else. You will go without me."

Her eyes narrowed. "Ahhh," she breathed, "you are truly ill."

I gave her a long, level look. "No, I have *been* ill, allowing you to smother me with grief, but I am well now."

She continued to regard me speculatively, her pale, lined face closed. Then she said slowly, "I will bargain with you, Aurielle. Respect your mourning period for my son and I will reward you handsomely." There was something exceedingly unnerving in her voice.

"I should respect my mourning period in any event, madame," I retorted.

"Then do lie down and rest." She gestured to my bed. "This has been a sad discourse between a—a mother and her daughter-in-law."

"It has been of your doing, madame," I replied, my voice unyielding.

Her black eyes glittered with a hatred that belied her soft words. "Then do forgive me and rest a while. I will send you up a brandy to relax you," and turning, she left the room, closing the door softly behind her.

She had been gone but an instant before Antoinette entered, her brown eyes round with astonishment.

"You heard?" I asked from the chair in which I had flung myself.

"Enough to say I am proud of your spirit, *chérie*. Now the old nannygoat will think twice before she crosses swords with you again."

"I do not trust her," I replied uneasily. "I shall drink no brandy she sends me."

"A wise decision. We shall both tread warily."

And tread warily we did. Two weeks slipped by and I discovered that Quentin Kincannon was wiser than I about such things, for I was not pregnant after all. It was with mixed feelings that I discovered this, for during sleepless nights I had envisioned a small replica of the captain in my arms.

Still I knew relief that morning as I breakfasted with the chill face of my mother-in-law across from me. She would surely have claimed my child as her son's and it would be another tie to a woman I had come to loathe. I noted that the servants were omnipresent and regarded me with alert interest. There was a difference in their observation that I could not name, but it filled me with dissatisfaction.

"I feel the same way you do," Antoinette responded to my remark on it. "And I saw madame talking very earnestly with Doctor Fourche the other day when he was here. I think she was complaining about you."

But Claudette remained cool and aloof toward me. No more was said about a will being probated and I remained secluded in the house, observing my mourning period with growing restlessness. Claudette made periodic trips not only to St. Louis Cathedral to pray but to the bank on business and to the lawyer's office. I learned this latter through Antoinette. "Not that she ever tells *me* anything, but I hear the servants talking. They think you are—unwell. I heard Trudi telling Pansy that the madame said they were to watch over you very carefully to see you did not harm yourself."

"Harm myself?" I responded indignantly. "It's much more likely that madame will poison me!"

After I had spoken the words, I found myself eating very lightly at the table with Madame Dessaultes, who remarked solicitously and with poorly concealed satisfaction on my lack of appetite.

At last there came a day in April when Roxanne came calling alone. When Antoinette told me she was there, I hurried down from my room to find my supposed cousin seated demurely across from Claudette. After our brief greeting, madame ordered coffee.

For a while we chatted inconsequentially. Then Roxanne said over her cup, "Incidentally, Captain Kincannon was asking about you, Aurielle. He wondered if you are well and wished to express his regrets to you."

"Do not mention that man's name in my house," Madame Dessaultes said coldly.

Roxanne, unpredictable as always, retorted, "*Your* house? Valier's widow's house you mean, don't you?"

"I do not. In his will, my son left everything to me. And I do not propose to allow that man's name spoken in my presence."

"You're a stubborn, misinformed woman, Madame Dessaultes. Captain Kincannon offered your son his life after wounding him in the shoulder and Valier took mean advantage of the captain's lowering his own sword to make the offer. Had Kincannon not been so swift in turning aside, Valier would have killed him on the spot."

Madame Dessaultes's jaw fell, but she recovered quickly. "That is a lie—otherwise I would have heard it before."

"It is the truth. You haven't been told in order that you might not grieve further, knowing that Valier's life could have been spared and he chose to lose it instead."

Claudette bit her lip and took refuge once more in her bereavement. "Alas, Roxanne," she said mournfully, "I do not see how you can speak so to me, knowing I have lost my heart and soul with Valier."

"I am sorry for you, Madame Dessaultes. I truly am. But Aurielle looks too pale. I have come to take her riding in my carriage while I do some shopping today. Tante Ondine sent me for that express purpose."

"Aurielle does not wish to leave the house. She is in mourning for her—beloved," Claudette said stonily.

"Going for a ride will do her no harm and it will not be unseemly. Any woman in mourning can go out for the air—and should. Aurielle, do you want to go?"

"Yes," I replied evenly.

"I cannot permit it!" Claudette's eyes glittered.

"You cannot prevent it," I retorted. I saw Roxanne's green eyes glint at the prospect of a fight.

"Get your bonnet, Aurielle," she said impudently, "and we'll be off."

I felt sticky and rebellious in the long, dull black dress I wore, but I rose eagerly and went to my room, flying up the stairs two at a time. My spirits soared at the thought of being in the sunlight once more, of seeing the shops and pretty clothes in them. I had no black bonnet so I seized a Lavinia hat of pale straw and tied it beneath my chin as I peered into my dressing table mirror. I did look thin and white, but my eyes were a sparkling blue as I turned and ran back down the stairs.

When I stepped lightly into the sitting room, Roxanne said saucily, "I would ask you to accompany us, madame, but I'm sure your grief is too much for it."

Claudette glared wordlessly. Ulysses, who had been standing beside the door, opened it for us and saw us to the Chaille carriage.

I turned to Roxanne as we settled ourselves and said, "Roxanne, you don't know how welcome your invitation is. I owe you a great debt for releasing me from my prison for even a little while." Then because I could not help it, I launched into the miserable details of my life in the Dessaultes house since the death of Valier. I finished with, "I have quarreled horribly with her and I do think she would see me dead should I smile or be happy over any minor thing. I cannot even eat my food with relish."

"Why don't you tell the old dragon to go straight to hell?" Roxanne asked bluntly.

I was silent. I had carried a burden of guilt all these weeks. I knew Kincannon had killed Valier for his threat on my life. Feeling as I did about Kincannon now, even Roxanne herself was part of my burden of guilt. And I could not blame Kincannon. I blamed myself for becoming enmeshed in such a scheme. I had been so ambitious to be a *lady*. Now I was as much a prisoner of my own ambitions as I was of Madame Dessaultes's determination to make me suffer for the death of her son.

"Well?" Roxanne looked at me challengingly.

I replied moodily, "I'm doing penance, I suppose."

"Why should you? Quent says he regrets the death of Valier, but he left him no choice. And after all, he did offer him a chance to settle it honorably." She looked at me thoughtfully. "But I can't understand Valier leaving you to dine alone with Quent, knowing how you dislike him."

"It was a whim of Valier's. He insisted he didn't want

me to miss the fine dinner he had ordered. I would to God I had never gone—had pleaded a headache that night!" The noose of my guilty desire for Kincannon settled more heavily about my neck as I dissembled to her.

"Well," Roxanne said philosophically, "you're not to blame. Isn't this a heavenly day? Mmn, smell the air, Aurielle."

It was delightful in the open carriage with the sunlight gentle upon us and the breeze filled with the fragrance of flowers. My eyes, unused to the brilliant light, narrowed as I looked hungrily at the happy people strolling down the banquettes and riding their horses along the dusty street.

Roxanne chattered on. "Rodeur has been calling regularly and bemoans the fact he cannot come and see you. You see, everyone knows how Madame Dessaultes feels about anyone who had anything to do with Valier's death. But he keeps us abreast of the news."

"Tell me the news. I have had nothing but praises of Valier and prayers drummed into my ears day and night."

"*Alors,* Rodeur says the blockade has almost stifled business in the city. If he and Quent didn't have the Baratarians to fall back on—they slip in and out like eels—their business would have suffered. And as you know, Quent can't finish his lovely house at Pointe St. Antoine. Nothing in town is moving. The Planters Bank and the Bank of Louisiana both have suspended specie payments and credit can be had only by paying usurious interest rates. Only Valier's Bank of New Orleans is doing business with any regularity. Really, the people are getting anxious and rather depressed now."

"You mean New Orleans is taking the war seriously at last?"

She paused reflectively. "Anyway, it's said there is an American general, an Andrew Jackson, who last month punished the Creek Indians for their raid and massacre of those three hundred men, women, and children in Alabama. The American President has put him over the Louisiana Territory, I understand." Her brow creased. "He may well come to the city and bring a real army, if the rumors are true."

"What are the rumors?"

"That the British are massing an armada in the Caribbean with a view to invading Louisiana—and New Orleans in particular." Then as the carriage drew up before one of the dress shops, she called out, "Ulysses, stop here. I would look at the summer frocks."

Later, after she had bought three of the luscious gowns, we remounted the carriage to return and I said with a sigh, "Ah, Roxanne, enjoy yourself while you can. Marriage is not such a happy state—" then added hastily, "I mean, being a widow is miserable. Madame has promised to give me money of my own eventually and God knows when Valier's will is to be probated. The Poliets are running the bank now, even though the Dessaultes own much of the stock."

"Yes, I knew that. I only hope my money is safe in their hands. Ondine says the same. The Poliets never impressed me as being much for business matters."

"Antoinette says madame has disagreements with them when they call. They are the only ones in town who will loan with any freedom now and Antoinette says they quarreled about that when Eugene called the other day."

"Why don't you get out of that house, Aurielle? It seems to me Madame Dessaultes is seeking vengeance on you—is punishing you."

"She is," I replied grimly. "She is certain that I am the cause of Valier's death, but I know Valier fancied the captain insulted him because of the war. I was there and the captain *did* imply Valier was a coward."

"It all sounds very muddy to me—and pointless." She gave me an oblique glance from tilted green eyes. "I still think you a fool to stay there."

"And where would I go?" I responded, nettled. "I haven't a farthing."

"How typical of you, Aurielle." She lifted her shoulders. "If I had married Valier Dessaultes, the first thing I should have done was establish a bank account of my own. Or at the very least, I would have saved some gold in my bureau drawer."

"There's no use to tell me that now," I said with finality. "I persuaded him to pay off ten thousand dollars of debt for me. He was in no mood to give me an account of my own after that."

"Why don't you come back to Ondine's?" She gave me a cryptic little smile. "I'm sure your good *tante* would welcome you back even without a retinue of servants. She has been buying some lovely new furniture and has built a rough storage shed behind the rear courtyard to store all the old furniture—she is thoroughly enjoying the transformation."

"Do you think she would let me return?" I asked. "At least until I could decide what to do. Certainly I can't marry again before a year is up, anyway."

"You forget, *cousine*," she said cynically, "that you and I guard a dark secret of Ondine's. She would not dare refuse you."

"But I don't want to blackmail her," I said hastily. "You must promise to tell me the truth. If she seems reluctant, you must tell me."

"I promise. Here we are, back at the mausoleum." Her voice was petulant as we drew up before the Dessaultes house. "It annoys me that I should care what happens to you at all. I don't know how I ever became—friends with you."

"It is a mystery to me as well," I retorted, but I wondered myself how I could carry so much guilt and not show it in my face. My thoughts of Kincannon were full of wild erotic fantasy in which he possessed me again in a dozen different ways. And this girl who sat beside me wanted him more than anything in the world.

"I'll be back in the morning," she said roughly, "and you be ready to leave with me."

"You must find out first if Ondine will accept me," I replied stubbornly. "I imagine she holds it against me that I stopped her horrible—pleasures."

"Leave that to me," she replied as Ulysses descended from the box and helped me from the carriage. "I'll be here before noon."

Pointer met me and said, "Madame wants to see you in the drawing room, Madame Aurielle." He appeared troubled, but I was too happy at the thought of leaving this house to notice.

When I entered the room, I saw her sitting stiffly in a great straight-backed chair. The room was in semi-gloom because of the drawn drapes and it was warmly stuffy with an unpleasant, dusty odor.

"Come here, Aurielle, and sit down. I want to talk with you."

I did as she asked without speaking.

When I made no attempt to speak, she said coldly, "You should not be running out with your cousin in this unseemly manner. You must restrict yourself to the house and you should start attending mass again with me."

"Will that be all, madame?"

"No, it will not. I have told Antoinette Desmottes to find another place. Things are not going well at the bank. We may have to economize even further. You have no need of her when there are Helen, Pansy, and Esther to serve us both."

"But you can't do that!" I exploded furiously. "You had no right! Antoinette is my *friend* as well as my maid—"

"I know that—all the more reason for her to leave. You need no friends, Aurielle. You are in mourning and should devote yourself to it entirely."

I looked into the harsh, drawn face before me, my mind racing around the fact that this woman meant to draw my prison so tightly about me that I might well do as she intended—die. Some canny instinct of self-preservation warned me not to tell her now that I was leaving in the morning, providing Ondine could be persuaded. She might well become violent. Violence lurked in those anthracite eyes.

"Have you already—told Antoinette?"

"Indeed. While you were gone, I saw her out, bag and baggage."

"Did she say where she was going?"

"No. And if Roxanne Deveret comes again, you should politely discourage her from calling. Is that clear?"

I made no reply. I began silently praying that I could

control myself until tomorrow. I wanted to scream, to rise and run from the room, out the front door and through the streets until I reached Ondine's house—despite the repugnant memories it held.

With strange insight Claudette Dessaultes said, "It will do you no good to run away from me, Aurielle, for I shall alert the police and tell them you have gone quite mad with grief, as I have already done with all my friends and acquaintances. The police would only bring you back to me and I would then post guards around your room and you would not even be allowed the freedom of the house after that."

I was chilled to the marrow. Real terror took hold of me. What if she refused to admit Roxanne in the morning? I said quietly, "That will not be necessary, madame. I will do as you ask; only I urge you to admit Roxanne to see me. Otherwise, she will think it strange, for she knows I am nowhere near madness."

Her voice took on imperious authority at my seeming meek acceptance. "You will discourage her from seeing you the next time she comes. I shall stay with you to hear you tell her that in your grief you wish seclusion—even from relatives."

"Yes, madame. You will excuse me, please? I would wash up before dining."

Later at the table, I was scarcely able to eat under her wild, devouring gaze. She stared at me fixedly and I thought, *There is madness in this house, but it is not mine.*

After dinner, the woman saw me to my bedroom, cautioning me, "Aurielle, I know you will do nothing foolish. You have no money and there is nowhere you could hide from me."

I closed my door. Wind from it snuffed the candle I held and I stood in the dark room, holding tightly to my self-control. Roxanne would be here—she was not a girl to be turned off by a cold greeting or a fabricated excuse.

Still I crept to bed in the darkened room with the sweet late April air blowing across me like a scented kiss, shivering with fear and desperate hope. For a long time, I lay there thinking that I should creep about in the dark and try to pack whatever I could take with me. Then I thought, *No, if she knows I plan to leave there is no guessing what she will do.* Far better to face her with Roxanne and Ulysses to back me up.

I rose very early and looked out over the courtyard below to the stables beyond. In the cool gray light there seemed to be a mist over them all, as if I were in some weird and eerie castle, lost in limbo. The panicky feeling that I would never get away from this place enveloped me and I moved swiftly to overcome it. Stripping off my nightdress, I went to the bowl and poured water from the pitcher into it and bathed myself briskly.

After dressing, I began surreptitiously to pack my large valise. I looked at the row on row of lovely dresses in the armoire and regretfully closed the doors on them. I would be lucky to get away from here with my toilet articles and a change of chemises.

Then I sat down to await the waking of the household. It was too long, for it gave me much time for thought, and in my mind I saw Claudette arranging for Pointer and Jacques to stand guard at my door, saw her even bringing food to me, saw myself grow wasted and wan.

My horror was increased when a faint rap sounded on the door and Trudi entered, bearing a tray. "Ma'am, madame say you like to eat in your room this mornin' so I brung your breakfast. She say you ain't feelin' well."

"Trudi, I feel just fine this morning. Let us take the tray back down and I will dine at the table."

"You do look mighty fine—all pink-cheeked an' bright."

"I am well," I repeated, pushing her gently out the door and following.

At the table, Madame Dessaultes sat alone and she looked at me with venom. "My dear, I thought you unwell. You were so pale last night. You should have stayed in bed."

"I feel perfectly all right," I said coldly, "and I will have breakfast here." But I was too edgy to enjoy the meal and forced down each bite. Only the hot strong coffee tasted good and I drank two cups.

"Where is that needlepoint I gave you, Aurielle? It will help you in your great loss to keep your fingers busy."

"I left it in my room."

"Fetch it."

Thus after breakfast, the morning found us both in the sitting room with handwork in our laps. My nervousness increased with every inept stitch, but I told myself to be calm, that Roxanne could arrive any minute. She did not come until nearly noon, and when she did, the rattle of her carriage brought Claudette Dessaultes to the window. She wheeled about in a rage.

"It's your dreadful cousin again! How dare she come twice in two days?"

"Perhaps because I invited her, madame."

"*Alors!* We will put a stop to that! Go at once to your room. I will tell her you are ill."

"I am not ill. I will stay and see her," I said evenly.

"Then I shall remain with you each moment and you will *not* go off with her again——I swear it. Indeed," she finished viciously, "you will regret this, Aurielle."

But Pointer was admitting Roxanne and her shadow, Ulysses. She entered blithely, remarking on the fine weather and how glad she was to see us both again.

"Really, Roxanne, Aurielle is not up to visitors today," Madame Dessaultes said icily. "After all, you kept her out an unconscionably long time yesterday."

"Oh? I thought she looked much better for it. And I bring a message from Tante Ondine. We feel Aurielle should come home with me, where she will be in the bosom of her family." Roxanne was imperturbable. "I have come to fetch her."

"But she is in mourning! She wants to be where her beloved husband lived. She can't possibly go with you to the Chaille house!" Madame Dessaultes's face was livid and her eyes glittered with savage light.

"But I can, madame," I said low and firm, though my heart was beating a wild tattoo in my breast. "It would comfort me to be with my cousin and my aunt."

"She shall not go." Claudette's mottled face turned toward Roxanne.

"I *shall* go," I said defiantly. "I am responsible for

myself and can move independently of you, madame."

A strange calm spread over Claudette's face; her lids drooped wisely and she actually smiled. "Then in that case, you must pack your lovely clothes, for after your mourning period you will need to wear them again."

I was astonished and disbelieving. "Do you mean it, Madame Dessaultes?"

"Of course, my dear. Run along upstairs and begin to pack now. Roxanne will stay here and have some refreshments with me." She sighed lugubriously, "Ah, I shall miss you, Aurielle."

I could scarcely credit my good fortune, but I fled the room in a blaze of relief. My breath was coming in little gasps as I reached the door. *Oh, Antoinette,* I thought, *if only you were here—but I will find you. We shall be together again!* I pulled out the big portmanteau from beneath my high bed and, running to the armoire, I gathered up an armful of gaily colored gowns. I flung them across the bed and began hastily and clumsily to fold them one by one. *God and the devil!* I thought as I pulled down the third armful and began to fold, *it is taking so long!* It was at this precise moment that the door to my room was flung open.

I looked up to see Madame Claudette Dessaultes standing there, a dueling pistol in each hand. With her foot, she kicked the door closed and advanced on me, her eyes gleaming with a dreadful kind of pleasure. The crossed rapiers on the wall behind her cast back the light from the windows like brilliant punctuation marks to the savage light in her face.

"Now," she gloated, "you will join my son, Aurielle. You will die for him who died for you!" and raising her right hand, she leveled the gun at me and fired. I heard the explosion and the ball as it whistled past my ear with stunned disbelief. I fell to my knees as she lifted the other pistol.

Abruptly the door behind her opened and Roxanne stood framed there for a brief instant before she turned and seized one of the crossed rapiers on the wall beside her. She moved so smoothly and so fast, for all her full pale yellow skirts, that she was a near blur in my frightened eyes. As she plucked the sword loose and held it high, she said in a low voice, "Madame!"

Claudette wheeled about, pistols in hand, and as she did so, Roxanne thrust the blade forward as gracefully as if she wore her tight breeches and soft boots. I saw her slender figure bend and rise with the strength of her thrust. I rose to my feet as Madame Dessaultes sank slowly to the floor.

I ran forward when Roxanne drew the blade from the woman's left breast and together we stared down at the still figure. The darkening stain slowly spread across her bosom where she lay. Roxanne leaned the reddened sword against the wall.

"My God, Roxanne," I whispered, "you've killed her!"

"So I have," she replied slowly.

I was thinking furiously. The servants would come. They would know one of us had done this. I could not let Roxanne take the blame for it. I owed my life to her now. What could I do?

"We must make sure that it does not appear you did this thing," I said huskily, a dreadful solution pushing its way into my mind. Could I do it? *I must!*

"Give me that pistol," I said thickly. "The one she didn't have the chance to kill me with—here." I took it in my slim hand and put it to the wound on Madame Dessaultes's chest. I squeezed the trigger, flinching at the sound. I turned to Roxanne, knees trembling, and spoke with forced calm. "Madame was so overcome with grief for her son's death, she has shot herself in a frenzy of despair—as I prepared to return to the bosom of my family." *After all, it was what she had planned for me.*

Roxanne whistled softly, then said, "By heaven, you are a cool one!"

There was the sound of hurrying feet in the corridor outside and I swiftly placed the gun in Claudette's hand, curling her fingers about the trigger just as Pointer and Jacques drew up in the doorway.

Roxanne turned and with perfect timing, cried out in distress, "Oh, Pointer—Jacques—Madame Dessaultes has shot herself! Oh, whatever can we do? Aurielle and I could not dissuade her!"

"*Mon Dieu*, Madame Aurielle, what moved her to do such a thing?" Jacques asked in French, as the two men stood back aghast.

"I—I was going to leave with Mademoiselle Deveret —going back to my aunt's to live—and Madame Dessaultes came in, crying to us that she herself could not bear to live without Valier. And then—she turned the pistols against herself." The lie was dredged from me. "This—the first time she missed. The second, though Mademoiselle Deveret and I tried to stop her, she fired into her breast." I glanced at Roxanne.

To my amazement, she burst into tears as if she had lost her dearest friend and sobbed, "Oh, what a tragedy!" and she began wailing in French.

I said painfully, "Jacques, send for the officials. Go to the Cabildo and get the coroner." I felt I could not speak another word.

Jacques departed at a run and Pointer was pressed into service by Roxanne, who insisted that he place the body on my bed. I felt a little sick, but I knew I had saved Roxanne as surely as she had saved me.

"I best get Pansy an' Helen," Pointer said shakenly. "I do b'lieve she's really dead. Po' lady—better she dead with him than 'live without him—so close was they."

"Pointer," Roxanne began, still tearful, "please go now and tell Madame Ondine Chaille to come. Poor Madame Aurielle needs her aunt. Oh—and have her maid, Antoinette Desmottes, come, too. As you can see, she is speechless with grief."

When Pointer had disappeared, she brushed away her ready tears with a firm, steady hand and observed me narrowly across the bed. Then she said, "You're pale as a ghost, Aurielle. I do hope you aren't going to let that oversized conscience of yours trouble you about this. The woman was determined to kill you, you know." She pointed to the floor before the door where a bag of bullets and powder were spilled. "You see, she even had additional bullets in case she missed you with the first two shots."

"I know," I said huskily, "but I killed her—"

"There you are, with that swollen conscience again. I'm glad I'm not afflicted with such. If ever a killing was justified, it was that old vulture."

"I'm going to sit down," I said shakily. "Her first shot missed my head by a hair."

"Do you suppose you could weep a little for your mother-in-law when the authorities get here?"

I shook my head and Roxanne sat down across from me, scowling with exasperation. "Then at least be so overcome with grief that you cannot cry."

"You—said Antoinette was to come. Where is she?"

"Antoinette came straight to me when she was fired by Madame Dessaultes. It served to harden Ondine's determination that I must come before noon today."

"How—how did you come to be there just as Madame Dessaultes fired at me, Roxanne?"

"She left me downstairs rather abruptly, saying she was going to help you, but I could see she was up to something. She looked to have a fever, so wild were her eyes. Frankly, I followed her. I meant only to give her time to think I had stayed with my coffee—and I waited almost too long, too."

"Another minute and you would have been too late," I murmured, remembering the stark instant when I looked into the barrel of the pistol above Claudette Dessaultes's burning eyes.

There was a burst of cries at the door and the black women servants stood there, their round eyes on the bloodstained floor. Roxanne said swiftly, "Go back downstairs, Esther—Helen—Pansy—Trudi. You must greet the authorities from the Cabildo and show them up here." Chattering with shock and excitement, they left precipitously.

In an amazingly short time there came the sound of male voices and the heavy tread of booted feet. Roxanne looked at me warningly. "Let me tell them. You can at least put your face in your hands and pretend to weep."

I put a hand to my face, gratefully shutting out the sight of the uniformed *corps de garde* as they entered the room. The last thing I saw as I closed my fingers was the sword, still red with Claudette's blood, leaning against the wall. I was electrified. My God, if they found *that* we would be undone, all our plans for naught!

I began to sob wildly and everyone turned to look at me with astonishment and compassion. My sobs grew louder and I threw myself out of the chair, wringing my hands and wailing, "Oh, I never dreamed she would do such! If only I had known—but she was so fast! Oh, *mon Dieu,* how can I bear it?" I paced up and down, all eyes on me now. "I can't bear it—so soon after my darling husband!"

The coroner stepped forward with his small black satchel, taking a bottle from it. "Here, madame, you are becoming hysterical. Put this to your nose."

I brushed it away, my sobs becoming wilder. If I could just keep their attention from that bloodied sword against the wall! It was back from the door and protected slightly by a jut in the wall. "But my dear mother-in-law is gone! My only link to my husband," I wept.

I noted from the corner of my eye that the authorities had brought a stretcher and were now examining the body on the bed. Oh, God, let them be quick and be gone! I paced faster and farther away from the wall where the sword leaned accusingly. Roxanne was observing me interestedly from eyes that were conveniently wet but speculative for all that.

The men bustled about the room and the coroner examined the bullet hole in Claudette's breast and the pistols, then ordered her body placed on the stretcher. He hastily wrote out a death certificate, verifying it was suicide. All the men looked at me nervously as I continued with my hysterics, alternately sobbing and wailing. I could see they were anxious to be away from me and I grimly renewed my efforts, improvising on my performance.

Very soon, they took the body and departed, still looking at me as I wept copiously. As he stepped out of the room, the coroner said, "Mademoiselle Deveret, here are some powders. See that young Madame Dessaultes takes two every four hours and get her to bed if you can. She will be ill if this keeps up."

Roxanne took them and, as the last of the men left,

carrying Claudette's body on the stretcher, I continued my moans and sobs. It was only when I heard the front door close on them that I ceased.

Roxanne looked at me mystified. "Now what was all that about, for God's sake?"

I flew to the wall and seized the incriminating sword. "This!" I cried, catching up one of my chemises from the open portmanteau on the floor. I wiped the blade but the blood was dried in places. I ran to the pitcher and bowl on the washstand to wet the chemise. Then I cleaned the sword neatly.

As I placed it back over the hooks on the wall, Roxanne remarked dryly, "I'll be damned, Aurielle. You're smarter than I thought. You've saved my hide now—and we're even, eh, *mon amie?*"

"Almost," I replied grimly, "almost."

Everyone had been very kind to me, and Roxanne was so convincing in the story she had told the authorities while I vapored with hysterics, I found myself half believing that Madame Dessaultes would, indeed, have taken her own life rather than see me go. Even the Poliets showed up, all five of them, the hour before our departure to Ondine's. Eugene was able to corroborate how distraught Madame Dessaultes always was at the bank, how the death of her son had warped her judgment. Indeed, it seemed to me he was hiding relief at the turn of events.

Before we left, Ondine and Roxanne had taken care of most of the plans for the funeral and burial the following day.

Back in my lovely room at the Chaille house, Antoinette left me with Roxanne as she and Ondine went to supervise the servants bringing in my considerable wardrobe.

Roxanne's green eyes twinkled as she remarked thoughtfully, "After all, in a way, Madame Dessaultes *did* commit suicide, you know. The moment she pointed that gun at me she, in fact, took her own life." She paused, then added critically, "You're still green about the gills. You take everything too hard."

I flushed. "Is that so? Well, you take everything too

lightly. You are a conscienceless trollop, Roxanne."

She tossed her red-gold head back and laughter poured from her. "That's much better. Now you look like the feisty wench I know. I'll leave you to rest." With the click of the closing door she was gone.

It wasn't until the following day after the funeral that Eugene Poliet called to tell me that my mother-in-law had died intestate and, as Valier's widow, I was now a very wealthy young woman.

Eugene was ardent in his sympathy. "My dear Aurielle—in view of our long friendship, may I call you Aurielle once more? I will see to all the details, as I am executor of Valier's estate. You need not bother yourself about it. I will see you receive ample funds each month and I will continue to manage your share of the bank for you."

"That is most kind of you, Eugene."

"What disposition do you wish to make of the house on Toulouse—the Dessaultes mansion? Will you wish to live there later?"

I shuddered. "Let me think about it. Is it necessary that I decide at once?"

He hastened to assure me that I might take my time. I felt myself between Scylla and Charybdis, in that I had no love for the Chaille mansion, while the Dessaultes house was filled with equally terrible memories.

I said, "I would, however, like to take one step immediately. I wish to manumit the slaves working for the Dessaultes." At his start of surprise, I lifted my hand. "Tell them they may stay on at good wages and keep the house ready for my return—whenever that shall be. But they must be freed."

"Of course, Aurielle." Eugene spoke my name with more assurance now. "I will bring you the papers to sign in the morning. I regret that we were unable to secure a marble vault for Madame Dessaultes, but the blockade—" He lifted his shoulders.

"Yes, it is regrettable that she had to be placed in one of the ovens," I replied. "Oven" was the term given

325

the long half-circle vaults of brick, smeared with stucco just above the ground. Usually only the poor were buried thus. "But there was no more room in the Dessaultes mausoleum." I added finally, "I do thank you for your kind help, Eugene."

Rising reluctantly, he said, "I will be here by ten tomorrow morning, Aurielle, with the manumission papers." Taking his hat in hand, he added, "May I take you driving—just for the air, of course, at the week's end?"

"I think I would enjoy that, Eugene," I replied with a little smile as I gave him my hand. In an excess of pleasure, he bent and kissed it fervently.

Over luncheon, I learned that Ondine had buried another servant only the week before. Roxanne let this slip when she remarked, "Poor Madame Dessaultes was buried in a grave no better than the one you buried Mondu in the week before, *tante*."

"Mondu?" I looked up over my cold sliced chicken.

Ondine looked at her plate with a faint frown. "One of my new servants, *chérie*. He had some dreadful disease and wasted away. We did all we could to save him but nothing availed."

I stared at her accusingly. "That is very strange—coming as it does after your promise to me."

She glanced behind her at the door to the kitchen. "Shh, *mon ange!* You know nothing like that has occurred since you were last here. You may be *sure* of that. Mondu was simply ill. He was ill when I bought him."

"Then why did you buy him?"

"I did not know it—I thought him only thin."

I looked at her innocent face and tried to believe her. I had lived so long with apprehension at my elbow, it was now an old familiar, gnawing at my heavy heart. "I should like to take a tour of the attics," I said quietly.

"I myself will escort you," Ondine said coolly. "Really, Aurielle, if you are to accept my hospitality, I should like to have your trust."

Immediately after we finished our meal, Ondine

took me with her to the attics. Sebastien lit an oil lamp for us and led the way. His eyes on me were inscrutable, his chiseled lips tight, and I felt the wave of hostility that emanated from him.

Ondine insisted on touring each small room and we covered several before we came to the one I had so unerringly found that night long ago. As I stepped into it, a wave of nausea struck me, for the odor, though faint, was the same. The shackles and the whip, the brazier and the tongs were gone, but I saw the places on the floor and in the walls where they had been. I stumbled slightly as we left and murmured, "This is quite enough. I believe you, Ondine."

"I want you to be sure, my dear. We will examine the rest, if you are up to it." So I was forced to follow along behind her and Sebastien as we covered the entire area. Most of the other rooms were filled with a jumble of old furniture and bric-à-brac.

Roxanne had refused to accompany us as she was expecting to go see a new theatrical troupe perform at the Theatre d'Orleans that evening and she wished to nap. Roxanne went out often with both LaRonde and Philip Poliet. Ondine said both men would marry her in an instant if she would have either. "But Roxanne is still yearning after that social outcast, Captain Kincannon," she said as we finished the last room of the attics.

It had been hot and terribly stale up and under the roof and I was perspiring profusely as we descended to the cool third floor and the still cooler second one, where Sebastien left us.

"Have I your trust now, little one?" Ondine asked, smiling without restraint.

"Yes, Ondine—"

"Why do you not call me *tante*, love? Everyone in town believes me to be."

"Yes, *tante*," I replied, turning in at my room.

Her smile grew and was beautiful to see. I should have known from her luminous beauty I was wrong—I who had been wrong so often in these past two years. But I believed her.

Chapter
16

During the month, Governor Claiborne made another attempt to destroy Barataria and the men who inhabited the area, and once again, the pirates slipped away. A gibe in the *Louisiana Gazette* set the whole city laughing.

Roxanne came home from an outing with Pierre Denis LaRonde to pull off her bonnet in my room and laugh. "I just learned from *le bon* Pierre Denis that he attended a meeting of American merchants and bankers. A friendly grand jury had been chosen under the auspices of our good governor—all very quietly. Before this jury there has come a long line of witnesses who have sworn to acts of piracy by Lafitte and his men."

I smiled. "It appears your captain got out just in time —with the proceeds from his *privateering*. And what, if anything, does this grand jury propose to do?"

"Pierre says that indictments have been found against both Jean and his brother under pseudonyms. It is all very hush-hush. I promised I would say nothing, of course." She laughed again. "Jean is so strong and so very clever—nothing will come of this grand jury." Then, with a grimace, she added, *"Dieu!* I will be so glad when I no longer have to look at you in those terrible black dresses!"

"I shall dress in my pretty clothes as soon as I can," I retorted, vexed, for I loathed the long, hot, black garments I wore.

"I suppose you will sit up here like a crow by yourself next month, when Ondine has her May ball?"

"I suppose I must, in order not to shock all these very proper New Orleans dowagers. What will you wear tonight to the Salle, Roxanne?" I asked enviously.

"I shall wear that new sea-green taffeta I bought last week. And if I were *you,* I'd put on that gorgeous pale blue watered silk you bought and come with Ondine—and to hell—I mean to blazes with the old cats who rule New Orleans."

"You don't mean that. You want to be respected as much as I. You'd stay home and burn, too."

She laughed again. "Well, at least you *admit* to wanting to go. I sometimes think you're turning into a complete milksop."

"God and the devil!" I exploded. "You haven't the faintest conception of what I've had to go through since I married Valier. Don't you *dare* judge me a milksop!"

"It's good to prick you into life. You are far too glum these days," and still laughing, she took up her bonnet and left me.

That afternoon late, while Roxanne was preparing for the ball with Antoinette's help and Ondine was engaged with her own toilette, Kincannon and Rodeur called upon us. Sebastien silently ushered them into the large sitting room, where I greeted them. Rodeur took my hand and lifted it to his lips.

"Ah, so pale—the beautiful young widow. But how good to see you, Aurielle!" The blue eyes twinkled and the smile was as devil-may-care as always. I would have thrown my arms about his neck, so glad was I to see him.

Instead, I smiled decorously. "It is nice of you to

call." Then turning, "Sebastien, will you tell Madame Chaille and Mademoiselle Deveret these gentlemen are calling?"

He nodded and disappeared as I looked up into the challenging eyes of Kincannon. It was our first meeting since that rainy winter night he had taken me, made me his. He took my hand for a moment, but did not bend to kiss it. Instead he said, "You are indeed pale, or perhaps it is widow's weeds make you so."

"I have been out to take the air but three times since—my mother-in-law's death. No doubt that accounts for my pallor."

"I had hoped to find you flourishing," he said with a slight smile. "Have you forgiven me for my part in the duel with your husband?"

"There is nothing to forgive. I know you offered him his life—at very nearly the cost of your own."

He bowed slightly, saying, "May we sit for a while?"

"Indeed—do," I responded, embarrassed at being so nearly mesmerized by his presence. "I shall ring for coffee," and I gave the silver bell beside me a swift pull. He was taller than I remembered, his shoulders broader, and his face was already darkly tanned from the spring sun.

Cheviot remarked, "I fear we bring bad news. Our old friend Pierre Lafitte has been caught unawares near the Place d'Armes and is now languishing in the calaboose." He used the slang term for the city prison back of the Cabildo. "He is not well and they have him in chains."

"Can you not get him released on bond?" I exclaimed.

"I have already tried that," Kincannon responded, "and they will not accept bond for him. It is only by a miracle of luck that Jean was not caught with him. The governor is determined to put an end to their base at Barataria."

"How fortunate you left it when you did, Captain," I said with irony.

"Indeed," he replied imperturbably. "I was only being prudent. Now I am in a position to assist Jean

330

and Pierre in any way I can—within the law, of course."
His little smile matched mine.

Ondine swept into the room, followed by Roxanne, who looked charming in a pale blue afternoon
dress, with her hair tied back with a matching ribbon.
Antoinette had not yet finished dressing it and she
looked the prettier for her déshabille, I thought enviously.
Both ladies had to be apprised of the news that Pierre
was incarcerated in the city jail.

Ondine made a sound of distress. "Our dear governor is so determined to stop smuggling—"

"The governor sees how smuggling is harming
the regular merchants, madame," Kincannon said seriously. "As one of them now myself, I can see why."

"Nonsense, Quent," Roxanne scoffed. "Some of
your merchandise comes from Barataria and you know
it."

"I must stay afloat somehow in this sea of blockades
and embargoes," he replied as solemn as a judge, but
his black eyes twinkled wickedly.

A lean and somewhat haggard black girl I had
come to know as Ruth came in bearing the coffee service. I looked at her sharply, thinking as always that
all of Ondine's new servants looked ill. Sebastian,
standing in the foyer doorway, gave her a sharp glance
as she scurried away. His smooth, dark face and strange,
slanted eyes gave me the usual queasy sensation as
Ondine gracefully served all of us from the steaming
silver pot.

"Will you be at the ball tonight, Quent?" Roxanne
was asking eagerly.

"Later, perhaps."

"I know what will keep you and Rodeur." She
pouted prettily. "The gambling rooms at the Salle
d'Orleans."

"Sometimes the gaming tables are more fascinating
than the balls," he replied smoothly. "Not that you
ladies are anything but lovely."

Rodeur laughed at him affectionately. "You dropped
a goodly sum last time we were at the Salle."

"And I must regain it—tonight," Kincannon said,

but his eyes were on me and there was a quickening in their gleam that made my breath shorten.

We continued to chat inconsequentially for the half hour of their call. Then as they prepared to leave, Rodeur made me a courtly bow. "A pity we will not see you at the Salle, Madame Aurielle."

"I shall be there—when my mourning period is over."

"And when will that be?" Kincannon asked swiftly.

"Oh," I was vague, "whenever Tante Ondine says it has been long enough."

Ondine said firmly, "I think it has been long enough already, but, alas, our good friends expect several months of mourning for young widows. Still, I shall urge Aurielle to at least come and sit in on my ball next month. There will be no harm in that."

My heart lightened at the prospect. Just the thought of being where there was laughter and dancing and good company set my pulses to pounding.

As the door closed on the two men, Roxanne cried, "I must fly to be ready—and *he* will be there, *peut-être*. Oh, I am so happy!"

With my hand still tingling from the clasp of Kincannon's in farewell, the old burden of guilt settled on me once more. It depressed me terribly, for I knew if it were possible, I would wed Kincannon myself. The mere thought of it was intoxicating. Even though he had plainly told me he would not marry such as I, or Roxanne, there was something in his manner now, something in his eyes. And he had said, *I want you* with a warm urgency that was undeniable.

As the evening wore on, Philip Poliet called for Roxanne. Then Ondine set forth alone in her carriage, except for the ubiquitous Sebastien. It was quite permissible for unescorted ladies of Ondine's age and station in life to attend these balls without an escort, sitting in the loges of the Salle d'Orleans and gossiping with their peers in society.

I went to my room with a thick new book, given me by Eugene, a novel by an English writer. An hour later, I was surprised by a rap on my door. I saw Ruth there, smiling at me haggardly.

"Madame, they's one of them mens come back here to see you."

I put down my book. "Which one?"

"That tall one with them black eyes. Does you want ter receive him?"

Kincannon! "Yes," I said quickly. "Tell him I will be down in a moment."

What had brought him back? I looked excitedly into the mirror at my tightly coiffed hair in a large bun at the back. In a fit of exasperation, I pulled the pins from it, brushing it vigorously until it flowed in soft curves about my face and down my back. Tying it with a black satin ribbon, I slowed long enough to put on lip salve and very delicately rouged my cheeks. Finishing, I looked into the mirror at my vivid face and sparkling blue eyes with something like shame.

But I was glad I had done it when I entered the lamp-lit sitting room and he rose to meet me, hands outstretched to take mine. "Now," he said exultantly, "we can talk alone—and be honest with each other."

"I have been honest with you—this afternoon."

He laughed. "In widow's weeds, mourning that crazed cripple you married? That's honest?"

"I swore I would never tell of his—mutilation. And you gave me your word to keep the secret!"

"And so I have—but between you and me, my dear, there are no secrets."

Oh, but there are, I thought in despair. The secret that I had come to want him more than he ever wanted me. I said, "None that we can reveal to each other anyway, Quentin."

"You sound mysterious. Is there something I do not know?"

"You know all that matters," I replied carefully. "And you know Roxanne loves you dearly. Oh, Quent, why do you not meet her halfway?"

His face hardened. "I have told you. Roxanne is a friend and nothing more. The matter is closed."

"It isn't closed as long as she loves you so, and

you know it. As for what has happened between us, I have put the reason for your duel with Valier out of my mind and I have forgotten that night at your house —that night aboard the *Wind* as well. I hope you have, too,"

"But I haven't." His face was suddenly intense. "Don't think I haven't tried to forget with a dozen women—but I keep remembering *you*. I could damn you for it, Aurielle, but you're in my blood and I *will* have you no matter the cost."

I looked into that dark face, and in the lamplight it appeared frighteningly predatory. I stepped back but he followed swiftly and I looked into his eyes and saw the small raw flame that flickered behind them. Before I could take another step, he caught me in his arms and, tipping my face to his, he brought his mouth down on mine hard, bruisingly.

I closed my eyes, feeling his flesh fuse with mine, and my lips parted to receive his kiss, which grew suddenly tender and ardent. *For just this little moment,* I told myself, *just this once and no more.* But we were like drowning swimmers, clinging to each other in a river of passion, held swaying together, and for the first time in my life I felt whole in his arms.

It was a long time before he lifted his head and muttered huskily, "Now you know what is between us—and we are only half complete. I want you, Aurielle, I want all of you. There is no one here to know—Can we go to your room?"

He had not mentioned love or marriage and I realized with renewed shock that love and marriage were not in Captain Kincannon's plans for me. I pulled from his embrace and said tightly, "I have not suffered so much, nor come so far as to act the wanton with you again, Quent. No matter how great the attraction between us. There is Roxanne—"

"Damn Roxanne and her obsession," he blazed. "Do you not know, Aurielle, that Roxanne wants most what she cannot have? She is like a child, full of whims, little caring where true love lies for her."

"But you slept with her on the *Wind*. You wanted

her then!" I wasn't sure how much of this accusation was prompted by jealousy.

"I wanted her for the moment. She knows that. She knew it then—" He reached out, catching me in his hard embrace once more, but this time I struggled.

"Let me go, Quent—you have no right to do such!"

"Lady be damned—I have every right. You know you want it as much as I."

"I do not! And you will have the courtesy not to intrude on my grief again."

He burst into laughter. "Grief? For what? For whom? You know damned well you were relieved to be rid of Valier—and his sharp-nosed mother as well."

"I am not the unfeeling creature you think. I grieve for what might have been," and I knew I spoke the truth. He seemed to recognize it as well, for he sobered, but his long arms reached out and closed about me strongly once more. My voice was muffled in the frilled cravat he wore.

"Quent, there are many reasons I cannot give myself to you again. And you are not where you can force me this time."

"I did not force you before—in the end."

"I know that too. But I am determined it shall not happen again." I pulled away, looking up into the angry, frustrated face. "You must leave now and you must not call on me alone again," I said firmly, biting my lower lip to keep it from trembling.

The black eyes swept my face and narrowed. Then without another word he turned and left. The door closed hard behind him and I sank to the sofa, allowing racking sobs to shake me. I wept hard for the first time since my tears of relief when the coroner had determined my mother-in-law's death a suicide. And this time I wept harder for might have been—not between Valier and me, but between Quent and me.

The summer days slipped by and Ondine's May ball a great success, though I stayed for only an hour of it, sitting on a sofa watching the others dance merrily by me. Kincannon was there. He danced with Roxanne but once and was not to stay to the end, though Rodeur did so. The dashing Frenchman came to my side and talked to me for a while.

"You are wearing a very fine uniform—as is the captain," I remarked, my eyes on his fitted, scarlet-trimmed gray uniform.

"*Oui*," Rodeur smiled. "We have just come from a meeting of the troop. With news of the fall of Napoleon, all of the Americans, and I include myself, are preparing to face a renewed British effort. New Orleans would be a fine prize to take to the peace table."

"What peace table?" I asked, forcing my eyes away from Kincannon, who was making his way to Ondine, where he paused with a courtly bow.

"It is rumored there are already negotiations proceeding, even as the British blockade us and attack the east coast at will."

"That is bad news—that they are attacking even with peace in prospect."

"But I have some good news for you. Though our friend Jean Lafitte is still unable to walk our streets without fear of the calaboose, and though his brother is still there, none other than John Randolph Grymes and Edward Livingston are undertaking the defense of the brothers."

My eyes rounded. "Indeed?"

"Indeed," Rodeur said solemnly. "Two of New Orleans most respected lawyers—Grymes has even resigned as district attorney in order to take the case. Though there are those who are unkind enough to say it is all for a twenty-thousand-dollar fee, I like to think they are doing it for justice for the two. You and I know they are not pirates."

"You may know it," I replied dryly, "but I have reservations about such a definite statement."

"Oh, come now, *ma petite*." He laughed. "There were a few like Belli, who were out-and-out pirates, but you know that Jean himself put out the order that they were not to fire upon American vessels, and for the most part they did not."

"That is true," I responded grudgingly, looking

336

across the floor to see that Kincannon had made his adieux and none other than the impeccable Edward Livingston, the former mayor of New York, was dancing with Ondine and smiling down into her upturned face.

Rodeur sighed. "You are looking very beautiful, Aurielle, despite those dreadful dresses you wear."

"Thank you, Rodeur," I replied gratefully. "I wish I could dance as the others are doing—but that will come in time."

"It is as great a tragedy as the bereavement itself," he said gravely, "that the young are forced into such seclusion."

I rose. "But it is the custom and because I am"— I paused, then smiled at him with a touch of mischief —"such a lady, I must observe it. I bid you good night, Rodeur." He took my hand and kissed it lightly and I left the room.

On the way out, I glanced again at Ondine. She had not once left the room with Sebastien. Though Sebastien stood beside the foyer door, his arms crossed over his broad chest, he had not left that post since the beginning of the ball. This was reassuring despite the fact that Ondine still employed the caterers she had used in the days before my marriage to Valier.

She saw me leave and gave a gay little wave from the arms of Governor Claiborne, who seemed to be enjoying her company immensely. Thus I spent the rest of the evening in my room beside the oil lamp, reading *The Storm*, by Hervey Lawrence Dinsmore, Esq. Once a group of laughing ladies passed my door on their way to Ondine's room where they would repair their coiffures and avail themselves of her beautiful cloisonné chamberpots, but they did not see me through my partially closed door.

Eugene Poliet was faithful in his efforts to cheer me. He took me riding in his barouche occasionally and would have taken me oftener if I had permitted it. His calls—business calls according to his explanations —were my sole diversion. I was grateful to the ardent and courteous young man, but each time he took my hand in his damp one, I felt distaste. However, he kept me apprised of all the news about town, the flurry of the men trying to ready themselves for the defense of New Orleans. But, he said, there was so much jealousy and envy among them that they remained isolated little groups that would not work together. The Creoles scorned the Americans and the Americans were contemptuous of the Creoles. Considering all he told me, I concluded we were ill prepared for any sort of attack.

Edward Livingston and John Grymes, for all their vaunted expertise, were unable to secure the release of Pierre Lafitte from the city jail. It was whispered that Jean himself came to the city from time to time but was very surreptitious in his comings and goings.

All through the summer months, Pierre languished in irons—though the eminent lawyers were able to secure the favor of exercise without the irons for his health each day. Meantime, New Orleans went its feckless way, with occasional communications from the legendary general, Andrew Jackson, who was in charge of the Louisiana Territory.

In all these weeks only Rodeur called twice for coffee with the three of us, but we saw no more of Quentin Kincannon. He sent word by Rodeur, inquiring politely after our health and extending his good wishes but, according to Rodeur, he was very taken up with his business.

In August, Ruth, the painfully thin and wan-looking black maid, died in her room, and another funeral was necessary in the St. Louis Cemetery.

Ondine was upset, but she remarked, "It's just the way Mondu died. They must have had the same disease. Dear me, I hope it's not catching!"

On the heels of Ruth's death, came word that the British had invaded Washington and burned the White House. Dolley Madison, the President's wife, had managed to escape with only a copy of the constitution and the portrait of George Washington, before she fled. Things were looking bad indeed for the young republic.

I found myself filled with unaccustomed ire and wished I might join a militia myself.

September came in a gust of heat that was almost unbearable. No more than five days of it had passed when I suffered a devastating headache. After the evening meal was long over and I sat in my suffocating room, I decided to go down into the courtyard, seeking a cooler spot.

I crept down the dark stairs, not desiring even a single candle to intrude upon my misery. I found my way to the front courtyard, knowing it was always empty. Moonlight was a spill of silver over the center and the side where the fountain splashed coolly. I went to the far side and flung myself down in the black shadows of the thick moonflower vine that arched above a woven wicker chaise longue. It was cooler there. My black dress seemed less heavy and hot, and after a long while, I dozed.

I awakened with a start at the sound of low-pitched voices just beyond me. In the moonlight I saw the tall, dark shadow of a man and the slighter one of a girl before him. I knew the girl immediately for Roxanne Deveret, but I did not recognize the man, though he had removed a hat and held it in one hand. The outline of a large knapsack was beside him. I could hear them distinctly, so close were they to my shadowed spot. I started to rise, to make my presence known, but it was too late.

"*Chérie,* you are beautiful in the moonlight—and we miss you still at Barataria." He bent his head and kissed her lightly. I knew the man then. It was Jean Lafitte. I sank back in the dense darkness, holding my silence. It would not do to interrupt this secret tryst.

"I miss Barataria more than I care to admit, Jean. This being respectable is not half so exciting as the old days. What is it that brings you to the city when it is so dangerous? Ulysses fetched me, but with no explanations—"

"I would have given my letters to Ulysses, for it is he who must contact Quent for me. But I longed to see you, *mon amour,* and I wanted you to know of

339

my messages—to give them to Ulysses with instructions. It is very urgent." Indeed, his voice was vibrant with urgency, but there was not a trace of desperation.

"What letters?"

"From me and from our enemies. Letters from Captains Lockyer and McWilliams of the British Navy. They would pay me well to join them in their attack on New Orleans. I have stalled them, asking for time to think over their offer of a captaincy in the navy and thirty thousand dollars—ha! Thirty thousand, when I have more than five hundred thousand in booty in my warehouses!"

"Are you going to join them, Jean?"

"Of course not! Why would I be turning letters and offers over to Governor Claiborne? All I want in exchange is a complete pardon for myself and my men—and a chance to offer my brother's and my services in defense of my country."

"Oho! What a high-flown patriot you've become!" she mocked.

His deep laughter was a touch wry. "Indeed, *chérie*, you know I have always been a patriot—in my way. And so are my men, my poor Beluche and my fine Dominique You, who are under these indictments for capturing Spanish vessels—*legal* prizes under our letters of marque." His voice grew angrier. "When the governor sees these letters, all these unjust indictments will be removed!"

"How came you by these letters, Jean?"

"The British captains themselves came to Barataria in their war vessel and to my house under a flag of truce, bringing their offers personally and in writing. You will see it is their plan to use me and my men as guides through the bayous and rivers of the Louisiana coast. They plan to penetrate the upper country and act in concert with their forces in Canada." There was a moment's silence before he added, "And finally, they plan to free and arm the slaves and turn them against the whites—Roxanne, you will see that Quent receives and delivers this packet to the governor?"

"You know I will, Jean. I have long grieved over the jailing of my good friend Pierre—"

"And what of me, my pretty one? Have you had no thought of me, under a dread penalty, accused so falsely and with a price on my head?"

"I think it's a great miscarriage of justice that you are so persecuted. But you know well enough I hope to marry Quent. *You* will not marry me! All you offer is—"

"Love, Roxanne! Quent is no marrying man—any more than I, and you know it. I would make a queen of you! I have long thought of going to Tortuga and establishing a kingdom there." His voice roughened. "Don't be a fool, Roxanne. Come with me tonight!"

"Ah, Jean"—she swayed near him and her voice was a breathy murmur—"you are so—strong—"

He dropped his hat besides the pack and, with a quick, violent movement, his arms shot out and pulled her to him. In the moonlight, I saw the figures merge in a silent, passionate kiss. She clung to him, as I had clung to the elusive Kincannon, as if she were drowning in desire.

Her voice was shaken when she pulled away. "You—disturb me, old friend—"

"I wish to disturb you"—his voice was muted—"and I am not your old friend. You know it well."

"Jean, you know I love—"

"Do not say that again! You only think you care for Kincannon. Your lips told me you care for me, *ma chérie*." His voice lightened. Then with the old insouciance that was so much a part of him, "I must make haste. You will see my letters reach their destination?"

"I will, I will! Jean, you must be careful. I fear to think what would happen were you caught. They can easily claim these letters to be forgeries—"

"I have stalled the British for only a fortnight and these letters are not forgeries, Roxanne." He spoke in French now. "And I do not count on these letters for the release of my brother. I have much more to do this night and my pack is heavy with gold." He laughed recklessly, adding, "Dawn will find me well away from the city." In the shadowy light I saw the dark, square shape of the packet of letters change hands. Then he said, "Kiss me once more, the way you did just now, my faithless little

341

one, for we may not see each other again for many long nights." Once more they clung to each other.

I half rose in my silent hiding place at the intensity of that long embrace.

Hoisting the heavy pack from the ground beside him and replacing his broad-brimmed hat, Jean Lafitte said huskily, "*Adieu, mon ange*" and with the lithe grace of a big cat, he was gone past the fountain, a blur in the darker shadow of the gate, which closed noiselessly behind him.

For a moment, Roxanne stood poised, then from the darkness beside the house, a towering figure approached and Ulysses said in French, "I stayed—I heard, Roxanne. Shall I take the letters to the captain tonight?"

"Yes, Ulysses, but not before I have read them. Surely such information will be invaluable to the authorities! No doubt the so-famous General Jackson will want to see them. The British are really going to attack at last."

"You had better hurry. Time is what the *bos* has least of this night—" and the two of them vanished in the dark toward the house.

I lay back, willing my tense muscles to relax, and I thought about the British plan to turn black against white in this country where the black outnumbered the white fifty to one in the plantation country—and were near equal in number in New Orleans. Still, I knew there was a troop of free black men who had been training along with the white troops since the war threat had darkened the horizon. Perhaps it might not be so easy to turn all of them against their white friends.

I rose at last from the chaise in the courtyard and made my way swiftly into the house and up the long, dark steps to my room. The hour was very late and I noted that light filtered through the crack in Roxanne's door. I knew she must be studying the letters. Before I could enter my own room, the door to hers opened and Ulysses stepped out, clad in his decorous black suit, a small packet in his hands.

He glanced down the hall and in the dimness saw me. He nodded, then strode to the steps and vanished in the blackness of the stairs.

The following morning at breakfast, Ondine was full

of news. Sebastien had been to the marketplace early and brought back the latest uproar.

"And no one knows how he escaped, but he was gone in the night—and now the governor is posting a thousand dollars reward for his capture!"

She was speaking of Pierre Lafitte's miraculous escape from the calaboose the night before. Roxanne laughed delightedly. "He's far away by now," she said, pleased. "They'll never find him. I'm sure much gold changed hands at the Cabildo in the dark hours of the night!"

"You think it was arranged?" Ondine asked, surprised.

"I *know* it was arranged—the reward is merely sop to public opinion."

"I'm relieved. Jean and Pierre have always been perfect gentlemen with me," Ondine said, then added pensively, "I must go down to the auction block and secure a maid to take Ruth's place. I hope to heaven I get a healthy one this time."

"Why don't you advertise for a freewoman and hire her, Ondine?" I asked coldly.

"They are hard to find, Aurielle, and not so appreciative of good treatment and kindness. You know that. Besides"—she gave me a wounded glance—"you know very well I have—given up—*that*."

Elsie, the cook, a neat black woman with her hair tightly braided, appeared with a plate of fresh, hot biscuits. She had heavy puffs under each eye, but she was plump and appeared healthy. To my silent annoyance, Ondine required formal, long-sleeved black uniforms no matter the weather. They were high-necked and relieved by a small stiff white apron.

"Anyway, I'm delighted that dear old Pierre has escaped," Roxanne returned to our previous subject as she took a hot biscuit and buttered it lavishly. "I had begun to fear for his life. He's not as strong as he appears."

I knew the bond between the Baratarians and I knew Roxanne's part in delivering those secret letters. Until and if she chose to reveal it, I determined to keep my own mouth shut.

When we finished breakfast, she turned to me and

said, "Come, little black crow, and let us go shopping. The people must get used to seeing you in shops. Tante Ondine, don't you think it has been a very long time since Valier's and his mother's deaths?"

"Indeed I do, and shopping together is a splendid idea. Sebastien and I will go and find my new maid while you are gone, my darlings."

Later, as Roxanne and I went to the rear courtyard and into the drive to mount the carriage, I glanced again at the new storage building, a rather large, square shed near the stables. It was of raw wood and not very attractive, but new young banana trees had been planted about it and were growing taller each day, nicely screening the ugly building from view. Ondine was too extravagant, I thought for the hundredth time. She was forever changing her furniture about, buying new for old. As the carriage pulled out into the brown dirt of the street, I dismissed it from my mind. It was a beautiful, bright September day.

It developed that Roxanne took a great deal longer about her shopping than I had anticipated. We had luncheon at Victoire's and it was near three in the afternoon before she had Ulysses turn the carriage homeward.

"Wait, Ulysses," she cried in a low voice, as we neared the Place d'Armes. "I see Captain Kincannon coming from the Cabildo. I would talk with him."

I saw the tall figure swinging away from the Cabildo. He stepped up his long stride on the banquette as he caught sight of us. He did not smile as he drew up beside the carriage and Roxanne greeted him with, "Good afternoon, Quent. Will you ride a few blocks with us? I would speak to you about—our mutual friend."

Without speaking, he swung himself up in the carriage and Ulysses moved the horses slowly forward. Roxanne slipped from beside me to the seat beside him. Her voice was low and clear. "You received my messages last night?"

"Aye. And delivered them at dawn. I have just come from a meeting with the governor, General Jacques Villere, Commodore Patterson, and Colonel Ross of the regular United States Army."

"What of—Jean's letters?"

"They were deemed lies and forgeries—with only Jacques and myself dissenting."

"Ah, that is very bad—"

"It is worse. Patterson and Ross are agitating for a force to go to Barataria and destroy it, making prisoners of the remainder of the Baratarians. Pierre's escape has made the governor amenable to their suggestions."

"What fools they are!" Roxanne exploded, red-gold curls tossing. "To make war on their friends while their true enemies will soon descend upon them!"

"Upon *us,* my dear Roxanne," he said, his dark eyes on me with hidden amusement.

"Is there nothing you can do?" I asked, and Roxanne glanced at me with surprise, as if she had forgotten my presence.

"I can and will send word to Jean and his brother."

"Will it be in time, do you think?" I persisted.

Roxanne's voice was anxious. "There's time! It will take some time to muster a force here. But whether Jean and Pierre and the others will believe it—who can say?"

"They feel very secure in their little islands," Kincannon said.

"Will you go yourself to warn them?" Roxanne asked.

"That I cannot do, but Rodeur has said he will take my letter and corroborate my story. And now, if you ladies will forgive me, I must take leave of your pleasant company and be about my business. Rodeur and I are to meet at Newlett's Coffee House." He turned. "Ulysses, I will leave you here," and as the carriage stopped, he swung down, closing the door and strode away.

"I presume," I said carefully, "that Jean and Pierre are in considerable new danger."

"That is right," Roxanne said absently, her green eyes following the captain's diminishing form. Then with sudden intensity, she said, "Aurielle, Jean sent word to me—last night. The British have contacted him with plans to invade New Orleans. He put them off for a fortnight for his answer and offered his aid to the Americans, and the fools here do not believe him. Oh"—she broke off

345

with real fear in her face—"I am so afraid for him! If the army and navy go to Barataria—" Her face smoothed as she said, "Ah, but Jean is so wary. They will not take him unawares. He is like an eel. He will slip away!"

"A pity the authorities do not believe him. It would have made him quite a respectable ally."

She looked at me sharply. "They may yet be forced to accept him. When the British come, I imagine they will be glad enough for his expert help."

"That is possible," I replied soberly, "if he lives to that day."

She gave me another frightened glance. Then, with a lift of her rounded chin, she said, "He will live. Jean is very brave and very clever."

"I agree," I responded, but I thought of the massing of the American government forces that might very well be going on right now, and I had a presentiment that Barataria's days were numbered.

A week went by and there burst upon New Orleans the sudden news that the "pirate's nest" at Barataria had been destroyed; many men had been taken prisoner, but some had escaped in the marshes.

The brothers Lafitte had, as always, somehow eluded capture.

I could visualize the consternation of the privateers —and pirates—as the American vessels and soldiers hove in sight, because the story told was that they did not fire on them nor take measures to protect themselves, as *le bos* had long enforced the rule not to fire on American vessels.

Not long after this news, Rodeur paid us a visit and gave us more details. "They did not believe me in Barataria when I told them they were to be attacked by the American forces. They thought Quent's letter a practical joke. Only Jean and Pierre gave any credence to my warning. It is said that Commodore Ross and Colonel Patterson set fire to all the houses—burned them all to the ground and took nine vessels and burned one to the water's edge."

Roxanne lamented, "That is dreadful after they offered to help against invasion!"

"Oui. The authorities at the Cabildo believe the letters from Jean and the British offers *now,* but excuse themselves on the grounds that the Lafittes were outlaws. Personally, I believe that what made them determined to capture Barataria was the five hundred thousand dollars' worth of goods in the warehouses on Grande Terre. A fine booty for them and their men."

"You have put your finger on it, Rodeur," Roxanne said bitterly. "It was greed more than anything else that brought on the attack."

We talked on about it over coffee at some length. Ondine's new kitchen servant, a timid, very young black girl named Christine, brought in pastries to go with our coffee. Ondine had secured two new servants at the slave block. The man—Zeke—looked intimidated as well, what little I saw of him as he scuttled about, doing Sebastien's bidding, which was mostly yard work, pruning the courtyards. These two new ones brought the number of Ondine's servants to four, the other two being the black cook, Elsie, and the upstairs maid, Millie.

Rodeur took his departure regretfully, promising Roxanne he would return soon in company with Captain Kincannon.

The rest of September went at a snail's pace for me, for Ondine had said it would be the last of my mourning days. She had announced she would have a very decorous gala for my coming out of the dead black which I felt, by now, grew on me.

The talk in the city about the Lafittes was varied. Some said that in the inventory of the warehouses were found jewelry and articles belonging to a Creole lady who had sailed from New Orleans and had never been heard from since. It made things look black for the brothers.

October brought an unseasonal chill to the city and the weather was gray and dismal. The city's streets became seas of mud, and Ondine's gala for me was held on one of the worst nights. The guests came anyway, with their servants carrying their shoes and stockings and lanterns to light the way, as they made the trip from carriages to the house in the cold mist.

As a special treat for her, I had arranged that Antoinette should take the evening off after helping me dress. I had bought her a ticket to see the new troupe of players at the St. Phillip Theatre. With the income I had now from the Dessaultes estate, I was a very affluent young woman. I had even insisted that Ondine let me pay her a goodly sum for my residence in her home. I still could not stomach the thought of returning to the grim mansion of the Dessaultes with all the vivid and terrible memories it held.

For the gala, I wore a pale pink silk and taffeta dress, a new one Roxanne and I had picked out on one of our shopping tours. Ondine's guest list was, as usual, very exclusive. As I unobtrusively made my way into the room, I saw the Poliets were much in evidence. The governor and his lady and the two lawyers for Pierre and Jean Lafitte, Edward Livingston and John Grymes, were there as well. Among the others were all the planters from Pointe St. Antoine and a few of the old families in the city.

They were all kind and courteous to me, but I could see in the women's eyes that they thought I had not mourned long enough. But none of them spoke of my bereavement to me and I felt my heart grow lighter with each passing moment.

Though the high-born Creoles were chill to them, Rodeur and Kincannon were there. I danced with both, my feet as light as thistledown despite the pall that hung over the city with the threat of the British lying but a few short miles out in the ocean.

But it was at this gala that my old suspicion of Ondine and Sebastien returned for the first and last time. It was because she and the black man absented themselves midway and were gone some time. When they returned, her face was glowing with the incandescence of youthful beauty that she had worn so often in the old days.

It stunned me so that I immediately left the bright salon, making an excuse to repair my coiffure. Once in the foyer, I took a candle and made my way secretly to the attics. But I found nothing there. Only rooms full of cast-off furniture and odds and ends met my eyes. And the single, still-fetid room, whose stench I seemed unable to rid myself of, even after I returned and danced the balance of the evening.

Kincannon claimed me for the last dance, asking blandly if he might call on me, now that my mourning days were over.

"You may call on Roxanne and me at any time."

"This scrupulous loyalty to Roxanne baffles me," he mused. "You two began by hating each other and I still think Roxanne has but little use for you. Will you tell me why you feel such a burden of debt to her?"

"It is only that I owe her a great deal," I replied evasively, "and as long as she loves you, there can be nothing between us."

"This great debt that you owe her," he said thoughtfully as we swung to the sprightly music of the Creole dance, "surely you can tell me how that came to be."

"Well—she introduced me to Ondine, persuaded her to take me on as her niece. You know that. It was a great favor."

He looked down into my eyes, his own impenetrable, as he said, "I think there is a great deal more you do not tell me." He laughed mockingly as he added, "And you must remember you owe me as well."

"Owe *you?*" My eyes widened, grew hot. "What, pray, do I owe you?"

"I have kept your secret as well as Roxanne's, the secret of your origins."

I stiffened. "And I have held my tongue about you—"

"What for?" His laughter grew. "Nothing you tell about me would matter. Already stories about my background and my early life are rampant in this city, stories that are much worse than the truth. I am not received in any Creole home but Ondine Chaille's." Then as the music came to a halt, he released me slowly, adding, "What a pity. The last dance of the evening and you are so cold to me."

"You're impossible," I said between my teeth.

"On the contrary, I am very possible—more so than you imagine."

"I must leave and join Ondine and Roxanne to

bid our guests farewell." I moved away from him toward the foyer where the guests were slowly gathering, with Sebastien and the hired servants bringing cloaks and lanterns belonging to each group.

He followed closely, bending to my ear. "Then you must bid *me* farewell, for I am a guest—" and he caught my arm, his big hand warm on my bare flesh. He pulled me back into the salon.

Because I was fluid with sudden desire at his touch, I allowed myself to be pulled along through the salon and, beyond, to the sparkling glassed French doors that opened on the rear courtyard. He reached down and flung one open. We stepped into the cold night air.

I did not look back at Ondine and Roxanne and the many guests who took note of our sudden departure. Instead, I followed him through the long windowed doors into the clean-scented, damp darkness of the courtyard. Once beyond the French doors, I let him take me into his arms. His big body was warm against the night-chilled silk and taffeta I wore. He was very deliberate as he tilted my head up and put his mouth over mine quite leisurely.

I clung to him dizzily as the clouded sky swung above us and my breath quickened. Hard thighs pressed against me and his arms drew me even closer against his broad chest. Abruptly, the memory of the candlelit salon on Bourbon flooded me and, with it, the remembered feel of our bodies as our bare flesh touched and struck fire in that blaze of glorious fusion. It was like strong drink and I was drunk with it.

He released me slowly, lingeringly, and murmured, "Now that's a proper kiss, for it promises more on our next meeting."

"Please," I whispered, "please, Quent, don't do this to me—"

"But I will until you admit it, until you are—" He broke off suddenly, his head lifted, his body tense. "My God, Aurielle, the Chaille stables are on fire!"

Chapter
17

I turned and looked beyond the courtyard to see a spout of red licking up among the young banana trees. *Fire!* The terror of a city that had been nearly destroyed by two devastating fires.

"Oh, Quent!" I cried, "that's not the stables—it's Ondine's storage shed."

A thin scream floated across the rising wind and I was abruptly chilled to the marrow as Quent said, "Hell, there's someone in there!" and on the heels of his words there came more screams from the small building, terrible rending wails that quivered in my ears.

The truth burst upon me with stunning shock. *I knew!* Ondine had merely changed the locale for her brutalities and perversions from the attics to this shed at the rear. I started to speak, but Kincannon had left me.

He stood in the glassed French door and roared, "Rodeur, Etienne—men, come! It's fire!" Then he was gone, running strongly toward the outbuilding beside the stables. I followed as fast as my entangling skirts would permit, the cold, damp wind against my bare arms and breast forgotten in terror for the servants in the blazing building.

The screams reached a searing crescendo as other guests poured from the house and caught up with me. I glimpsed Rodeur and Eugene as they passed, and Rodeur called out, "The governor has sent for the firefighters—stay back, Aurielle!" But I did not heed as I sped along behind them.

I slowed as I saw Kincannon rip the burning door from its hinges. Other men began tearing at the walls. The screams from inside were agonizing. Then from the inner fire there stumbled two figures, which Kincannon immediately knocked to the ground and rolled over and over, quenching flames that engulfed their bodies. I felt my satin slippers sinking in the cold ooze of the ground about us, but my face and arms were hot from the heat of the fire before me.

"They's two more in there," cried one burned figure, tottering to his feet.

By now the men had secured sticks of wood; some had torn off their fine coats and were beating at flames, prying at walls with the pieces of wood they had secured. The guests were in a circle about the scene and I saw Ondine crying into her hands, with two of the women fluttering about her. But others were staring at the burning shed and listening to the screams in open-mouthed horror.

After what seemed an eternity, the fire wagon lumbered up the drive, rattling over the courtyard, smashing the delicate wrought-iron lace that separated the courtyard from the rear where the shed and stables lay. Men flung themselves from the horse-drawn water barrels and pumps and began to pump water as fast as they could into the buckets they brought. Among the onlookers now were many blacks who had come from houses far down the street in order to help. Terrified of fire, the people of New Orleans had no thought now but to quench the flames before they could spread.

Wind from the south was rising fast and a wet mist had begun to fall. Flames now blew in the direction of the stables. The fire wagon pulled nearer to the blaze, with every man busy on the pumps flinging the water steadily as the now-blackened and singed men pulled away the last walls of the building. By the light of the remaining fire, the horror of the shed lay revealed, for one of the women, very young, was still chained to a flattened wall by manacles of steel at her wrists. She did not move, her body blackened and smoking. I knew it must be Christine and I knew she was dead. The other body was barely discernible as a woman and she lay face up in the center of the charred ruins.

As the last flames were slowly extinguished, I heard a murmur welling up from the crowd, questions being asked and Ondine attempting to explain. I noted suddenly that Sebastien appeared from nowhere, materializing beside her just as she collapsed.

He caught her easily, and as I drew near, I heard his deep rumble, "The shock has been too great for madame. Make way—I must take her to her house!" and he swung the slight figure into his arms and made his way through the crowd.

I came suddenly upon Roxanne, who looked at me with narrow green eyes. "This has been a night for revelations, eh, *cousine?*"

I had no chance to answer, for a rough voice beside me said, "So this is the way you punish your servants, Madame Dessaultes?" and I looked into the angry face of Etienne Poliet.

"We did not know they were there, m'sieu," Roxanne retorted for me. "And we certainly do not approve of our *tante's* punishments." She took my arm and began to pull me from the scene.

"But we must stay to see how they are!" I protested, my body thoroughly chilled and my clothing damp.

"We are chattering with the cold. And we know two of them are dead," she replied angrily, releasing my arm. The last embers were being tamped out by the grim firemen and others about them. The angry murmur of the crowd was growing louder as bodies were lifted from the ashes. The groans of the man and woman who had escaped the outbuilding were heartrending.

"Come," Roxanne urged, "these people are angry.

Let us get into the house," and I followed, stumbling a little in the rain-soaked earth.

When we reached the house, Roxanne closed the open French doors behind us, but we faced a room with a dozen people in it. She said quickly, "We shall be ill of the cold, my friends. Forgive us if we retire. We know nothing of our aunt's treatment of those servants." She picked up a candle from a nearby table.

"There are punishments provided by law for those who mistreat their slaves, mademoiselle." It was Governor Claiborne himself and he was helping his wife adjust her cloak. His voice was cold and his demeanor contemptuous. "The slaves can be sold and the owners fined heavily."

"I assure you, governor, *ma cousine* and I knew nothing of this terrible thing," Roxanne said defiantly, lifting the candle with a steady hand.

"That seems incredible to me," Madame Claiborne said, her dark eyes flashing. She was a delicately boned Creole, with all the fire of her Spanish ancestors.

"Nevertheless," I said, "it is the truth. When first we discovered our—aunt's abnormality, we put a stop to it. She had given us her word that she would not repeat these cruelties—"

"You are only making it worse by explaining," Roxanne hissed, tugging at my arm.

"And she did not, for a long time," I went on stubbornly. "But we—we did not know of the shed. She said it was for storage only."

"Hmmnn," Madame Claiborne said in obvious disbelief. "It is a disgrace to our Louisiana. And now you run away from your questioners!" She swept past us on her husband's arm and made her way out through the foyer to the front door.

I turned to those left in the room. "My cousin and I will return and answer any questions we can as soon as we change from our wet clothes." I lifted my chin and faced the angry contempt in the room.

"It is two of the clock, Aurielle! We cannot come back and argue with these outraged people," Roxanne whispered. Then to the others, "My cousin and I will be ill if we do not get into dry clothing." Again she pulled at me.

"We will return," I promised the accusing eyes around us. Then I followed Roxanne from the room. As we took the stairs, I turned to her. "Where is Ulysses? I haven't seen him all evening.

"I do not know," Roxanne said. "I told him this morning I would not need him. I suppose he is off on some errand of his own."

"With all the commotion going on here, you'd think he would hear and return."

"He will return when he is ready," she said shortly. Then, as we reached the top of the stairs, "I saw you— the two of you."

My heart sank. "What do you mean?"

"You and Quent, of course. In the courtyard, just before the fire. I was not surprised at him—but I was very surprised at *you*." She waved one hand and, in the other, the candle fluttered as I turned to face her. She said, "Don't deny it, Aurielle. It was plain enough that you returned his kiss." Her voice dropped, grew bitter. "I know he's a handsome devil and I suppose you are no stronger than any other woman would be in the circumstances." We had reached her bedroom door and she tightened her grip on me, adding, "Do you deny it?"

There was faint hope in her voice and I could not bear to face her, but I did squarely. "Yes, I returned his kiss because I have—been a long time without kisses. But I told him there would be no more. It meant nothing. I will never come between you." It cost me dearly to say it.

Her eyes were startlingly green and her mouth twisted in a wry smile. "I know Quent. Do not make vows you cannot keep, Aurielle."

"Still, I make you that promise, Roxanne. I will never come between—"

"You already have."

I winced. "It will not happen again." I added firmly, "Now we must get on dry clothing to face the tragedy that Ondine has wrought."

I left her and opened my bedroom door. There were two lighted candles by the bed and I was met by an agitated Antoinette, who closed the door behind me. She had stirred up the fire in the bedroom fireplace but the room was still cold.

"Aurielle! Aurielle! I came home just as it all began! The people are so angry. I heard them talking in the salon before I came up here," her words tripped over one another. *"C'est vrai?* Madame has been torturing her slaves? I heard them say Zeke is not dead and he has been telling of hideous depravities!" I made no attempt to stay her hot flood of words. "One man said Zeke himself tipped over a brazier to start the fire rather than go on living under Sebastien's whip and madame's—" She broke off at last, her face pale with shock and sorrow. Then, "I should have known! The servants have always been so cowed, so *worn.*" She put out her hand to me, then cried, "You are wet!"

As we began stripping the dampened garments from me, I told her about it from the beginning, of my having discovered the attic room, of Ondine swearing never to commit such acts again, of my belief she would keep her word after I forced her to release the previous slaves.

"I owed her so much," I said bitterly. "She had been so good to me—to *us,* Antoinette. So generous. Somehow I thought, I had hoped—" I broke off as I slipped into a warm, wine-red woolen dress, the long sleeves cozy on my chilled arms.

"My poor little one—do not blame yourself," Antoinette murmured, brushing out my long, curling damp hair. "I know what you thought. I thought it myself, you resemble her so."

I turned and looked at her searchingly. "You thought it, too? The mere mention of it is like a knife in my vitals now, Antoinette. Do not think it! I forbid it!"

"It cannot be," she replied firmly, tying my long hair back with a matching wine ribbon.

"And now I must go down and face those people, see to the burns of poor Zeke and Millie. Elsie and Christine perished in the flames." I looked into the mirror at my pale face, then rose to my feet. "But I shall see Ondine first—despite her convenient faint."

"I will go with you, *chérie*," Antoinette said bravely, but I knew she was afraid.

"No, Toinette, you wait here. Roxanne and I will face those people together. I am not afraid," I said, but I lied. Those condemning faces had justice on their side and I knew, despite Zeke's disclosure to the contrary, they believed that Roxanne and I must have been well aware of the incredible brutalities that were committed here.

I walked lightly down to Ondine's closed door. I hesitated and took a deep breath. This time there would be no holding of tongues for Ondine. This time she must face her guilt. I took the knob firmly and opened the door without the courtesy of a rap. I was astounded at the chaos that met my eyes.

Clothing was strewn over the bed, the chaise, the chairs, and Ondine herself poised over a large portmanteau. She looked at me with tear-wet eyes, her beautiful face unchanged for all the weeping, her lovely hair lovelier in disarray.

She cried, "Ah, *ma petite fille*—come in and help me. Oh, you must help me! Sebastien has gone to hitch up the carriage." She came to fling her arms about me. "My darling one, you must give us haven!"

"I cannot give you haven, Ondine," I replied, thinking with deep shock of her term. *My little daughter*. Was she, in her extremity, admitting what I had dreamed of, then feared?

"But look—look there on my bed!" I followed her trembling finger and saw a small figure among the clothes. She snatched it up and held it toward me. "It is an effigy of me! Observe the pins in the heart—the noose about the neck. And that hair is my hair, *my own hair* on its head. That dress is made from bits of my own clothing—" Her voice was near hysteria as she continued. "Even my nail parings are in the wax. I know Clothilde LaVaux has made it. She has cursed me for years and this is the final step. *Mon Dieu*, Aurielle, as my daughter, you must save me."

"Your daughter? Ondine, I think you lie." My heart was sick because I thought she spoke the truth.

"Oh, I have cursed the day I had to flee Paris and leave you to a nursemaid's care. I would have taken you with me, my angel, but I barely escaped with my life. Hide me now, Aurielle—hide me!"

"There is nowhere I can hide you, Ondine. You must face the people of New Orleans and publicly admit and do penance for your deeds in order to win their respect once more—if ever that can be."

"I am not afraid of *them!* It is the voodoo I fear! Can you not hide me in the Dessaultes house?"

"How can I do that? You know word will leak out of your presence there. Servants will spread the—"

"Ah, that is all too true. I can only do as Sebastien says—flee to St. John's Bayou where a ship is readying to leave. He knows of it—a smuggler bound for France. Help me pack, my darling child." Distractedly, she began flinging clothing into the portmanteau. "Ah, I have loved you so well in these short months we have been together."

"I cannot believe it," I said numbly, unable to grasp the reality she was forcing on me. "Why didn't you tell me before?"

"You *can* believe it," she said with a suddenly vicious glance. "Your father was killed in the political wars in France and I was caught up in intrigue myself. What good would it have done you to know? Now help me pack."

"I must go see to Zeke and Millie; they were badly burned. I must face those people below."

"You owe them nothing! You owe your mother everything! Help me, my darling child, help me!" She began cramming the clothing into the portmanteau with renewed vigor.

"I will help you, madame." Sebastien, silent as always, had entered. "I will see you safely out of this. I have secured the gold from the attics and it is in my packs even now. We must hurry. The smuggler leaves at dawn."

"Are there many still down below?" she asked.

"A great many—even some of the guests. They have put Zeke in the sitting room and Millie is still alive. They have told everything." The strange Egyptian eyes flicked over me contemptuously. "Even that your nieces knew nothing of their mistreatment. But there are authorities from the Cabildo there now and we must face charges if we do not escape, and soon. I have the carriage hitched and ready. The trick will be getting to it and leaving undetected."

"Then Aurielle *can* help," she said in a calmer voice, still cramming clothing in the portmanteau. "You and Roxanne go down and talk to them, Aurielle. Tell them I am ill and will come down to the Cabildo tomorrow myself. You will do that for your mother, will you not?"

I felt ill with the knowledge that this perverted woman was my mother. "Yes, I will do that one last thing for you, Ondine."

Sebastien said, "Madame, you cannot take all these clothes with you. We will buy more in Paris. Get your long, hooded cape so you will not be recognized."

A rap sounded and the door opened to Roxanne, who looked pert and fresh. "Are you going somewhere, *tante?*" she asked impudently, glancing around the littered bedroom.

"You know I must flee! Look! There"—and she pointed to the small wax figure on the table. "I know voodoo and I know that is deadly! I must escape it!" She paused, then said urgently, "You and Aurielle must go below and tell the others I am ill and will answer to the authorities in the morning. Give me a chance to escape with Sebastien."

"It is a long drive to Bayou St. John," Sebastien said. "Madame must make haste." He snapped the portmanteau closed and picked up her reticule. "You have your toilette articles in here?"

"Yes, yes—but we must wait until the girls go down and occupy the people with explanations." She reached into the armoire and took out a long, black velvet cloak. "We will wait ten minutes, then leave by the servants' rear staircase."

I could not bring myself to look upon that lovely, unmarred face again. "Come, Roxanne. We must face Ondine's accusers."

As we took the stairs, she said cheerfully, "Zeke

has told them we knew nothing of this. *We* will not be accused."

"But our relationship with Ondine is undeniable and we are guilty by association. We should have known!" I said in low anguish. "It is my fault."

"Well, I don't feel in the least guilty. Ondine's getting what she deserves."

"No. She is escaping what she deserves—and I know that wherever she goes, she will do these things again." I paused. "Roxanne, she says now that she is my mother." The words were thick in my throat.

She gave me a judicious look. "Well, you do resemble her—somewhat. But I thought Ulysses said once she came from Santo Domingo in 1800."

"That is when I was brought from France to England. She could have fled Paris to the islands. It all fits very neatly—"

"You don't have to be like her. What do you care if she is your mother?"

"I care," I replied dully, remembering Marianne's clubfoot and her clubfooted baby. What if my children should be like their grandmother? "I think perhaps Ondine has ruined my life."

The foyer was full of people, as was the salon and the sitting room. Roxanne and I went about, explaining that our aunt was ill and would appear at the Cabildo to answer charges the next morning. We expressed our sorrow and our horror at the evening's events. Though Zeke and Millie had absolved us of knowledge and blame, the people were cold. The blacks who had gathered near the doors eyed us balefully.

Kincannon, his face sooty with smoke, appeared and said, "I have ordered an ambulance to take Zeke and Millie to the Ursuline nuns' convent. They are badly burned and need the greatest care. Where is Madame Chaille?"

"She is ill," I lied, "and will appear at the Cabildo in the morning."

Kincannon smiled grimly. "She will be charged with murder and she is ruined in New Orleans society. No one will accept her after this."

Roxanne said, "I expect that means us, too, as her nieces." Her voice was surprisingly light.

Eugene Poliet, as smoke-grimed as Kincannon, found me and hovered near, saying reassuringly that it would soon be forgotten, that I could go live in the Dessaultes house and become a leading social arbiter if I chose. He finished by adding, "You know how I have long felt about you, Aurielle, and I offer you my good name in marriage."

I smiled at him painfully. "You are kind, Eugene. I will think on it."

The ambulance rumbled up and took Millie and Zeke away. Their bodies were dreadfully burned and I feared they would surely die. The crowd finally began to disperse, grumbling among themselves about Ondine, and it was not long after the last of them had gone that I heard the Chaille carriage wheels spew shells as it rumbled past the side of the house.

I ran to a window and, in the darkness of the night, I saw the darker bulk of it careening down the muddy street in front of the house and I knew Ondine and Sebastien had made good their escape from her accusers.

It was well after three in the morning when Roxanne and I finally made our way to bed. Antoinette was waiting for me. Her face was white and drawn when I entered and she came to me without a word and put her arms about me. We stood thus for a moment until I pulled away and said, "I don't know what we shall say in the morning, when Ondine does not appear before the justices at the Cabildo, Antoinette."

"You will tell the truth. This was none of your doing."

"But both Roxanne and I aided her by lying to those who would punish her. We lied so she could make good her escape."

"So she has run away. I heard the carriage a few moments ago." Then she added thoughtfully, "You don't have to tell them that, *chérie*. Just say she is gone."

"Poor Elsie and Christine—poor Zeke and Millie."

"Perhaps Zeke and Millie will live. Do not give up hope."

When at last she pulled the warm covers over me, I made a conscious effort to relax and still my racing thoughts. I could not bring myself to tell Antoinette of Ondine's confession that she was my mother.

I shuddered and twisted restlessly. The feeling of horror I had known when first she said *"ma petite fille"* swept over me. Far better to be a bastard of unknown parentage than this! I thought of Kincannon then and my desire for him, which I must somehow overcome. And now I could not hope to find happiness with any man. I would not dare marry and have children.

I slept at last, little dreaming what new horror the following day would bring.

On rising, I discovered the house was still terribly disordered. Antoinette was in the kitchen. I could hear her rattling pans, but the salon, the sitting room, the foyer and drawing room showed much wear. There was mud tracked in on the beautiful Aubusson carpets, some chairs were overturned, and an air of desertion hung over all of it. It was very quiet now, for there was no one in the mansion but Roxanne, Antoinette, and myself.

I had dressed in one of my brightest silk dresses, a pale yellow with a little round collar of brown velvet and long, fitted sleeves. It was dismal outside, with intermittent cold rain, and I was depressed as I joined Antoinette in the kitchen.

The coffee was boiling cheerfully over a warm fireplace and she greeted me brightly. "I thought I would start breakfast for us." She was kneading biscuit dough.

"I'll help," I volunteered and went to the pantry for eggs. As I did so, Roxanne came into the room wearing a bright green dress even more spirited than my yellow one.

"Good morning," she caroled, as if the previous night had never happened. "You are both feeling well, I trust?"

"As well as we can," I replied glumly, "knowing that you and I must go to the Cabildo and answer for Ondine's sins later."

"Must we?" she asked lightly. "Let them come to us. Then we can tell them she has run away in the night."

"That sounds like a good plan, Roxanne," Antoinette said as she finished patting the biscuits into a pan and popping a cover over it to set it in the fireplace.

"No. We told them she would come and we must go in her stead," I replied, breaking the eggs in a bowl and beating them vigorously. "I wonder how Zeke and Millie are. We will go to the Ursuline convent to see them afterward." Then, with sudden passion, "And I will tell them they are free people now. That should put heart into them."

I gave Antoinette the beaten eggs and went to the back window to peer out at the long drive toward the charred ruins of the outbuilding. It had come very close to setting fire to the stables. I could see the flattened look about the scene and remembered the charred bodies of the two dead women. *What a dreadful way to die,* I thought, and shivered.

"You and I will likely be ostracized by the highborn New Orleanaise who took us so readily to their bosoms, Aurielle," Roxanne said without rancor or bitterness. "All our hard-won ladyhood goes for naught—because we had a pervert for our supposed aunt. I wonder if Philip or Pierre LaRonde will come to see me again?" She laughed easily. "I suspect we will have no more callers, and any ball we attempted to give in this house of horrors would be coldly ignored."

"You are right," I replied with a faint smile. "But there is one door still open. Eugene asked me to marry him—in all the melee of last night."

"You *would* receive a respectable proposal, Aurielle." Roxanne's laughter rang out. "You are so much more proper than I."

After breakfast, we washed up the utensils and plates, and Antoinette began to mutter about trying to clean up the disorder and drying mud from last night.

I said abruptly, "It seems passing strange that Ulysses has not yet put in an appearance. He is always your shadow, Roxanne."

A disturbed look flitted across the vivid face and was gone. She said calmly, "I can only assume he is still with friends and has heard nothing of events here. I feel sure he will be returning at any time now."

It developed that Roxanne was wrong about callers, for we had two after all. Mid-morning, just as we were readying ourselves to go to the Cabildo and report on the flight of Ondine, Rodeur and Kincannon arrived.

They had no sooner been ushered into the still-disordered sitting room than Rodeur spoke up. "My dears, we have sobering news for you." He gave his hat and cloak to Antoinette. Kincannon's dark eyes were on my face and there was compassion in them. I braced myself and Roxanne, beside me, stiffened.

"What news?" I asked.

"Ondine Chaille was found dead in the St. Louis Cemetery a few hours ago."

"Mon Dieu!" I burst out. "How did she—how did it come about?"

"It was clearly murder," Kincannon said, "but the authorities seem strangely unwilling to pursue the matter. And Sebastien cannot be found. The carriage was overturned on a side street near the cemetery."

"How—did she die?" I asked haltingly. *My mother,* I was thinking dismally. How could it be?

"Rather terribly, *ma petite,"* Rodeur hesitated. "It would be better not to give details. Suffice it to say she is dead."

Roxanne said disgustedly, "This means another funeral. It seems to me that all we have is funerals and I hate to attend them!" She was not in the least disturbed over Ondine's demise.

"Where is her body?" I asked.

"At the Cabildo in the mortuary with the bodies of her servants. You will have to claim them and make arrangements, Aurielle," Rodeur said gently.

I murmured, "And she was my mother—"

Rodeur started violently. "What is it you are saying?"

Antoinette, by the door, had wheeled about with an involuntary cry.

"Last night she told me she was my mother—that she had to desert me in Paris to flee for her life."

Rodeur gave vent to a stream of French oaths. Then he said, "I cannot—I do not believe it!"

"Then I do not understand why she said it," I said.

"Don't you?" Kincannon asked skeptically. "For the very reason you are worrying now. That—and the chance you gave her to escape while you lied to the angry mob in her house. Would you have done *that* for anyone but your mother?"

I shook my head slowly, still unconvinced. "Still, her crimes were so great, I do not think I can bear to look at her."

"Then you shall not have to look at her." Kincannon's voice was rough. "Rodeur and I will go to the Cabildo and make arrangements for five funerals. Millie and Zeke did not survive the night. So you see, her crimes are even greater than you thought."

"Oh," I said, my eyes filling, but I blinked the tears away. "That will be most kind of you both." I looked at Antoinette, still standing by the door. Her eyes, shining with unshed tears, told me plainly she would have taken me in her arms. I added, "I'm sure Roxanne feels much as I—"

"More," Roxanne replied emphatically. "We will give you money now for the coffins."

"Nay, ladies," Kincannon smiled grimly. "Your reputations may be in tatters because of your aunt, but your credit—especially yours as Valier's widow, Aurielle —is very good indeed."

"And after all," Roxanne remarked, the green eyes narrow, "we are *tante's* nieces and I expect we are her only heirs." Then turning to Rodeur, she said with intensity, "Tell me—did you find any gold with our—Ondine—or any in that overturned carriage?"

"Non, Roxanne." Rodeur spoke in quick, angry French. "Ondine was nude, garroted and spread-eagled over the oven grave of Selina in the Chaille burial area. There were hatpins thrust into her nipples. No gold anywhere."

I felt my stomach churn at the horrid picture conjured up. Roxanne was unperturbed. She said, "Sebastien said last night he had put a great deal of gold in that carriage. Well, Aurielle and I will seek out a lawyer. I'm sure she has a great deal of money in the Dessaultes Bank of New Orleans."

Kincannon's short laugh was derisive. "Always the practical little pirate. No doubt you can produce papers to prove you are her nieces?"

"I don't want any of her money," I said with revulsion. "I shall lay claim to nothing, Roxanne. And I shall leave this house as soon as possible."

"You are very foolish, *cousine*. With enough money, even this great blot on our social lives can be slowly erased. People will forgive anything but true poverty." She paused, then added thoughtfully, "I doubt if we need any papers, Quent. Ondine admitted freely to many that we were her nieces. I'm sure they would have to so testify before a judge, if it came to that."

Kincannon slowly rose to his full height, picking up his hat. "I wish you luck in pursuit of Ondine's treasures, Roxanne. But for now, I will go to the Cabildo and arrange the burials of your aunt and her servants. Her death has relieved you both of the necessity to explain her absence before the authorities."

"Before we go," Rodeur added, picking up his cloak, "I would tell you ladies some better news." Antoinette moved from her frozen stance as he spoke. "The remaining Baratarians have set up business at Isle Dernireè, at the mouth of Bayou Lafourche, about sixty miles west of the Temple. Grande Terre itself has been made a base for the officers of the United States, because it is so important a waterway to the city. Jean and Pierre, I might add, are not at Isle Dernireè, but they are quite safe and in close touch with their comrades." He laughed suddenly, his warm, reckless laugh. "The respectable Messieurs Grymes and Livingston also keep Jean informed about Dominique You and the others in the calaboose. All are ready to obey Jean's commands on their release."

"I should think Jean and the Baratarians left would go kill off those officers at Grande Terre," Roxanne said tartly. "The way they descended on the islands and killed and captured his men and his warehouses—all that after Jean's offer to help, too!"

366

"On the contrary," Kincannon replied. "Jean still stands ready to help in event of a British attack on the city." He paused. "And there will be an attack. You ladies had better start thinking of what you will do in the event this city is taken by them." He moved toward the foyer, following Rodeur. Antoinette, Roxanne, and I trailed after them.

Kincannon stopped at the door, his cloak over his arm. "I will come back and tell you when I have accomplished my mission. Will tomorrow noon be all right for the time of the funeral?"

"Yes," I replied, "and thank you both for your kindness."

It rained all the rest of that day and far into the night. Drenched New Orleans was a sea of mud when the cold gray day of the funeral dawned.

Over breakfast, Antoinette said, "Aurielle, let us return to the Dessaultes house this afternoon. At least you and Roxanne will have more help then."

"I'm for closing up this house and leaving it—just the way it is," Roxanne said with an uncharacteristic shiver. "It seemed to me I heard things in the night."

"I heard nothing," I said, "but I slept poorly enough. We will pack our things after the funeral and move into the Dessaultes house. After all, though they never really liked me, I suppose the servants will stay."

"They liked you well enough," Antoinette said, picking up our empty dishes and putting them in the pan of water at the dry sink. "But old Madame Dessaultes saw to it they didn't show it."

There was a rap on the back door and we turned as one. Antoinette moved to open it on the tall, lanky form of Pointer. When she admitted him, he took off his broad-brimmed black hat and said, "Mister Cheviot come by an' tol' me to fetch the carriage over here this mornin' fer you ladies to ride to the fun'ral in. He say him an' the cap'n be along soon."

"I'm glad to see you, Pointer," I said quietly.

He shifted uncomfortably, "Thank you, ma'am.

When Jacques quit, I done took over as coachman an' carriage man, if that's all right with you."

"It's fine with me, Pointer," I replied.

"We all 'preciates you manumittin' us, ma'am, Helen, Pansy, Esther, Trudi, an' me, though we ain't seen you since to thank you."

"You know I do not hold with slavery, Pointer," I replied. "Have you heard how the others Madame Dessaultes fired, the ones from the Chaille house, are doing now?"

"Yes'm. They all done found work in the city. Tressa, she's a ladies maid an' Pearl's a upstairs maid to the Broussards. Jasper an' Couri works down to the levee now." He stood there, holding his hat awkwardly.

"Come, Pointer, sit down and have a cup of hot coffee," I said. "Mademoiselle Deveret and I will soon be ready." The black man took one of the chairs at the kitchen table.

At the door, I paused, "Pointer, did M'sieu Cheviot say he and the captain would attend services with us?"

"Yes'm. He say they's comin' 'bout 'leven o'clock." he replied as Antoinette set the steaming cup before him.

It began raining again midway through the funeral services. A cold south wind blew, and Roxanne and I were shivering as we stood, perched on a portable banquette in the midst of the muddy land about us. Philip and Eugene Poliet were the only two representatives from the respectable element in New Orleans. I sensed that Eugene had pressured Philip to come, for he did not look at us and his greeting had been chill and distant. No servants attended, with the single exception of Pointer, who stood well back from the graves. Antoinette stood firmly beside me through the brief services. Kincannon and Rodeur had secured a priest who had recently been assigned to the diocese directly from France and he conducted the brief ceremony in French.

Later, only Eugene and Philip followed us in their carriage as we dispersed from the cemetery. Roxanne, Antoinette, and I sat in the Chaille carriage alone. We did not speak again until we were rattling down the street;

I asked Roxanne, "Are you serious about trying to claim an inheritance from her?"

"I certainly am," was the quick retort; then she added petulantly, "I thought sure Quent and Rodeur would come back to the house with us. I wanted to talk with them about it."

Antoinette, Roxanne, and I had finished packing and were preparing, with the assistance of Pointer, Eugene, and his brother, to load the carriage when Ulysses walked up the shell drive to us as we stood in the misting rain. He moved with the peculiarly lithe stride so well suited to his large frame. His close-cropped hair sparkled with raindrops. I noted immediately the darkly bruised cut, just scabbed over by congealing blood, that formed a half-moon on his cheek.

Roxanne scowled with relief. "Well, it's high time you showed up, *mon ami*. Have you heard?"

"I have heard," was the short rejoinder as he stepped up and swung a huge portmanteau into the carriage. Pointer moved back deferentially for the big black man. "I was with friends and knew nothing of the affair until it was all over."

I looked into the inscrutable face and a chill swept me. I knew unerringly that Ulysses knew more than he would ever tell us of that dark night's events.

Roxanne asked cryptically, "And what if *I* had needed you, Ulysses?"

"You yourself told me I might have some time off when I spoke with you about it, Roxanne." He took another large case from Eugene and swung it lightly into the back of the carriage.

"That's true enough," she said, her narrowed eyes meeting his. "But with all of New Orleans in an uproar over the fire and Ondine's death, I thought sure you would return before—now."

He shrugged. "I was across town, Roxanne. It was over, when word came to me. You and Madame Aurielle are moving into the Dessaultes house, I hear."

"You hear very well for one so long gone," she retorted. "But you can go upstairs to my room and bring down the last of our baggage."

"Mademoiselle Deveret," Eugene said eagerly, "Philip and I will be delighted to take you three ladies in our carriage."

"How kind you are," she said with a melting smile at the two Poliets. But the stiff Philip did not thaw. I felt his animosity. His fondness for Roxanne had vanished with the disgrace that had come upon us.

Later, we made an odd little cortege as we traversed the muddy streets, one carriage behind the other, the wheels spattering through puddles and potholes. From the window, I saw two ladies of long acquaintance, Madame Broussard and Madame Deliquet, who saw us from the banquette where they were walking. We nodded and smiled, but they appeared not to see us as we rumbled past.

"Old cats," Roxanne muttered under her breath.

"As soon as the shock wears off, mademoiselle, I think they will regret this," Eugene said kindly. "Aurielle, you know they will come around if given time." Philip said nothing.

"Oh, they'll come around quickly enough, if our *tante* has left us a fortune," Roxanne said with a grim smile.

Philip flushed a dull red and Eugene said, "Your aunt had quite a sizable fortune as you well know, mademoiselle. And as her nieces you are sure to inherit."

"That you will not know," Philip said coolly, "until you have seen her lawyer, Mr. Richards."

"We shall call on him as soon as possible," Roxanne said, giving him an equally cold glance, which he affected not to notice.

Later, when we stepped down from the carriage and made our way along the stone steps leading to the Dessaultes front door, we were met by the black servants, Helen, Pansy, Esther, and Trudi, the cook. They stood just inside, all trying to look sober but fighting smiles of pleasure.

In a short time, we had found our rooms with the help of the men who moved our baggage into them.

370

We bade the Poliets good-bye below. I saw to it that Antoinette occupied my old room, while I set my jaw and took Valier's room. Ulysses, by his own wish, refused separate quarters over the stables and moved into one of the rooms on the third floor with Pointer Dessaultes as his neighbor.

After the funeral, we settled down to what proved to be the dullest two weeks of my life. If I was bored, as time went on, Roxanne was like a caged lioness. Mourning did not set well with either of us and I reflected, as I sat looking out at the steady rain, that not even life at the Boar's Head Inn had been so miserable. Even our last faithful friends, Eugene Poliet, Kincannon, and Rodeur, were not in evidence, the latter having sent word by Ulysses that there was much in the air militarily speaking and they were very busy.

Nothing alleviated our boredom until one afternoon Pointer came home with the news that Governor Claiborne had sent for the famous general, Andrew Jackson—the man to whom so many of our former Creole friends referred as a Kaintuck.

"Seem like the British is sure 'nough comin', Madame Aurielle. Folks at the market say they done set sail out'a the Indies. They bound ter take New Orleans for England," Pointer concluded.

This was the topic for a whole afternoon, the day before Roxanne was to go see the lawyer, Mr. Richards. We no longer discussed the snubs of the highborn Creoles. When Roxanne returned the following day with the news that Richards had affirmed Ondine Chaille had died intestate, she was jubilant.

"He says the estate belongs to her nieces by right of descendance. They can't trace another relative," Roxanne said merrily.

"You take it all," I said coldly.

"Sitting on the Dessaultes fortune, you can afford to be cavalier," she retorted. "I've long thought you and that conscience of yours should be in a convent."

Antoinette, nearby, gave an audible sniff.

"Think what you like," I replied. "I'll have nothing that belonged to that—pervert."

"Still think she's your mother?" she asked maliciously.

"I try not to think about that at all," I said painfully, aware the thought—no—the *knowledge* depressed me terribly.

The old year 1814 had but a month and a half to go and the weather remained absolutely abominable. It had kept Roxanne and me and most of the servants inside the house for the past two weeks. The streets were so muddy we dared not risk even walking on the banquettes for fear of being splashed.

When the sun came feebly forth on November eighteenth, we both rejoiced and prepared to go out, though the streets were still like soup. We dressed quickly with Antoinette's help. Neither of us wore mourning any longer, for as Roxanne had so aptly remarked, we were ruined in New Orleans anyway.

Ulysses and Pointer brought the carriage out and helped us mount. Antoinette, smiling now herself, accompanied us. Though the wind was chill, we kept the side curtains rolled up to see the city streets with the pale sunlight filtering over the buildings.

As we rattled down Royal Street where many of the businesses were, we noted a large crowd of agitated men and women, many well-dressed blacks among them. As we drew nearer, we observed that they were in a wild state of disorder. Some shrill cries could be heard.

"What is it?" Antoinette was mystified.

Roxanne asked, "What do you suppose has them all—Look! They are clustered about the doors to the Dessaultes Bank of New Orleans! *Sacré bleu!*—can there be a murder? Or worse, a fire?"

We hung out the windows of the carriage, staring apprehensively. I called out, "Ulysses—Pointer! Go find what is the matter with all that crush of people about the bank."

They pulled the carriage to the side, Ulysses dismounting quickly to leave Pointer in charge of the horses.

"Something very bad has happened," I murmured. "I see women with their faces in their hands, weeping." I kept my head out the window, the better to see.

Roxanne, who was keeping watch on the other side, said, "I see two men on horseback, dashing away like couriers with the devil after them—and some people are beating on the doors! Whatever can be the trouble?"

Antoinette, who was craning out the other side of my window, said slowly, "It is something to do with the bank, *mes petites*. Something has happened inside the Dessaultes Bank. Here comes Ulysses and he looks very serious." She pulled her head back inside like a turtle and rearranged her disordered skirts.

Ulysses drew up beside us and opened the door on my side, entering to sit beside Roxanne. "You must prepare yourselves, ladies, for very bad news indeed. The Dessaultes Bank is in default—it has failed. These people are distraught and hope to get their money out of it, which, of course, is impossible at this time."

"But how can that be?" I cried. "M'sieu Poliet sent my money to me only last week and he said nothing of such—"

"I fear the Messieurs Poliet have been putting on a good face. This must have been brewing for months."

Roxanne's face was white and stunned. "Then all the money I have been accumulating—all of Ondine Chaille's fortune is gone?" Her hair, so bright, seemed to have drawn all the color from her face, leaving the wide eyes like emeralds.

Antoinette's little sigh was piteous as she murmured, "All that money you repaid me—have been paying me each month, Aurielle. Is it—can it all be gone?"

There was a shadow in the pale sunlight by the window and suddenly the hard, tanned face of Quentin Kincannon looked in on us. "Good morning, ladies—Ulysses. A fine day of sunshine, is it not?"

"Quent!" Roxanne was at the door in a flash, opening it, bidding him in, but he stood back. "You must tell us the details of this disaster, Quent. Surely *you* know. All your money! All your gold and silver in the bank, too!"

I leaned toward the open door. "We don't understand, Captain. How could such a thing happen? You don't seem at all disturbed." It was a relief to see his dark, audacious face wearing the careless smile.

He stooped then and looked directly at me. "My dear, I am wiped out, even as you are. It can happen very easily. All the bankers must do is loan their depositors' money to bad risks—and believe me, there are many bad risks in New Orleans in these days of blockades and embargoes. I am sorry for you, but I blame only myself for my misfortune—for I knew Valier Dessaultes was playing fast and loose with his loans. And so were the Poliets."

"Then you should have told us!" Roxanne stormed, brows drawn. "It was the least you could do—warn us. Now we have nothing, nothing at all. Whatever shall we do?"

Kincannon shrugged. "I thought Dessaultes and the Poliets had resources. They *said* they had plenty of them. All the depositors, the stockholders believed them. It seems I—and they were wrong." He was as nonchalant as if he were discussing a meal he had finished, as he added, "The other banks, the ones who have been playing it close to their vests, withholding payments of specie, are now rejoicing over the fact that their competition is less."

I was appalled. "Have we no recourse at all?" I was thinking of the few gold pieces and greenbacks that nestled in my reticule and realizing there would be groceries to buy and servants to pay and there was not enough for all that.

"You can ask your suitor, the estimable Monsieur Eugene Poliet, what the bank plans to do in the way of restitution—or if there is a chance for such." His smile was white in the sunlight as he tipped his hat and bade us good day.

The air was warming under a sky with only a few fleecy white clouds in it, but I was chilled by the immediacy of our financial ruin.

Chapter
18

A week went by before Eugene Poliet called on me. It was a week during which Roxanne, Antoinette, and I pooled our meager resources and figured we could keep the servants and run the house for no more than eighteen days if we were very careful—and Antoinette took no wages. I protested that she could be very well paid as a milliner, or by doing coiffures, or even as a couturier.

"We've been through too much together, Aurielle. I will stay until we get on our feet." She smiled at me encouragingly.

About four in the afternoon of that day Eugene rapped on our door. He appeared drawn and weary as Ulysses admitted him to the sitting room. Antoinette went to arrange for Trudi to serve coffee. Without any preliminaries, he kissed my hand, greeted the cool Roxanne, saying, "Dear ladies, I would have been here days ago, but you understand that things at the bank have been in such disarray that I could not leave."

"Yes—I know. We are bankrupt, are we not?" I

asked. He bowed his head in silent agreement and I went on, "Surely you saw this coming on, Eugene. Surely you could have taken some precautions to see that we were not left destitute."

He lifted his head and said in a low voice, "It is even worse than that, Aurielle. We must sell everything to pay back the depositors even a little—and under law, we are bound to do that."

"You mean this house?" I was stunned.

"Yes. You are a stockholder and, as such, responsible for repaying as much of the default as possible. *Mon Dieu,* Aurielle," he burst out suddenly, "I would have done anything to prevent it! But the whole city is in a great turmoil. The British are coming and we have only the promise of an ill, old Kaintuck general to come to our rescue. I fear the city is doomed." He looked into my eyes with his dark ones and I saw something strange and unsettling flicker in their depths as he concluded, "I—my family—we are in quite as dire straits as you ladies, if it is any comfort to you."

"I am sorry, Eugene," I murmured, but Roxanne sniffed.

"Why didn't you stop all that lending so freely, paying out so lavishly when you took over?" she asked bluntly.

"My father, my brother, and I did the best we could; we tried desperately to collect on the loans after Valier's death, Roxanne." He turned back to me, "Ah, Aurielle, I would offer you a safe marriage, backed solidly by my fortune, but it has all melted away."

I replied gently, "Though I am fond of you, I do not wish to marry, Eugene."

"What are we supposed to do in the meantime?" Roxanne asked with hostility. "We have barely enough money to last another week."

Eugene said, "I myself will secure a job with another bank—a menial one, I fear, as soon as we have liquidated the last of the bank's assets and paid off what we can to the depositors." He paused, then said rapidly, "It is reported that the British are sending an armada and thousands of men to capture Louisiana and we do not know where they will first strike. In the conflict, I may reverse my fortunes, Aurielle." He spoke with great confidence. "Would you think on marrying me in the future?"

"I will think on it," I lied.

"I wish I had your allotment for you, but alas, my dear, I have nothing to give you and only the bad tidings that this house must be sold."

"How long have we before it goes on the block?"

"A week, perhaps."

"Just long enough for our money to run out." I laughed wryly, as Trudi entered with the silver service and coffee.

In the following half hour, Eugene elaborated about General Jackson and the kind of man he was reputed to be. "He has fought many duels and he has inflicted a great defeat on the Indians at Horse Shoe Bend in Alabama for their massacre of all the people at Fort Mims last year. He has even been down to Pensacola and *le bon Dieu* only knows what the situation there may be with the Spanish. He is said to have run the British, who the Spanish allowed to garrison the fort there, back to their ships. It was then he wrote Governor Claiborne that the English fleet was on its way to New Orleans."

"He sounds very formidable to me," I said.

"Our only hope is that he is formidable enough to keep the British out of New Orleans. One thing this threat has accomplished—it has unified our city. Creoles are now perfectly willing to fight alongside the Kaintucks and the Americans to keep our city free."

"More than New Orleans is involved here," I said abruptly. "It appears the entire American nation is in peril. For if we in New Orleans fall into their hands, they will have sealed us off from the east by the blockade and by an army from the west. America will be a sandwich to be eaten at their leisure."

Eugene brightened as he said, "Once the war is over, Aurielle, all the land—of which I own so much—will become valuable once more. People will come to

New Orleans and we shall become one of the world's great ports. If you will wait and ———"

"Perhaps," I cut in, then added, "I am going to seek employment myself. I may find work as a teacher at least, with some family not devastated by the bank's circumstances. But I shall always consider you a dear friend, Eugene."

"You would be much dearer," Roxanne said, getting to her feet, "if you could manage to salvage some of our fortune, Gene. I suppose because Aurielle is one of the heirs, our aunt's house will be sold also?"

Eugene spread his hands expressively. "You will recall, Mademoiselle Roxanne, that you, too, became one of our stockholders by your own wish, when Valier was still president of the Dessaultes Bank of New Orleans."

Roxanne's little laugh was rueful. "That is true. I sank nearly all my fortune in stock long ago. So be it. Like Aurielle, I will find—employment." She hesitated over the word and her glance at me was wicked with mischief. I knew Roxanne would never settle for anything so prosaic as teaching small children. She was far too hotheaded and impatient.

After Eugene had made his adieux and Ulysses closed the door on his slender form, Roxanne turned to me. "I am going to see Jean tonight. Ulysses knows where he is hiding, just beyond the city. He will have— means to help us."

"Why not Quentin?" I countered.

"Like us, he is ruined. He had all his fortune in stock in the bank. He has nothing left."

"Surely you don't love him just for his fortune?"

"I love him for many reasons, but his fortune was part of it."

"Truly, Roxanne," I smiled, "you are even more practical than I thought."

She shrugged. "Nothing lasts forever, Aurielle— not even love. Surely our change of fortune has taught you that."

"You are wrong. There are many things that last forever," I replied angrily.

"Name one," she retorted.

"They are things of the spirit. Real love, real courage. Decency—honor—true kindness and loyalty."

She burst into laughter. "You are indeed a fool, Aurielle. Has the defection of all our former kind, honorable, and *loyal* friends taught you nothing?"

I shook my head. "They taught me that Ondine's cruelties are unforgivable, so much so they cannot face us because of our—supposed relationship."

Roxanne sniffed. "You are more than a fool, my friend. You will find a job teaching little ones to be very dull indeed."

"And what will you do when they sell these houses from under us, Roxanne? Put on your breeches and boots and become a footpad?"

Her laughter rang out. "That would be much more to my liking. I have discovered respectability to be a poor substitute for wealth and love." Her voice was bitter on the last word.

I said no more, and that night Roxanne ate her supper with Antoinette and me, wearing her breeches and boots. Ulysses, having eaten earlier, was saddling two of the horses for them. The servants were restless but quiet and I knew they were conferring as to where they might go to find jobs in the less than a week left to us in the house.

As we finished the meal, Roxanne said fiercely, "I know Jean is strapped himself, since they have destroyed Barataria and robbed his warehouses of their goods. *Bon Dieu!* He had half a million dollars' worth of merchandise—and those so-called sailors and men of the government now have it all! Damn their souls!" I said nothing and she continued, "At least he is free and in contact with his men. He will be able to lend me some gold—enough for you two as well," she added rebelliously. Then motioning to Ulysses, who was standing by, she went into the hall leading to the rear kitchen door.

Antoinette said tentatively, *"Chérie,* I heard at the marketplace that this General Jackson calls the Lafittes

379

and their men a 'hellish banditti.' I fear he will have little use for them in the coming trouble."

"Coming trouble?" I replied. "*Alors,* Toinette, the trouble is *here* now. It is hard to think of it being worse."

"It could be worse," she said glumly. "When they sell the houses at the end of the week, we could be out on the streets, for we have no friends who would come to our aid, thanks to Madame Chaille's dreadful past."

"I know that, Toinette, but for now let us try to keep abreast of the news. As Eugene says, the city is in real peril —Oh, I wish I could help!"

"I don't know how you could do that, Aurielle."

"I could put on a pair of Roxanne's breeches and boots and join the men when the fighting starts."

"*Sacré bleu!* What madness is this? A small girl like you, fighting alongside men? You would be killed!"

"I could take my chances," I replied recklessly, excitement at the thought welling up in me. Quentin Kincannon would be there, too.

"Let us hear no more of that," Antoinette reproved.

Late that night, Roxanne rode in from her trip to see Jean Lafitte. I was wide awake, being unable to sleep for worry about our future. She was not very quiet coming up the stairs to her room. I slipped out of bed, donning a warm woolen wrapper, and made my way down the hall.

Rapping lightly on the door, I whispered, "Roxanne, let me in."

She opened the door immediately and her face was flushed from the cold night wind. Her eyes were brilliant. She had thrown a leather bag on the bed, a nice fat pouch. "Jean has given me enough gold to last us quite a while. He says Jackson will have none of him and his men now, but he is playing a waiting game." She gestured to the pouch and added, "He was most distressed to learn that we are to have the houses sold from under us. Not that I could bear to live in Ondine's house." She made a wry face. "I think it must be truly haunted—Ulysses says that voodoo got Ondine." Her voice fell to a whisper as she added, "He saw her body early in the morning before anyone knew it was there and she looked dreadful. Her eyes were open and staring, he said, and there was blood about her throat where the wire garrot cut it." Roxanne looked at me narrowly.

Again my stomach twisted and I paled. My suspicion that Ulysses knew a great deal more than he was telling was confirmed. His long absence, beginning the night of the fire, made me certain he had a connection with Ondine's death and the disappearance of Sebastien. *And how much did Roxanne really know?*

"Have they found any trace of Sebastien?" I asked.

She shrugged. "No. Nor will they. It was a fit enough end for two such people."

"I suppose it was," I said slowly. "Yet I loved Ondine in the beginning. And in the end she revealed herself as my mother."

Roxanne said cynically, "She *could* have fled Paris, leaving you as she said, and wound up in Santo Domingo before coming to New Orleans."

"That is what I think," I said haltingly. "I fear my mother and Ondine are the same."

"Very probably," she agreed. "Now let's start thinking of where we shall move. The bank agents will be here to sell this house by week's end."

"I am thinking of seeking rooms in some stranger's house. American preferably, since the Creoles no longer receive us," I said.

"And we cannot go to the plantation beyond the city where Jean is staying." Roxanne tugged at a stray curl. "Our presence might give him away. And I must admit that Quent, poverty-stricken, does not appeal to me as much as the rich privateer he was. I, too, have had a stomach full of respectability. Ulysses and I are going back to Jean as soon as he gets his organization set up properly."

I was astounded. "But Jean's organization has been destroyed!"

"No, it is only underground and a few are in the calaboose." She added confidently, "They will all be pardoned when the attack on New Orleans comes, for this ill-prepared city desperately needs every man. He will come out of this stronger than ever. You will see."

"Then you have transferred your affections to Jean Lafitte?"

Her eyes grew narrower. "Jean and I understand each other and I have always had a fondness for him." Her face changed subtly and grew wistful. "But I wanted Quent for my *husband*. It would be hard to give him up."

"I didn't think you ever gave up anything you wanted."

"That's true," she said, then added maliciously, "Still, it pleasures me somewhat to see him humbled by this bank disaster."

"I haven't seen him since that day at the bank. Is he humbled?" I could not imagine the tall, arrogant Scotsman humbled by any circumstance. I remembered him as he stood by our carriage that disastrous day. He had appeared untouched, even amused. I received the distinct impression that he was already looking forward to seeking new fortunes.

"If he isn't humbled," Roxanne's smile was wicked, "at least he is inconvenienced—with that half-finished house and all that land on Pointe St. Antoine."

"In the morning, we will start seeking lodgings in the city," I said, dismissing the disturbing subject. "I bid you good night, Roxanne."

I had thought that finding lodgings would be difficult, but I was dismayed to discover it impossible, except in the lowest section of town, where greasy slatterns would take us in for a cheap price. Everyone, even the Americans, had heard of Ondine's perversions and at each place we tried, the mistress of the house was cold to us.

"You are the nieces of Ondine Chaille? I am so sorry but I have nothing available in my home."

It became a litany, and the three of us, Roxanne, Antoinette, and I, returned to the Dessaultes house weary and depressed. We were preparing for bed when Ulysses answered a knock at the door and admitted Quentin Kincannon.

The three of us hastily redressed and went down to the sitting room to greet him. He came directly to the point.

"I am told this house is to be sold this weekend,

ladies," he said bluntly, "and I have heard rumors today that you have been unsuccessful in securing lodgings."

"That is quite correct," I replied.

"This miserable town is full of small minds," Roxanne said sullenly. "They all have heard of Ondine and think us part of her life."

"And weren't you?" He grinned.

"We certainly were not," I flared. "I threatened her with exposure. We did everything we could to make her stop."

Kincannon said smoothly, "At any rate, I have come to offer you help. Though my town house has been sold, as has my importing business, I have managed to put ownership of Sugarhill, my estate on Pointe St. Antoine, in Rodeur's name. While the house is still unfinished, it is at least shelter. I offer you ladies the use of it——"

"With you in it as well, I suppose?" I interrupted rudely.

"Naturally." He appeared amused. "I am not in much better circumstances than yourselves. However, I shall be gone a great deal of the time, as our troops are drilling to prepare a welcome for the British."

"It is most kind of you to offer us harbor, Captain," Antoinette said quietly. "I am sure when the ladies have time to reflect, they, too, will be grateful."

"Oh, I'm grateful enough," Roxanne remarked, giving Kincannon a sultry glance from beneath her thick lashes. "I just wonder what prompts such an offer, when you have repeatedly shown yourself immune to *my* charms."

"It's obvious, isn't it?" he asked mockingly. "I'm not immune to Aurielle's charms and it seems she bears you great friendship—so much so, she will have none of me. And therefore I include you all in my invitation."

"Hein—" Roxanne looked at me sourly. "I saw that kiss you shared in the courtyard at Ondine's before the fire. Aurielle told me it meant nothing to her."

"I'm sure of that," Kincannon laughed, "but perhaps when she sees the generous and courtly side of my nature, she will look more kindly on the lusty side as well." His eyes twinkled and I knew he did not mean a word of it.

"You offer nothing but yourself, Quent," Roxanne taunted, "and that's not enough for Aurielle. She wants a wealthy marriage *and* respectability, and you lost the one when the bank failed and the other you have never achieved."

"Hush now," Antoinette said severely. "Roxanne, you are always too quick with your tongue. You know well enough we should accept the captain's kindness without these sharp exchanges—unless you want to sleep in the lower section of town, where your door would never be safe from entry."

"And I'm perfectly able to speak for myself, Roxanne," I broke in. "If all the captain offers us is shelter, I'll accept that gladly."

Roxanne shrugged. "It is better than going to one of the rooming houses by the levee. And we at least have Jean's loan so we can buy food."

"Jean gave you money?" Kincannon lifted a brow.

"Naturally. Jean has always been kind to me," Roxanne retorted. "Much kinder than you!"

"I have told you on more than one occasion that I am a bad risk, Roxanne."

"If you don't mind," I put in stiffly, "we will move in the morning, with what few belongings we can bring. I fear the agents will come any day with prospective buyers. Some of the Americans who have flooded the city seem to be very rich and they are looking for places to live."

He nodded. "I will send my carriage to assist—"

"Then they left you your carriage?" I asked swiftly. "Perhaps we can take ours as well?"

"I'm sure you can"—he began to laugh again—"if you are quick enough."

"I don't see how you came out of this failure with your lands and carriage still yours," I said accusingly.

"I told you. I was very quick to put them all in Rodeur's name. He was no stockholder and they cannot attach what belongs to him." He added, "You had better bring your bedlinens and other personal requirements, as I had no time to stock such things. And I will come, or send my carriage at ten in the morning if that is satisfactory, Aurielle."

"It is most kind of you," I replied, looking away from his challenging eyes.

The following morning, it began to drizzle again. The sky was cold and overcast. It looked to be a wholly miserable day as we took our leave. Rodeur Cheviot came instead of Kincannon and drove our carriage with us in it. Ulysses drove the otherwise empty Kincannon carriage, with all our personal baggage. It was the first day of December, 1814; we drove into the heart of town and were surprised to see crowds gathered. Far down the street we saw an imposing array of men approaching on horseback.

"Nom de Dieu!" Cheviot called down to us, "I believe it is the famous General Andrew Jackson, arrived at last in the city!"

We immediately craned our heads out the windows the better to see the approaching riders. Cheviot and Ulysses pulled the two carriages to the side and we all sat watching the growing crowd. New Orleans loved a show and this promised to be a big one. As the people continued to gather and the riders drew nearer, it was a sight to behold. I could see the city fathers had done the best they could on short notice.

Plauche's guards were there and St. Geme's carabiniers and the chasseurs of Captain Guibert. I knew that somewhere in the midst of the riders was Kincannon himself, with the Louisiana Grays. Rodeur was muttering from the box at his own disappointment in having to escort us rather than be among those coming toward us now.

My eyes fell on the central figure and I was shocked at the sight of Jackson's almost skull-like face, grim and taut, with his direct, to-hell-with-you eyes. Closely around him and forming his bodyguard and his guard of honor were the glittering blue-and-silver Feliciana dragoons, about which we had heard from Rodeur and Kincannon.

I must say that in such surroundings the commanding officer of the United States 7th Military District cut a drab figure. I was, like the rest of the city, terribly disappointed in the outward appearance of General Andrew Jackson. But he rode with his back ramrod straight, his brilliant eyes looking directly ahead, and his dirty, unpolished boots flapping senselessly at his bony knees. In fact, he looked to be all knees, elbows, and angular joints.

We saw that Ulysses and Rodeur had jumped from their seats and were mingling with the crowd, Rodeur speaking excitedly with some of the men on horseback, while Ulysses lost himself in the crowd. Suddenly the main body of the parade was directly across from us and we saw them from just a few feet distant.

"Dieu!" Roxanne muttered, "I never saw a less likely general. He looks worse than the Kaintucks—as if he'd as soon kill you as bat a lash."

"Did you look at his eyes?" I asked.

"Yes."

"They're different from the Kaintucks—from most Americans, for that matter."

"So they are, Aurielle. There may be more to him than appears." Then she said abruptly, "Did you bring that precious little poniard of yours?"

"Of course. That belonged to my father. I'd never leave or lose it."

"I packed my sword and breeches and boots. If the British win, we may need all of them. And despite his eyes, I don't know if this general can hold them."

Rodeur pushed his way through the crowd to us. *"Ah, mes petites*—and Toinette—I caught a word with Quent. Did you not see him?"

"No," I replied sharply. "Where was he?"

"On the far side, with a company of our Grays. He will ride with the general to his new headquarters on Royal Street. He shall have much to tell us when he returns to Sugarhill this afternoon! Ah, there is Ulysses."

Ulysses came to the window. "I have been talking with my people. This general is organizing a battalion of blacks with regular army pay."

"I suppose you want to join with them?" Roxanne asked.

"I would like that. But I cannot leave you unguarded, Roxanne. You are my prime interest."

"If you wish to join up, I can't stop you," she said coldly. "You are a free man, you know."

"I will think on it," he said with a little smile and

went to mount the box of the Kincannon carriage. The two vehicles rolled out into the muddy street.

In an hour, we reached Sugarhill, which looked strange to me, for so much of the building was yet unfinished. "Good lord," I said, releasing an old Boar's Head expletive, "it looks as if there is only half of it barely habitable."

Roxanne said dubiously, "I thought it was only the marble for the mantels that Quent was unable to procure."

"At least there is a roof on it," I answered, "and perhaps there are rooms well finished on the left side. It looks more complete there."

When we dismounted with Rodeur's assistance, he confirmed my assumption. "The left half of the house is quite comfortable. The fireplaces are bare of trim, but they are installed and the chimneys are complete. I think you will be warm—at least part of the time."

We made our way up wooden steps, which I knew were meant to be granite or marble, and into the half-finished foyer. The floor was raw, uncarpeted wood. The stairway curved as gracefully as a woman's body into the upper floors, and up this stairway we went, followed by Rodeur and Ulysses laden with portmanteaus and bundles. In the hall above, Rodeur directed us down to the far left end where our rooms were located.

"You must be very careful of your fires, ladies," Rodeur said, throwing open the first door, "for there is no marble at the hearths. The fires must be contained within the recessed brick area. A fire at this time would put us all into the cane fields!" He laughed merrily, but looking into the barren room, empty but for the high beds, one at each side, I was unable to smile. He went on cheerfully, "There is a bed here for you, Toinette, in Aurielle's room. We thought you might like to be together." He and Ulysses briskly set down some of the luggage they had carried. "Roxanne, you have the bedroom next to this. We men will be sleeping in the left half downstairs in what will be the kitchen and a small dining hall. Ulysses will join us there, for we have a third cot."

As they were leaving to put Roxanne's portmanteaus

into her room, I asked, "Where do we prepare food—if you occupy the kitchen?"

Rodeur turned in the doorway, his vivid blue eyes gleaming. "*Alors, chérie,* we have made room for cooking about the fireplace. There will be room for all of us. It is a very large kitchen."

Antoinette and I stood looking at each other in dismay after they departed. Then I said with forced cheer, "It can only be for a short time, Toinette! Surely we will soon be back in the city."

"I do not see how, Aurielle," she replied mournfully. "This war has dragged on near three years—and it becomes worse all the time."

Rodeur suddenly thrust his head around the edge of the door and laughed. "I am on my way back to the city, ladies. I feel I have missed out on much of the excitement! We will return before dark, Quent and I. There is much food in our kitchen. Do make yourselves comfortable." And he was gone, his booted feet echoing hollowly along the bare rough wood of the hall.

Antoinette turned and began striking flint to the brush that was laid beneath the small logs already in the fireplace. "I shall be much surprised if we see either of them for a week," she muttered unhappily as the twigs caught and a flicker of warmth began to penetrate the cold dampness in the room.

Antoinette was wrong. We were seated about the small rough table, the four of us, Roxanne and Ulysses, Antoinette and I, eating a rather early and spare supper, when we heard the drumbeat of hooves coming up the long drive. Ulysses picked up the rifle he now carried since our coming to this country place and lithely left the room. In minutes, the three men were back in the kitchen. Rodeur and Kincannon were laughing together with Ulysses. They shook the heavy mist, which was still falling, from their capes and hats and flung them over one of the plain straight-backed chairs.

"Ladies, how would you like to make a second debut in society tonight?" Kincannon asked, his eyes brilliant with amusement.

"What are you talking about?" Roxanne spoke up. My heartbeat quickened as excitement gripped me.

"It appears," Kincannon said softly, "that General Jackson has renewed acquaintance with his old friend, Edward Livingston—"

"Who is," Rodeur cut in, "also attorney for and good friend to our troubled friends, the Lafittes."

"And Mr. Livingston is having a reception for the general this evening in his home—with the best of New Orleans invited." Kincannon's grin widened. "We, as military men of influence, have been invited to attend with the ladies of our choice."

Roxanne clapped her hands delightedly. "And we are the ladies of your choice?"

"And Antoinette will attend as your maid, for someone must carry your slippers. The streets are a sea of mud." Rodeur laughed.

"We may find ourselves soundly snubbed by all present, with the possible exception of the general, who cannot know about Ondine," I said soberly, "and perhaps Mr. Livingston, who might forgive our relationship."

"Are you so cautious," Kincannon looked at me narrowly, "that you are unwilling to risk going?"

"No," I replied recklessly. "I shall go and I shall wear the finest dress I possess." I laughed suddenly, freely. "I will shine as brightly as the richest woman there, for all that I am a penniless widow!"

"That's much better," Kincannon said. "Now let us make haste. Ulysses, you will want to drive the carriage for us. While the reception is in progress, you can see about that legion of free blacks that has been formed."

Roxanne looked at her guardian sharply. "So that is the legion you spoke of, eh, Ulysses?"

"I have thought to help defend our new country, Roxanne," he replied without smiling.

Perversely she said, "And who will defend us when the men are gone—in this great empty barn?"

Ulysses smiled then broadly. "I have been thinking on that, Roxanne, since we spoke of it earlier. You were ready enough then to let me go and I know you have brought your sword and pistols."

389

I said grimly, "I would say the three of us would be a dangerous enough trio." I was remembering the moment my poniard had sunk so easily into Tucker's chest, the moment Antoinette had fired her musket into Durket. As for the slender, sinewy Roxanne Deveret—there was Belli and Madame Claudette Dessaultes, who had died even as she clutched an unfired pistol. *Indeed,* I thought dryly, *we are a deadly* ménage à trois.

Kincannon was looking at me with sharp intensity and I remembered his words once more. *I tell you only this, I want you. I have wanted you over a year, while I dallied with the pretty ladies of New Orleans.* It was there again, the hot desire, and my own rose up to meet it.

I dropped my lashes and suddenly became aware of Roxanne's scrutiny. Turning, I said slightly, "Come, Roxanne—Antoinette, we must look our best. Who knows? Our fortunes may rest on tonight and the opportunities it presents!"

Later we went up the stairs, each of us holding our skirts high with one hand and a bucket of hot water in the other. Antoinette followed more slowly with two buckets of hot water. In a remarkably short time, we had all bathed and were dressed.

Roxanne came into our room with her hair down in a great copper mane along her back and said, "Toinette, would you put my hair up when you are finished?"

"Yes, Roxanne," she replied in French. "Sit down and wait."

I looked at her. She wore her favorite, an emerald-green satin, bare across her lovely shoulders, with sleeves that fitted closely to her wrists. Her full breast was tightly outlined in shimmering satin, before the dress fell into fullness just below the waist. I wished there were a mirror in which to look at my own finery, but there was not one in the entire house.

My own dress of pink silk gauze over satin was the finest I owned and it fitted me much as Roxanne's fit her; it was trimmed in pale pink satin ribbons and tiny roses around a flounce at the bottom. Each of us had laid out our fur-lined cloaks, for the misty evening was very cold.

We moved downstairs, Antoinette sedate behind us

in her cape and her neat black dress trimmed in white; the men were waiting for us below. We had put out all fires as a precaution and the house was cold as ice. I looked admiringly at Rodeur and Kincannon, for they were resplendent in their gray uniforms trimmed with scarlet, their sabers at their sides and their cloaks thrown carelessly over their shoulders. Even Ulysses looked imposing in his black broadcloth, his golden earrings glinting in the candlelight.

We were soon rattling down the road in the Kincannon carriage, which was somewhat larger than the Dessaùltes. Ulysses, in his leather cape, sat the box. Inside, I sat beside Rodeur and Antoinette, for Roxanne had put herself beside Kincannon. It was a useless ploy, for both men talked of nothing but military matters.

"Jackson will find the arms inadequate, the supply of ammunition pitifully small," Rodeur was saying.

"And worse, there is a shortage of flints for the guns," Kincannon responded. "But that is what I count on for getting Jackson and Claiborne to change their minds about the Lafittes. Jean has over seven thousand flints hidden in a warehouse not far from the Temple, one unknown to those tacticians, Ross and Patterson, who cleaned out Barataria. I'll wager the offer of the flints will change the official feeling about Jean."

"Jean will want all his men out of the calaboose, too." Rodeur laughed. "Ah, but there will be some bargaining! It will take some persuading to change Jackson's views on the 'hellish banditti'!"

"I think not," Kincannon said dryly. "Jackson strikes me as being a practical man above all else. He *needs* the Baratarians." He chuckled suddenly. "And that has included you and me, old friend—for we are Baratarians still, in our own way."

"*Bien!* We are as penniless as they," Rodeur replied. "We must seek our fortunes all over again—even as our so charming companions."

"Being penniless sits poorly with me," Roxanne put in, her voice sulky. "It is something I shall not long endure."

"How shall you remedy that, Roxanne?" Kincannon asked curiously.

"When Jean is free, I shall throw my lot with him once more. Privateering is a good field." Her eyes on him were smoldering. "I suggest you join us."

"I have other plans," he replied casually, "but I think you have chosen wisely. Unless you still want respectability—as Aurielle does." His black eyes fastened on my face. "You are determined in that, are you not, Aurielle?"

"I want to live an honorable and decent life," I retorted. "If *that* is respectability—and I am no longer so sure the two are synonymous." I was thinking of Valier Dessaultes, who was quite respectable but neither honorable nor decent.

"Ah," Kincannon smiled, "I detect the beginnings of a certain hard-won wisdom in that remark. Then how do you plan to remedy your penniless state?"

"I could marry myself out of it," I said sharply, but that brought Ondine to mind and the taint in my blood—and therefore in my children. But I said with bravado, "This evening should find me with some likely candidates."

"And you are very beautiful," Rodeur said in a troubled voice. "You would not marry coldly would you, *ma petite?*"

"I don't know," I replied moodily. "It all depends."

"Then I hope you will make no rash decisions this evening," Rodeur said softly, "for I would see you happily wed—the next time. We will reap a large crop of cane next year and perhaps the war will be over." He spoke with a hopefulness I did not share. "Then perhaps you will let me be—your guardian again."

Kincannon clapped him on the shoulder. "My optimistic Frenchman! How will we reap the crop? We have no slaves and we cannot hire help without money."

"Something will turn up," Rodeur said stubbornly, and the two fell to discussing military matters once more.

As the carriage was splashing through the muddy streets of the city, Antoinette spoke up, "If Ulysses can draw the carriage up close enough to the banquette before M'sieu Livingston's house, you ladies will not need to remove your shoes and stockings this time."

"Yes," I said, hoping it would be so. It was always such an awkwardness to take off our shoes and wade through mud, as we did when attending the opera or a ball at the Salle d'Orleans if it had been raining. There was always that moment of washing our feet once inside and redonning our footwear.

It developed that the carriage was halted a few feet from the banquette. However, Rodeur, Kincannon, and Ulysses solved our problem by lifting each of us in turn from the steps of the carriage to the soggy, wooden banquette.

Lamps glowed at the windows and, as the door was opened to us, I saw candles shimmering in the great crystal chandelier above our heads in the broad foyer. The black butler divested us of our cloaks as Ulysses spoke a quiet word to Roxanne and vanished back into the night.

I was dazzled by the sight of the crowd in the salon. New Orleans' loveliest, blue-blooded belles in their finest dresses were there, attended by equally elegant men, most of whom wore beautiful and varying uniforms. New Orleans, I decided, was preparing for the British in the only way she could, flamboyantly.

Again, the greatest shock was the tall figure of General Jackson himself. For this time, he was shaved, powdered, boots agleam and his uniform, new and exquisitely tailored, fit his lean form perfectly. His hair was a white crest above the lined, arresting face. As I was presented to him he made a courtly bow and in a deep resonant voice remarked, "I thought I had seen New Orleans' fairest, but they were only a preliminary to you, Madame Dessaultes," and he bent over my hand, kissing it lightly. I came away somewhat stunned by the personality of the man. He was as courtly as any highborn Creole, more so than most of them, in fact.

I clung to Rodeur's arm and he murmured in my ear, "I think most have underestimated the general, *n'est-ce pas?*"

"Indeed, I think you are right, Rodeur. He is—a bit overpowering and every inch the gentleman I had thought him *not* to be."

We were mingling with others now. I had lost sight of Roxanne and Kincannon as we went to the snowylinened table, which was laid with great bowls of punch and dozens of crystal cups.

"Oh, Aurielle," came a feminine voice at my ear, "I have not seen you since—ah—that dreadful night of the fire at Madame Chaille's. I am so glad to see you out and about again!" It was the loquacious little Lisette Poliet and she was smiling so warmly that I returned her greeting with equal warmth.

As we stood chatting, two other women, the imposing widow, Madame Broussard, and Madame Villere joined us. To my amazement, both treated me with an aplomb that would indicate no animosity whatsoever. The Macarte nieces, Belise and Marthe, also greeted me with friendliness. I could scarcely believe it. Truly, the excitement that was permeating the city on the eve of its battle for life was a great leveler. There were American men and women mingling with the Creoles as if they were old friends.

Rodeur bent down to my ear and whispered mischievously, "The fortunes of war make strange bedfellows. Did you ever see such a spirit of camaraderie, *ma petite?*"

"No," I murmured. "I find it quite comforting."

And as the evening wore on, Roxanne and I renewed old acquaintance with many of those who had dropped us after Ondine's macabre death. Even the governor's wife, the petite Madame Claiborne, was coolly polite and I had thought the night of the fire, she would cut me entirely if we ever chanced to meet.

I began to feel even better, for Eugene Poliet hung about me and along with him Gabriel Villere who had, months ago, wanted to pay court to me. I began to feel that Kincannon was right in his remark that this would be a second debut for Roxanne and me.

Later, when I went up to the room that had been set aside for the ladies to refurbish their toilettes, I whispered to Antoinette, who was there with the other maidservants, "Toinette, I believe they are accepting us once more, penniless though we may be!"

"That is good, Aurielle. It is only natural and right, for you have done no harm."

I squeezed her hand and made my way back down to

the salon, where I noticed that a number of men were clustered about the general and Mr. Livingston and all were involved in tense discussion. I had another glass of punch as Roxanne came up to me, her green eyes gleaming wickedly.

"All is forgiven, *cousine*. We have been invited to a tea at Madame Broussard's next week."

I did not disguise my astonishment. "With all the city aboil over the war, Madame Broussard is going to have a tea?"

"Amazing, isn't it?"

"Did you tell her we would come?"

"Of course. Now we are respectable once more, you will make a good marriage, but I"—she shrugged eloquently—"I shall be *sans peur et sans reproche* only so long as it suits my fancy and that will not be too much longer, I think."

"But you could also make a very advantageous marriage, Roxanne. I saw Pierre LaRonde and the way he looked at you—"

"The prospect bores me, as the tea will bore me. When I saw Jean again, I knew—I must go to sea again." Her eyes lifted defiantly. "And who knows, now that Quent is ruined financially, he may return to Jean's organization."

"For all your talk, you love him still."

"I love him still, but I know now I may lose him and I am prepared for that. I wasn't before."

I knew a strange pang of sympathy. Roxanne was always so independent, such a headstrong, hot-headed girl, it was painful to see her wrestle with deep disappointment. But I was wrestling with my own surging passions and disappointments just below the skin of outward calm. I knew I wanted Quentin Kincannon myself and nothing could come of it but a brief and illegitimate liaison. How could I marry anyone, loving children as I did, with the possibility that mine might inherit Ondine's twisted brain?

Toward midnight, the guests began leaving, picking their way down the steps of the house to the banquette and the carriages which were lined up there. We found Ulysses had returned, but Roxanne did not ask him about his visit with the free black troops and he volunteered nothing as we all ascended the carriage.

As he closed the carriage door behind us, Rodeur laughed jubilantly. "That was a thoroughly successful reception, eh, old friends?"

"It was," Kincannon agreed, striking flint to the lantern as the carriage pulled out into the quagmire that was the street. By its flickering light, I could see his serious face and dark eyes. "Livingston made a good plea for Jean, and I think you and I clinched the bargain."

"Where do you think the British will strike?" Rodeur asked.

"There are only those five miserable gunboats stationed off Lake Borgne. If I were the British, I'd strike through Lake Borgne. Patterson's *Carolina,* with her fourteen guns, would give me too much trouble if I came directly up the river to the city."

"Damn Patterson," Rodeur said quietly. "It was he, with Ross, who destroyed Barataria—and I had to be civil to both of them this evening."

"It cost you nothing, Rodeur," Kincannon grinned, "and they accorded you a civil enough greeting." He laughed aloud suddenly. "Cheer up, Rodeur. Remember our friend Jean has been cool-headed enough to have Livingston file suit for recovery of the property that was confiscated last September. The wheels of justice being what they are—I wouldn't be surprised to see it all restored to the Lafittes eventually."

"No," Rodeur said positively, "it will never be restored to them. They will be lucky, he and Pierre—and the others in the calaboose—to be pardoned."

"You may be right," Kincannon shrugged, "but knowing Jean, I would say his fortunes will improve in any event."

Roxanne, beside him, gave him a sooty look from under her thick lashes. "Then why in heaven's name don't you rejoin him and make a new fortune, greater than ever, in privateering?"

"The day of the privateer is over, Roxanne. I intend to make another fortune when the war is over—and I have in mind how to go about it."

"Privateering will never be over," she said belligerently, "and how would *you* go about making a fortune any other way? Your *honorable* methods ended in disaster."

He laughed good-naturedly. "I'll admit buying into the Dessaultes Bank was a big mistake and it cost me, but I learned something from it."

"What did you learn?" I asked ironically.

"Loose credit practice is the mistake I won't allow in my next venture."

"And your next venture?" I persisted.

"When the time comes, you'll know of it," he replied evasively and this time he smiled at me. I caught my breath. I had first seen that smile on the *Wind,* just before we wrestled together in Rodeur's cabin and it had weakened my resistance. And it was his smile, his warm laughter that had won my love and its consummation that night in his home. My cheeks burned as I remembered, for the thousandth time, the moment of yielding. My eyes fell, for I knew intuitively that he was remembering too and savoring it even as I was.

Roxanne sniffed loudly. "I'll lay money you don't have any plans beyond the Louisiana Grays!"

"None that you'd approve of anyway, Roxanne," he countered.

"I hope you will include me in them at any rate, *mon vieux.*" Rodeur chuckled, then exclaimed loudly, *"Mon Dieu!* This road is impossible!" and he put out a hand to keep from falling against me as the carriage lurched, then righted itself. Antoinette, who had not spoken, apologized softly as she fell against me from the other side.

The two men then talked on of the troubled military situation in the ill-prepared Louisiana Territory, and we arrived at the Sugarhill drive in somewhat gloomy spirits despite the colorful evening just spent. The long road to the house itself was boggy and deeply rutted.

Kincannon remarked on this mockingly. "I regret it, dear ladies, but it is one more privation you must endure —or did any of the good ladies of society offer you the hospitality of their homes this evening?"

"They invited us to a tea, but not to reside with them," I said coolly, "nor would we have accepted such

397

an offer. Charity has been too much my diet in life—and I still do not have a taste for it."

"I hope you don't consider my hospitality as charity," Kincannon said derisively.

"I consider it more like misery loving company," I retorted.

The carriage drew to a halt and, once again, the men helped us to the rough wooden steps that led to the gallery around the house. Ulysses drove the vehicle around the side to the stables in the rear, which, luckily enough for the animals, had been completed before the house. I knew he would rub down and feed the hot animals before coming to the house.

It was black as pitch inside the foyer, but Rodeur had brought the pale carriage lantern in with us, and by its feeble light, Kincannon lit candles for all of us.

After Antoinette and I reached our bedroom, we talked of the reception and its distinguished guests, of the undercurrent of excitement that had filled the gathering this evening and of the fact that Roxanne and I were once more accepted and accorded courtesy. She informed me that the other maids in the toilette room upstairs had questioned her about us and seemed properly impressed with the fact that we were guests at Sugarhill.

I smiled wryly. "They evidently don't know how rough it is here."

"No. And I certainly didn't inform them." She gave me a French gamin's grin. "Ah, Aurielle, you could marry any of the young bucks that swarmed about you tonight. Nothing is so alluring as a beautiful young widow!"

A peculiar coldness settled over me at the thought of another marriage. Kincannon had ruined other men for me and it was one more depressing thought among the many that peopled my mind. "I don't know," I said slowly. "I am afraid to marry. My children might inherit Ondine's madness."

We snuffed the candles and crept into the chilled beds. Antoinette was silent, unable to offer me any comfort.

Chapter

19

The following week found us, without Antoinette in attendance, at Madame Broussard's tea. Ulysses drove us in the carriage, for he planned to sign up with the legion of free men of color that day. Roxanne was acquiescent one moment, then railing about needing him the next. Before we arrived, she said to me broodingly, "I suppose you and I can drive ourselves in the carriage when we wish to come into town, eh, Aurielle?"

"Then tell Ulysses he can't leave you." I was exasperated.

"I won't do that. He wants to join and I cannot blame him," she replied disconsolately.

Once inside the Broussard house, we were greeted pleasantly. No one mentioned Ondine or the fire, nor did the ladies remark upon our lack of mourning clothes. They politely refrained from asking about the empty, half-finished barn where we resided. They ignored the fact that we were two unattached young women living in the same house with the bankrupt Kincannon and Cheviot.

The constant topic of conversation was the approaching British and what the city could do to fortify itself. There was much conjecture as to where the British would first strike, and on this each lady had her own opinion.

Lisette, who had clung to my side since I arrived, finally asked in a surreptitious voice, "What do Captain Kincannon and M'sieu Cheviot think, Aurielle?"

"They think they will come by way of Lake Borgne, then up the bayous from there."

"Then you and Roxanne will not be safe, Aurielle—Sugarhill would be right in that path of march!"

Roxanne shrugged. "It is all a matter of conjecture. No one really knows where they will choose to strike."

Madame Villere drew up beside us, cup of tea in hand, and said, "I hear that man Jackson, the general, is going to put a curfew on our city and restrict travel from one place to another." She was frowning. "I do not think I shall like that."

"But it is necessary, *chérie*," Madame Broussard spoke up. "He must keep strict account of the comings and goings of all citizens. We might have a traitor in our midst."

"Then I will have to stay in our town house, for if I go out to the plantation, I will not be able to come back without a special pass," Madame Villere said peevishly.

"That is true," Madame Broussard agreed, "and I am not so sure I wish to stay in town. New Orleans will be the first place the British will come. You might be safer in the Villere house on Pointe St. Antoine."

The chatter went on endlessly until late afternoon, when the tea was over. Roxanne and I went back down the steps to the banquette and saw that Ulysses had returned from his errand. He was sitting calmly on the box of Kincannon's carriage, waiting for us.

"I suppose you signed up?" Roxanne asked, as Ulysses helped her mount the step. She paused, awaiting his answer.

"*Oui,* Roxanne," he replied in French. "We have few enough men in New Orleans. Only a little over two thousand, and rumor has it that the British have many more, all veterans of the Napoleonic wars."

"Where did you hear that?" she asked sharply.

"At headquarters for the men of color. We are to be

paid just as the whites, with equal standing. It is the general's own orders." He laughed softly. "They say one of the paymasters objected and the general wrote him a scorching letter that he was not to question whether the troops were white, black, or tea-colored. He was to pay them as he, the general, ordered. I think I am going to like serving under this Jackson." Roxanne entered the carriage and, putting his hand under my elbow, Ulysses assisted me in beside her.

Later, as we were driving past the Cabildo, Roxanne suddenly shouted, "Stop, Ulysses! Look, look, Aurielle!" I followed her pointing finger as she cried, "It is Dominique You and Beluche and the others from Barataria!"

She was right. Streaming from the Cabildo was a sadly bedraggled group of men, all gesticulating and talking happily among themselves. Conspicuous by their cleanness and their well-cut gray-and-scarlet uniforms were Kincannon and Rodeur. They were talking to the men while their horses stood patiently hitched to the posts before the building.

Roxanne and I slipped from the carriage and made our way among them. "Oh, Beluche—and Dominique!" Roxanne was laughing. "I could hug you villains."

"How is it you are freed?" I asked, unable to keep from grinning back at the two bearded privateers. The main body of men were moving away from the building under Rodeur's direction when he caught sight of us and gestured to them to stop as he turned back to join us.

"Roxanne—Aurielle," he said, smiling broadly.

Kincannon, beside me now, took my arm. "We have only just reestablished your entry to polite society," he murmured, laughing into my ear. "Do you wish to give it all up just to greet some disreputable old friends?" I noticed then that passersby on Chartres and St. Peter were slowing, eyeing the odd mixture of humanity with interest.

I heard Dominique say in French, "Ah, Roxanne, how good to see you—and the sunlight once more. We have been freed by our good friend, General Jackson. We are going to serve our Louisiana under his command—"

"And we are to be accorded a command of our own

under him," Beluche said proudly. "We are seasoned artillerists and shall captain the artillery."

"Here, we must get on with our business," Kincannon said, taking my arm and steering me purposefully to the carriage, where Dominique was already assisting the smiling Roxanne inside. He added, "I will relay all the news to you both when I return to Sugarhill."

Ulysses sat the box, his grin broad and white, but he did not call out to the men as I stepped inside to take my place beside Roxanne in the shadowy carriage. As we pulled on our way once more, I suddenly laughed aloud.

"What is it?" Roxanne asked as we bumped along.

"I was thinking what shreds our reputations would be in, were this any time but now. And how, all at once, it scarcely matters anyway."

"Now you are talking sense, Aurielle," Roxanne replied, settling back against the cushions. Then she added carelessly, "Perhaps you'll want to come with the privateers later. Jean would no doubt let you and Antoinette cook for them once more."

I shook my head. "That's not what I mean, Roxanne. I meant only that it no longer seems to be the whole aim in my life—to be proper. But I still feel as strongly as I ever did about honor, decency—things of the heart."

"And don't forget real love and real loyalty," she retorted sarcastically. "You would find yourself sacrificing them all when your back is against the wall."

I looked out the window where the houses were thinning out to fall behind us. "I think not," I replied quietly.

"Pah," Roxanne replied. "Where were all those spiritual values you prate about when Durket was trying to rape you—and old Claudette Dessaultes had it in her mind to blow your head off?"

I looked into her hard emerald eyes and replied, "I know what I owe to you and Antoinette, and I intend to repay each of you—"

Her little laugh was as hard as her eyes. "I know how you are trying to repay me—by ignoring the attractions of that devil Quent. Well, you need not bother, Aurielle. I shall get him on my own terms or not at all."

Stung, I retorted, "Then get him! We have been over

this too many times before. I mean to marry and marry well."

"Here we are, back to propriety again," she jeered. "What if Kincannon offers *you* marriage."

"We both know he won't."

"I know," she said sourly, "and perhaps one of these days I will not care at all. It is only when I see those shoulders, that mouth, and his eyes when he smiles—" She trailed off and I was seeing him too as she spoke of his individual features. In my heart I silently cursed him for having put his mark on both of us.

When we arrived at Sugarhill, we found Antoinette had prepared a remarkably good meal, a roast goose with side dishes of vegetables which Ulysses had fetched from the market in town the day before. And her hard loaves of crusty French bread with the still warm, feather-light interiors were superlative. We ate, all four of us, at the kitchen table just as darkness fell.

We were all a little edgy, thinking Rodeur and Kincannon might come at any moment with additional news, for we had gleaned from Ulysses all he had learned while he circulated about town after signing up for the black troop.

In his deep, faintly accented voice he had told us there were many aristocrats among the strange mélange of men who were to defend the city. Brawling riverboat men had mixed with lean, hard-faced strangers who had come down the Mississippi aboard flatboats, each carrying a rifle in the crook of an arm. These men had come to help protect New Orleans because Louisiana was now a part of the United States. And from the prairies and bayous of inland Louisiana had come the bronzed Acadians, ready to take their place in the lines. Even flaxen-haired Germans from the coast of Mississippi had come. And lastly had come his troop, a company of mulattoes and Santo Domingans, the free men of color. Weapons for all these men were in short supply.

Of all his news, the most unsettling was the fact that Ulysses himself would ride off on one of the horses to join his troop. Though he promised he would return, Roxanne was long-faced and remarked with bitter truth, "You don't know if you'll return or not, Ulysses. Even if the British lose, you could be killed in what will surely be a hard-fought battle. And if they win, you will be a prisoner and certainly be punished as an enemy."

The big black shrugged his massive shoulders, then said in French, "Roxanne, what is to be, must be. You have never learned to accept that." Then abruptly holding up his hand, he added, "Listen!"

We heard the distant thud of horses at a gallop in the muddy drive. Ulysses caught up his musket and left on his way to the front of the house. In a moment, he was back, accompanied by Kincannon and Rodeur. They brought the chill damp of the night into the warm kitchen, but the room filled immediately with the challenging vitality that was so much a part of each of these men.

Rodeur, with his reckless laugh, spoke first. "Ah, my friends, we have been given commands under our good general. Small ones to be sure, but a measure of his trust and his need."

"And after tonight, we shall come even less frequently to Sugarhill," Kincannon said. "That should please you, Aurielle—and possibly Roxanne." His smile became a grin at the scowling Roxanne.

"Ulysses leaves to join his troop in the morning, as well," I replied, refusing to look into those twinkling black eyes. "We shall manage of a certainty."

"You will have as neighbors all the great houses on Pointe St. Antoine. And we shall see you are left horses."

"That is most kind of you, Captain," Antoinette said, when Roxanne and I made no response. "Aren't you both hungry?" she asked tactfully, gesturing at the main portion of the roast goose which still graced the table.

"Indeed we are," Rodeur said joyfully, seating himself before the table. "We haven't eaten since early morning. Come, *mon vieux,* let us do justice to Toinette's goose."

"And do tell us of the day in the city," Antoinette said, pouring coffee and setting two new places at the rough wooden table.

"We had the pleasure of bringing Jean to meet with the general this afternoon," Rodeur began, as he helped himself generously to the food before him.

Ulysses smiled. "So the rumors at headquarters were true."

"I thought he considered them—Jean and all his men —as hellish banditti," I said, unable to restrain a touch of sarcasm.

"They are 'these privateers' now, Aurielle," Kincannon said lightly. "Indeed, there is almost a camaraderie between the general and Jean since he told Jackson of his secret storehouse in the marshes, where he has thousands of flints for all the useless guns now in the hands of the men. As you saw earlier, the Baratarians are all released— recruited into the hodgepodge of Jackson's army."

"Jean is to station himself and a group of soldiers in the bayou area of Barataria in case the British come from that direction," Rodeur put in. "The rest of us are to train just outside the city, where Jackson has set up a camp for the army." Then he added with diffident pride, "Quent and I are captains."

"I wish there were something I could do," I said enviously. "A woman's lot is such a sorry one—waiting, always waiting."

Kincannon shot a swift, dark glance at me. "You will wait, all three of you. We will have no easy time of it, for it is said that the Iron Duke, Wellington himself, is coming to head up the British army. Some of our men are stationed along the Chef Menteur Road and on the Plain of Gentilly—but Rodeur and I have elected to stay with the main body of troops."

We all sat about the table while the two ate, Ulysses conversing with them about the situation. It was fascinating and exciting to me, for I found myself caught up in an unexpected and newly discovered love of my country. I realized suddenly that over the long months I had become a patriot.

When at last the repast was finished, Antoinette and I cleared away the supper dishes and put away the food. Even Roxanne did her share, albeit with poor grace. She had no use for the domestic side of life and made no bones about it.

In less than an hour, the kitchen had again become the barracks for the men and we three women retired to our cold, damp rooms. The feeble fire Antoinette and I lit

405

took but little of the chill off and we undressed hurriedly and got into our beds.

At dawn we were up, for we knew the men would need breakfast before leaving and we did not know when we would see them again. Antoinette and I prepared eggs and ham, with hot French bread, with little help from the dawdling Roxanne. It was soon over and the men were off. They left us but two horses in the stable, for Ulysses needed one.

"I will ride into market in a few days," Antoinette said, "for we must keep provisions on hand."

But, for the following two days, we chafed under idleness. Roxanne was as fidgety as I. She cleaned her pistols and polished her swords. I even took out my poniard and buffed the blade to a shine, slipping it once more into my waist.

Roxanne came to me the fourth day and said, "No one is coming to see us—not the Villeres or the Rodriguez's—the Macartes—none of them. So I'm going to put on my breeches and boots."

"I wish I had some," I said enviously as Antoinette clucked in disapproval.

"I have an old pair and we are of a size," Roxanne said grudgingly. "I suppose I can let you have them."

"That is generous of you," I replied briefly, but my spirits lifted as the exchange was made.

Later, Antoinette was baking bread in the brick oven beside the fireplace, and, as usual, we were all in the kitchen, which was the warmest room in the house.

"It will soon be Christmas and a thin one it will be," Antoinette grumbled, "with a curfew in the town and everyone scared out of their wits about an attack."

"We will spend the holiday alone in this half-finished old house," Roxanne brooded. "I'm certain all the parties and galas have been put off and no operas or musicals are being given, let alone balls at the Salle d'Orleans. The city is probably as dead as it is here at Sugarhill."

"Unless the British have come up Bayou Lafourche and taken it," I said, voicing a fear that had been with me for some time.

"Nom de Dieu!" Antoinette muttered, crossing her-

self hurriedly. "That cannot be! We are low on supplies. In the morning I will ride into the town market and pick up the latest news while I'm at it."

"We shall go with you," I said firmly.

"There are only two horses," Roxanne objected. *"I will go with her."*

"And leave me? You will not!" I exploded.

"Then you can ride double with Toinette," she said angrily.

"You can ride double with Toinette," I retorted.

"I shall go alone," Antoinette injected with some heat. "There are all kinds of men loose in the city, strangers and ruffians drawn by the prospect of blood-letting. I remember Paris when Napoleon was rising to power—*sacré bleu!* I will not have either of you pretty things tagging after me."

"You are not so old and unattractive as to be left alone yourself, Toinette," I told her.

"I *will* be—with one of Roxanne's pistols," she said grimly.

Thus it was that in the early morning of the next day, Antoinette, well armed with one of Roxanne's pistols at her side, set forth on her mission to buy provisions and find what the circumstances were regarding the impending invasion. Roxanne and I looked down the drive from the open front door as she vanished in the heavy fog. Each morning for the last four days we had wakened to a shrouding mist that seemed to swirl in baffled coils from the river and its environs, obscuring our view. It was very depressing, and Roxanne and I turned away from the door, closing it behind us slowly.

"I hope she can find the road in this fog," I said shortly.

"I should have gone with her," Roxanne replied, glaring at me.

"So should I." I lifted my chin stubbornly.

"Let's ride down to the Macarte plantation," Roxanne said suddenly, "and see if the girls and madame are there. We can ride double that far and they may have news of the men."

I looked down at my slender legs, encased in Roxanne's fitted breeches, ending in the soft, comfortable knee boots. I was enjoying them immensely and had decided that men had much the advantage in their wearing apparel. "We could do it and get back long before Toinette returns," I agreed.

"Let's go then," she cried, and we ran to our rooms where we donned the hip-length leather coats that Roxanne had especially tailored for herself. She came into my room and tossed a broad-brimmed black hat on the bed. "Here. Put your hair up in that and no one will know but we are boys."

I did as she suggested and wished once more for a mirror. Sliding the poniard in my belt, I was comforted as always by the hard feel of it pressed against my side.

In the heavy mist we took the horse from his stable and saddled him quickly. "I wish we had a curricle," I muttered.

"We'll be comfortable enough and it's much less bother," she replied as, riding double and astride, we trotted around the curve of the house and down the drive, fog cold and damp against our cheeks.

We were doomed to disappointment, for when we reached the Macarte plantation, all the Macartes were in town, including the two nieces, Belise and Marthe, so the two black maidservants said. Once their astonished disapproval of our raiment wore off, they offered to serve us refreshments, but we decided to return to Sugarhill instead. We were a disgruntled pair as we followed the thin, soggy road back to the unfinished house.

"We could go on to the Villere's to the south," I said without enthusiasm, "but I'm sure Gabriel is with the army and so is his father. Probably Madame Villere and Solange are in the city as well."

So we rode up through the mist to the house and were surprised to see another horse, tethered to the hitching post at the front. I said, "Maybe Solange has come to see us instead—"

"Very likely—since she has evidently gone in and made herself at home," Roxanne replied carelessly. "You go on in and make her welcome. I'll circle around and put our horse in his stall."

I dismounted and, as Roxanne cantered slowly around

the house to the rear, I took the wooden steps to the gallery. Opening the door, I started to call out, but the silence of the house aroused a sudden instinctive alarm. I made my way silently through the foyer and into the salon and from there to the kitchen. I stopped short at the kitchen door, for there, eating bread and a haunch of Antoinette's roasted beef, sat a bearded, unkempt man. He was young and his eyes on me were alert and interested. They glittered blackly in his full face as they took in my breeches and boots and came to rest on my pointed breasts which were undeniable under the open jacket and the full white shirt I wore.

"Well-ll—so you're a girl!" He grinned broadly. "I didn't find nobody at home and I thought if you was here, you'd surely give a hungry traveler a bite to eat." His smile grew ingratiating as he wiped the greasy, long-bladed knife he had been using on the beef across his sleeve. He slipped it in a leather case at his belt.

"Here," I said coldly, "I will wrap you some of the beef and you can be on your way again."

"Aww, no—that ain't no way to be hospitable, ma'am —even fer a girl in britches. I'll finish here an' we can have a visit. All alone in this big house, eh?" He wiped his wet mouth on his sleeve. "All yer menfolks marched off to jine the army, eh?"

"They're due in on leave at any minute," I said. Where was Roxanne? "They won't like finding you here."

He laughed easily, exposing bad teeth. "Aw, now. I jis' come from th' army an' I know they ain't givin' no leaves to nobody. Fightin's gonna bust loose hereabouts any minute an' that's why I'm clearin' out o' here." He got up from the table, wiping his mouth once more, and came toward me.

I backed away. "Get out of here," I said, holding my voice firm.

"I'd like ter see th' woman under them britches," and, reaching out, he seized my hat, pulling it off. My hair tumbled down, an unruly chestnut mass. "Ah, see there! You're as tasty a bite as I ever seen!"

He grasped my arms, pulling me to him. With lightning agility I slipped the dagger from my waist, but he was quicker than I, catching my wrist to send the poniard flying under the table. We grappled together and his breath was hot and foul in my face. We struggled silently before he put his leg and foot behind me, tumbling me to the floor where he pinned me beneath him. Panic struck with renewed horror. He meant to rape me! I writhed furiously in his grasp. I dragged in a great gulp of air and opened my mouth to scream.

"If you scream, I'll kill you right off," he said viciously, putting a hand to my throat.

With the other he caught at my breeches, snapping the leather belt with a forceful pull that cut my breath off. Fleetingly I remembered Tucker in the dark, fetid little cabin on board the *Sea Warrior*. I fought harder under this man's heavy body as he wrestled with my breeches, tearing them with a loud rip. The rank, unwashed smell of him filled my nostrils. As he lifted himself to better straddle me, I glimpsed again the bone handle of the knife at his waist, but he now had my arms pinned above my head. He pulled at his own belt, loosening it, exposing himself to me, his lust erect and pulsating visibly.

I lay bare and vulnerable beneath him and I groaned as he came down upon me with such driving force that each thrust was a burning agony in my shrinking, trembling body. It seemed an eternity before he expelled his passion with a shuddering sigh.

Still, he lay across me and I was finding it difficult to breathe. Twisting, moving, I stirred him and he lifted his hairy face to mine. The little eyes were bloodshot now and his mouth twisted like a snarling animal's as he muttered, "As tasty a piece as I ever had—"

"Get off me now," I said hoarsely, "unless you want my brothers to find you. I meant it when I said they would be here any minute."

His eyes narrowed. "They with th' army?" He was still breathing rapidly.

"Yes," I replied, trying to pull myself from beneath the heavy body. "They have leave to come home for a few hours—and they'll kill you!"

"By God," he said viciously, "I ain't leavin' you here to describe me—th' army's already after me!" and he released my arms, only to place both his huge hands about my throat.

My God, I thought in terror, *he is going to kill me!* I felt the blood singing in my ears as he tightened his fingers. With despairing and abnormal strength, I reached to his waist where I knew the long-bladed knife hung and with an instinctive and unerring grasp I had it in my hand. The room swam before my eyes as I lifted the blade high above his back and plunged it in to the hilt. With that same terror-driven strength, I tore it out and plunged it in again and again as his thick hands left my throat and sought his back.

"God damn—you little bitch—" he mouthed and struck me a sudden, stunning blow on the side of my head as he slowly collapsed on me.

Gulping the sweet cold air, I shoved myself from under him. I reeled upward, swaying precariously, and looked down, my head still ringing from his blow. He lay upon his face and his heavy blue shirt was darkening across the back with his blood. I looked down at the long, razor-edged knife still clutched in my hand and silently thanked God that I had been able to reach it and drive it home. My bruised throat ached and I was still sobbing for breath when Roxanne came into the kitchen from the rear and halted abruptly to stare in astonishment at the corpse on the floor.

Then she took in my torn raiment and nakedness and burst out in French, *"Bon Dieu!* What has happened—and so quickly?"

"He was running away from the army," I said, still panting. The knife in my suddenly nerveless hand clattered to the floor. "And he has raped me—I killed him before he could strangle me. Where in heaven's name have *you* been?"

"All I did was unsaddle the horse and rub him down a little when I put him in the stall," she said defensively. "I had no idea——"

"I feel filthy!" I interrupted, my voice hoarser now, "and look what he did to the breeches and shirt!"

"How did you—" she began.

"I managed to pull his knife from his belt. Otherwise

411

I would be dead now." Then urgently, "I must bathe. Oh, he was foul!"

She peered into a wooden bucket that stood on a shelf under the cupboard. "There's water here. It's cold, but it will do."

I shuddered. "Will you let me have another shirt and breeches?"

"I suppose so," she replied unwillingly. "What are we going to do with him?" She looked down at the body with distaste.

"Bury him, I suppose," I replied, fresh revulsion sweeping me. "I'd like to do it before Antoinette returns."

Roxanne eyed me with reluctant admiration as I caught up a small towel and began washing myself at the cold bucket of water. She looked at the pool of torn clothing at my feet. "You surprise me, Aurielle. I didn't know you were so—"

"Just because Madame Dessaultes caught me off guard, doesn't mean I couldn't have handled her," I interrupted, then added angrily, "And I'm well aware *you* saved my life then."

"Yes, that was one time you could have been killed. Your knife is no good against bullets, Aurielle. I will go fetch the breeches and shirt for you."

She was gone and I shivered as I washed myself vigorously from the bucket. I wanted to scrub and scrub and I was scrubbing still when Roxanne returned with the clothes for me. Later, I dressed rapidly and my shivering ceased as I warmed slowly.

Roxanne stood looking down on the body and said doubtfully, "Do you think we can dig a grave—the two of us with no shovels?"

I paused. "No, I guess we can't. But we must get him out of here." I stooped and took up his knife once more, this time thrusting it, blood and all, into the leather case at his side.

"Let's take him out to the road and dump him beside it," Roxanne said, her green eyes narrow. "We can put him across his horse and haul him out there."

"Then we'll keep his horse," I said practically. "It will give us three mounts."

We scrubbed the bare floor clean of blood after wrapping him in a blanket to keep the blood from seeping out again. I picked up my poniard from under the table and thrust it once again into my waist. Then we undertook to dispose of the man.

But he was very heavy and it was all Roxanne and I could do to drag him out of the house. We discovered that our combined strength was not enough to lift him across his horse.

"We can never get him up there," I panted, "even with both of us lifting."

Roxanne reflected a moment, then said, "There's rope in the stable. We'll tie him to the horse and let it pull him out to the road."

"Good. I'll get it."

In a few minutes, we had tied the rope beneath the man's thick arms and were dragging the body down the long drive toward the river road beyond. The blanket had come off in the drive and I said, "Never mind that now. We'll burn it later."

As we reached the road, Roxanne said, "We could drag him farther—across the cane field and down to the river and push him in."

"A good idea. That would eliminate any questions if he were found in the road before Sugarhill."

So we led the horse across the cane field and down to the riverbank, where the Mississippi slowly swallowed up another secret.

"We won't tell Antoinette," Roxanne said, as the body disappeared into the slow, coiling currents of the water. "It will only make her more nervous and protective of us."

I agreed. "I'd like to forget—I wish I *could* forget it all." I shuddered, then said, "But we must be very alert, for there may be others fleeing the city and we don't want to be caught again—as I was." I felt raw and violated, and my terror and rage were still hot within me.

When Antoinette returned late in the day with two sacks of provisions and a head full of gossip, Roxanne and I were in the kitchen with the fire crackling warmly over the ashes of my torn, bloodstained clothing and the blanket. The room was cozy, and we looked for all the world as if we had been there an entire and uneventful day.

As we prepared supper, Antoinette was full of talk. "Oh, but I feared I'd not get back at all, for the city is under martial law," she said, basting the fat ham on a spit over the fire. "They say Jackson is feverishly busy. Supplies are being brought in from everywhere. He is dispersing his troops, little groups of men to every spot where he thinks the invasion may be mounted. And the women in New Orleans!" She looked at us and rolled her eyes heavenward. *"Mon Dieu,* the women are scared to death! The servants at the marketplace said they were talking of the rape of Norfolk, just a few months ago, and many of the ladies are securing weapons of their own to defend themselves in the event the city is taken."

"So the women are fearful?" I asked, exchanging glances with Roxanne, knowing our secret was hopefully halfway to the gulf by now.

"Indeed they are, and rightfully, I think." Then she added with firmness, "We are much safer here in the country—for it is the city that the British will take first."

Once again I looked at Roxanne, then looked swiftly away. "You are likely right," I replied, little dreaming of what the following day held in store for us.

I did not rest well that night, for I dreamed the rapist was pursuing me, wet from the river, with blood streaming from his wounds as he chased me through the stubby, cut cane fields. I tripped on the dry stubs and fell sprawling, turning frantically to face him, only to find it was Ondine standing over me with whip in hand and a ring of blood about her throat. I wakened with a violent start, perspiring despite the night chill that permeated the house.

The broad windows that looked out on the road, the cut cane fields, and the river were graying with the first light of dawn. Antoinette in the bed next to mine was sleeping peacefully, so I made no sound as I slipped from the feather mattress to the cold, bare planking of the floor.

Tense with chill, I dressed swiftly and silently and made my way down the hall to the stairs, where I felt my way down in the dark. It was a little warmer in the kitchen, where the fire was banked on the hearth, and I began to relax as I placed more wood on the swiftly stirred coals buried in the ashes. In minutes, I had a glowing fire and I put the heavy pewter pot of coffee over the rack to boil. Seating myself at the table on which bowls of fruit and a few raw vegetables were set for the day's use, I put my chin in my hand and reflected on my uneasy dreams.

Ondine was in these dreams now, more than anyone else. I had finally determined I would have no children—for my mother was quite mad and that madness would be passed on by me. I brooded over my bleak future, knowing that my love for Kincannon could come to naught, even were he ever to go so far—unimaginable as the thought was—as to propose marriage. I no longer spoke of my relationship to Ondine, for Roxanne and Antoinette were impatient with my worries and inclined to discount them.

I did not discount them. They were deadly, those possibilities, and quite irreconcilable with future peace and happiness for me.

I heard approaching footsteps, and Roxanne stepped lithely into the kitchen, sniffing the air appreciatively as she said, "Mmmn, smells good. What has *you* up so early?"

"I had a nightmare—about that awful man I killed. It was useless trying to sleep."

"If I had nightmares over all the men I've run through, I'd never sleep," she said irritably. "I suppose your conscience troubles you?"

"No," I retorted sharply. "He was trying to kill me after—he used me. Still, I don't have to *like* killing in such a manner."

"Is that coffee ready?"

I went to the fireplace and lifted the pot to pour us each a cup. We hadn't finished before Antoinette joined us and began busily frying bacon and cooking eggs. She was full of inconsequential chatter.

"Just think! In two days it will be Christmas and we will likely spend it alone here at Sugarhill—no gifts, no parties, no decorations." Her cheerful voice held regret before her irrepressible optimism asserted itself. "Ah, but next year, little ones, it will be different. All this will be over. We shall celebrate a marvelous Christmas."

Roxanne said acidly, "I, for one, do not intend to spend many days such as these past, isolated from all activity and pleasure."

"You are still of a mind to go back with Jean's privateers?" I asked dryly. "It seems to me he has suddenly become quite worthy and his organization may be no more. He may turn shopkeeper."

Her laughter rang out. "Jean? Never! He'll tire of his newfound acceptance in short order. He'll always be a corsair at heart—and that is the life for me."

"This is useless chatter," Antoinette said suddenly. "We do not know what the future holds in store for us. We must be prepared for anything."

But we were not prepared for what burst upon us the late afternoon of that twenty-third of December.

After our noon meal, the restless Roxanne declared she was going for a gallop and I decided to accompany her. We went out to the stables to saddle the horses and returned to the house to fetch our coats, as it was cooler than we had at first thought.

I was becoming more accustomed to horseback riding and I enjoyed sitting astride. Now I said impatiently, "Hurry up, Roxanne. It is as warm as it will be all day now—the best time for a ride. We will go as far as the Villere's this time and see if they are there."

We were just ready to leave when there sounded a great banging on the front door and the hoarse voice of a man crying in French could be heard. All three of us ran from the kitchen through the halls to the foyer, where I flung open the door.

Gabriel Villere stood there, his usually impeccable attire in disarray, torn and rent in places; he was perspiring profusely. In rapid French he said, "Dear ladies—I must have a horse! The British have come—*le bon Dieu* knows I barely escaped with my life as they surrounded my home. I have come through the swamps to escape capture, for they fired on me as I ran. I need to reach the general in New Orleans with word of this invasion—and I warn you to follow after me as quickly as you can."

"You can have one of our horses—" I began, as Roxanne and Antoinette hovered behind me.

"Yes—quickly then. There is little time. They caught

416

me on my own gallery—taking a nap." He made a grimace of disgust as we all hastened through the house to the rear door. He added breathlessly, "And if I hadn't been quick —I think they fear the swamps, which I know well—I should never have escaped. I believe they plan to camp there for the night, which may give us enough time to prepare a hot welcome for them."

"Roxanne and I were just about to ride to your house," I said as we reached the rear door. Our horses were tethered just outside.

"Thank God you didn't," he said, as he mounted a big gelding. He added roughly, "They will be coming this way eventually, ladies. I urge you to leave—ride your other horses to the city as soon as possible. There are thousands of them. Thousands!"

He wheeled the horse about, striking a gallop around the side of the house. We ran after him by instinct until the three of us stood looking toward the road that led past the Rodriguezs, the Chalmets, the Macartes, toward Montreuille, the last of the great cane plantations on Pointe St. Antoine.

As soon as he disappeared, Antoinette said worriedly, *"Mes petites,* we must leave immediately, for if they come here we would be made prisoners at least—and it is possible we would receive worse treatment."

"I have no desire to go into New Orleans and beg harbor from any of our acquaintances," I murmured, my thoughts racing.

"But we cannot stay here—directly in the path of the enemy!" Antoinette's voice rose.

"And I am not going to leave all my beautiful clothes and jewels here for them to plunder." Roxanne spoke between her teeth. "We will go in the carriage and take our belongings with us."

I looked at her astounded, as if clothes mattered at this point. But Roxanne was ever materially minded. "We can travel much faster on horseback," I pointed out, "even with one horse carrying two."

"I've a fortune tied up in those clothes and jewels. They are all I have left now," she said stubbornly, "and I *will* take them with me. Besides, Gabriel said they will likely camp overnight at the Villere's. That gives us plenty of time."

"We can't be sure of that!" I accused.

"I don't care. I'll take a chance on it. Come, let's go pack our portmanteaus."

So we spent that precious bit of time packing clothes and jewels and loading the Kincannon carriage. It was very late afternoon when we pulled out of the drive to Sugarhill and started at a fast clip down the narrow dirt road.

Roxanne was gloating, "You see—we had plenty of time." But she spoke too soon.

We had passed the Chalmet, Rodriguez and Macarte plantations when we saw, in the fading light, Jackson's army assembling on the Montreuille place. I was dumbfounded to see Plauche's natty battalion and the free men of color, the Santo Domingans. They were dragging two six-pounders and there was a company of what I was to learn were Mississippi Horse and Beale's Rifles, expert shots, all local and volunteers. They wore blue hunting shirts and wide-brimmed black hats.

All three of us sat on the box together, and Roxanne, who held the reins, snorted, *"Bon Dieu!* Did you ever see such a mad mixture of troops? Can they possibly be going to attack them *tonight?* Jackson must be insane!"

I was looking for the Louisiana Grays and saw them near the rear. "I'll wager Kincannon and Rodeur are among these men," I said.

"But not Jean," Roxanne spoke with disappointment. "Jackson's sent him to the bayous near Barataria." I looked at her curiously in the failing light as she added, "I have not seen him since I borrowed the gold from him."

Roxanne had slowed the horses, and the men, who had spotted the carriage, suddenly dropped to the ground, rifles raised. Those on horseback behind drew to a halt as well. "God and the devil!" I cried, "they're going to fire on us!"

Roxanne rose up, reins in hand, and cried, "We are friends—from Sugarhill—" It was then we saw two big roans break from the rear ranks and heard deep bass voices shouting commands as they thundered forward to meet us.

In seconds, Rodeur and Kincannon were beside the carriage, their voices mingling angrily.

"By God, what fool's errand brings you here at this late hour?" Kincannon's voice rose over Rodeur's.

Over the smothering beat of my heart, my own anger, composed of terror and relief, rose to meet his. "You should know! We were alone at Sugarhill and the enemy was coming——"

"Villere said you were the first he told—hours back. You should have been in the city long ago," Kincannon interrupted. I looked out over the plain and in the dusk saw that the men numbered more than a thousand—could it be as many as two thousand? I drew a deep breath as surprise and a warm flood of emotion I could not quite name tingled in my fingertips. In Kincannon's face, the rapacious expression was the one he had worn when first I saw him on the bridge of the *Wind*. There was exultation in it and a kind of absorption that made me somehow lonely. He was going to do battle for the country that had given him a home and I could only wait until the battle was either won or lost.

"You should have an escort," Rodeur Cheviot said, his blue eyes troubled, his lean face anxious.

Kincannon turned on him. "Who the hell can we spare to escort them, Rodeur? Jackson's scraped up the dregs to fling into the breach."

"Not all the dregs, *mon vieux*. It is the dregs they will meet between here and—Where are you going in the city, ladies?"

Antoinette spoke up. "We will have to rely on the courtesy of our recently renewed friendships, Rodeur."

"*Alors!* You mean you have nowhere to go?"

"Lisette Poliet might give us shelter," I said hopefully.

"Since the bank failed, the Poliets are living with their cousins," Kincannon said harshly. "They have no room for you."

I noted the men were marching purposefully on, now that our presence was explained. Wave after wave went by on the double; the Louisiana Grays mounted on their fine horses were passing now, and Kincannon looked at them, then back at us with frustration.

"Come," he said roughly. "Rodeur, you and I will see them back to the Macartes. Edmond Macarte is in Plauche's troop. His nieces and wife can put the women up until we can see them better situated."

We said nothing, and Roxanne now turned the carriage about and we rattled along behind the silent army. The only sound was that of the thud of horses' hooves in the soft dirt and the creaking of the carriage.

The ride seemed interminable as we passed Languilles's place again in the twilight and made our way down the dirt road until we at last came to Edmond Macarte's country home and turned into the long, tree-shaded drive to the house.

Below us, Rodeur and Kincannon dismounted and reached their arms up to us on the box.

I was not surprised when we were met at the door by a frightened black maidservant who cried, "Law me! Madame Macarte an' her nieces been gone inter New Orleans ever since M'sieu Villere rode by this afternoon an' tol' us the British was at his house."

"You mean you are alone?" Kincannon asked.

"All our men folks is in the army. Just me an' Maybelle is here. Madame Macarte say we mus' stay here an' see that the house don't be 'bandoned." She craned around him to peer into the dusk. "I thought you was the British come fer sure."

"We are on our way to stop the British and we want you to give shelter to Madame Dessaultes, Mademoiselle Deveret, and Madame Desmottes."

"Madame Macarte be glad ter have 'em, was she here. Come in, ladies." She flung the door wide. "How come you ladies ain't goin' ter the city?"

"We were," Roxanne said shortly, "before these gallant gentlemen put a stop to it. What is your name?"

"Katie, ma'am."

"Katie," Kincannon cut in, "you see to the ladies and we'll try to see the British don't get here." He turned to leave, then wheeled around. "Katie, do you know if all the people between here and the Villere's have gone to the city?"

She shrugged. "No, sir."

"You haven't looked out on the road today?" Rodeu[r] asked.

"No, sir. Maybelle an' me been hidin' the silver a[n] things."

Rodeur grinned. "Come on, Quent. The Grays will b[e] halfway to the Villere's."

Still Kincannon hesitated. "Ladies, we're going [to] take your horses. You won't be needing them and we will

"*Chien!*" Roxanne scowled in the semi-gloom of th[e] foyer. "I believe that's the only reason you stopped us fro[m] going on."

He looked at me and laughed softly. "If I had thoug[ht] of it first, it would have been reason enough. *Au revoi[r]* Aurielle—ladies."

Rodeur blew us a lighthearted kiss and, smiling, fo[l]lowed Kincannon out the door, across the gallery, a[nd] down the broad granite steps. As my eyes followed them, [I] saw that mist was rising from the river, easing across t[he] batture and up above the levee to coil sinuously over t[he] cane stubble in the fields between us and the Mississip[pi] Below, the two men swiftly unhitched the horses. With [a] knife he took from his belt, Kincannon cut the reins, lea[v]ing them just long enough to accommodate a rider lat[er] Tossing one pair to Rodeur and holding the others, [he] mounted in one easy, fluid movement and the two m[en] cantered down the avenue of trees, our horses followi[ng] obediently.

All of us stood looking after them somewhat fo[r]lornly, I thought, as they turned at the road that wou[ld] lead them past the Rodriguez plantation. The army h[ad] already disappeared in the evening shadows. If there w[as] not fighting going on now, there soon would be, I thoug[ht] turning back into the darkening foyer.

Katie called, "Maybelle—you Maybelle! Bring in t[he] tinderbox an' some lamps. We got lady company."

There was a rustle in the hall, and a short, stout bla[ck] woman entered. "I been waitin' ter make sure it ain't [the] British." She struck flint to a candle as she spoke, th[en] from it lit a candelabrum on a small gleaming mahoga[ny] table beside the staircase that curled upward. "I thou[ght] you ladies was—boys," she added, still looking frighten[ed]

Roxanne said peremptorily, "Come with me—Maybelle, Katie. Put a chimney on that candle and bring it with you. We must collect our things from the coach." Then to us, "You'd better come too, Aurielle and Toinette. Now, Katie, where did you hide the silver? I have jewels I want to hide there."

"It's in a sack at the bottom o' the well out back."

"That sounds as good a place as any," Roxanne responded as we all converged on the carriage. In a short while, we had transferred all its contents to rooms upstairs and Roxanne was in the process of dropping her precious jewelry, neatly tied in a cotton cloth sack, to the bottom of the well. The few I had, I did not bother to hide. I merely wrapped them in a chemise and thrust them a little deeper under the clothing in my portmanteau.

As I did so, I reflected that this war had been fought for so long, on so many fronts in America—ever since June, two and a half years ago. The British had invaded and taken Washington, even burned the house where the American President lived. Now it appeared they would do the same to New Orleans. It was this latter thought that hurt, for it meant that the brave men facing them now would in all likelihood die.

I knew Beluche and Dominique You well enough to know they would have to be overrun before they could be captured. And Rodeur Cheviot and Quentin Kincannon would die before they would be overpowered.

Well, Kincannon had been right when he prophesied they would come by way of Lake Borgne, which was actually an arm of the Gulf of Mexico. It was easy to imagine what a long, torturous march it had been for those intrepid Englishmen from their landing to the Villere plantation. Most of it must have been made partially by boat through the bayous and partially by marshy land.

We were finishing a cold, scant supper when we heard a dull boom, followed by another and another, and we looked at one another in consternation across the table in the vast dining room of the Macarte house. Maybelle and Katie rushed from the kitchen, their eyes wide with fright as the cannonading continued. None of us spoke.

The battle for New Orleans had begun at last.

Chapter
20

Sitting together in the great Macarte salon, it seeme[d]
hours to us that the cannonading sounded from the riv[er]
below. I knew the two schooners, the *Carolina* and t[he]
Louisiana, were stationed below the city on the bro[ad]
Mississippi. The distant crack of musketry and rifle f[ire]
could be heard, too. But as time passed, the cannonadi[ng]
ceased and the gunfire grew less. I rose from the smoo[th]
satin sofa in the salon and went to a window.

Looking out, I saw that the mist was thick enough [to]
cut as it moved cloudlike past the window. *"Bon Dieu,"* [I]
muttered, "how can they see to fight?"

Roxanne, who had silently joined me, replied, "Th[ey]
cannot see to fight. That is why the gunfire is ceasing."

"What will they do now?" Antoinette asked uneasi[ly]

"Probably wait until dawn and fall on each oth[er]
again," I replied with a touch of bitterness.

But I was wrong. After I had retired, still fu[lly]
clothed except for my boots, I was routed up by a lo[ud]
banging on the locked door below and the sound of ma[ny]

423

male voices, the clink of bridle bits, and the snuffling noises of horses.

In the darkness, I hastily struck flint to a candle. The British! They had taken advantage of the night to advance on the Macarte house!

Running into the hall, I met Roxanne and Antoinette, each still dressed and clutching a candle. Antoinette's was chimneyed, but Roxanne's and mine fluttered wildly with our movements as we all made our way to the stairs together. I took the steps two at a time, reaching the foyer before the maidservants, who were coming reluctantly down from the third floor with wrappers over their nightdresses.

At the barred door I cried, "Who is it?"

"Andrew Jackson, madame—open the door."

I did so and we three women stared up at the men who filled the doorway. The general was very tall, and thin to the point of emaciation, the pallor of his chiseled features bespeaking his illness. But there was nothing of weakness in that gaunt face or those blazing blue eyes under the crest of white hair. I saw recognition in his eyes as they rested on my face and my tumbling hair. I saw then that among those behind him were Rodeur Cheviot and Quentin Kincannon.

The general spoke again. "Madame Dessaultes—can it be?" There was faint contempt in his voice as his eyes rested on my apparel. He added, "I understand you—ladies have taken refuge here. We must take the house for headquarters, for we have taken up our position a few hundred yards from here in the Rodriguez canal."

I knew that canal, having passed it many times. It was just a man-made irrigation ditch with a muddy bottom at this time of year, leading from the river, which was low now, to empty in spring in the cypress swamps behind us. It would afford the men precious little protection.

"Where are the British, General?" I asked.

"We have given them cause to regroup," he replied with a wintry smile. "They are still some distance away." His eyes were still disapproving of our male attire, but the contempt had softened. "You will have to double up in one bedroom, ladies, for I and my officers have need of the rest," he finished with real regret.

The men had come into the foyer behind him and were speaking, low-voiced, to one another as Jackson added, "As soon as I can spare the men, I will have you escorted back to the city. We have taken a few prisoners and they will be sent with you. Is there any food in the house?"

Katie spoke up from the shadows behind us, "Y-yes, sir. Want me ter heat up some fer you?"

"I would like that, and some good hot coffee for my officers and me," he replied as more men filed through the door—there were at least twelve of them. "You ladies may retire again—in *one* room." He dismissed us and went into the dining salon with the men following. Kincannon gave us a half smile and Rodeur bent to kiss my hand briefly.

I looked at the hall clock and saw that it was five in the morning. I turned to Antoinette and Roxanne. "I'm not going to bed again. I haven't slept a wink anyway."

"Nor I," they said in unison. Then Antoinette said, "Let's go in the kitchen and have breakfast ourselves."

Roxanne was muttering, *"Bien!* I am glad I hid my jewels. I do not trust soldiers of either side."

We went into the warm, fragrant kitchen where Katie and Maybelle were busily preparing eggs, biscuits, and ham. In moments, the mouthwatering smell of boiling coffee rose on the air. It was turning colder outside. I could feel it in the air, and it had begun to rain. I could see it slashing against the windowpanes. I shivered, thinking how miserable the troops on both sides must be in such weather. I was thankful for the soft leather coat I wore over my full white shirt.

In a very short while, the men had been fed and were making themselves comfortable in the beautiful rooms of the Macarte mansion, catching some much needed sleep. They had paid us scant attention, so preoccupied were they with the coming battle that would be waged between the Macarte and LaRonde plantations.

As the morning wore on, the fog became thicker despite the misting rain. Outside one could scarcely see

425

hand before face. Jackson went up to a south dormer on the third floor and peered out the window with his telescope, but the fog was too dense for visibility.

We caught scraps of information, some from Kincannon in passing. They were going to throw up a breastworks at the Rodriguez canal and hold the line there. How they would create a breastworks there was a mystery to me, for there were no rocks or dry dirt, nothing but mud which would sink as fast as it was piled up. But later, Rodeur told me they were breaking off limbs in the cypress swamps, making fascines.

Still, all through that foggy day, the Americans worked busily on their fortification and, at last, toward evening when the fog began to melt away, we could look out the upstairs windows and see that they had piled a rather impressive breastworks along the canal. But there was no sign of their adversaries.

That evening, when Katie and Maybelle brought our supper up to the three of us, Katie said excitedly, "Termorrow'll be Christmas day an' the general says we'll all be escorted ter the city. He's a mighty sick man," she added cautiously.

"Sick?" Roxanne asked alertly. "I know he looks bad and is so painfully thin, but—"

"He got dysentery," Maybelle said succinctly, "but don't nobody say nothin' about it. He a powerful determined an' firm man. He can't hardly ride his horse, but he hobble all around, ferever inspectin' an' talkin' at the sojers."

"This is fine broiled chicken, Katie," I murmured over the browned drumstick. "I'm surprised the general is going to let you go back to the city with us."

"I ain't cooked this," she sniffed. "The general got some big ol' mens what say they cooks and done took over my kitchen. They cookin' up everything in the smokehouse fer them officers, who taken over Madame Maçarte's house."

"I'll be glad to get shet o' this house," Maybelle said, looking nervously at her companion. "I heard that boy what rid in a few minutes ago say the British done been paddlin' canoe after canoe loaded with sojers up Bayou

Bienvenu. This ain't gon' be a very safe place ter be. Come on, Katie. We gets our supper an' be out'n they way."

That night we disrobed and donned nightdresses. As I lay in the big bed between the sleeping Antoinette and Roxanne, I pondered the fate of the little more than two thousand men who were spending this Christmas eve in the bone-chilling rain that was silently falling upon them. The sporadic crack of rifle fire and the hoarse shouts of the Kaintucks along the Rodriguez canal came to my ears. Despite the down comforter across us and the warmth of the bodies near mine, my feet and hands were icy, and sleep eluded me. Where was Quentin Kincannon in the cold darkness beyond the windows? And what of Rodeur Cheviot with his French blue eyes and reckless, warm smile? And somewhere far to the southwest among the bayous of Barataria, Jean Lafitte stood guard, watching for another invasion I felt sure now would never come that way. The British were all massing below us—and the fate of New Orleans hung in the balance.

The faint rap that came on the door before dawn startled me out of light sleep, and before the two beside me could rouse, I called out, "Who is it?"

"It's me, ma'am, Katie. The general say to get you up. He got a escort fer us after we eats breakfast."

"All right. We'll meet you in the kitchen and take our breakfast there." The prospect of all those men stamping about the dining salon and frowning on us and our apparel was unnerving.

This proved to be a groundless worry, for later the house was nearly empty, all officers having joined the men in the field. Only a minimum guard and three bedraggled British prisoners remained and they huddled about the kitchen fire with the two male cooks. So we ate at the long mahogany dining table after all. The house was chill, with only the kitchen cook fire blazing.

When we had finished breakfast, one of the two soldiers standing easily against the wall behind us approached and said diffidently, "Private Johnson at yer service, ma'am. We'll be leavin' soon as the officer in command of the escort gets here. Me an' Joe Burnside back here are part o' your escort."

427

"Everything is very quiet, Mr. Johnson," I remarked. "Is there no fighting?"

"The British're pretty well pinned down by fire from the *Carolina* an' the *Louisiana*. An' besides, 'tis Christmas day." He smiled a little then.

"We don't need an escort," Roxanne said acidly. "We are only five miles from the city and, given horses, we could make that in an hour alone."

The soldier said stubbornly, "We got prisoners to take inter town. Besides, the general says you must be escorted, as yer ladies."

"Will we be able to take our baggage with us?" Antoinette asked.

"Everything you kin carry on a hoss," replied the man laconically.

"Good," Roxanne said relievedly. "I can strap my portmanteau, the largest one, behind me." Then with some urgency, "There *will* be a horse for each of us?"

"Yes, but you can't keep 'em. We got to bring 'em back—the men need 'em. The cap'n has orders to round up all the horses an' firearms an' extry men he kin find while we're in the city, 'fore we come back."

Thus, as dawn was breaking, we found ourselves mounted on three big geldings with our portmanteaus, including Roxanne's wet but safe jewels, strapped on behind us. Beside us on horseback were the two blue-shirted soldiers, Privates Johnson and Burnside, as well as Katie and Maybelle. Then out of the dim grayness there cantered another big horse and, to our surprise, we saw that it was Kincannon.

He greeted us easily and said, "I have further duties in the city, ladies, so you have an escort." On the heels of his words there came the loud boom of the cannon resuming from the schooners on the river. "Come along," Kincannon said sharply and we trotted down the long drive from the Macarte house to the river road. The war was to continue then, I thought, despite Christmas day. Kincannon asked, "Have you given thought to where you will stay?"

"Yes," I replied firmly, little dreaming the circumstance that would send me riding pell-mell and alone back down this same narrow road in less than a fortnight. "We will go to Madame Broussard and ask her if we may stay with her until this is—over."

In the gray light, I saw his smile. "Yes, for all her gossip and sharp tongue, Madame Broussard may very well take you in on Christmas day—even in breeches."

In a remarkably short time, our entourage of eleven was within the city of New Orleans, where Kincannon spoke with two armed men who halted us just inside the town. He showed his pass and the papers on us and they nodded us on. Less than half an hour later, in the cold morning light, Kincannon was rapping on the Broussard door. The prisoners, under Burnside's and Johnson's surveillance, as well as the two Negro women who were destined for the Macarte town house, waited outside the courtyard in the muddy street.

A black maidservant opened the door, her round eyes revealing her astonishment. Obviously she was scandalized by the appearance of Roxanne and myself. Madame Broussard, when she came into the foyer, was equally disapproving.

After Kincannon explained the circumstance which brought us to her door, she said a touch loftily, "Young ladies, you may stay with me. I have four other young ladies whose parents have left them with me for safekeeping." She hesitated, then said firmly, "But surely you have some—decent clothing?"

"In our portmanteaus, madame," Roxanne said impatiently. From the mutinous look about her full mouth, I reflected she probably had little taste for her exquisite clothing at this moment.

Madame Broussard invited the captain to coffee in her salon and remarked that the maid was to show Roxanne and me to a room upstairs, which we would have to share. Antoinette would be shown a room on the third floor with the rest of the servants.

"I regret, madame, that I cannot stay for coffee—nor can my men. We must see our prisoners deposited in the jail. After that, I have other business to conduct," Kincannon said and he was bidding madame a gallant adieu as Roxanne and I went up the stairs behind the maids.

Madame Broussard had made an attempt to honor the season with a few greens and red and green candles in the sconces along the wall. There was the spicy scent of mince pies baking in the kitchen. The fragrance of roasting meat mingled with it and I was suddenly hungry.

Once in our room, Roxanne and I shook out two wrinkled silk dresses and began to don them. "Whatever shall we do in this dull house with all these dull women about?" Roxanne demanded angrily.

"Wait," I replied briefly.

"I would rather be back at the Macarte house with all those men and the action going on," she retorted. "At least things were happening. *Dieu,* how I miss Jean and the life I used to lead!" There was something in her voice that made me uneasy. Roxanne was predictable only in her unpredictability and I wondered what her dissatisfaction portended.

But we descended the stairs sedately and greeted the other girls who were under Madame Broussard's care. For a while, our adventures the night of the twenty-third were a sensation and we were pelted with questions. But after Christmas dinner, things settled down. It was then Roxanne and I discovered the women of New Orleans were in complete terror, for rumor had it that the British motto was "beauty and booty." Some of the girls, even as I, carried daggers at their waists.

By the end of the week and after the New Year, Roxanne was pacing the floor. Neither she nor I took to handiwork. But under Madame Broussard's lofty tutelage, I was attempting to crochet. I had absolutely no talent for it and came close to swearing as I dropped stitches regularly. Roxanne made no pretense of learning to sew in any fashion, and in her private conversations with me she spoke more and more often of Jean Lafitte.

Madame Broussard had twice refused to give up her two carriage horses to the military and she had somehow managed to make her refusal stick. Thus it was that one day when the sun promised to shine, madame and we six girls went for a brief ride. But before we had covered three blocks a deluge of rain descended and we returned hastily. That was our one attempt at diversion. The city was like a morgue. There were no entertainments and even the merchants had closed some of the shops in fear. Only the French marketplace did business and it was subdued, according to the Broussard cook, not at all the raucous, cheery place we had known.

Such news as there was, however, was brought in by the servants. Rumors were rife and occasionally a friend would walk over to see Madame Broussard and bring the city gossip to us. It was said there were members of the legislature who were planning to open up the city to the British, to surrender rather than have the city sacked and burned.

When this news reached Jackson, he did not explode as was expected. Instead, he coldly dissolved the legislature and ordered Governor Claiborne to investigate. The upshot was that the rumors vanished like a mist and Claiborne wrote that it was nothing to cause concern. Whereupon Jackson allowed the legislature to reconvene, but it was whispered that that august body would never be the same.

Conflicting reports came in from the battlefield itself, skirmishes and encounters, while more and more British were being transported up Bayou Bienvenu to the Villere plantation where they had made their headquarters. And it was not the Duke of Wellington who had come to command the invasion after all, but the next best thing, the duke's own brother-in-law and right-hand man, General Sir Edward Pakenham.

I listened to it all and had little to say. Truth to tell, like Roxanne, I was extremely restless, and Madame Broussard finally gave up my crochet lessons in disgust.

I was not too surprised when, one morning, I awakened to find the bed beside me empty. Roxanne was gone. She left all her dresses, but she took her precious jewels and wrote me a terse little note. She was going to Barataria where Jean was stationed, watching for another invasion army.

She took one of Madame Broussard's pet fillies and that good lady was most irritated. In fact, she viewed me askance and was quite cool after Roxanne's disappearance, for I did not reveal where she had gone.

431

"Humph! I knew when I saw you two in those dreadful boots and breeches that you were not accountable," she said acidly. "And though you have stayed, I feel that you, too, are unaccountable, Aurielle."

Still the days dragged by and brought news from the battlefield that most of the action consisted of brief sorties and skirmishes. The *Carolina* just down the river from us suffered a hot shot in her magazine and blew up with a great roar that could be heard all over the city. It had frightened all of us, until we discovered that every man aboard swam to safety before the explosion. After this, we heard that some New Orleans men and Kentuckians were forming a line on the west bank in the event the British decided to outflank Jackson and march on the city from that side of the river.

The middle of the week brought the event that was to alter my life forever. It began with a rap at the door. No one was near, so I opened it myself and admitted Rodeur Cheviot and a prisoner he was bringing to town, a Colonel George Carleton.

When I saw Rodeur, I could not resist hugging him, as he smiled so warmly at me and said, "I had to stop by and see how you are, *ma petite*. I have worried about you." Then as an afterthought, "And Roxanne. Where is she?"

"In the deeps of the bayou country with Jean Lafitte, I imagine, Rodeur. And I am very anxious and restless, closeted as I am in a houseful of terrified women." I spoke low, so that Madame Broussard, who was now bustling up, did not overhear.

As she reached us, she said graciously, "Ah, M'sieu Cheviot—how good to see you." Her anticipation of news was visible. "Will you not stay and take your noon meal with us—you and ah—" she hesitated, observing the high rank of the man with Rodeur. "You are both welcome and it is almost ready."

Rodeur, with his finest Gallic charm, kissed madame's hand and complimented her effusively, and I could see she held him in high esteem. There was such an air of aristocracy and breeding in Rodeur Cheviot that, I found myself wondering, as always, about his life in Paris so long ago.

"I would be delighted. And I am sure the good Colonel Carleton would welcome fine French cuisine. Field rations are not too palatable."

Thus we all sat at table, with the girls asking Rodeur dozens of questions. There was almost a festive air about the meal, for the tension and fear the girls suffered most of the time were lacking. Only the colonel was silent and stern-faced. Rodeur held forth on the lack of weapons and how much each one was worth to Jackson's mixed army. It seemed there were still men on the battleline without musket or rifle. Even pistols, he said mournfully, would be most welcome.

After the meal, the unmarried girls regretfully took their leave. As a young widow, though only eighteen, I was left with Madame Broussard and the two men for afternoon liqueurs. As we finished, Madame Broussard said reluctantly, "M'sieu Cheviot—I—have several pistols that were my brother's and my husband's, God rest them. I hate to part with them, but I feel I must do so, knowing your dire need."

"Ah, Madame Broussard, you are a true patriot," Cheviot said. "I will try to see they are returned to you afterward."

"Come with me," she said, rising, "and I will get them for you."

I was left alone with the grim-faced but gentleman colonel as they departed the sitting room. For a while we chatted inconsequentially and pleasantly. Then I said, "I hope your imprisonment will not be too hard on you, Colonel."

He smiled meaningfully. "It won't. It will be for such a short time. Tomorrow I will be back with my regiment."

"You seem very certain," I said curiously. "How can you be so sure?"

"Tomorrow at dawn, General Pakenham will smash them in a frontal assault. My only regret is that I shall not be among them."

A coldness settled in my vitals. "You know this?"

"I will say you lie if you quote me," he retorted, even voice still pleasant, "but by this time tomorrow, it will all be over and we will occupy New Orleans. I have

433

learned Jackson has but two thousand men. We have near twelve thousand massed to the south. You haven't a chance." He smiled benignly.

I was stunned. Rodeur and Kincannon, Dominique You and Beluche, all the Baratarians and those amazingly rugged Kaintucks mingling with the Creole and German and Irish recruits would be slaughtered. The sheer momentum of numbers would overcome them. My hands grew cold with fear and I realized suddenly this disaster was certain—and Andrew Jackson did not know the British planned to strike, I was certain. He must be told!

"You are a very beautiful widow, Madame Dessaultes," the colonel said now, leaning easily back in his chair, completely in command of himself and the situation. "I will see no harm comes to you during the occupation." He looked to be in his early thirties and was handsome in a rugged sort of way. His tone intimated many things. And for all he was an officer and evidently of good blood, his intimations frightened me.

Rodeur returned with a beaming Madame Broussard and he carried a leather sack which contained the weapons she had given him. His eyes twinkled and he said, "We must leave immediately, for I will see the colonel to the Cabildo jail—a cell suitable to his rank," he added, with a glance at the colonel. "But you do not know the vast gratitude your generosity engenders, my dear Madame Broussard!" She bridled and reiterated her pleasure to be of help.

The colonel kissed my hand lingeringly, murmuring, "I have very much enjoyed your company, madame," then added enigmatically, "and I will see you again, sooner than you expect."

I wanted to blurt out what he had told me to Rodeur, but there was a warning in the blue eyes of the colonel and I knew he would make good his threat to tell them I was lying. No doubt he would express astonishment if I came forth with such vital information. Then they were gone, leaving me in a hidden turmoil.

The balance of the day I was miserable. Kincannon would be in that thin line facing a massive attack. I paced my room and eluded the other girls who were staying with

Madame Broussard, protesting that I wanted to rest. I ate supper with them all and was silent through the meal. Several jokingly made reference to Rodeur and said I was mooning over him, that I was in love and that was why I ate so little.

But in my mind a plan was stirring. Madame Broussard had one horse left and I knew the way to Pointe St. Antoine like the back of my hand. I would ride to the Jackson line and tell them that the devastating frontal assault was to take place in the morning. The more I thought of it, the more feasible it became. I would don breeches and boots, push my hair under the broad-brimmed hat, and no one would know but what I was a boy. It was dangerous to ride that five miles at night, I knew, but I had my poniard which had stood me in such good stead. With all the men concentrated at the battle-lines, there would be none on the road, I was sure—none who would stop me.

I waited until all had retired before I put on my male clothing and pinned my hair under the hat. Shrugging into the leather coat, which this time I buttoned firmly to hide my breasts, I crept silently down the curving stairs. It was very late and all in the house were sleeping. I felt my way through the foyer, the hall, and into the kitchen. There I took the door to the back where the stable stood behind the rear courtyard. I would be taking Madame Broussard's last horse and she would call me a thief, for I left no note —but I *must* warn Kincannon and Rodeur.

Ah, Kincannon! A dull ache was in my throat as I thought of that tall, powerful man. I realized anew, and with bitterness, that I had loved him from the moment we rode that tide of passion in Rodeur's cabin aboard the *Wind*. All I would ever have was remembrance of those piercingly sweet moments of fulfillment we had shared before I knew I was Ondine's daughter and tainted by madness. Now, at least, I knew I would not stand by and see him shot down in the morning.

The air was damp and cold against my flushed face as I made my way silently to the stable. The filly nickered softly as I reached her stall. I moved swiftly, putting on the bridle and bit. I did not try to saddle her. The saddle

435

was heavy and I was unfamiliar with all the straps, having never saddled a horse in my life.

In a matter of moments, I was leading her quietly down the drive beside the house, keeping to the grass so her hooves would not sound on the shell drive. Once beyond the house, I mounted swiftly and cantered through the dark, muddy streets until I reached the road to Pointe St. Antoine and the plantations that lined the long plain before the Mississippi River.

It was very dark. The sky was overcast and there was no moon, no winking stars. The city thinned, and suddenly I was on the narrow dirt road. The first plantation, Montreuille, was dark back among the trees, and I increased the gait of the horse. I couldn't gallop five miles without tiring her too much, but there was something eerie about the silence. We had heard cannon and gunfire in New Orleans faintly during the days and we had worried, but this silence was more unnerving.

I passed the Languille plantation and it, too, was deserted and dark back among the towering oaks. I was almost there—the next would be the Macarte house. Surely Kincannon would be there! And Rodeur as well. I would go straight to them with the revelations of the British colonel.

I knew a moment of panic as I looked at the sky. The fog had rolled in from the river, but it was luminous, too. Was it near dawn already? I kicked the flanks of the filly and she struck out in a gallop. I peered through the trees and the stubbled cane fields, straining to see what lay ahead, but the fog was a barrier.

There! There at last was the Macarte house and a little light came dimly from two windows. I turned the horse down the drive and galloped wildly to the house.

Slipping from the horse, I ran swiftly up the steps and beat a rapid tattoo on the door. It opened almost at once on a blue-shirted soldier.

"I must see Captain Kincannon or Captain Cheviot— or even General Jackson. I have important news!" I said breathlessly.

"They're all on the line, boy. They expect an attack by the British at any moment."

They were expecting it! My ride had been for nothing, I thought. Then it occurred that possibly they did not realize the magnitude of the attack—and I fled down the steps once more, mounting the filly swiftly.

I heard the soldier call out, "Hey, boy—come back here!" but I was gone, his voice fading as I rode swiftly to the south. The Rodriguez canal, which was their line, was only a few hundred feet from the Macarte house and I made for it rapidly. In the dark and fog, I could scarcely discern the men, but there were hundreds of them. Some were sitting about small fires that lit the darkness for a few feet about them. I went to the first of these and asked for Kincannon.

"He's with the general farther down the line, boy. What you want?" The soldier rose leisurely to his feet and reached out for my reins. I jerked them back, but quick as lightning he had them in his hands. "Now, lad, you'll wait here until Ed c'n get the cap'n." He jerked his head at the man who had crouched beside the fire wtih him and the latter disappeared on foot among the scattered campfires. His voice was low as he added, "Git off that hoss, sonny, and set."

I slid off the filly and realized suddenly that I was trembling, not only from the cold but from tense excitement. I lowered my voice gruffly, "I'll have a—cup of that coffee there, if you can spare it." I motioned to the rack across the coals.

Still holding the reins to my horse with one hand, the man bent and filled a metal cup he had been using himself and silently handed it to me. I drank slowly, for it was very hot. I held my chilled hands around the cup, and after a few sips I felt my hands and feet begin to tingle with warmth, but I shivered a little still.

I had finished the cup and refused another when the man returned with Kincannon, both walking, but the captain held the reins to his big horse in his hand. "There he is—the boy who says he's got a very important message fer you." He jerked a thumb at me and, squatting back down on the damp ground, reached for the pot over the fire.

I looked up into the lean, loved face above me, at

the black eyes glittering in the firelight. Catching his arm, I pulled him away from the fire. "Come away—and I'll tell you," I said, my lowered voice muffled. Mist was rolling in heavily now from the river, wreathing around the men, but through it the campfires winked cheerily. What were the British doing now? I wondered as we moved back. It was so silent beyond the breastworks on the canal. At some little distance from the men, I felt Kincannon's grip on my shoulder. "Now, what news do you bring me, boy, that's so important?"

I looked up at him once more. The sky was definitely lightening now. In a few more minutes, dawn would be upon us. He was looking down at me intently and suddenly his hand shot out and he jerked off my hat, sending my hair tumbling down my back.

"Goddamn!" he swore under his breath. "Aurielle! What fool's errand brings you here at this time?"

"There was a prisoner, a colonel, brought to the house by Rodeur, and when I was alone with him, he boasted the British would occupy New Orleans by the end of the day—today. They plan a massive frontal assault that will smash you. I had to bring word of their plan."

"Don't you know we are aware of Pakenham's plans? We have taken prisoners and questioned them and know full well that reinforcements have arrived—enough to attack us in force."

"Then I—I didn't need to come?" I asked forlornly.

"No, Aurielle. Why did you?"

"I—I thought of you—and Rodeur and Dominique You and Beluche, all being taken by surprise and killed." My throat was thick with unshed tears and I could not understand why. It had to do with this man, standing here before me, tall and broad—and unattainable.

"You thought of me?" he asked, pulling me still farther into the shadow of a great live oak.

"Especially of you," I confessed almost inaudibly.

He put his hand under my chin and tipped my face upward, slowly bringing his mouth to mine. At its cool touch in the mist, my arms went about him of their own volition and I clung to him, suddenly boneless with desire. He caught the back of my head, slipping his big hand into

438

the mass of hair, holding me thus while he kissed my li[ps]
my face, and at last, the hollow at the base of my thro[at]
I wished with sudden violence that this moment could
on forever.

"You must go back. It's too dangerous for you her[e]
he said huskily. "You should be safe. Marriage is for y[ou]
lady, and children as well."

We were silent for a moment. Then I said, "I c[an]
never marry, Quentin." My heart was leaden in my brea[st]

"What idiocy is that?" he asked roughly.

"I can never bring children into the world for fear
passing on Ondine's insanity."

"You are talking like a fool! Ondine's depravit[ies]
were a cultivated taste."

"No. They were born into her. It was someth[ing]
over which she had no control. I know I carry the se[ed]
within me, for I am her daughter."

"You have only her word for that. I never thou[ght]
you looked so much alike." His voice was restrained, [as]
if he held back a violent declaration. Then he said for[ce]
fully, "We will discuss this later. Now you must get b[ack]
before the attack begins." In the dim light from
paling sky, I could see his face set like iron.

"I don't want to leave you, Quentin," I blurted tru[th]
fully. He could not know of the wealth of love I carried
my heart for him and I must never tell him.

"I have to return to my post and you must go." [His]
voice grew more urgent as he added, "We'll get your ho[rse.]
You must be on your way before sunrise."

I stuffed my hair back under the hat and follow[ed]
him to the campfire where the men were now eating bre[ak]
fast. It looked to be cornbread with whiskey from
bottle which one of the men had produced.

"Want some breakfast, sonny?" asked one, as he t[ook]
a great swig from the bottle, washing down his cornbre[ad]

"The lad is returning to the city," Kincannon sa[id]
handing me the reins and holding his cupped hand for
foot as he assisted me in mounting.

I looked down at him and said in a small voice, "Y[ou]
will be careful?"

His smile by firelight was a touch derisive. "Oh, v[ery]

439

careful. Now be off with you," and slapped the filly's rump resoundingly.

I cantered through the mist only a little distance before I brought the mare to a halt. *I could not leave.* The thick, moist fog that usually dissipated with the rising sun was thick around me as I turned the horse about. I would know the outcome of this clash at arms. I *must* know Kincannon survived, that Rodeur was unharmed. I might get my head blown off, I thought recklessly, but without Kincannon, what did it matter? And I might be of some use. I could fire a pistol!

I walked the horse slowly back to the campfire and the two men looked up at me, unsurprised. "Wanter get inter the thick of it with us, eh, laddie buck?" the one with the whiskey bottle grinned.

"Yes," I replied gruffly. "I heard the general needs every man, so I'm going to stay."

"Yer a long way from bein' a man yet, sonny," said the other, peering at my slender form in the firelight as I slid off the horse. "You got a weapon?"

"Only a knife," I confessed.

"Ed, give 'im yer pistol. You got yer long rifle. Come on and set, sonny, an' have a bit o' breakfast."

So I squatted down in the canal by the two rough, bearded men and ate some of their cornbread and even took a swallow of the corn whiskey. It went down like fire, causing my eyes to water, but it generated a pleasant warmth and took the edge off my apprehensions. Dimly I could see the breastworks before us and it was only faintly reassuring. A determined foe could scale it easily. The man called Ed followed my eyes and said comfortingly, "It don't look too high, but you gotta remember we're on this side o' it, sonny, an' we'll shoot 'em before they get to it."

It developed that the two men were from Georgia and their names were Ed and Joe, and as we waited for dawn to break, they told me they had come in answer to Jackson's call for volunteers to help defend Louisiana.

Ed said, "You ain't a day over fourteen, I bet, laddie buck, but you got a man's determination—comin' back ter help us."

I nodded, speaking as little as I could for fear of giving myself away. After a while the men dozed, sitting up, but I was too tense to relax for even a minute and the time dragged interminably as the sky grew lighter. I was aware of being cold and hungry now.

Abruptly, I was wrenched to sudden terror by a great roar and hiss. A flame shot high in the air, bright and terrifying despite the fog that clung to the land.

"That's a Congreve rocket, lad," Joe said calmly. "They're supposed to scare the hell out'a you but they don't do much harm. I figger that one's a signal fer the British to mass fer their attack." He took another swallow from the bottle and both men began to work with their long rifles, priming, polishing, loading.

Ed handed me a pistol, which was so heavy I could scarcely hold it steady in my hand. "It's loaded, sonny, but it don't shoot far. Wait til they git right on us before you use it."

Even as we watched, the fog began to shred, revealing open places, for the sun had risen and now I could see the might of the British Army! They were drawn up in two long red columns, with their big guns shining in the middle between their lines. They stood in their fine scarlet coats in perfect order. I glanced along the canal at the hodge-podge accumulation of men and arms and my heart sank.

I started violently as their cannons belched fire. They were answered immediately by big American guns emplaced both at the canal and across the river. I longed to clap my hands over my ears and shrink down in the bottom of the canal as I heard the dull boom when the ship *Louisiana* fired her cannon. Instead, I crouched against the breastworks, peering beyond, with the pistol wobbling in my hand.

Suddenly, before my horrified eyes, those beautifully arrayed and ordered troops began to fall. Some of them swayed and fell to the ground, some sank to their knees as if in prayer and some simply crumbled, while the men in the Rodriguez canal held their fire.

"But no one's shooting them—" I began, my voice high.

Joe looked at me curiously. "That's th' round shot from th' river doin' all that damage, lad. Yer voice changin'?"

I gulped and nodded wordlessly and he laughed, "After this, it oughta be a full bass."

I did not see how the British could withstand the havoc, but the command must have been given and the men responded bravely, for still in perfect order they advanced. Yet the men crowded around me along the length of the canal held their rifle and musket fire. It occurred to me they were doing so until the marching men came within range. My assumption was corroborated when Ed muttered, "Now, sonny, don't fire that pistol until they're less'n twenty yards from you. In a minute, we can fire our long guns."

Joe said jubilantly, "An' don't them crossed white bands on their chests make a fine target—" and his voice was chillingly convincing.

Then, suddenly, those beautiful troops reached a point nearer the canal, and all around me, the riflemen opened up fire. I was stunned to see the redcoats cut down in a swathe. The round shot had been bad enough, but these Kentucky and Tennessee riflemen were wondrously accurate and swift to reload. What the British faced was an almost continuous sheet of fire and I rose up higher to peer over the parapet and saw the field between the two armies was so thick with fallen men the ground was red.

Suddenly Joe knocked me to the ground roughly. "They're firin' at us now. It ain't smart to stick your head up too far, laddie."

I rolled to the bottom and my hat fell off, allowing the mass of chestnut hair to spill out about my shoulders. The two men gave me a startled look and Joe blurted, "My Gawd—she's a girl—" before he turned his attention once more to the battle waged before him.

I crouched rebelliously below the breastworks as I stuffed my hair back under the hat, looking along the line east and west to see what casualties the Americans were suffering. I saw no one down. All were leaning over the breastworks as far as I could see, continuing their deadly and accurate fire.

Slowly, I crept back up to the edge of the parapet to see the British coming doggedly on, stepping courageously over the bodies of their fallen comrades. And still the guns of Jackson's men roared out their death and destruction. Despite it all, the British continued to fire and march in order until they were cut down.

I held the pistol, but I did not fire it. I was sickened by the wholesale slaughter. I leaned against the damp, cold breastworks and it seemed hours to me before some of the British broke ranks and fled. I felt a wash of relief. It was a measure of their fear that they took to the dreaded swamps to escape the devastating accuracy of the long guns of the Americans. And down the line, I could see that we had suffered casualties, too.

I had thought it much longer, but the holocaust had actually been a matter of about an hour, when the firing died away as the red-coated and valiant British retreated. There was jubilation in the canal behind the breastworks. Jackson and his men did not pursue the retreating British, but some of the soldiers leaped from the canal and went among the fallen men, some helping, some seeking souvenirs.

Joe and Ed reloaded their rifles and turned to study me. "Now what're we gonna do with a girl—a little girl at that," Ed asked dubiously. "The gen'l will skin us alive if he finds out—My Gawd, here he comes now!"

True enough, the tall, painfully thin Jackson was walking among his men and congratulating them. I jammed the hat down lower and tried to make myself as inconspicuous as possible. Ed and Joe began cleaning their rifles with enthusiasm. Still, the general stopped before us, looking at me curiously.

"You're a mighty young lad to be in this man's army," he said and I felt the piercing eyes on me. "What's your name. Speak up, boy!"

I looked up and our eyes met, his cold and blue, mine round and scared. I felt my thick black lashes pinned to my brows. He looked at me for an interminable minute before he said, "I'll be damned if it's not young Madame

Dessaultes, wearing boots and breeches again. I sent you to New Orleans. What are you doing back here?"

"I rode in last night to warn you of the assault this morning. A British colonel had told it to me in the city— and I didn't know you were already expecting it—and I stayed because I wanted to help, General Jackson," I finished defiantly.

"And did you?" He looked at the big pistol still in my hand.

"I never fired a shot," I said shamefacedly.

He laughed shortly. "Then maybe you can help with the wounded. We have more than a few, madame."

I looked down the canal and saw now that the fallen men had been stretched out on the ground behind it and my heart sank accordingly. Kincannon and Rodeur! But I could not discern the identity of the men from this distance, and as the general was leaving, I asked hurriedly, "Who was—has been wounded?"

"I don't know. But I suggest you get to the Macarte house, for that is where we will bring them and you might make yourself useful as a nurse." Then he was gone.

I looked back out over the breastworks at the devastation beyond and my heart caught, then raced wildly. I could not believe my eyes!

From among those piles of fallen redcoats, soldiers were rising slowly in the clear, sunlit air to face the men with their long rifles at the ready—and their hands were raised above their heads. Some were pulled from under the limp bodies, others pushed the bodies off themselves, some rose from the edge of a group of fallen comrades. I let my breath out silently. *Thank God they are not all dead,* was my first coherent thought. These surrendering men had remained beside their fallen brothers, lying still, until the slaughter was realized by their commanders and retreat had been sounded. Now they were surrendering themselves to the brave few who had wrought such havoc among Britain's finest soldiers.

"Well, ma'am," Ed was saying, "yer a brave woman an' though you didn't fire a shot, you wanted us to win an' we knew it." Then tactfully, "If I was you, I'd git on my hoss an' beat it fer the Macarte house if you want ter help now."

I turned to see that a beehive of activity was all about the canal. Several men on horseback broke from the body of milling men. With two riders on each mount, I could tell from the sag of some of the bodies that they were wounded. As far as I could see the cypress swamps to the east were aboil with the mixture of Jackson's oddly assorted troops and the surrendering redcoats.

With a brief word of farewell to my two companions, I climbed out of the canal and looked about for Madame Broussard's filly. It was nowhere to be seen. It had probably bolted when the firing started, or some soldier could have commandeered it. It could even be somewhere in the swamps by now. I pulled my hat down firmly and struck out on foot across the cane fields toward the Macarte house. It was a long walk, and several men on horseback passed me as I moved steadily forward.

When I reached the house, it was already filling with men who paid me little heed in my male clothing. I kept the hat on my head as I pushed my way into the foyer. Soldiers continued to bring in their wounded comrades, seeking to make them as comfortable as possible. I saw no familiar faces as some of the wounded were being carried up to the bedrooms and some were laid carefully on the rugs and couches in the salon and the sitting room.

I stood uncertainly in the foyer, at a loss as to where I might offer my services, when I heard a familar husky voice behind me.

"Step aside, boy—I've a—"

I spun around and faced Quentin Kincannon, who carried Rodeur in his arms. I cried, "Oh, Quent—Rodeur! Is he badly wounded?"

"Good God, Aurielle, why are you here—"

"I stayed," I broke in. "I want to help. I couldn't leave without knowing—" I stopped. No words of love had ever passed between us. I could not start now. "Is Rodeur —can it be a flesh wound?" I asked hopefully.

"No," Kincannon replied, grim-faced. "It is bad."

Chapter
21

Kincannon shouldered his way through the men and I followed hastily. He spoke over his shoulder. "I'm going to put him in one of the upstairs bedrooms. Fetch bandages and any medication you have. He has taken a ball through the chest."

I drew even with them and looked down into Rodeur's white face, saw that his vivid blue eyes were alert. As mine met them, he grinned the old reckless grin and said, "I am tough to kill, *chérie.* I will be all right," but as he spoke, blood flecked his lip and a cough rattled ominously.

"Rodeur—" I said with a half sob, then turned and ran fleetly up the stairs ahead of them. At the landing I ran down the hall to one of the linen closets and pulled out two heavy sheets. Then on my way downstairs to the kitchen, I met with half a dozen wounded men, supported by their unwounded comrades.

"Where'd ye get them sheets, boy?" several asked in unison and I pointed them toward the closet, the door of which I had left open.

Downstairs in the kitchen, I searched fruitlessly in every cupboard for salves or emollients, knocking off my hat in my efforts. I paid it no heed in my anxiety for Rodeur, but ran from the room to the stairs. Mounting, I met with a young Tennesseean with a bloody bandage on his forehead, evidently made from his torn shirt.

He grinned at me jauntily and said, "We licked 'em, lassie. Ye can put on yer dresses now."

I sensed a vast euphoria among the men, both well and wounded, a triumphant spirit that was very nearly tangible. Despite my fears for Rodeur, I felt their triumph seeping through my veins. They were so few! And they had turned back so many. They had every right to feel exhilarated. If only Rodeur had not been so grievously wounded! Hurrying down the long hall, I entered two bedrooms before I found the one where Kincannon had chosen to place Rodeur. It was a small room near the end of the hall.

"No medicines or salves—only bandages," I said briefly. "If we bandage it tightly—" He began tearing the first sheet, and in moments we were both working to staunch the flow of blood.

"Leave me some room to breathe," Rodeur said, still smiling, but his voice was breathy, shallow, and it struck fresh fear to my heart.

"Are you in pain?" I asked tenderly.

"Not as long as I can look at you, *ma petite fille*."

Ma petite fille. Ondine had called me that when she was faced with an angry mob—when she was trying to escape, she had let the truth come out. Rodeur's words were but an endearment stemming from deep friendship.

"I will nurse you, Rodeur. I will not leave your side until you are well, I swear it. Do you want a sip of water?"

"I'd much prefer French brandy, Aurielle." His white grin was as impudent as ever.

"I'll find some—if I must turn the house upside down!"

"*Non, chérie*—stay with me." There was a touch of desperation in his voice.

"I'll find it," Kincannon said swiftly and strode from the room.

I put a pillow under Rodeur's head and wiped the blood from the corner of his mouth. His eyes on me were so vivid, so intense I felt tension begin to build within me. What was behind that look? It was a look of radiant and deep love and a kind of despair. It came from some deep, inner source and he never took his eyes from my face.

"Aurielle, I have something I must tell you." His voice was growing more whispery.

"Tell me? What, Rodeur?" I asked anxiously, a sudden sense of impending shock spreading through me. "What is it?"

A look of great pain crossed his face, made it haggard, and the blue eyes clouded, then cleared. "It is something I should have told you months ago, but I was a coward—I was afraid I would lose your love."

"How could you lose my love, my friendship?" I asked in swift French. "It is yours forever, Rodeur."

He groaned, then said, "Have you not seen it, my little one? Have you not realized that you resemble me much more than you did Ondine Chaille?"

The implication stunned me into silence. I looked into the chiseled features, the blue eyes, the tilted dark brows, and realized for the first time the truth that had been there for me to see all the time. My God! I was but a feminine version of his reckless charming face.

"I am your father, my darling. The poniard in your belt is mine. Jean Bayard Sechere—J.B.S.—"

"Oh!" I cried poignantly. "Why didn't you tell me at first—why did you wait?"

"Because in a way I am guilty of your mother's death. If I hadn't—left her, I might have saved her. I couldn't have you hate me for that!" He coughed thickly, then said, "But I find at last I cannot leave you thinking that mad woman, Ondine Chaille, was your mother. She was nothing—*nothing* to you!"

"Oh, Rodeur—Papa—how did it happen—that we were all parted?" My eyes had filled with unshed tears, and the handsome, devil-may-care face I looked down into was blurred.

"Intrigues. I was very young—I was a royalist. I

had pledged my honor and my life for my king. I am
duke—one of the hated aristocracy, as was your mothe
He drew a shallow breath. "Napoleon's soldiers w
coming to take me. Your mother gave you to our Engl
friend, John Warren, that night. He was to take you
England, where you would be safe, where your mot
could come to you. Your mother—her name was Aurie
too—she insisted that I leave immediately to escape c
ture. It was *I* who left that note with her for John. I
tell you the rest of it for the words are burned into
brain. 'I am discovered and I must flee for my life. T
Aurielle to England with you—tell her how beloved
is to us and she is never to forget her mother is of
nobility. She is our hope for our future. Tell her that
papa fought for a just cause—his king and his coun
We love her and trust you, John.' Your mother sta
behind, thinking they would not harm a defensel
woman—" His voice was whispery but full of bitterne
"How wrong we were. They guillotined her—and I h
roamed the world since. If I had stayed, I might h
protected her, or at least we could have died togethe
shall never forgive myself—so how can I expect you
forgive me, my daughter?"

Hot tears rolled down my cheeks as I leaned my f
down to his and murmured, "Oh, Papa—Papa, you m
not condemn yourself. You were so young. How co
you know they would kill Mother?"

He sighed deeply. "I feel relieved somehow. For r
you know your parentage—and I know only too well h
it has troubled you through the years, my little one."

Kincannon strode into the room with a bottle of c
whiskey. "This was all I could find and I had to fight
it," he said grimly. "Here, take a swallow, old friend
will give you strength."

Rodeur let Kincannon put it to his lips and too
long swallow. It did seem to give him some strength,
his voice was stronger as he said, "Quent, I took y
advice and I have told Aurielle I am her father. May
bon Dieu put it into her heart to forgive me."

"There is nothing to forgive," I said in a cho

voice. "My mother was a brave woman—and at least one of you escaped."

"Now that you are aware your father and mother were a duke and duchess, you *know* you are indeed a lady," Kincannon said dryly. "Does it afford you much satisfaction, Aurielle?"

"No," I answered violently. "I want only for my father to survive. Oh, Papa, you *must* get well!"

He lifted a hand and I caught it to me. It was cold—*cold*. Frantically I took up the other hand and began rubbing the two of them between my warm ones. Rodeur—I could hardly think of him as my father and le Duc de Sechere—smiled faintly.

"It will take the fires of hell to warm those hands again, *chérie*," he whispered.

"No, no!" I cried, putting them up to my tear-wet face. "Rodeur—Papa, you must try to hold on." Then I cried distractedly to Kincannon, who stood by, his black eyes full of compassion, "Get a doctor! Isn't there one in the whole of the American Army?"

"He is coming," Kincannon said quietly. "I told him of Rodeur when I secured the whiskey—but there are many he must see."

"Why isn't he here then? Rodeur—Papa needs him now!" I struggled to keep my composure. It would not do to let my father see me weep. I wanted him to think me as brave and courageous as my mother. Oh, in my heart I agonized that I had not known all those long months at Barataria—the long months at Ondine's when I dreamed of her as my mother. If I had only known, I would have sought his company so much more often. I would have been kinder—I would have shown my love more!

I knelt beside the bed and put my cheek against his. *"Ma petite, je t'aime bien—"* His voice trailed off and his lids closed, the long, double-thick black lashes, so like mine, fanned along his lean, tanned cheek.

Kincannon stooped over him and said urgently, *"Mon vieux,* try! Two are coming up to see you in a few moments. They just rode in. You will want to see them—old comrades come to congratulate you."

The brown lids fluttered up and the half smile ap-

peared once again. "I'll wager it's Roxanne and Je
non?"

Kincannon laughed, "Ah, you are not near dea
Rodeur. You are as sharp as ever and you are right. B
of them are in a fury over missing the battle. Gene
Jackson is of the opinion the British might renew th
attacks later in the day and he is going to send Jean a
General Humboldt to aid Morgan on the west bank
the river. As a matter of fact, he is keeping Jean at
side while he is penning a personal note to Morg
probably this very minute."

"They will not attack again," Rodeur whisper
"We have beaten them."

"Jackson can't take chances, Rodeur."

Again that whispery prophetic voice. "They are e
now returning to their ships to sail back to England—
America is established now as a power that can hold
own." A spasm of coughing shook him and blood v
thick in his mouth. I seized the remains of the torn sh
and held it to his lips.

"A bowl of water!" I cried. "I must bathe his face—

"I'll fetch it," Kincannon said and left the ro
swiftly.

While he was gone, I did the best I could with
sheet, tearing the other one into squares and wiping
lips repeatedly. His face had taken on an ominous pa
beneath the tan.

With great effort, he opened his eyes and loo
searchingly into mine and then said distinctly, "Aurie
my daughter, I want only your happiness. Be happy
petite—" His voice trailed away and the hand in m
was suddenly flaccid and cold as ice.

I became aware of Kincannon behind me and I s
numbly, "Too late. He is gone."

I heard him place the bowl on the washstand beh
me and his big hands cupped my shoulders. They w
gentle and comforting. I turned, looking up at him v
tear-blind eyes. "I only just found him. Now I've lost
again."

"Nay, you found him in June near three years a
Aurielle. He has been your father since then. He thou

451

of your welfare constantly from that moment on. He had feared you dead all these years."

"Why didn't you tell me?" I pulled from his embrace. "You've known all this time and you never said a word!"

"I've known only since I widowed you under the oaks—and the truth was not mine to divulge. He swore me to secrecy." His smile was grim. "And all to insure your happiness."

"Oh." I wept and he again took me into his arms. "I was so unhappy! I was so sure Ondine was my mother—"

"He knew that, too, but he knew you loved him as a daughter and he didn't want to risk losing that. He was so sure you would hate him for deserting your mother."

"But he didn't desert her." My voice was muffled against his dusty blue uniform. "He *had* to leave—"

"He might have taken her with him," he said softly.

"But she herself thought she would be safe—"

"You can make excuses for him. He could make none for himself." He tilted my wet face upward and put his lips against mine in a warm, salty kiss. Pulling my chilled body tightly against his big, hard, warm one, he murmured, "This makes a difference about children for you now, doesn't it, Aurielle?"

"Oh, yes," I whispered, quivering with the desire he always evoked within me. I clung to him, reveling suddenly in being alive, in being young, in being with this man I had longed for ever since the first time he had taken me in his arms.

"So," came the contemptuous, lilting voice from the doorway, "it *is* as I thought, eh, *mes amis?* Come then, Aurielle, take Quent's sword and let us settle once and for all who is the better woman!"

Kincannon released me, turned as I did, and his quick, "Fool!" stung the girl before us. Behind her stood an impassive Ulysses. She had drawn her sword and now bright color flamed in her cheeks. Kincannon said coldly, "You and Ulysses have lost one old friend this morning. That should be enough, Roxanne."

"Lost an old friend?" Bewilderment filled the bright green eyes. "Jean, Dominique—Beluche I have seen below—"

"Rodeur Cheviot is dead of wounds suffered in battle this morning."

"Never!" she cried in French. "Rodeur has r lives! He has escaped too often to be caught now!"

Ulysses muttered an oath in French and moved i the room behind Roxanne.

Kincannon pulled me aside and the bed holc Rodeur was visible to them both. Roxanne drew a s breath, her face whitening slowly.

"And if you have lost an old friend," Kincan added quietly, "Aurielle has lost more. He was her fath

Ulysses's dark eyes swung to me and there was c passion in them but no flicker of surprise.

Roxanne blanched whiter. "But no! That cannot She, *his* bastard? Ondine was her mother—"

"A lie," Kincannon said dispassionately, "to pre upon Aurielle to help her escape—and to punish her her disapproval."

Her eyes on me narrowed once more. *"Who was I*

"He was Jean Bayard, le Duc de Sechere," I rep levelly. "My mother, his wife—Aurielle de Sechere, guillotined by Napoleon's zealots because she was mar to a man who dared to conspire for a return of monarchy."

Ulysses glided smoothly up to the bed and cros himself swiftly. Roxanne slowly replaced her sword followed Ulysses to look down on the classic feature my father. "I should have guessed," she drew a s breath, "the way he loved you—how much you res ble—" She reached out and put her hand on Rodeur's tanned one that lay at his side.

My eyes filled with fresh tears as I moved to s beside Roxanne, looking down into that beloved and face.

Like hundreds of his British counterparts, Jean yard de Sechere, known only as Rodeur Cheviot, buried in an unmarked grave that afternoon in the stub cane fields along the banks of the Mississippi River. I Lafitte, Roxanne, Ulysses, Kincannon, and I were at graveside as the last shovels full of earth were pac down on the mound by a detail of soldiers, who left immediately to prepare other graves.

As we walked slowly back to the Macarte house, Roxanne remarked to Kincannon, with her old arrogance, "Ulysses and I are going with Jean. He has some very interesting plans for the future and I mean to be part of them."

Lafitte looked down at her with mingled admiration, amusement, and desire. "You will not regret it, Roxanne. I shall make a queen of you." Then to Kincannon, "And you, old friend, you can be part of my future," he paused, his voice taking on a deeper tone, "as long as Roxanne is not part of yours."

"I have plans of my own, Jean," Kincannon replied laconically, "and privateering is not among them."

"Then what will you do to regain your fortune?" Roxanne jeered.

"I am not yet ready to say," he replied evasively. Then turning to me, "You are very quiet, Aurielle. What are your plans?"

I shrugged. "I shall go back to Madame Broussard's and get Antoinette. Then we will make plans together."

The three men walked on ahead of us and Roxanne and I, our soft boots easy among the stubble, fell slightly behind as the men spoke together. I heard Ulysses say, "The general has released me to serve with *le bos* on the west bank—"

I did not hear the rest, for Roxanne looked at me and spoke suddenly in soft French. "A duke's daughter, ha! And I know you have the great love for Quent, for all the good it will do you. He will take what he wants and leave you." Her eyes were green ice. "And for all your lineage—you'll be no better than the little bitch I first saw aboard the *Wind*."

I paled with fury and lashed out in kind. "And you are the whore I first knew you to be."

She laughed shortly. "Well, at least I'll not be seeing you again, thank God! When Jean and Ulysses finish their soldiering for Jackson, we will soon leave New Orleans for a far more exciting life. It's a pleasure to bid you good-bye, Aurielle. Good-bye and good riddance."

I made no response, stepping up my stride to
distance between us. How like Roxanne! For a time,
were almost friends, I thought wryly. But Roxanne co
be friend to men only. She would never have any use
women, I reflected, and I shared her relief that our pa
were parting.

At the Macarte house, she, Jean, and Ulysses secu
their horses and cantered away toward the river road. J
and Ulysses were on their way to take up the post Jack
had given them, and I knew that at last, Roxanne wo
stay by Jean's side.

Kincannon left me in the broad foyer to sec
a leave from Jackson in order to see me to New Orle
to find Antoinette. In a short time, we were mounted
his big gelding, I seated behind him with my arms ab
his broad chest. Our proximity was almost my undoing

I longed to lay my cheek against his broad back
let my body flow against his. Roxanne had spoken
truth. I knew what Captain Kincannon wanted of me
if I yielded, I would no doubt know a few weeks
intense pleasure with him. Then I would be cast off fo
new adventure and surely wind up like Marianne
scullery maid in a local tavern, with a handsome l
bastard baby to care for.

My dismal thoughts so preoccupied me that I
not realize that he was as silent as I, until we neared
city. A murmurous sound rose to meet us the nearer
drew. We entered to find a New Orleans gone wild
the news of Jackson's victory; many of the citizens w
both literally and figuratively drunk with the triumph.
soldiers were being hailed as heroes. When Kincann
uniform was glimpsed, hands were waved, cheers ye
invitations to stop and drink with them were called
People clustered about us so thickly we moved only in
at a time. But the evening was waning and the celebra
I could see, were tiring from a long day of frenzied
and relief.

We wended our way slowly through the well-wis
and tipsy celebrants to the Broussard house, with t
young boys following after, firing questions at Kincann
He answered them good-naturedly as he tethered

455

horse at the iron post before the Broussard gates. I slipped from the horse without his help as he opened the gates for us. The late evening sun was setting as he lifted the knocker. The black woman who answered it seemed hesitant at first to admit us and I realized that despite my hat and clothing, she recognized me before hastening to inform her mistress.

When Madame Broussard rustled up, her large bosom heaved with righteous indignation. By the lamp held by the maid, she viewed me with icy eyes. "I cannot take this irresponsible girl into my home again, Captain," she addressed Kincannon. "She and her cousin have stolen my two pet fillies and where are they now?"

"Probably where they are doing the most good, madame—with the army," Kincannon said shortly.

I cut in coldly. "I do not wish to stay here, madame. I came only for Antoinette Desmottes."

"Antoinette wishes to stay with me," Madame Broussard replied haughtily. "She is expert at coiffures and I am paying her ten dollars a month."

"But I am not staying with you, Madame Broussard," Antoinette said from the shadows and stepped forward. "I am maid to Madame Aurielle and I shall go with her."

I wanted to throw my arms about dear Antoinette's neck, but I said coolly, "If you will pack our things, we will leave now, Toinette." Then with a touch of sarcasm, "Unless, of course, madame chooses to keep my clothing in exchange for her fillies."

"Indeed, I want nothing left to remind me of your presence in my home. You are no lady, Madame Dessaultes!" Madame Broussard lifted her sharp nose like a fox scenting the wind. "And the sooner you are gone, the better." I could not restrain a faint smile. *Lady.* How little the term meant to me now. She added venomously, "I'm sure you do not expect me to receive you in my salon. You will wait *here* for Antoinette."

When she sailed away into the darkening rooms beyond the foyer, Kincannon said with a lazy laugh, "Mean old nannygoat, isn't she?"

"She certainly is," I replied.

"And where do you and Antoinette intend to go? Do you have any money?"

"I haven't a sou—and not the slightest idea where we shall stay," I responded bleakly.

His husky laughter grew. "For a penniless and questionable lady, you are very independent and saucy with your elders."

"Perhaps we can find a hostelry that will take us until we can find work," I said without any real conviction.

"I'm penniless myself right now," Kincannon said, frustration and anger mingling in the deep voice. "There is Sugarhill though. It is mine once more since Rodeur's death. I plan to sell it to Eugene Poliet, who seems to be the only man in town with any cash."

"Then he has survived the bank failure better than most," I remarked bitterly.

"I would investigate that," Kincannon said evenly, "if I were going to stay in New Orleans, but it matters little to me now."

"You are leaving the city?"

"I have plans," he reiterated.

"Eugene wants to marry me," I said irrelevantly. "That would solve all my problems."

"Shall I take you and Antoinette to the Poliets? They have returned to their large house now and Eugene, due to a remarkably convenient old dueling wound, is not in the army."

"No," I said with sudden revulsion. "Better that I go to Sugarhill. I have no love for Eugene."

Antoinette came down the stairs, burdened with both our portmanteaus, and Kincannon stepped forward to help her. We went out the door without Madame Broussard or servant to close it behind us, but I felt that from some window, madame was peering down at us as Kincannon strapped the portmanteaus to his gelding.

As the three of us walked down the street, with Kincannon leading the horse, he said, "I will deposit you ladies in the old Chaille courtyard where you will be safe until I can secure a curricle or carriage of sorts. You cannot walk all the way to Sugarhill now." There was exasperation in his voice with that faint hint of protectiveness he had revealed that long ago night when we had reveled in our physical union.

It was cold and dark and I felt uneasy as we waited in the courtyard, which was all unkempt and overgrown. I looked up at the blindly staring windows in the attics and shivered. We sat on the hard, wrought-iron furniture for what seemed hours before Kincannon returned with a light curricle, into which he put first our portmanteaus, then assisted us to a seat atop them. He did not explain where he got the vehicle and we did not ask.

I was very tired, but I straightened my shoulders and said, "This is very good of you, Quentin. We appreciate your letting us stay at Sugarhill until we can solve our problems." I realized I had never felt more bereft and lonely in my life.

Rodeur was gone. He had been my only security in an insecure world and I realized it fully now. I wanted to burst into tears, but I bit my lip and refused to let my face crumple. Once I started to cry, I might never stop. Kincannon, who was my heart and soul now, gave no indication that he would do other than furnish us this temporary shelter.

It was a long, cold drive back to Sugarhill, during which I softly told Antoinette of what had transpired. She was quietly sympathetic and put her arms about me, drawing me to her soft warm bosom. By the time we reached the house, we were all so fatigued we went to bed without supper.

I slept deeply, dreamlessly at last, and when I wakened in the morning, it was to find Antoinette preparing a breakfast of toast and coffee. Kincannon was gone on his own errands.

Five days dragged by and our food supplies were dangerously low, when Kincannon showed up on the sixth morning with a sack full of provisions. "I have been discharged from the army, ladies—and we will dine sumptuously in celebration of that fact," he said cheerfully. "Further, I have sold Sugarhill to Eugene Poliet, which gives me cash for my plans. Have you ladies solved your problem of what to do?" There was something mischievous in his voice, but underlying it was steel.

"We will go into town and seek employment in women's clothing shops," I said resolutely.

"You will not like that in this town, after having been a social success and a lady of quality, Aurielle," he said soberly.

"No, I don't suppose I will. But I must."

"Marriage with Poliet would make you a member of New Orleans' best once more."

I looked away. The thought of going to bed with Poliet repelled me. Once again, I thought that his whole body must be moist and sweaty and the prospect of touching it, being touched by it, was revolting. I restrained a shudder. "I told you. I don't love Eugene," I said slowly.

"We shall do quite well, I believe," Antoinette spoke up, her voice light. "I shall teach Aurielle the art of making fetching bonnets."

Over the delicious dinner Antoinette and I prepared, we talked further about our plans until night drew on and it was time to retire.

Antoinette took a candle and went up to her bed in the half-finished house. I was about to follow when Kincannon caught my arm. He took the candle from my hand and set it on the clean kitchen table.

Then slowly and deliberately, he took me into his arms and began to kiss me, my temples first, then my throat, and at last, hungrily, my mouth. Fluid with desire, I made no resistance. Ah, Roxanne had been right, so right!

His lips were warm and tender, growing ever more demanding. He pressed my body in its lightweight muslin dress against himself and I could feel him hard and eager against me. I was aware that he was about to seduce me once more and I had no strength against my pounding pulses and shortened breath.

Even on the kitchen floor, I thought dimly, and remembered the soaring, intense, and fiery delight that had been mine in his house on Bourbon Street. Yes, I knew what he wanted of me and, God help me, I was succumbing. I would love his bastard child all the days of my life. It would be better than to go through life without any part of him.

I swayed as he released me, and his voice was thick with passion. "I told you once, I couldn't get you out of my mind, Aurielle. You have become a part of me. I find I cannot leave you."

"Leave me?"

"I have secured supplies, horses, wagons, much equipment, and I am going to Texas y Coahuila in Mexico. The Mexican government is giving out hundreds of thousands of acres to settlers who will come and help tame the wild country. I have three men and a contraband Protestant preacher who wish to accompany me." Suddenly, violently, he kissed me again and said, "You must go with me— I will take you and Antoinette. I have already bought horses for you. We will cross the Mississippi tomorrow morning, heading west to Mexican territory."

"Oh, Quentin—"

"There will not be the security, the finery and social graces you would have with Poliet. There would be only me and our life together." He paused, his voice deepened, the words dredged from him, "I find—I love you—I want to marry you."

"Marry me?" I was stunned. I had steeled myself to the knowledge that Quentin Kincannon would never marry.

"Did Roxanne speak the truth when she said you had great love for me?" he asked, a timbre I could not at first define in his voice.

"You heard!" I accused. "You've known all this time!"

I recognized the timbre then as hope, when he said with more certainty, "I had *hoped* all this time. There is no place in New Orleans for us now, Aurielle, and I plan to build us a fine house on a great estate in Mexico. Now tell me, is it true? Do you love me?"

The dam within me burst and words rushed out. "Oh, yes, Quentin—I have loved you since that first night when you were too kind to rape me in Rodeur's cabin on the

460

Wind. And I loved you even more after that first time—in your house—"

"Then our smuggled Protestant minister shall marry us tomorrow at dawn." And he added urgently, "You will stay with me tonight, my darling—you will not make me wait longer?"

I melted to him and he began to unbutton my basque in the warm, fragrant darkness of the kitchen. I felt a torrent of passion rising in me, burgeoning, pulsing in my veins like fire. And when at last we lay unclothed on the narrow cot, our bodies tightly pressed together, I thought dimly, *I am home at last. I will be home no matter where we go, no matter the insecurity of our lives, I will be secure in my love for this man.*

THE BEST OF BESTSELLERS
FROM WARNER BOOKS

BLOODLINE
by Sidney Sheldon   (85-205, $2.75)
The Number One Bestseller by the author of THE OTHER
SIDE OF MIDNIGHT and A STRANGER IN THE MIRROR.
"Exotic, confident, knowledgeable, mysterious, romantic
. . . a story to be quickly and robustly told and pleasur-
ably consumed."—*Los Angeles Times*.

SCRUPLES
by Judith Krantz   (85-641, $2.75)
The most titillating, name-dropping, gossipy, can't-put-
it-down #1 bestseller of the decade. The fascinating story
of one woman who went after everything she wanted—
fame, wealth, power, love—and got it all!

DESIRE AND DREAMS OF GLORY
by Lydia Lancaster   (81-549, $2.50)
In this magnificent sequel to Lydia Lancaster's PASSION
AND PROUD HEARTS, we follow a new generation of the
Beddoes family as the headstrong Andrea comes of age
in 1906 and finds herself caught between the old, fine
ways of the genteel South and the exciting changes of a
new era.

A PASSIONATE GIRL
by Thomas Fleming   (81-654, $2.50)
The author of the enormously successful LIBERTY
TAVERN is back with this gusty and adventurous novel
of a young woman fighting in the battle for Ireland's
freedom and persecuted for her passionate love of a man.

LILLIE
by David Butler   (82-775, $2.25)
This novel, upon which the stunning television series of
the same name is based, takes Lillie Lantry's story from
her girlhood, through the glamour and the triumphs, the
scandals and the tragedies, to 1902 and Edward VII's
accession to the throne.

EVERYTHING YOU'VE EVER WANTED TO KNOW ABOUT EVERYTHING!

THE COMPLETE UNABRIDGED SUPER TRIVIA ENCYCLOPEDIA
by Fred L. Worth   (83-822, $2.95)

864 pages of pure entertainment. A panoply of sports, movies, comics, television, radio, rock 'n' roll, you-name-it, at your fingertips. The biggest, the best, the most comprehensive trivia book ever created!

MARY ELLEN'S BEST OF HELPFUL HINTS
by Mary Ellen Pinkham with Pearl Higgenbotham   (97-085, $3.95)

An invaluable collection of speedy, practical and handy tips for simplifying just about every household chore with a minimum of time and expense. More than 1,000 Helpful Hints on cleaning, laundry, home repair, cooking, babycare, and health and beauty aids have been assembled in this handy, spiral bound volume.

GROW IT INDOORS
by Richard W. Langer   (80-054, $4.95)

Hefty, information-packed, it has everything you need to know about over 250 different plants: specific details on light, warmth, humidity, soil and watering. Illustrated with over 100 drawings, it is a 'must have' for successful plant growing.

THE DREAMER'S DICTIONARY
by Lady Stearn Robinson & Tom Corbett   (79-825, $1.95)

If you have different dreams, chances are you'll find their meanings here. Lady Stearn Robinson and mystic Tom Corbett have gathered 3,000 dream symbols and arranged them alphabetically for bedside reference. THE DREAMER'S DICTIONARY is the most complete and revealing guide to interpreting your dreams ever published.

BIORHYTHM: A PERSONAL SCIENCE
by Bernard Gittelson   (81-326, $2.50)

It is our newest scientific discipline, the computerized study of biological clocks, built-in natural cycles that powerfully influence our behavior. BIORHYTHM: A PERSONAL SCIENCE will teach you everything you need to know to chart your natural body cycles and forecast your good and bad days so that you can plan your life with confidence.

THE WONDERFUL CRISIS OF MIDDLE AGE
by Eda Le Shan   (91-199, $2.50)

Over 40? The best is yet to come. Tune in on Eda Le Shan as she talks good sense about you and herself and the unique problems and pleasures of being middle-aged today.

AN UNFORGETTABLE ROMANCE IN AN ERA OF VIOLENT REVOLUTION

LILIANE
by Annabel Erwin   (79-941, $1.75)

Born for love . . . this is Liliane—a beautiful woman swept by the storms of history from the embattled France of Napoleon to Virginia where violence simmered beneath the surface of slavery-dependent plantation life. Warm, passionate—a woman alone—she sought refuge, but found instead turmoil, with two handsome, powerful brothers vying for her. One tantalized her with desire but would not marry her. The other proposed marriage, but concealed a dark secret that tinged his love with terror. LILIANE is truly an unforgettable romance—set in an era of violent revolution and smouldering rebellion. A wonderful saga that spans wide oceans and probes the recesses of a lover's heart.